Lockett's Betrayal

A Novel by

T.J. Johnston

James Lockett Novels

The Boys From Kalamazoo

Volume 2

Johnston, T.J.

Lockett's Betrayal : a novel / by T.J. Johnston

ISBN 978-0-578-68837-4

1. Michigan—Tennessee--History—Civil War, 1861-1865—Fiction.   2. Shiloh, Battle of, 1862—Fiction.   3. Corinth—Western Tennessee—Fiction.   4. Civil War Spies—Fiction. I. Title. II. Series: Johnston, T.J. James Lockett, Boys From Kalamazoo novels.

Foreword

Lockett's Betrayal is a work of historical fiction, but like all of the books in the series, I have taken great pains to be as accurate with the history and the context as possible.

Part of the fascination with the time period is that history itself does not need a boost from the writer's imagination very often. It is vibrant and full of surprises on its own. All it really needs is some fictional characters to live it and weave it together.

While James Lockett and Blair's Independent Regiment are fictional, their travels, travails, battles, and observations are straight from history.

===============================

Section I – The Angel and the Enemy

Section II – A Prayer for Redemption

Section III – Decision

===============================

I

The Angel and The Enemy

Chapter 1

April 8, 1862
Pittsburg Landing, Tennessee

The heat and humidity would have been suffocating alone, but it was the overpowering smell of the corpses that truly made this hell on earth. The stench of thousands of bodies, already blackening and bloating, hung like a vile fog over the remains of the battlefield.

A troop of cavalry rode by. There was a perplexing jauntiness and galling ease to them. How could anyone display such relaxed oblivion to this visage? It was beyond comprehension to those digging the burial trench.

"Would you look at them?" Private Patrick McManus said aloud, leaning on his spade, "Forrestt and the rest of the Reb cavalry ride circles round 'em, but they always stay high 'n mighty, out of the mud!" He spoke for infantrymen everywhere, and his comrades caked in Tennessee muck bobbed their heads and muttered agreement.

But Lieutenant James Lockett did not hear the grumbles of his men. His eyes were fixed on the scene before him. The morning mist was finally burning off, revealing more of the cataclysmic destruction. The fields and thickets of Pittsburg Landing, or the Battle of Shiloh as his men were calling it, were trampled and battered flat, littered with the debris of war – bodies, muskets, haversacks, hats, scorched wadding, the accoutrements of an army.

McManus and the rest of Lockett's little company had been up before the dawn, digging. The past two days of battle were not forgotten, and their aching backs and weary bones protested, but the men lifted the heavy, wet Tennessee soil without interruption. The sooner the bodies were buried, the better. It was already agonizingly hot and humid, and certain to get worse as the day wore on.

The burning pyre of horse flesh caught their attention as the wind shifted direction ever so slightly. It wasn't just the soldiers who had suffered at Shiloh. Hundreds of mutilated horses covered the ground as well.

Tall and wiry, young James Lockett looked with steady gray eyes at their efforts. "This was to hold 250 bodies." He paused. It was obvious that they would be digging more than one pit.

McManus and a few others peered out across the field that had drawn Lockett's attention. Beyond the field was a thicket, a tangled snarl of branches and briars where they had fought so tenaciously two days ago. It was no exaggeration that General Grant's army had fought for its very existence there, and the landscape showed their desperation.

With trees uprooted and shattered, they could have been looking at the aftermath of a tornado, such as the one that ripped through Lockett's native Kalamazoo ten years ago. But all of Lockett's mismatched company were not from Kalamazoo, and to the others, the carnage of the blackened brush and torn bodies looked like Biblical Gomorrah after fire rained from Heaven.

Yet, it was not from God that this destruction had derived. It was their own doing, and Lockett knew this all too well. He had seen as much of Shiloh as any man.

From Major Powell's opening skirmish, to the fight for the sunken road, and to the final charge across Barnes Field, James Lockett had seen too much in the last two days. The waving Rebel flags and hordes of brownish butternut clad soldiers were etched in his memory. It was men as far as the eye could see, all bearing down on them, over and over again. The yelling Rebels would fall like reaped wheat only to be replaced by twice their number.

So many times it seemed impossible that he would live another minute as wave after butternut wave advanced. He had felt the Minié balls whip by overhead, felt the earth shake with the impact of artillery shells, and seen men at his shoulder fall dead. Yet, miraculously, he was still alive.

Sergeant Milton Bosworth crawled out of the pit and gazed at the view that was becoming increasingly clear as the mist lifted. Even the vociferous Ohioan was moved to silence. Bodies blanketed the Tennessee soil so that it seemed one could walk a half mile in any direction without actually laying a foot on the ground itself. In some places, the dead were stacked three or four deep, forming a grotesque wall.

A fatigue party emerged from the thicket. Their hand cart was full of corpses. Lockett's eyes followed the squeaking, protesting dray, but his mind saw the sunken road located deep within the thicket. That road had been their best defense, and for six hours they had clung to that scrap of land like a drowning man clutched at a rope thrown from shore.

The Rebels were calling it the Hornet's Nest, and before it had been surrounded and crushed, Lockett and the others had given General Grant enough time to form one last line of defense.

It had been just after the fall of the Hornet's Nest that James Lockett's life had taken a sudden and decisive turn. To him, it had been a case of mistaken identity and a mindless act of bravery, driven more by rage and insanity than valor. He had been a mere sergeant, yet jacketless and coated in blood like a butcher, carrying his fallen Lieutenant's sword, the 15th Michigan mistook him for an officer.

Those Michiganders had been in their uniforms less than two weeks and were still without their first rounds of ammunition. They were a poor excuse for a last line of defense. The Rebel surge seemed certain to overwhelm them, but the 15th had followed Lockett on a mad bayonet charge that blunted the Rebel advance.

His life would never be the same now, he thought. His moment of delirium had caught the eye of no one less than General Grant, leading to his instant promotion from Sergeant to Lieutenant.

Most men would have been honored and greatly pleased at such good fortune, but Lockett would give it all back if it meant that his friend, Lieutenant Ainsley Stuart, could have his foot back. The slight, bookish son of Senator Stuart had once given him the benefit of the doubt. Lockett could only pray that God had given Ainsley his own second chance.

The clang and scrape of the spades brought him back to the present. It would be a long day of taking care of the dead.

"Sir? Rider a'comin'," one of his men pointed behind him.

Coming up the dirt path, the rider avoided the overloaded cart and trotted towards him. "You Lieutenant Lockett?" the fresh-faced Lieutenant asked.

"I am," Lockett answered wearily.

The other officer's uniform looked oddly orderly and clean. Curious, Lockett looked at his own. While he had possessed the new jacket for only a day and a half, it was already thoroughly soaked with sweat and mud. He toed his muddy boots in the grass in a ridiculous effort to raise the standard of his appearance.

"Lieutenant John Walsh," the other man said, seemingly unaware of Lockett's peculiar behavior, "Part of General Grant's staff."

Lockett had figured as much. Only a staff officer could keep his uniform that clean.

"Colonel Webster sends his regards and requests your presence at eight this evening."

Grant's Chief of Staff was the man who had seen Lockett's act of mindless bravery and brought it to the general's attention.

"Yes, sir," Lockett answered automatically.

"And may I say," Lieutenant Walsh added in a conspiratorial tone, "The colonel told me of that charge you led. Bayonets and no ammunition! Outstanding! And then you lead this band of shirkers across Barnes Field yesterday. Bravo!"

Lockett's gray eyes turned cold, and his face stiffened into a determined mask. It was how he often appeared before a fight. His men had quickly come to love that face because they knew that nothing would faze him.

"These men are not shirkers," Lockett said in a low, menacing voice. He spoke softly, so that his men would not hear, but the weight behind his venom was clearly visible to Lieutenant Walsh. "These men have always been as brave as their officers allowed them to be. Always! Do you understand me, Lieutenant?"

"O-of course," Walsh stammered, "I did not mean to imply… I only meant to…"

"I deserve no praise. The men do."

"Yes," Walsh said tightly, more than a little put off by the impertinent man who had been a sergeant two days earlier.

Walsh quickly remounted and left, leaving Lockett to ponder his own men.

Other than McManus, with whom he had grown up, Lockett had known "his men" for little more than a day, but he had already become intensely loyal to them. They had followed him when it would have been easy not to. For that, he would be eternally grateful.

They had been patched together at the end of the battle's first day from various shredded units and even a few genuine shirkers. With members from Ohio, Michigan, Indiana, and Illinois, this company of remnants was one of eight that had been formed into a special reserve regiment. They were supposed to be held only in reserve. No commander wanted to stake victory on such a bunch, but the day proved to have a different outcome.

They had been needed, and they had surprised everyone, even themselves in some cases. When the firing was the hottest, and officer after officer went down, these men stayed together. Lockett would never let another man speak ill of them. After all, he knew first hand how reputations could be affected by the context of events.

He knew that all too well...

Lockett turned around and stared at the men.

Sergeant Bosworth was talking incessantly as they swung bodies unceremoniously into the pit. Round-faced and always full of comments, the burly Ohioan's voice could often be heard dominating conversation. He had once been part of the 53rd Ohio, a regiment that had broken and run when its colonel had lost his nerve. So full of boasts and bluster, Lockett had initially been worried about the sergeant's true character. But such worries proved to be unfounded. Bosworth was a good man, as were most of the others.

Sweat poured off their brows in the hot morning sun. Somehow, the sun-blotched Irish face of Patrick McManus turned an even deeper shade of red as the day wore on. While still a strong-necked farmer, Lockett's old friend was not the bull of a young man who had departed Kalamazoo with him less than a year ago. Illness in Missouri and the death of Patrick's wife while they had been away had seen to that. Patrick was a different man now. He had once been full of teasing humor like Bosworth, but now he was as tight-lipped as Lockett himself.

McManus and Bosworth tossed a Mississippi corporal on top of an armless Ohio sergeant. The Union and Confederate boys were being buried together. There was no special designation for either. It was the same mass grave for both now. Lockett listened to the squeak of another fatigue party's wagon disappearing into the distance.

"We finally have union," McManus remarked in a detached voice.

Lockett turned, startled. He had not noticed McManus coming up next to him. "What?"

McManus pointed to the assortment of soldiers in the grave. "We may not be united as one country right now," he explained, "But here, these boys are finally united."

"In one grave," Lockett murmured, understanding. He looked squarely at his friend, "If that is the case at the end of all this, then maybe all these men have not died in vain."

He looked over to the next man to be tossed into the pit and stared directly into the unseeing eyes of an Alabama private. The young man's arms were frozen upwards in rigor mortis, as if he was reaching out for help.

Privates Holmes and Thickle bent down. Holmes reached forward and grabbed for the Alabamian's shoulders; he couldn't bear to clasp onto the man's outstretched arms. They lifted and swung the lifeless body into the pit.

Just beyond the mass grave, one tree had been split down the middle, as if by lightning strike. A second tree, sheared off at the bottom, lay in the cleft of the first tree. With the rising sun behind the two trees, it formed a shadow above the mass grave. The shadow bore an uncanny resemblance to Christ's cross.

"Jesus, please save us from ourselves," Lockett prayed silently.

* * * * *

The blackened timbers of the mill opened up to a starry night sky. The place still smelled of charred wood, but the stone floor and walls were undamaged by fire. Most of the machinery in the mill had burned or been removed. All that remained was the massive grist stone and one rough wooden chair, whose occupant sat defiantly with his arms tied to the back of it.

Three other men stood around the prisoner. The lanterns and cook fire on the stone floor burned bright, illuminating the spiteful looks on their faces.

"You'll be shot in the morning if you don't tell us," one of the Yankees growled at the prisoner. He wore the uniform of a major and had a long black beard that gave form to an otherwise pointy face.

The prisoner, who wore his Confederate gray, snapped back, "Y'all kill all your prisoners? Officer and private alike?"

The major went over to the fire and poked it with his prisoner's sword. He said nothing as he watched a few embers float upward into the black sky. It was the broad-shouldered Yankee sergeant who answered instead. "You ain't a captured Reb officer. You're a God-damned spy."

"I am Captain Harry Riley of General Beauregard's Army. My uniform should be proof enough of that," the prisoner answered resolutely.

The Yankee major gave a sinister laugh, "My sergeant is right. That gray was underneath the blue uniform that you were wearing… at least that is what my report will say." The major turned around with the sword, whose tip now glowed red. "Captain Riley," he sneered, "You were captured in our uniform, which makes you a spy."

Riley gave no response. He tried to look calm.

"Either you tell us who you intended to meet, or…" There was a prolonged silence.

It was the Yankee sergeant who finally spoke. "You ever seen how quick the red tip of a heated sword turns an eye into a black puckered mess?"

When Captain Riley did not answer, the sergeant provided his own response. "Damn fast, Secesh. That's the answer. Quicker'n an eye blink. Course, I'll leave it in there longer than that."

The sergeant hovered near the prisoner. Then commanded with only a slight nod, he swung his foot and pushed on the back of the chair, sweeping it forward. The bound Captain Riley pitched forward, unable to prevent his head from cracking against the stone floor. The chair was yanked back up by the sergeant, and in nearly the same motion, he back-handed Captain Riley so violently that the prisoner toppled over backward, smacking the back of his head too.

Bleeding from his nose and the back of his head, Captain Riley couldn't remember the chair being uprighted a second time. He could vaguely hear a buzzing but had no idea that the Yankees were addressing him again.

The major snorted at the lack of a response. "Sergeant, see what you can find out." He pointed to the other soldier still standing by the door-less entrance to the mill. "Private, take a spade and dig his grave. No need to make it too deep. I want to be out of here by dawn. But we'll work our way up to that, right, sergeant?" He gave a sadistic chuckle. "I'm nothing if not fair. The faster he talks, the quicker it will end for him."

* * * * *

Lieutenant Orrin Long studied his reflection in the dull shaving kit mirror. Alone inside the tent with the dim candlelight behind him, he could still make out the bruising on his neck. Gently, he adjusted his red kerchief, a memento given to all of the Kalamazoo Sharpshooters when they departed in 1861.

If he shifted it just so, it would cover the marks that James Lockett had made.

He swallowed with difficulty. Even a trickle of air across his windpipe still rasped painfully.

And how long would it take for the tell-tale discoloration to go away?

Thankfully, the red garment could hide it with some adjustment, because it would be difficult to explain away the strangulation marks. It would be clear to even the most dull-witted observer that someone had tried to choke him. The individual finger marks could be distinguished on his neck!

If necessary, he supposed that he would claim that he had gotten the bruising from some murderous Mississippian, although that excuse could be a bit problematic. After all, his regiment, Birge's Western Sharpshooters, had seen plenty that day, but no hand-to-hand fighting.

14

Still, the day had been as confusing as could be, and he had been separated from the rest of the company, or at least that was what he was telling everyone. In any case, the story would have to suffice.

He would finish his communication to Big John Moffat and his powerful friends back in West Michigan tonight. It would fully detail his bravery under fire and incredible leadership capacity. After that, he would rejoin his uncle and the rest of the Kalamazoo Sharpshooters, who were now part of Birge's Western Sharpshooters regiment. They probably thought him dead, and some would doubtlessly be celebrating that, assuming that those fools were still alive themselves.

Fools, he thought again, one-time friends of Lockett, utter ignoramuses, worthless farm boys for the most part!

His lips curled into a snarl. They would get theirs too. Someday. But first, he would take care of Lockett, somehow.

He would never forget the encounter down at Pittsburg Landing, just after the first day of battle. The shock of seeing his old private was one thing. After all, he thought that he'd effectively removed the man from the army forever, but worse yet was the sight of Lockett in officer's clothing!

The rumors of General Grant's drunkenness must surely be true for him to make an ignorant farmer like Lockett into an officer!

He had believed for a moment on that fateful night that he would die as Lockett crushed his windpipe. It wasn't the first time that day where he thought his brilliant life would meet a premature end.

The fear had been overwhelming from the start, and while he had been able to choke it down for two hours, he had seen an opportunity to run and took advantage of it.

Fortunately, that day had been so chaotic and confusing that no one understood that it was cowardice and not confusion which caused him to separate from his men. Even now as he stood here in this tent, only one man knew the truth, and that one man was going to suffer for getting in the way of Orrin Long's ambition.

There were two things that Orrin Long knew with Biblical certainty. One, he was destined for greatness. Two, James Lockett would suffer for his impudence.

Chapter 2

Darkness had fallen across Pittsburg Landing, yet the heat remained. Lockett felt completely sapped, as if he could sleep for a hundred years without waking up, but orders were orders. Patiently, he waited outside of Colonel Webster's tent.

He knew that he smelled something fearful, but there was nothing he could do about it now, and besides, how would one notice his smell above all of the other putrid elements that hung in the air?

"Lieutenant Lockett?" Webster called, and Lockett entered the tent.

It seemed impossible that it had only been two nights since he had stood here and been rewarded for his timely actions. It was still difficult to believe that he had been promoted far above where an ordinary farm boy should ever aspire, especially considering his past troubles in the army.

Of course, Colonel Webster knew nothing of the fact that Lockett had been dismissed from the Kalamazoo Sharpshooters, sent back to Kalamazoo for killing an innocent Missouri girl. Though he had been trying to protect her from Lieutenant Orrin Long and his cohorts, the fact did nothing to ease Lockett's conscience. From time to time, he would snap out of a dead sleep with the girl's face burning bright in his mind.

But as powerful as his conscience was, there was something equally strong that coursed through James Lockett's veins, an inexorable hate for Orrin Long – the man who was really responsible for Amelia's death. The mere mental image of the Orrin's oily smooth face! His jaw clenched at the thought.

Even the knowledge that Orrin had disgraced himself by running at Shiloh did nothing for Lockett.

When he had stumbled across him hiding at the Landing with the other shirkers, he had nearly strangled the man, but that was no balm. Orrin was responsible for the death of a young girl, not to mention forever tarnishing Lockett's reputation. Even his new promotion would not erase that stain from some people's eyes back home, and nothing would ever bring little Amelia back.

And coward or not, Orrin Long would go back to his privileged life, probably marry into the Moffat family, and he would achieve a stature and power that a poor farmer like James Lockett could never reach.

Lockett knew that he should forget, if not forgive, but he couldn't. Orrin Long! God, how the hate surged in him!

"Have a seat, Lieutenant. You look tired," Colonel Webster said, gesturing to a rough three-legged stool.

The aging colonel with the flowing moustache looked exhausted himself. It would not have surprised Lockett that Webster had slept only five fitful hours in the last seventy-two.

"Thank you, sir. I have felt better," Lockett admitted, sitting down.

"It's been trying, but we have emerged victorious, Lieutenant, in no small part due to efforts from men like yourself. The general was greatly pleased to hear of your unit's gallantry in Barnes Field."

Lockett doubted that General Grant took that much interest in him, but he nodded nonetheless.

"Clearly, we did not make a mistake by promoting you."

"Thank you, sir. But it was the bravery of the men that led to our success."

Webster smiled tiredly at the modesty. "The question now, Lieutenant, is what do we *do* with you and your men? Now that the smoke has cleared, many of these regiments will be put back together again."

Lockett stiffened noticeably. He had not thought about what would happen *after* the battle. Somehow, he had assumed that they would remain together as a company and as a regiment. Rag-tag as they were, he liked the unit.

"However," Colonel Webster continued, "In a few cases, there are a number of men with nowhere to go, which brings me to you..."

* * * * *

Colonel Webster had been all too correct when he said that there was no good place for some men, men like James Lockett. While it was not an official policy, it was sometimes assumed that in the rare cases where a man was raised from the ranks, that he should be assigned elsewhere, away from old comrades, some of whom might question his new authority. While Lockett doubted that would be a problem for the 12th Michigan, he was not about to argue the point.

In many ways, he preferred his new men, however brief their time together had been. On the face of it, many officers would find that strange. They were not exactly the crop of the litter.

They were men like Milton Bosworth, whose entire company was being broken up after its disgrace. There were also cases like Privates Holmes and Graham. Their old commanders thought them to be cowards. And finally, there were men like the rough looking Private Klugge, troublemakers to be sure. This was a convenient way for those commanders to get rid of their garbage.

So James Lockett found himself with a shrunken company of sixty-six soldiers, unwanted all of them: cowards, troublemakers, or men with no place to go. They were his men.

There were two such companies of flotsam. One commanded by Lockett, a second by the mild-mannered Enoch Pope.

Colonel Calliford and the rest of the reserve regiment were to be sent back to their old regiments, while Lockett and Pope were to become part of a new regiment, one that had been hastily raised out of Detroit, so hastily that it had only three full companies.

Lockett had never heard of his new commander, Colonel Laurent Blair, but he did not harbor high hopes. He knew only one thing about the man – he was a wealthy banker, and to James Lockett, that meant Blair knew nothing about this bloodbath.

He pondered all this for hours before finally falling off into a fitful, yet exhausted sleep. A cool breeze ruffled the tent, and the half moon provided some illumination on the cloudless night. It was a perfect night for sleeping, and the tired men in James Lockett's company slumbered gratefully.

But Lockett bolted upright in the tent, and it was not the hog-like snoring of some of the men that had awakened him. The searing whites of his eyes scanned the tent opening, but he saw nothing – none of the flame, fire, death, and blood that filled his dream. Absently, he saw the rifles stacked outside in their teepee like fashion, one against another. He looked down to his side where he unconsciously squeezed the hilt of his sword.

No, not his sword, he realized, the Stuart family's sword.

The memory drifted back to him: the sight of his friend, Lieutenant Ainsley Stuart, writhing in the smoking dirt, his foot seared off by cannon fragments.

"We'll not be able to stop them this time," McManus yelled in James's ear. He wore a pained expression as another shell slammed in behind them.

"We don't have enough ammunition as it is," James shouted back in agreement, "Unless Ainsley gets back here with more, we'll have to give ground."

"He'll not try to come back through all this."

The earth spouted in smoke and dirt again.

He watched behind them as shells rained in. Finally, through the spikes of flame and dirt, he saw the familiar outline of Ainsley Stuart running towards them. With his hand clamped to the bouncing scabbard at his side, he ran half bent over, his head tucked into his bony shoulders like a turtle trying to protect itself.

Other than the spare rifle the young officer carried in his left hand, he appeared empty-handed.

Another shell screamed by overhead, and James buried his head in the ground, knowing this one was close. When he looked up through the smoke and falling dirt, he did not see anyone.

"Ainsley!" he cried, jumping to his feet and spotting a body on the ground near where the shell had landed.

Oblivious to the other shells crashing down, he sprinted to his friend's side. Sliding to a stop, he automatically covered Ainsley's body with his own as another shell sent deadly shards in all directions.

"Ainsley," he croaked, looking at the contorted face.

With a sickened feeling, he saw nothing where Ainsley's boot had been. The top of the boot deteriorated into a blackened stump.

Ainsley choked out unintelligible words.

"We have to get him out of here, back to a surgeon!" he yelled, looking at Patrick.

A shell thunder-cracked nearby, showering them with debris. Patrick had not heard James's words, but he didn't need to.

"McClernand and Sherman gave away... had to warn you," Ainsley finally blurted out in painful gasps.

"Hang on, Ainsley. We're getting you out of here."

They began to lift him when Ainsley spat out the words, "The sword, James!"

Seeing the scabbard that had been cut from his body nearby, James ran over and grabbed the precious Stuart family heirloom. "I have it, Ainsley! I won't lose it, I promise!"

That sword, Lockett mused as the crickets rang in the night air. That was what had confused the 15th Michigan into thinking that they were following an officer on their heroic charge. He had bloodied the sword on that charge. Had the Stuart family ever bloodied it? Ainsley had said that the sword dated back to the Revolution, that his great-great-grandfather had fought with George Washington. Had the sword been made wet with blood then? Or had it always been a showy mantle piece, with bronze and inlaid silver vines that arched as a guard over the hilt?

"Ainsley's sword," he muttered softly. They had taken his friend to Savannah, north of the Landing, with many of the other wounded. But was Ainsley still alive?

April 12

The night cloaked the two men on horseback.

"Where's Captain Riley?" one asked the other. His face was hidden by the stiff, wide-brimmed hat that he wore.

"Captain Riley's been captured, may even be dead." He looked up at the man in the wide brimmed hat, literally, but only because his steed was a good head shorter. His smaller horse shuffled impatiently in the cool midnight air, as if it could pick up on the young rider's nervousness.

He waited and waited, but there was no reply from the man in the wide brimmed hat to the dreadful news about Captain Riley. He wasn't sure what to say next, but then finally, the man in the wide brimmed hat answered.

"Shame. Rest his soul, if he is dead." The man with the wide brimmed hat paused and looked around them, more suspicious now.

But he saw nothing in the gloom of the night, just the outline of trees to his left and the empty blackness of a small pasture to his right. Their horses stood on the narrow dirt trail that bisected them. In the subsequent silence, he listened intently but heard nothing except for the flutter of a slight breeze through the leaves.

"And how might it be that you are here then?" the wide brimmed hat eventually continued.

"The colonel sent me. Ah'm Lieut…"

"Stop!" the wide brimmed hat snapped. "Better for all of us if I don't know. Fools!" he muttered to himself. "Not sure if the colonel sent me fools or damn fools, but they sure as hell are young fools. I don't need to see your face in the daylight to know that." He shook his head and adjusted the reins in his hands, unsure if he should just leave now.

The young lieutenant winced. He couldn't tell how old the man in the wide brimmed hat was. His tenor was older, like that of his father, but there was a vibrancy to that voice that suggested he was younger, maybe not even much older than himself.

"A fool in the dark of night," the wide brimmed hat muttered softly, but still loud enough for the officer to hear.

When the colonel had approached the young lieutenant with the mission to replace Captain Riley, the young man had been excited, but now, he was not so sure. His nerves were already stretched to the breaking point by being so many miles behind the Yankee line, and the spy was treating him like they were not even on the same side. Worst of all, he knew the Yankees who had hunted down Captain Riley were out here too, somewhere.

"The colonel wanted me to express how valuable your services are to the Confederacy," the officer said stiffly, "And that despite Captain Riley's unfortunate demise, your identity is still safe."

"Of course, it's safe!" the wide brimmed hat snorted. "Captain Riley didn't know who I was. That was quite intentional and will remain so! And the colonel can save his platitudes. Patriots don't need those. This is the best way that I can serve my country. No fear, Lieutenant, I will continue to provide him the best intelligence that I can."

The wide brimmed hat lapsed into silence, aware that his volume had risen as the emotion worked its way into his voice.

"I'll need a new drop location now that Captain Riley may have revealed my last one."

The lieutenant nodded. He wanted to defend Captain Riley, that the captain would never reveal anything, but the colonel's message was to deliver a new drop location. "Yes, the colonel suggested altering your schedule by plus two days in terms of the frequency. The new location is Yoder's Corner. There is a large rock there with a natural cavity."

"I know it," the spy nodded in agreement.

"The Yankees seem to be setting up headquarters in Savannah."

If it meant anything to the spy, he gave no indication in the dark of the night.

"Your country applauds your service," the officer added, unsure how to end the conversation.

"We ain't got a country yet, not fully," the spy laughed gently. As he did so, his horse stirred beneath him, sensing something in the night air.

"You were followed!" the spy snapped in a harsh whisper. His eyes quickly scanned the inky night.

"Impossible," the officer answered, but he had a sudden terrible feeling. He abruptly yanked his horse around in the opposite direction.

The movement triggered a voice in the distance, and there was a bright flash, a red eye winking in the night.

The young lieutenant's head snapped back, and the spy felt something warm splatter on his face. The army officer would have fallen to the ground except one boot was still hooked firmly in its stirrup. Even when the panicked mount bolted, the young lieutenant stayed latched to the saddle, upside down. His startled mount galloped away, dragging him so that his shattered head bounced off the ground as they went.

The spy tried to assess multiple things at once. The lieutenant was dead. He was sure of that, which at least would keep the new drop and schedule safe, but it would do him no good if he was caught or killed himself.

He heard commands being shouted to capture him alive and saw two horsemen coming hard at him, one from each side, and he was sure that whatever marksman fired the shot was already reloading.

Without hesitation, the spy urged his horse into the pasture. The powerful animal leapt forward and was instantly flying with the wind.

The two pursuing horsemen had the angle on him as his horse dashed into the pasture, but the spy had complete confidence in his mount. Faster and faster, it ran. The wide brimmed hat flew from his head, but he paid no attention. He leaned forward over the horse's neck, urging even more speed.

The cool night whipped by and made his eyes blur with tears. Even so, he was sure that he was starting to outrun the Yankees, surely to their surprise! He yipped without thinking in his excitement.

Pistol shots rang out, but to no effect. If they were shooting at him from astride their own galloping mounts, then there was little chance they could hit anything smaller than a house, much less something moving as quickly as he was moving.

It was just after that when disaster struck.

One problem with riding a horse full speed in the dark of night was the inability to see the ground clearly, and in the slight undulation of the turf, his animal stumbled, putting it off stride.

It did not seem to have injured itself, but momentarily, it slowed, and he could hear his pursuit coming. One of them even reached his flank.

"Surrender!" the voice yelled.

The spy half-expected a crashing pistol shot next, but none came. Apparently, the man had an order about taking him alive.

The spy's horse was quickly gathering speed again, and he could feel himself pulling away.

But would the horse lose its footing again, this time spilling the rider and killing both of them? Or would there be another pistol shot? It was one thing to take him alive; it was another to let him ride to freedom.

And then something loomed in front of him, appearing almost at once out of the night!

It was a fence, and they would be upon it in the matter of seconds. The spy did not hesitate, nor did his animal. It quickly gathered itself and sent hundreds of pounds of man and horseflesh upward. He heard his pursuer screaming a cry of terror.

There was that moment of pure exhilaration, when time seemed to slow oddly, and he wasn't sure that the timing was right or that his horse's vault was high enough.

But his horse tucked in its hind legs perfectly, and they cleared it with inches to spare.

The shrieking rider behind him was not so lucky. The screech came to abrupt end, and there was a great crashing bellow and clatter.

The spy looked behind him after a few more yards. The closest pursuer was done for, and the other had pulled up at the fence.

He smiled a toothy grin and could not resist thrusting a triumphant fist into the air.

Up ahead was the marsh. He knew it like the back of his hand. Even if the Yankees were to resume the chase, they would not be able to follow him through the muddy waters and tangled brush.

And with that, the spy charted a course back to Savannah.

* * * * *

April 13
Our orders are clear, and they come with great relief. Savannah! I can only pray that Ainsley still lives. It will be a quick march there, but I am sure that it will take an eternity. On top of being anxious to find Ainsley, I have the discomfort of knowing that I must report to Colonel Blair first. I don't know the man, but I fear that it will be a bad mix.

Humorously, when I first told the men that we were to march to Savannah, some of them thought we were invading Georgia! I had to explain to them that Savannah, Tennessee is just a little town not far from here.
--- the diary of James Lockett

* * * * *

Sergeant Bosworth reformed the men into column, and from his spot in the third row, Patrick McManus was only half-aware of the slow progression of the men. They were near the midpoint of their march to Savannah, but already the men were not entirely eager to end this rest break.

Levi Thickle was grumbling about his old bones. Prosper T. Rowe earned a few chuckles with another well-timed joke. Otto Klugge muttered something in his impenetrable German tongue.

Yet despite all of the distractions, McManus's attention was fully on his friend, James Lockett.

He was standing near the head of the column, silently letting his sergeant do his job. To an ordinary observer, James Lockett probably looked disinterested, even to the point of flaccid ignorance.

But McManus knew better. James was thinking, thinking hard on something.

McManus had known him for as long as he could remember. In fact, they were more like brothers than friends. Since he was the only boy in the McManus family, James would always be like the brother that he didn't have.

They were not generally alike in terms of personality. McManus had his father's Irish temper and a tendency to act before thinking, while Lockett had always been slow to anger and usually deliberate in thought.

But this war was changing them, both of them. McManus found himself thinking, maybe brooding, more than he ever would have thought possible.

And as for James, there were occasional cracks in his expressionless demeanor. He had seen a few times now where anger had poked its way through James's mask of a face. It might take a lot, but there were moments.

James had told him of the encounter with Orrin Long, how he had nearly strangled the man with his bare hands. McManus, of course, believed every word that James said, but it was still hard to fathom. Before this war, James had not been a man of violence, much less one to move to fury so quickly. In fact, in the past McManus had wondered how James could be so slow to anger and so contemplative. It was not something that he understood as an Irishman.

He used to view it as a short-coming in James, something inexplicable, but at this moment, he was concerned, very concerned about the change in his friend.

Yes, what they had seen, and what they had gone through was changing them. It was changing them in ways that they never would have imagined when they left Kalamazoo only a matter of months ago; it was changing them in a manner that could never be undone.

McManus was sure of all this, and he worried. It did not occur to him that James would find this vein of thought quite ironic. In the old world, Patrick McManus never seemed to worry about anything, but here he was.

The column was finally satisfactory, and Sergeant Bosworth reported their readiness to James.

James nodded curtly, and the march continued. There was chatter in the ranks, mostly positive sounding. In spite of their reluctance to end their rest break, the men were ready to be away from Shiloh, far away from the smell of death. Most of the men realized that the smell would travel with them, or at least be embedded in their nostrils for quite some time, but with some optimism, they were ready to be away.

His old friend marched alongside the small company in silence, lost in what McManus knew to be deep thought. McManus hung onto that realization with some sense of buoyancy. Despite the apparent changes, James could still lose himself in trancelike thought. There was something reassuring about that, but he still worried. Was James's mind centered on Orrin Long? Was there some growing, unhealthy predilection to rage churning below the surface?

He was glad that they were done with Orrin and would not see him again. He didn't want to think about what James would do next time.

Lockett said little during the march. His brain was tying itself in knots, just as McManus had surmised. In a way, the repeating, pounding thought did revolve around Orrin Long, just not in such a direct way as McManus guessed.

The thought was not of revenge, not immediately, although the torturous swirl was about violence. His brain latched onto the image of little Amelia again, of the blood on the floor, of remembering the incredible exhaustion that emptied his spirit like a physical blow, and lastly, of how immediate and utterly complete the feeling had been.

He could not get it out of his mind or heart today.

The impetus for this latest bout had only been the passing image of another little girl. This one was peeking out the window of a small, dilapidated cabin as the troops marched by.

Lockett tried to shake the images from his consciousness. The girl who looked out the window had not looked anything like Amelia and was significantly younger, yet it had been enough to surface the despair and guilt once more.

It was one death. It was one death from many months ago. Since then, he had literally seen hundreds of men killed. There was no shortage of death around them, but it was still this one death that haunted him.

His finger had been on the trigger. No amount of rationalization spared him from that knowledge. Yes, he had been trying to save her. Yes, it had been precipitated by Orrin Long and his cronies. But time and time again, what Lockett remembered was his hand on the gun. One moment, he was tussling with Hiram Walker over the weapon. The next moment, there was the ear-shattering bang, louder than any cannon that he would ever hear, and then... little Amelia and blood.

* * * * *

The men were still setting up camp when Milton Bosworth returned from their new regimental headquarters, leaving the lieutenant there to deal with more of the abuse from his new colleagues.

"God damn officers," Bosworth muttered.

He thought that it had been under his breath, but Levi Thickle and Prosper T. Rowe heard him as they finished staking their tent.

"Problem, sarge?" Rowe said good-naturedly.

"What's the story?" Thickle chimed in. "What's the colonel like?"

Bosworth bit his tongue and debated what he should say. He didn't want the reputation as the camp gossip. After all, he was supposed to be the go-between for the lieutenant with the rest of the company.

But he truly had nothing good to say about any of them, save Lieutenant Lockett.

"C'mon," Thickle prodded. "It's not good. I can see that on your face."

Bosworth scowled at him. "You can't read my face anymore than you can read a newspaper."

"I cain read," Thickle responded, aggrieved. "Read a damn sight better'n you, I'll wager."

"That ain't sayin' much," another man snickered.

"Ain't nothing to tell, Thickle," Bosworth answered, ignoring the swipe.

"C'mon, sarge," Thickle persisted. "Ain't we got a right to know?"

Bosworth paused and squinted at him with one eye while he debated with himself.

And what could he tell them? That the other officers sure as hellfire hadn't seen the elephant yet? Or that they were a lean crew: no captains, one measly lieutenant for each company, and just the colonel? And why should he bother to describe his first impressions to them?

There was a Lieutenant Fulkerham, polished buttons and all. He looked like a West Point cadet and apparently had actually been one, based on the comment from the French Detroiter lieutenant, Renaud.

The third lieutenant was Lieutenant Williams, but he seemed to melt into the background, although maybe that was because Bosworth was focused on Fulkerham's rude reception, complaining about the condition of their uniforms, mud spots, dull buttons, and most of all, the smell.

As if they had stopped to clean themselves up? Bosworth thought indignantly. They had marched hard to get here as quickly as possible, and that was their reward?

He hated officers, had even before his old officers had abandoned him at Shiloh. There wasn't a good one between all of them, except for maybe Lockett. Of course, Lockett was not a real officer like these. He had once been a private and sergeant. That made him different.

Of course, it made him different to men like Lieutenant Fulkerham also.

"So, you can read, eh, Thickle?" Bosworth said, trying to change the subject.

The leathery faced private returned the gaze with a dubious, unsure look.

"Then I got a task for you. I assume that means you can write too."

"Yeah?" Thickle answered cautiously.

"Well, the new colonel was a banker. He likes nice, neat records, and he needs our roll call and such. Guess who is gonna help the Lieutenant gather that up?"

Back at Colonel Blair's headquarters, Lockett quietly seethed at the reception.

The colonel sat behind neat stacks of paper and had already described the importance of orderly records to his newest lieutenants. Now, he had moved onto a dissertation on how camps should be organized and maintained.

Lockett nodded dumbly from time to time, if only to give the impression to his new commander that he was listening, although the words seemed to dissolve into a fog in his brain. Instead he found his mind drifting onto thoughts about how small this new "regiment" was and pondered at least his one good fortune: there were no captains. He would get to maintain command of his own company.

It was strange how quickly he had come to value that, even though part of him nagged that the responsibility wasn't worth the hassle. Lost in his own thoughts, he barely heard the colonel's parting words.

"Parade in one hour, gentlemen. I would like to see my men."

Lockett hid his frown. Parade? It had been a long, hot march. The men would not like that, but he supposed that it was not wholly unexpected, especially from a new commander in the field.

The officers departed the colonel's quarters and headed back for their companies. Lieutenant Tyler Fulkerham immediately took up stride alongside Lockett, and then as if to provide balance, Lieutenant Pierre 'Pete' Renaud took up station on his other side.

"So, you were in the ranks?" Fulkerham said, gently pulling on his wispy goatee, "I hope your men pay more attention to their uniforms than you. The colonel likes a proper parade."

Lockett allowed himself a spiteful look. He didn't care whether this man was from West Point or not. He was too tired. "Fulkerham," he said, impulsively grabbing the man's hand.

Tyler Fulkerham stiffened but seeing that Lockett meant no harm, he let Lockett inspect his hand for a second, as puzzled as could be.

Finally, Lockett looked up, and he said simply, "Girls dress pretty, Fulkerham. Fighters have ragged fingernails." He held up his own scarred and dirtied hand while the words sunk in. Fulkerham's face reddened, and his thin eyebrows sliced down like poised daggers, but Lockett did not give him a chance to reply. "I would rather have fighters than polished buttons, and so will you after your first battle." He turned and walked away, half-expecting a blow or at least Fulkerham to follow, demanding satisfaction.

Still, Lockett did not look back. Only when Renaud appeared at his shoulder did he look up.

Renaud had thick brown hair, a bushy moustache, and a relaxed air of good-nature about him. He grinned at Lockett with bemusement. "Lockett," he chuckled, "Odd zat I seem to like you, becos you 'ave a talent for making enemies, eh?"

Chapter 3

Parade went off without incident, and Tyler Fulkerham steered clear of Lockett to his surprise.

From Renaud, Lockett learned that Fulkerham had indeed been at West Point and then expelled.

He wondered if it was for ineptitude in his studies. In his experience, the blatant rudeness seemed more of a prerequisite than a disqualifying mark for professional soldiers, at least in terms of how they treated the volunteer, citizen soldiers.

As for Renaud, Lockett found himself liking the Detroiter of French descent. The short, brown haired officer was friendly and unassuming. He seemed to have his men's respect. Interestingly, his company was all of French descent, and he had proudly told Lockett that his grandfather had been part of Dequindre's Rifles, sharpshooters of some renown during the War of 1812. Renaud added wistfully that his men were all farmers now, and not trappers such as many of Dequindre's men had been.

From the top of a small rise, they looked down on their tiny encampment. Cook fires burned, and the smoke trickled up in swirls before disappearing into a nebulous haze. The brown skein lingered above camp, dimming the reddish glow of the setting sun. Beyond the camp, a small cotton field lay vacant and untended.

"Not exactly ze ribbon farms," Renaud commented.

"Ribbon farms?"

Renaud chuckled and stuck a pipe between his teeth. "Oui, Lockett, but we're not growing ribbons in Detroit." He grinned and took a satisfying puff from the pipe. "Our fields are all long and narrow, up against ze Detroit River. Long and narrow like a ribbon, eh?"

Lockett thought about his own farm in Kalamazoo. Were his younger brothers able to maintain it without him? The burden had been all his for so many years after his father's death. At times, it seemed that they had scarcely helped him at all. Now the burden was solely theirs.

He was pondering this when he heard the inscrutable sound of German. Looking over at the cook fire, he saw the fresh-faced Adie Graham and the rough looking Otto Klugge sitting there, conversing in German. They made quite a contrast.

"Evening, Lieutenant, sir," Adie said cheerfully. "Care for some coffee?" He fished for the battered tin pot that dangled above the fire on their makeshift set up.

"No thanks, Adie," he said.

Adie Graham beamed, surprised that the Lieutenant knew his name already.

"Was that German you were speaking, Adie?"

"Yes, sir. Otto doesn't speak much English, and my mother was German. I guess you could say I'm about the only one in camp who talks to Otto."

The big German stared into the fire, ignoring the officer. He looked a bit like a heavy, stone gargoyle, Lockett thought to himself.

"He have anything interesting to say, Adie?"

"Sir?"

"Just a joke, Adie, never mind."

The raucous laughter of the encampment wafted by. Privates John Messern and Prosper T. Rowe were singing with mule-like harmony. It was the popular tune, *Kiss Me Before I Die, Mother*. More and more men joined in as they went about cooking another dinner of hardtack, bacon, and grease.

It amazed Lockett how resilient these men were. The horrors of Shiloh were only a few days old.

"…You will stop that song at once, Lieutenant Lockett!"

Lockett heard the order, snapping him out of his wanderings. He looked away from the dirty, tired men and into the serious, ice blue eyes of his new colonel. "Sir?"

What was so damning about the men's singing, besides their utter lack of tune, was beyond him. Was the colonel simply in a foul mood, he wondered.

"I said, stop that singing at once!"

Perhaps, the glum news of the day had soured Colonel Blair's spirits? It had certainly soured Lockett's own outlook today. When word had first worked its way into camp, he found it impossible to believe. Surely, it must be yet another daft rumor that army life seemed to generate on a regular basis. But then the official dispatch confirmed the impossible.

Despite winning at Shiloh and Fort Donelson, General Grant had been removed from command! Again!

Even if General Grant had not been James Lockett's personal benefactor, the removal of the cigar-chomping leader of the Army of Tennessee would have struck him as the height of idiocy. Grant had shown the one thing that no other Union general had, an ability to fight and keep fighting.

Yet somehow, the desk bound General Halleck had again usurped Grant. Lockett had seen Halleck in Missouri and didn't like him. Halleck could no more lead this army to victory than he could flap his arms and fly like a bird.

The mournful refrain from the boys broke through his consciousness again, and he saluted Colonel Blair, "Yes, sir, Colonel. I'll stop the men from singing that song."

"Bad for morale. Have them sing something gallant, something patriotic," Blair explained, his stout chest inflating like a balloon.

His pose was so full-chested that it reminded Lockett of the horribly bloated bodies that they had buried. How quickly the human body swelled up after death, he reflected. It had been more than grotesque. Some of the bodies had looked like a furnace bellows had been placed in their mouth and then filled to the bursting point with air. So many men...

"Lockett, when I give an order, I expect it to be done immediately," he said with visible annoyance.

"Yes, sir," Lockett repeated automatically. His face did not acknowledge any hint of his true emotion.

Problems with a song? Not patriotic? What was patriotic to the colonel, walking into the blinding flash of cannons and seeing friends turned into pulped offal?

Had Colonel Blair ever seen any action? Did he have any idea of the incredible courage it took? Did he know that his so-called "gallant" behavior was driven by fear - fear of dying, fear of losing the respect of a unit, fear of losing a reputation at home, fear of abandoning a friend?

Fear, Lockett mused, as he walked down to the men.

"Private Rowe, pick up that fiddle. The colonel would like to hear *Lorena*."

He knew that he should have said something like *Hail, Columbia*. There wasn't anything patriotic about *Lorena*, but he could not squelch his sudden rebellious streak and spontaneous disgust.

Colonel Blair be damned, he thought savagely. He might have the men change from a pure melancholy song, but he couldn't stop himself from slightly disobeying the order.

"*Lorena*? That is a good 'un," Private Messern agreed.

"Ah, Lorena." Prosper T. Rowe gave a gap-toothed smile, showing horse like teeth, "I knew her once..."

"Jus' play the fiddle, Prosper T.," Private Thickle broke in, "We don't want hear your tale about a rundown Chicago whore again."

April 13
I write again this day for I feel the need to talk to someone, if even myself. We have a new commander. Does he know this war? The war will not soon be over. I have never been more convinced of that. Hopes for an easy peace are foolish now. Any dense fool must see that. So much blood has been shed. So much blood! Men were slaughtered like pigs. I must keep

Daniel from the war, but that becomes more difficult with every passing day. When my brother realizes that the war will not soon be over, I will no longer be able to keep him from volunteering. Even the weight of the farm will not tie him down long enough.
   --- *the diary of James Lockett*

* * * * *

The lingering odor of infection met James Lockett's nostrils as he neared the tent filled with wounded Union officers.

He had wanted to come last night, but as soon as he had set down his diary, he had fallen into an exhausted sleep. There was little time this morning before his duties would call him back, so he made haste.

But now, the nauseating smell that surrounded the tent slowed him. The foulness made him fear the worst, and cautiously, he stepped inside. By strange chance, the first face that he saw was Ainsley Stuart's.

Pale, gaunt, and glistening with beads of perspiration, Ainsley did not look all that well, but he was alive. The son of Senator Stuart was still with them. For a moment, Lockett felt a great weight of concern removed from his aching shoulders. Ainsley was still alive! But then despite that initial comfort, Lockett felt the weight come crashing back down.

There was a shadow of despair that shrouded the entire tent. All around him, men were in wretched suffering. Many of the wounds would never heal, or if they did, it would leave them broken men. He could feel their misery as he looked into their faces.

Agony and gloom enveloped and inundated this place. It was like a thick fog that touched every corner. There was no escaping it.

But then a strange thing happened. A ray of light entered the dismal tent. Like a solitary, brilliant star on a dark sky, she moved through the tent, casting a cheerful glow onto each cot.

Water for one captain, a reassuring word for a legless major, a relaxed smile for one young lieutenant, and a promise to an armless one that she would write his letter later.

Her round cheeks dimpled when she smiled, and her curly brown hair constantly needed to be swept from her face as she bent over to attend to them. She was mesmerizing to watch because she was oblivious to the despair. She left each soldier's spirits better than before.

She adjusted the bandage on one man's stump. The blood and dried surgical plaster clung to the bandage in leeching gobs, but there was no hint of distaste on her face, and the soldier swallowed his grimace, not wanting her to see his pain.

"James!" Ainsley Stuart suddenly croaked. His voice was weak, but the sight of his friend gave it a joyful chirp.

The girl looked up at the visitor and eyed him carefully while his gaze flickered between the wounded lieutenant and herself.

She saw a tall and serious-eyed man, one with the beginnings of crow's feet etching into his otherwise youthful face. He wore an officer's jacket, but he was as soiled as the lowliest private. His gray eyes followed her despite his friend's call, and then he must have realized that he was staring because he began to blush.

Lockett felt himself redden and tried unsuccessfully to turn his attention solely back to Ainsley. He walked towards the cot, but his eyes still flitted one last time to the girl before reverting back to his wounded friend.

"By God, I prayed you were still alive, Ainsley," he said, clasping his friend's bony hand.

Ainsley tried to lift his head, but the effort was too much, and it immediately drew sisterly consternation from the girl. "Lieu-ten-ent Stuart, you know not to exert yourself so!" Even when scolding, she had a pleasant Tennessee lilt in her voice with a friendly exuberance that matched her outward appearance.

"This is the man I was telling you about." Ainsley's voice was weak, scarcely more than a whisper. It reminded Lockett of how his father had sounded just before he had died.

"Shush now Lieu-ten-ent, you must save your strength." She looked at Lockett. "I tell him that he doesn't need to talk, only to listen, to save his strength, but of course, he must tell me about it."

Lockett blinked, unsure what '*it*' was. "I'm, uh, James Lockett," he began awkwardly.

"Oh, I know exactly who you are – though he told me you were a sergeant?" A look of puzzlement crossed her pleasant features.

"I was," Lockett said with a nod, "They've made me a lieutenant since then."

"Hah!" Ainsley cried out in a surprising loud voice. The momentary exertion made him catch his breath, and he continued in a weary but pleased voice, "I knew it." There was triumph in his voice. "I told you it could happen."

"You were right as usual, Ainsley," Lockett agreed, but with growing concern. It seemed that the excitement was making Ainsley even more pale.

The girl noted the look of concern on his face, and she turned to her patient. "You must promise to rest, Lieu-ten-ent, to save your strength." Ainsley's eyes nodded in agreement, and the girl continued. "I'm Anna Tucker, Lieu-ten-ent Lockett."

She paused and dazzled him with a smile.

"It's looks like what Lieu-ten-ent Stuart told me was true, judging by the fact that they made you an officer. The saving of a man's life should be rewarded."

"Well," he began, uncomfortable with the sudden attention, "Actually, they made me an officer for something that happened afterwards."

"Really? Do tell."

"Uh," he blushed. Why did women always seem to have this effect on him? "It's a long story, miss. I'm just grateful Ainsley's alive."

"Thanks to you," Ainsley whispered.

Anna Tucker admonished Ainsley with a look. The comedy of it made Lockett chuckle, and even Ainsley had a brief look of amusement surface through his pain tightened features.

"Actually, Ainsley, you should thank God that you're alive, not me. It's some sort of miracle if you ask me."

Anna Tucker raised an eyebrow at the comment. "You are saved, Lieu-ten-ent? Washed in the blood?"

"Her father's a preacher," Ainsley chipped in hoarsely, drawing looks from both Lockett and Anna this time. He lifted a palm off the cot in mock surrender.

Lockett knew he would not have used such a dramatic word to describe his faith. *Saved.* It reminded him of something that Luke Bailey would say. Perhaps, it was something about being the offspring of a preacher.

"Well, Lieu-ten-ent?"

"Oh, of course!" he replied, realizing that he had never addressed the question.

She seemed pleased with the answer.

Anna Tucker excused herself and went back to tending the other soldiers, leaving the Yankee officers to talk but under the strict orders that Lockett do most of the talking. "You're doing a sight better than when I left you, Ainsley," he remarked, deciding that it was at least partly true.

Ainsley nodded but grimaced as a bolt of pain passed through him again. His gaze returned back to Lockett, but the agony was still carved into his features.

"Should I go?"

"No," Ainsley croaked. "The pain is always there. It is just worse sometimes more than others."

Lockett nodded, and they were silent for a moment.

"I don't remember much after the explosion," Ainsley choked out. "I remember being in a field of wounded. Then, all was black again."

Lockett nodded. "It's probably just as well that you don't remember, Ainsley."

His mind flashed back to that night - how he and Patrick had searched the acres of wounded outside the surgeon's tent, finally finding Ainsley unconscious in a field of over-flowing agony next to the surgeons' makeshift shelter. The smell of the wounds and the echo of the maimed were still fresh in his mind.

"We found you in a field by one of the hospital tents, unconscious, didn't seem like you would make it through the night, especially after it started to rain. A worse sight I never saw, Ainsley. It rained so hard. It turned the field into a morass. Hundreds and hundreds of wounded soldiers, Ainsley, all suffering in the mud. A good number never saw morning. It's a wonder that they didn't drown where they lay."

"I don't remember any of that."

"Like I said, it is just as well. It didn't get any better after that either."

He paused and looked around at the scant resources of Ainsley's current home. As insufficient as they were, this little hospital tent was three times better than back at the Landing. "You don't remember any of it? Even Lieutenant Powell?"

"Who?"

Lockett shook his head in amazement. "Lieutenant John Wesley Powell. You don't remember him?"

"Should I?"

"If it wasn't for him, you would probably be dead."

Ainsley looked back quizzically, and Lockett continued. "I'll wager you that there is nobody else from Michigan in this tent."

"No, I don't think so now that you mention it."

"There is a reason for that, Ainsley."

Lockett's face furrowed into a frown at the memory. He knew the remembrance would eat at him for the rest of his days.

"Conditions were bad at Pittsburg Landing. They weren't ready for that many wounded. How could they be? There were some supplies provided by the U.S. Sanitary Commission for little hospitals like this one, but they were all north of the

Landing. So, they moved most of the wounded to the river landing and steamer after steamer came, taking the men back to Savannah and further north."

"And Powell was a ship captain?"

"No. Powell was wounded just like you. Lost his arm." Lockett clucked his tongue. "Somehow you made friends with him even though you were unconscious. You have a knack for that." He sighed. "Probably didn't hurt that I gave Powell my gum blanket for that night in the rain."

"You spent that night in the open field with me, didn't you?"

He nodded. "As much as I could. It was a long night."

"Then what happened?"

"Well, boat after boat came to get to the wounded. Steamers from Indiana came and got the Hoosiers. Steamers from Ohio got the wounded Buckeyes. Steamers from Illinois came and got their boys…"

"But Michigan isn't connected by river," Ainsley remarked with insight, "There are no steamers from Michigan."

Lockett nodded again. "That was exactly it, Ainsley. There are no steamers from Michigan so our poor boys languished there for days, scarcely attended. It was a whole bunch full of nothing but Michigan."

He gritted his teeth. The frustration was welling up in him again. He rubbed a hand fiercely across his face as if he could wipe off the image.

"Most of 'em died. It was three days until a steamer from Ohio called the Magnolia came and got any Michiganders."

"And me?"

"Invalided as he was, Powell demanded that they make room for you on the *Spirit of Chicago*, the first boat out. He's got quite the bark. It wouldn't surprise me if John Wesley goes onto something great, one arm or not."

"And where's Powell now?"

"Don't know," Lockett shrugged. "You took his spot on that first boat. He was on the second Illinois boat out. I heard some of the later boats went further north, even up to Paducah."

43

"So, I have more than one man to thank for my life."

Lockett nodded. "Most definitely."

* * * * *

"The British would have him hung," Lieutenant Fulkerham growled, "And flogged."

"And probably in zat order," Renaud quipped.

Lockett sighed, wishing that they would get back to the point. Paradoxically, he was hesitant to throw forth his own thoughts, despite the fact that they were debating the future of one of his men. The apprehension swelled in him as they discussed the "desertion" of Private Otto Klugge.

"So, your opinion is to hang the man?" Colonel Blair queried Fulkerham.

"It was desertion, sir."

"We 'ad already concurred ze man was absent wit'out a pass, not deserting," Renaud argued, turning serious. "'e was looking for a place to drink. No intent to leave. 'e was coming back."

"So he says," Fulkerham sneered. "It was in German no less, so who knows what he was really saying besides that other little runt German?"

"Sounded believable to me," Lieutenant Enoch Pope chipped in, but they all ignored him.

"Even so, he's a drunk, and there is no place in this Army for drunkards," Lieutenant Williams declared.

Blair sat quietly by, as if he was enjoying the internecine debate, but the reality was that he was not at all sure what to do with this situation. Was this a time to make an example of someone, to establish his authority? It would look a bit arbitrary, he knew. The man's misdeeds were not that great, despite what Fulkerham maintained.

"Should he be dismissed from service?" Pope wondered aloud.

"We need all the men we can get," Lockett finally commented.

"The man was dismissed from his last regiment for drinking, which is how you ended up with him in the first place, Lockett. He's of no value to this army." Fulkerham placed his palms on the table and bent forward. He scowled, but Lockett did not reward him with any of acknowledgement of this provocation.

"He was dismissed from them for drinking *and* brawling," Lockett corrected, ignoring Fulkerham and looking at Colonel Blair.

Williams jumped back in, "That is supposed to defend the man?"

"He fought three other men by himself and won." Lockett said pointedly. He was so tired that he just couldn't hold his tongue. "Can you?"

The lithe Lieutenant Williams launched himself to his feet.

"Sit down," Blair said a gentle wave of his hand, "So you still want this man under your command, Lockett? He has no respect for authority. That was clear from when he stood before us an hour ago. The disdain was plain. He doesn't even speak English. You want a man like that?"

"I do, sir."

"Can you control him, Lieutenant?"

"I can, sir."

"You've failed once on that already."

"Yes, sir. He is my man, so this is my failure to begin with, and I'd like the chance to show you that it won't happen again."

"We can't have the men showing such disobedience. Discipline is everything, Lieutenant. I want total obedience to me, and that means obedience to you also."

"Yes, sir."

Blair nodded. "Then four weeks of fatigue duty for the man, Lockett. If there is a latrine or grave to dig, I want him to do it. If there is some distasteful duty, I want the German to do it. It is your head in the noose now too."

"Yes, sir."

* * * * *

45

Lockett nodded towards two of Fulkerham's men who guarded the brooding hulk of Private Otto Klugge. He sat sullenly on the stump and did not look up at the officer.

"You're still with us, Klugge," Lockett informed him.

The German said nothing, and Lockett cursed under his breath, remembering that Klugge spoke little English. "Where's Graham?"

Klugge's eyes flickered upward.

"Follow me," Lockett ordered, but there was ignorance on Klugge's troll-like face.

Did the man really understand that little English?

"Come here," he tried again with the arm motion. The thick-chested German rose to his feet and grudgingly followed Lockett in search of Adie Graham.

It took a while, but the mismatched tandem eventually found Graham returning from the river with nearly twenty canteens over his shoulder. "Adie, what in tarnation are you doing?"

"Getting water for the rest of the boys," he answered sourly. "The others 'nominated' me."

"Nominated, huh?" Lockett gave a little grin, "Okay, but first you're going to help me and Otto have a little talk."

"Yes, sir."

The sun was turning warm, and he spotted the shade of a large tree. "Let's sit, shall we?"

Lockett sat without pretense; his long legs spread out in front of him. Languidly, he scratched the dirt with a fingernail.

"What's going to happen to Otto?" Adie asked.

"Do you think he cares?"

"Cares?" Adie said incredulously, "Of course, he cares." The innocent look of astonishment was plain on his youthful face. "We all care. That's why we volunteered, sir."

Lockett chuckled. "Of course," he assured Adie, remembering his own naiveté. It hadn't been that many months ago, but it seemed like years now. "Then, let's start by telling Otto that he's not going to be hung, nor kicked out of the army."

"Hung!" Adie cried.

"Desertion deserves a stiff penalty. There's few things worse in the Army. He might as well shoot an officer at that rate, and don't translate that, Adie. I don't want to give him any ideas. Now, if you don't mind, tell Otto that he's still part of the company."

"Oh, of course, sir."

There was the harsh staccato of German between Graham and Klugge. The puzzled look on Adie's face was unmistakable. "I don't think he was very happy about that, sir. I think he wanted to be discharged?"

Lockett grimaced at the words. That was what he was afraid of. Why had he impulsively stuck out his neck for no good reason? The man didn't want a second chance.

"Sir?" Adie prompted after a long pause.

"Ask him why that is. If he volunteered just two short months ago, what happened? Army life too hard for him?"

Adie translated, and Lockett knew when Adie reached the last sentence by the scowl that burrowed across Klugge's heavy, scarred face. There was an abrupt, harsh German burst.

"Uh, he says that it isn't too hard, sir," Adie translated delicately.

Lockett laughed at Adie's blatant diplomacy. "Let's go back to asking why he wants to leave," he added with a chuckle.

"He says that he didn't volunteer," Adie started with confusion while Klugge continued to speak. "He says that the judge ordered him to volunteer?" The curiosity was too much for Adie, and he started to converse with Klugge in German on his own.

After a full minute, Lockett cleared his throat and raised his eyebrow expectantly. "You mind letting me know what you two are talking about?"

"Sorry, sir. Otto says he didn't volunteer. He says that he was accused of murder, says he gave the man a whipping all right, but the man was beating Otto's sister to within an inch of her life. Then the man found a gun. Otto says that it was self-defense, but the judge wouldn't listen. The other man had been rich with too much power. The judge wouldn't listen, or he was paid not to listen. The judge told him he could go to the gallows or volunteer for the army."

Lockett's jaw hung open, and he blinked in recognition. Then he looked off into the distance, as if he saw something besides the empty pasture and the forest beyond. Adie could not have known that the tale would strike such a nerve with the young officer. In fact, little else would have made such an impact on Lockett. He had more in common with the big German than he would have guessed.

Otto didn't need to speak English to recognize the look on Lockett's face.

"He said it was self-defense, sir."

"I heard you the first time," Lockett replied cautiously, weighing the words and his own biases.

He looked Klugge in the eye. The big German stared right back without flinching, and Lockett knew he believed the man. The judge probably did too, seeing as how he gave the German stevedore a choice. If the judge had truly thought him guilty, he would not have hesitated on pronouncing sentence on a lowly stevedore. By giving Otto Klugge an out, the judge had revealed Klugge's true probity.

Lockett pursed his lips and took a deep breath. "Very well, Klugge. So, you didn't volunteer."

"Is that all, sir?" Adie asked.

"Not hardly, Adie. Tell him exactly what I say, and I do mean exactly."

With a nod, Adie carefully translated the following statements. "Private Klugge, I don't care how you got here, but here you are, and you are one of my men. You will obey Colonel Blair's and the rest of the officers' commands and rules. There will be no more midnight attempts for a drink. Besides, there is no saloon in Savannah. The closest tavern is five miles away from what I hear. And if you don't obey, it will be both our necks."

April 15

Milton Bosworth absently swatted at a fly buzzing around his face. Patrick McManus quietly dozed next to him, his floppy slouch hat tipped forward over his eyes. Even beneath the shade of the tree, it was hot, and it was only April. They were waiting for Lockett and the rest of Colonel Blair's officers to emerge from the meeting at the hotel headquarters. At one point, Bosworth had seen the fleshy face of General Halleck in the window as the old man had looked outside while speaking.

The march to Corinth must certainly be starting, the sergeant surmised. They had already let the iron grow cold by allowing the Rebels to retreat all the way back to their base, but there was no fixing that at this point. The only thing to do was finally begin the inevitable march towards the Mississippi railroad junction.

"Think Colonel Blair is receiving orders for us to join the march on Corinth?" Bosworth queried, turning to McManus. He was anxious to share his thoughts, as was normally the case.

"Never in a million years," McManus replied sleepily, not bothering to open his eyes beneath the hat.

"Maybe we're gonna serve as the general's personal escort."

"Personal escort?" McManus scoffed, starting to stir.

"Generals have protection, you know," Bosworth said seriously, not catching the incredulity in McManus's voice.

"Halleck is more likely to have us dig a ditch from here to Vicksburg than have *us* protect him."

Bosworth tried to interrupt, but McManus continued on. "The only way that could happen is if Colonel Blair knew Halleck, and they were personal friends. Now, it wouldn't surprise me if the colonel had a large number of powerful friends – he is a banker after all – but somehow, I doubt that 'Old Brains' Halleck is one of them. Remember, I saw Halleck up close in

Missouri. He's old Army through and through. Ain't an ounce of tolerance for us citizen soldiers, privates or colonels."

"Why do you always have to look on the dark side of things?"

McManus shrugged and responded, "No, I've a bad feeling about this, Milton. A very bad feeling. It's not good days ahead."

"What are you a gypsy or something?"

"Better. I'm Irish."

"Well, maybe we'll just ask the Lieutenant his'self," Bosworth said stubbornly as Lockett emerged, giving Colonel Blair a parting salute.

"Care to make a little wager now, Milton?" McManus asked. His hat was still drooped over his eyes, but apparently, McManus could see right through it.

Lockett did not look happy. His face was set in a mask of determination, chin locked forward and brow hardened.

"Uh, no. Not any more." Bosworth answered.

Lockett stopped momentarily when he saw Bosworth staring at him.

"So whad'd he say, sir?" Bosworth asked tentatively after Lockett joined them.

There was no immediate answer.

"Are we advancing on Corinth, sir?" His tone was far more cautious than it had been minutes ago.

McManus laughed. "You never give up, Milton."

Lockett shook his head. There would be no Corinth for them. The rest of the army was finally beginning the advance in that direction, but they would not be going.

And it would be slow going for those who did go, Lockett thought bitterly to himself. He had seen Halleck's style firsthand in Missouri. The only thing General Henry Halleck was in a hurry for was the next meal, he scowled. It would take weeks or months for Halleck to advance those few miles to Corinth.

No, he changed his mind, there was something else that also hurried Henry Halleck – power. If there was power or prestige to seize, he would hurry. The demise of General Grant was proof of that.

"Uh, Lieutenant?" Bosworth prodded once more.

McManus said nothing. He could tell by the look on his old friend's face that it was not what they wanted.

"We're staying here for the time being," Lockett answered stiffly, "Garrison duty here in Savannah. The Wisconsin boys will join Sherman. Our regiment is to stay here."

Bosworth kicked the dirt with the toe of his boot, sending a small stone thirty yards ahead. Few soldiers liked garrison duty. The boredom was excruciating and grew worse with each day. It was particularly bad in a town like Savannah where there were limited diversions to distract the men.

The news would not be taken well by the men. One half of the regiment was new and eager to prove themselves, and Lockett's half still yearned to remove the stain of their repute. Garrison duty would be a particularly bitter pill. There would be no chance to prove themselves here.

"…There's more," Lockett said slowly, the embers of fury growing behind his gray eyes, "General Halleck's reason was that we are an ineffective fighting unit, best used for guarding wagon trains and garrison duty. That's why he's sending the Wisconsin boys. As long as he is in command, we can expect nothing better than 'guarding women and baggage'. Those were his words to Colonel Blair."

"What! I'll show those Wisconsin boys how to fight!" Bosworth declared hotly.

Lockett made bleak face. "Let me know when, so I can have McManus come pull you out, and it's not the fault of the Wisconsin boys."

Bosworth ignored the good-natured jibe. He liked the fact that the Lieutenant already treated him like an old friend. "What does General Halleck mean we ain't up to a fight? What about our charge across Barnes Field? We closed that battle! Fought like a unit, an' we'd only been together one day! Why, General Grant his'self recognized our fightin' spirit!"

"I think you have your answer right there, Milton," McManus grumbled, "Grant ain't in charge anymore. It's Halleck now, and 'Old Brains' ain't the type to take a chance on ruffians like us."

"Besides," Lockett added, "At Barnes Field, we weren't Blair's Independent Regiment. Who knows how those Detroiters will react once the firing starts? They're all fresh fish."

"We all were once," Bosworth muttered to no one in particular.

They had walked the length of the road in Savannah and around the bend came the sound of pounding hooves. Stepping to the side to clear a path, they expected the hurrying rider to continue on, but the uniformed officer reined in his steed and stared down at them.

The cloud of dust hurried to catch up to the rider, and it swirled around the animal, obscuring the four legs for just a moment, giving the sense that he was on some celestial beast.

The grit of the dust clung to Lockett's mouth. Short-tempered as he already was, he inhaled sharply to bark at the man, but then the rider's shadow covered his face.

Before he had even seen the eyes of the rider, Lockett could feel the bile rising in his throat. Later, he would think it strange that he could sense who it was without actually seeing the man.

There was both a sinking feeling and a poison leeching into his veins.

"Coming back with your new orders, Private?"

It took all of Lockett's self control to stay still and not reach angrily for the man in the saddle.

Lieutenant Orrin Long smiled haughtily above them, running a finger across his pencil thin moustache.

There was the smooth as tallow face, wavy brown hair, manicured moustache, reptilian eyes, and new uniform – God, how he hated the sight!

Bosworth looked at the officer's uniform, so bright against the light sky with the buttons glinting in the sun. The rider also wore a bright red neck kerchief, but it was in such pristine condition that Bosworth never would have guessed that it was the same soiled Kalamazoo Sharpshooter symbol that Lockett and McManus bore.

He had heard the stories before from McManus about how they had fought in Missouri and eventually been subsumed into Birge's Western Sharpshooters regiment. They took pride in it, but he also knew that something particularly bad had happened, though he didn't know what it was.

"I see by your silence that you have your orders, Lockett," Long said with distinct pleasure. "Happy with garrison duty, my old Private?"

"What are you doing here, Orrin?" Lockett replied, trying to keep the emotion out of his voice.

"No? Not happy?" Long continued, ignoring Lockett's question. "I thought not. No, there will be no generals or colonels or even lieutenants to fool while you are on garrison duty. No, there is no way for Private Lockett to miraculously elevate himself while on a garrison post." He laughed, full of pleasure. There was pride in his voice. He had gotten the better of James Lockett, and he knew it.

"On your way back to Michigan, coward?" Lockett retorted, failing to prevent the emotion from coming through.

Long's face drew into a scowl, and he stared down from atop his horse. There was an evil look of vindictiveness that could not be missed. "You would do well not to spread rumors," he growled, "about any of General Halleck's staff officers."

Lockett let the threat pass by. So there was another reason why Blair's Independent Regiment had been relegated to the humiliating existence of garrison duty — Orrin Long. If he was one of Halleck's staff officers...

Still, Orrin's latest threat sounded empty in his ears. What more could the man do to him?

He stayed silent.

"Good day, soldiers!   And good riddance!" Long exalted. Satisfied with his small victory, he mockingly lifted his short-billed kepi as he departed.

Chapter 4

April 18

The boy on the cot to the left of Ainsley Stuart stared up at the parched tent roof with unseeing eyes. The soft-featured lad was sublimely peaceful in death.

For one more soldier, the constant pain felt in a missing limb was no more, Ainsley reflected. Young Peter Hensley of Illinois had gone to join his Heavenly Father.

In the faint early morning light, Lockett sat on a rough, three-legged stool next to Ainsley, and he too looked over at the expired Hensley. "Did he die in his sleep?"

"Quietly," Ainsley nodded, "That's how I knew he was gone."

"I guess I should go tell Doc McClutcheon," Lockett thought aloud after a long pause.

Ainsley gave no reaction other than to close his own eyes.

"You want me to fetch you a drink before I go?" He tried to sit with Ainsley each day when his duties permitted, and he always made it a point to offer Ainsley water. His friend's face was constantly pale and damp with perspiration, and he worried about all of the sweating that Ainsley was doing.

"No, not thirsty," Ainsley answered in a raspy voice. They sat quietly for a few seconds before Ainsley spoke up. "Feel better today. My strength is coming back."

Lockett smiled wanly. He wanted to believe the words, but Ainsley did not look any better. If anything, he looked even weaker. Ainsley had always been rail thin, and Lockett still remembered that first laughable sight of the scarecrow-sized officer in his uniform. It fit Ainsley like a half-askew drapery.

Even so, Ainsley looked to be half that size now, almost skeletal. The skin on his face clawed at the bony corners of his cheeks, seemingly growing tighter and tighter each day.

Ainsley winced. The taut skin beneath his left eye had begun to suffer twitching spasms again.

Each day, Lockett had been saddened to find that the grasp of their departing handshake was growing weaker and weaker. Even a small child had a firmer grip now. He tried to think in a positive light, but it was impossible. Ainsley was slipping away. His friend who had done so much for him was slowly dying before his very eyes, day by painful day.

Yet, Lockett knew Ainsley was lucky to be alive at all. So much blood had been left on his clothing after carrying Ainsley to safety that he couldn't believe his friend was still breathing. When he had found Ainsley again later that night, unconscious and on the cusp of death in the wretched Pittsburg Landing mud, it seemed impossible for his frail looking friend to survive.

He had been sure that if Ainsley could survive that night in the drenching downpour, lying like a hog in the thick mud, unconscious from the severity of his wound, that Ainsley Stuart could survive anything. But, it was as if Ainsley had used all of his strength to survive that initial threat. He seemed to have nothing left, and even daily visits from Patrick and himself could not lift him.

"You seem lost in thought today. Problems with the company?" The voice was tight. Ainsley was fighting hard not to show the pain that Lockett knew he felt.

"No," he answered, surprised that the weakening patient had picked up on it, "Something else, Ainsley."

"Go on," Ainsley prodded with a weak smile, "I'm a good audience. I'm not going anywhere, you see."

Lockett forced himself to chuckle at Ainsley's little joke. "No, it's something else, Ainsley. It's… It's Orrin Long. I saw him yesterday, here in Savannah."

While Ainsley was acquainted with Congressman Vincent's nephew from sharing the same West Michigan social circles, he knew more about the man from listening to Lockett. He had always taken an instinctive dislike to Orrin, so it was not hard for Ainsley Stuart to believe Lockett's account of the reprehensible conduct in Missouri, which led to the death of an innocent girl and Lockett's exile from the Sharpshooters.

"It's been a long time since you saw him. Did he see you too?"

"Well," Lockett said hesitatingly, "I never had the chance to tell you this, but that night when I first found you in that muddy field hospital…"

"Yes?"

"I had just run into Orrin before that."

"Wounded?"

"No, a shirker! He had run, Ainsley. Deserted the Sharpshooters! I saw him down near the Landing with the other skulking cowards!" That thought made Lockett burn. An officer had a responsibility to his men. Cowardice was bad enough for any soldier, but it was especially hideous in an officer.

Ainsley looked at him without surprise. "Should that shock you? You said he ran out on you at the Battle of Hallsville in Missouri, I seem to recall."

"A far less worthy battle at that! No, it didn't surprise me."

Ainsley patiently listened and waited for him to continue.

"He's here in Savannah, Ainsley."

"Well, he has to go somewhere."

"He's a *staff* officer now!" Lockett virtually exploded before bringing his voice back to a harsh whisper. "That no good yellow tail is a staff officer! Why couldn't he be sent somewhere else? It's a big war. Why do we have to keep crossing paths? Every time I see that face, it reminds me of that poor girl. I dreamt about her again last night, Ainsley. Couldn't sleep a wink. Every time I closed my eyes, all I could see was Amelia with her brains blown out!"

April 21

"It's good to be reminded of home," Milton Bosworth continued as he walked alongside Lockett. "Reminds me of home, a good dunking like that."

Though Lockett made no reply, it did not deter Bosworth in the least. He was used to carrying both ends of the conversation, especially when it came to his quiet company commander.

"A Sunday prayer meeting just ain't complete without at least one good dunking, but today, there were three baptisms. Yes, sir, good to see some more washed in the Lamb."

With Lockett purposefully leading the way, they walked past the branching pathway, ignoring the fork that led back to camp. Bosworth gave an imperceptible shrug and kept stride. Normally, he would think little of taking an alternate path, but today, the scorching sun was making him sweat heavily, and he was looking forward to the shade of his tent.

The regimental prayer meeting had been bearable by the cool of the river and the shade of the willows and river birches, but he could feel the day heating up rapidly. This was not Ohio. It felt like August to him.

"Beggin' your pardon, sir, but wasn't that the way back to camp?"

"You were the one who wanted to accompany me back," Lockett said with a hint of amusement. "I never said that I was heading straight back."

"Oh, well, sir," Bosworth hesitated, "I reckon that's true. It's just so hot out here. I think this uniform is five pounds heavier than when I started the day. I think I could wring it out."

Lockett chuckled. "We're almost there, Milton, but I'll take no offense if you head back without me."

"Well, I guess I could go a bit further. Where are we headed, sir?"

Lockett ignored the question and angled towards the shade of a massive willow tree. They were on the edge of town, and

Bosworth could not imagine a single reason for the detour. With some relief, they reached the cool of the willow and removed their hats, wiping their brows.

"Much better in the shade," Bosworth remarked, "Almost bearable."

Lockett grunted in acknowledgement but made no other comment and did not look at his companion. Instead, he intently watched the small, white church beyond them.

The curiosity pained Bosworth, but he bit back the impulse to ask. Clearly, the lieutenant did not want to talk about it. They stood there for a few minutes in a companionable silence that was foreign to the Ohioan.

"Good time for a rest," he said to himself and took a seat.

Leaning back against the tree, he tipped his hat over his brow, but not so much as to obscure the tranquil view that was keeping Lockett's attention.

Then, just as he was about to drift off, there was a peal of childish delight. Opening his eyes, two young boys dashed down the steps of the small church, followed shortly by the rest of the congregation. The first few parishioners were oblivious to the presence of the two soldiers beneath the willow's drooping branches, but then they were noticed.

They were not close enough to hear the murmurings, but it was clear that word was spreading. With a handful frowns and a hatful of suspicious glances, the parishioners headed off in a direction that would take them away from the willow.

"Some Secesh there to be sure, Lieutenant," Bosworth grumbled.

"They're leaving the House of God," Lockett chastised.

"House of God or not, sir. I can see a nasty look plain and clear when I see one."

"Let's not forget that we're not from around here, and we've filled their town with a few hundred wounded men."

"Beggin' your pardon, sir, but I could jus' as easily say the Rebs are responsible for that."

"Point taken," Lockett admitted, his eyes still watching the final few parishioners exiting slowly down the front steps.

An elderly couple took a particularly long time to depart, but then there was no one else. As the final couple disappeared, Bosworth could not contain his curiosity any longer. "Beggin' your pardon, sir, but what are we doing here? If we wanted to draw disapproving looks, we could have had the men parade in front of that Lieutenant Fulkerham."

When Lockett gave no answer, Bosworth rose to his feet and dusted off his backside. He was about to repeat the question one final time before heading back to camp, when the answer came down the front steps of the church.

Her yellow dress flapped briefly in a short gust of steamy air. Pausing, she adjusted the yellow ribbon on her flat straw hat. Satisfied that it was tied securely beneath her chin, she stared off in the other direction. But ever so slowly, she scanned in their direction until she saw the two blue coated soldiers.

Unlike the others, there was no look of apprehension or disdain. No, instead she smiled brightly and waved pleasantly.

"Who is that?" Bosworth uttered softly as it dawned on him why they were here.

She headed straight toward them with an energetic and bouncing stride.

"Why, Lieu-ten-ent Lockett, your prayer meeting ended sooner than you thought, as I can see!"

"I guess there were fewer dunkings than I expected," he said with an uncharacteristically unsettled voice.

Even so, her dark brown eyes never flickered from his face, and she did not seem notice, or care, about his nervousness.

Bosworth could not reconcile Lockett's timorousness with the man he had quickly come to know. How could this be the same recklessly brave and decisive young officer that he had seen at Shiloh? It was comically peculiar. He thought that he had kept himself from laughing aloud, but he must have snickered slightly for the brunette beauty turned her mesmerizing gaze on him.

"And who might you be?" she asked with curious grin.

"Excuse me," Lockett hurried, "This is Sergeant Milton Bosworth."

"Ma'am," Bosworth answered, snatching his hat from his head. For a brief moment, he better understood his officer's discomfort as her dancing eyes seemed to look right through him, all while the dimpled smile froze him in place.

"Milton, this is Miss Anna Tucker from Savannah."

Fortunately for Bosworth, the gaze turned back to the taller Michigander.

"I feared that you might not be here," she admitted, "I'm glad that you did not take your leave too quickly. I needed to help father with something after the service and thought that you might leave before I could stop you. You could have come in, you know?"

"I didn't want to cause any more of a commotion than we already were."

"Don't be frightened away by our curiosity, Lieu-ten-ent," Anna Tucker replied teasingly. "It's not often that Yankee soldiers come to visit our Southern churches. Y'all seem to prefer your own prayer meetings."

"Well…" he began hesitantly.

"Ma'am," Bosworth interjected, "Don't you worry about frightening the lieutenant here. Nothing scares the lieutenant, ma'am. In fact, he may be the most fearless officer in the whole army. Why, at Pittsburg Landing, he carried his wounded leader two miles to safety just as Ruggles's trap closed around him. Why, he had to shoot his way past twenty Rebs!"

"Milton…" Lockett tried to interrupt to no avail.

"How noble!" Anna Tucker answered in an impressed voice. She smiled, having already heard the story a half dozen times from Ainsley.

"Course, Lieutenant Lockett was jus' startin', ma'am. No sooner had he saved Lieutenant Stuart when he turned around and led a charge to stop the Reb advance. Not just any charge, mind you. Bayonet! That's how the Lieutenant led them. All green troops just off the steamer, so new that they didn't have one round between them all. But that didn't stop him, ma'am! Led'em smack into the teeth of the Rebs, waving Lieutenant Stuart's sword and sent them all runnin'!"

"Sergeant Bosworth, that's enough!" Lockett exclaimed, turning a deep shade of red. He turned back to Anna. "He has a tendency to exaggerate."

"Oh, I don't think so," she said cajolingly, "Sergeant, I believe every word."

"As well you should, ma'am, because that's the honest truth."

"Milton, you weren't even there when it happened. You hadn't even met me yet."

"I heard it all from McManus. I know truth when I hears it."

Lockett groaned in resignation, and Anna chuckled.

"Well, anyhow, the sooner the general gets Lieutenant Lockett back on the field, the sooner we can whip the Rebels!" Bosworth pronounced enthusiastically.

A look of sadness crept across Anna Tucker's face, and there was an awkward pause before she said, "I just pray that you don't come across my brother, for his sake."

Lockett could tell that Bosworth was about to say something, and he gave him a not so gentle elbow so that Anna could continue. "You see, my brother's no Rebel, but he's with that army of scoundrels. A month ago, just days before General Sherman's first men arrived, Curcy's Raiders came through town and forced every able-bodied man to join them. If they didn't join, they were to be shot. Most ran off and hid in the woods, but Ambrose refused to leave me unprotected with those bandits running loose in town. He didn't think father would be able to defend me well enough with his bad leg and all. Oh, my foolish brother! If only he had run off like the others... Now, he's with them and against his will."

The drain of melancholy on her face was out of place, but the sight of her father exiting made it a fleeting moment.

"Here comes Father now."

From the church entrance, the gray haired, but youthful faced preacher, limped slowly down the steps. His one leg was little more than dead weight, and he leaned heavily on a hickory cane. He stopped and raised a hand to his brow to block the bright sunlight. Seeing them conversing, he altered his direction and slowly stumped towards them.

"Father and his horse had a disagreement once," Anna explained, noticing that they were staring at him. "He is actually an expert rider, always has been. Even as he got older, he was still the finest horseman in the county. Unfortunately, even though the Bible tempered him in many ways, he never could resist a good race and the wind in his hair. Only just once did he ever have a problem."

"Must have been a distempered horse," Bosworth remarked.

"He can be a high-spirited horse," Anna agreed, "But Father loved riding him so. Thunderbolt is as fast as any horse you've ever seen. I can promise you that."

"Your father likes to ride fast?"

Anna nodded. "As fast as the wind. Even his fall hasn't changed that, although I won't allow him to ride Thunderbolt anymore."

The old preacher continued to rely heavily on the cane and plod towards them. He was sweating in the bright sun, but he bore a pleasant countenance, similar to his daughter. The corners of his mouth were slightly upturned, as if he was amused by some secret joke or just amused by their mere presence. An abbreviated gust of humid air buffeted his silvery hair, and he youthfully swept it back into place with a snap of his head.

"You must be the lieutenant that Anna mentioned to me," he declared cheerfully, proffering a hand as he reached them.

Lockett blinked in surprise and tried not to wince at the preacher's crushing grip.

The older man stared directly at him. "A shame that you missed today's message. All of the Lord's messages are dear to me, but this one was special. Nothing is as important as the

Lord's work, but family is a close second. The safety and security of one's family is paramount. Wouldn't y'all agree?"

Lockett shuffled slightly, feeling uncomfortable, sensing that the father was testing or warning him. He wasn't sure which.

The preacher then shook hands with Bosworth who introduced himself.

"We all do things to protect our families," Lockett answered, thinking about how he had enlisted to keep Daniel from the war.

"Indeed, of course, of course. You missed our service, but perhaps you will join us for lunch then? I can give you a brief summary of the message." He paused with a stone face. When Bosworth's eyes flickered toward Lockett with a fleeting look, not unlike a child being told to do an unsavory task, the preacher winked good-naturedly, though Bosworth seemed to miss that.

"Apologies, sir, but I have duties to attend to back at camp."

"I was not serious about having you listen to a sermon, sergeant," the reverend laughed.

"It's not that, sir. Duty and life in the army."

"Of course, of course, then. How about you, Lieutenant?"

Lockett's eyes darted quickly to Anna, who was smiling expectantly. "Thank you for the offer. It's most welcome."

"Splendid, splendid. Now, if you'll excuse me for a moment, I seem to have left my satchel back inside the church."

"And your hat," Anna added. She turned towards the two soldiers. "Perhaps I should help him find that. As wonderful as he is, he can be a bit absent-minded at times.

She looked at Bosworth, "And thank you for the story, Sergeant. I fear the good Lieu-ten-ent does not like to talk about himself."

"My pleasure, ma'am."

They tipped their hats to her as she followed her father back into the church.

"Milton, what was all that about?" Lockett demanded as soon as they were out of ear shot.

"All what?"

"All Lieutenant Lockett and his bayonet, this and that."

"Jus' helpin' you build yourself up, sir. A pretty girl like that, why, you should thank me, sir." Bosworth permitted himself a friendly grin. "'Sides, it's all the truth. Jus' tryin' to make you look good, sir."

"I don't care whether I look good to Miss Tucker," Lockett lied. "Anyway, from your description, she probably thinks that I'm some sort of blood-thirsty Yankee."

April 22

Lockett grinned to himself as he listened to Bosworth berate one of his men.

"Drop your ramrod?" Bosworth exclaimed, "Why don't you just drop your drawers in front of the enemy? Three shots a minute, Graham! Three! Every man needs to get three off in a minute!"

Bosworth paraded behind the men. He made it sound like they had far to go before reaching their goal, but he winked at Lockett as he walked by. All in all, the boys were doing well. A bit more practice, and they would be there, he mused.

Of course, Lockett and Bosworth both knew that three shots a minute was one thing in an empty pasture; it was quite another with sweaty palms and panting breaths between somebody shooting back at you. That would be the telling moment.

Lockett poured the black powder from his powder flask into the chambers on his Starr revolver.

While his men practiced with their rifles, Lockett practiced loading the still foreign revolver. As a private and then a sergeant, he had never used one until Shiloh. It still felt awkward and strange in his hand. And while his men had the goal of three shots a minute with their rifles; Lockett's goal was loading all six cylinders in the Starr in under a minute.

He had already thumbed the hammer back into a half-cock position and rotated the cylinder. Putting down the flask, he placed the ball over the chamber and pressed firmly with his thumb. Then, he rotated the chamber until it was under the loading lever which forced the lead firmly into place.

He would do the same process five more times before placing the primer caps into place. The men had already fired two volleys by the time he had finished, but they had not yet fired the third. He wasn't sure if it was a good sign that his speed was improving with the revolver or a bad sign that the men's speed with their rifles was not.

When completed, Lockett thumbed the hammer all the way back and took aim on the grass stuffed haversack that hung from a tree thirty yards away. His aim was sporadic. He was much better with a rifle.

He fired twice in close succession. On the second shot, the haversack spun as the heavy slug ripped through it. Lockett lowered the Starr revolver and smiled momentarily.

It was a weapon that he had picked off the field at Shiloh, and he liked it versus the Colt revolver that he had started the second day with. The Starr was a double action revolver. The front trigger pressing against an auxiliary trigger in the back allowed him to fire the gun without first cocking it.

The only drawback was that the second trigger, which allowed for the double action, was rather awkward, and sometimes it felt like it threw off his aim. He assumed that he would improve with practice.

Hitting the target from thirty yards was pretty good, he thought, pleased for the moment. If only he could do that more consistently.

Earlier, he had tested the gun from closer range and found that it packed quite a punch at close quarters. At fifteen yards, the slug had penetrated deeply into a tree nearly five inches in diameter. But it was the accuracy at a slightly longer range that he wanted.

He fired his last four shots and sighed as none of the others hit the haversack. Still, while Bosworth continued to drill the men over and over again, Lockett doggedly practiced.

* * * * *

The fire was starting to burn down to embers, and Adie Graham was already blissfully asleep. He dreamt that he was climbing the huge tree outside his uncle's farm. He was far up into the branches when the whole tree began to shake. Despite the blue sky, it was moving so violently in the wind that he could feel himself shaking in his dream. It took him more than a moment to realize that it wasn't a dream. It was Sergeant Bosworth relentlessly tugging on his shoulder.

"The boy sleeps like the dead," Bosworth complained over his shoulder.

"Jus' give him a good kick," McManus answered, "And be quick about it."

"What's going on?" Adie mumbled.

"Jus' throw him over your shoulder, Milton. C'mon or we'll lose him!"

Bosworth physically yanked Adie to his feet. "C'mon, Graham. We gotta go."

Adie stumbled after Bosworth, leaving the dim glow of the dying campfires. "Where? Where are we going? What's going on? I don't have my gun."

"Don't need no gun," Bosworth answered. "Now, shut up, or he'll hear us."

Adie had no idea who "he" was, but he followed obediently. They had gone a good distance when it occurred to him that they were leaving camp and heading toward the picket posts. He could see McManus up ahead creeping through the brush. Sergeant Bosworth grabbed Adie by the collar and dragged him after McManus. He wanted to open his mouth and ask what was going on again, but it was so quiet that Adie did not dare.

Then the solitude was broken by McManus's loud voice, "Wait one second, Otto."

As they cleared the cover of the brush, they saw McManus standing in front of Otto Klugge. The big German's silhouette dwarfed the smaller Kalamazooan. "What took you so long, Milton?" McManus growled.

"Sorry," Bosworth shrugged.

"You two took so long, I couldn't stop him before he knocked Levi on the head."

There was a low moaning sound, and Adie noticed for the first time that there was someone laying on the ground at Otto Klugge's feet.

"Never saw him coming," McManus said, "Levi's gonna have one heck of headache."

Klugge said nothing and looked belligerently at all three of them.

"Okay, Graham," McManus continued, "Do your thing."

"Huh?" Adie managed.

"Now, we don't speak German, do we? You have to tell Otto what I'm sayin'."

"Oh. Okay. What am I supposed to tell him?"

"Otto, we can't have you leavin' camp again. If they caught you…" McManus paused so Adie could translate.

"It's not that we don't like to partake none," Bosworth picked up, "A man got's a right to drink somethin' with a little fire in it, but you see, if you get caught leavin' camp again, it will be the end for Otto and look bad for Lieutenant Lockett. And we can't have none of that. The lieutenant is one of us. He started out as a private, and we like that. But those rich and powerful sons of bitches don't like the lieutenant for that same reason, and they don't need much excuse to make an example of him." Bosworth stopped so that Adie could rattle on in German, but before he could finish, Otto Klugge cut him off with a smattering of harsh sounding German.

"He says the lieutenant isn't like us," Adie explained, "He's an officer, and it doesn't matter where he came from. He's as… as worthless as any of them." There was an uncomfortable pause after Adie diplomatically finished.

Adie was beginning to think that they would have to physically drag the big German back to camp, a task that he did not relish, even with three of them, but before he could think much more on it, Otto Klugge responded in a more conciliatory tone. Adie smiled at the response, glad that the tension was passing. "Otto says that he'll go back to camp tonight, but only if the sergeant shares some of the Tennessee whiskey that he found on those dead Rebs back at the battle before we came up to Savannah."

"What!" Bosworth responded, "How did he know that I found that? And not a chance! It was just three flasks."

"And a canteen full," McManus pointed out with a small grin.

"It ain't gonna last if I share it. That stuff's more precious 'n gold!"

"C'mon, Milton," McManus laughed, "It's no good to drink alone, now is it?"

Bosworth grumbled under breath.

"Hey, what about Levi?" Adie asked after they had gone two steps.

"Good point," McManus answered, "Guess you better finish his picket duty, Adie. We'll carry Levi back and explain it all to him. Maybe a little whiskey will dull his pain and any sore feelings."

"What? But it's not my turn for picket duty tonight. I want to go back to sleep."

But Bosworth and McManus laughed, and Adie knew that he had drawn the short straw again.

April 23
"Gawl, if it gets any hotter, Lieutenant..." Bosworth moaned, melodramatically pulling his soaked blue uniform from his chest.

Lockett never heard the end of the sergeant's sentence. His eyes and attention were unblinkingly on the stagecoach that had just pulled up in front of weather-beaten Savannah hotel.

At first Lockett had chuckled as he watched the driver assist the lone female passenger down. Even though she was coated with a noticeable layer of dust from the road, moving a bit stiffly, and had her back to him, he could tell that she was a young woman, plus well-to-do judging from her bright patterned dress and expensive looking bonnet.

"Staff officer's wife?" Bosworth speculated aloud.

"Or his mistress?" Levi Thickle smirked.

"Mus' be a staff officer's wife," Prosper T. Rowe chimed in, "Ain't no one else stupid enough to have her travel to this God-forsaken place."

"That's why I said, 'mistress'," Thickle answered, "Generals wouldn't care about a mistress wanderin' around here, but he'd care if it was his wife." He paused. "Course, maybe it's the other way around?"

The woman's tall, slender frame also drew the attention of Halleck's officers standing on the hotel's front step. Lockett thought that she must be quite fetching from the stares that she was drawing.

"Ma'be it's the other way around, Levi, if the mistress looks like that."

"Maybe, Prosper T., maybe," Thickle grunted, "Won't know until she turns around."

Her expensive dress, full of frills, was a terrible choice for what looked to have been a long journey. She took a moment to try to put it back in order before giving up. She also seemed to have no idea that the hotel was now General Halleck's military headquarters and not taking any guests, as she announced to the driver, "I shall inquire inside about a room while you handle my baggage."

Dutifully, the driver lowered one large and one small trunk from the top of the coach, but Lockett was no longer paying attention to that. Bosworth, who had started to say something, stopped in the middle of his soliloquy as his lieutenant stared at the woman and started walking towards her. "Lieutenant, sir, where are you going?"

Lockett gave no answer and kept walking, slowly at first then building momentum. The voice, he thought, that voice sounded impossibly familiar!

Suddenly, the young woman stopped and turned around, as if she was aware that she was being watched. Immediately, her blue eyes flashed recognition. A wide smile broke across her face.

"James!" she exclaimed happily.

"Katherine?" Lockett said in a confused voice as he walked up to her with unbelieving eyes.

Impetuously, she reached out and hugged him warmly. His own hands hung limply at his sides for a second, only slowly did they reach up to return her hug and even then, without the enthusiasm shown by her.

"Katherine, what are you doing here?" he asked dumbfounded, wondering if this was a dream. If it was a hallucination, it was as realistic as his recent ones had been, though far more pleasant than the visages of Shiloh and little Amelia.

"When we heard that Ainsley had been wounded, I rushed here as fast as I could."

"By yourself?"

"Well, Father did not approve, but I would not be stopped this time! Ainsley may only be my cousin, but to me, he is more like a brother!"

Her chin jutted forward defiantly as if she anticipated an argument, but when he said nothing her eyes softened as she stared at the blank look on his face. "He isn't... I mean... Ainsley isn't..." She couldn't complete the sentence, and her voice softened and choked.

"Dead?" he finally filled in, "No, he isn't dead, but he is in bad shape, Katherine. If..."

"And that's why I'm here," she interrupted, as she was prone to do. Gathering strength again, she added, "I'm going to nurse him back to health."

"He certainly could use some care, but you shouldn't be here, Katherine."

Her eyes flashed with such anger that Lockett mentally took a step back.

"Don't you tell me what to do and what not to do!" she said hotly. "It wasn't easy to get this far."

Her cheeks flushed with color, and he knew that he had spoken too hastily. Obviously, her father, and certainly her mother, did not approve of this trip and could even be a few miles behind her – ready to take her back to Michigan, but that hadn't stopped her.

Katherine Moffat was a stubborn young woman. He had known that before, but he didn't realize how stubborn until now. "At least, your heart is in the right place," he thought aloud, a relenting look on his face.

The words relaxed Katherine, and like a Plains thunderstorm, the obstinate face and aggressive tone disappeared instantly. She put her arm through his, "Come, help me get a room, then you can take me to Ainsley."

"That won't work, Katherine."

"Why not?"

"The hotel is now General Halleck's headquarters. There are no rooms."

"Well, then I'll find another."

"There are no other rooms in Savannah. No rooms for 20 miles as far as I know."

"No rooms? But where am I to stay?" she asked, mystified.

"That I don't know, but..." he started before noticing Anna Tucker coming across the dusty street, a breadbasket under her arm. Instinctively, he looked down at his elbow, acutely aware that Katherine still clung to his arm.

"Why Lieu-ten-ent Lockett, have you found yourself a southern Belle?" she said in her melodic voice.

Anna eyed where Katherine had her arm wrapped around his.

He blushed a deep red. "Ah, no, no," he stammered before catching himself.

"I'm no Southerner. I'm here to find my wounded cousin," Katherine immediately answered, wary of the Tennessean. There was a bit of a challenge in her voice. "He's been wounded here."

Anna Tucker paid the challenge no attention. She smiled casually, which only made her cut an even sharper contrast to Katherine Moffat. Anna was shorter than Katherine with a more curvaceous build, but it was the brown curls of hair that framed dimpled cheeks and a vivacious smile that made her stand out against Katherine's tall, lean figure and austere stare.

"I was on my way to give the good major some freshly baked bread," Anna explained, turning her attention back to Lockett. "I'd ask you to accompany me, but I see you are already occupied, Lieu-ten-ent," she added teasingly.

"Actually, I am occupied, but not how you think," Lockett replied. He glanced over to his men who were lounging on the hitching post, entertained by the whole affair. "However, perhaps you could help me?"

"It would be my sweetest pleasure, Lieu-ten-ent. Whatever can I do for you?"

"Well, Lieutenant Stuart, you see," he said, trying to figure out the best way to open the subject.

"Yes, brave Ainsley," Anna gushed, her liquid brown eyes turned to Katherine, "You must have Lieu-ten-ent Lockett tell you the story of how he saved Lieu-ten-ent Stuart — a most courageous and noble story indeed."

"Another time," he resumed quickly but politely, "You see, Miss Tucker, allow me to introduce Miss Katherine Moffat, Ainsley's cousin. She's traveled all the way from Kalamazoo, Michigan to help nurse him back to health, but the hotel..."

"Say no more," Anna interrupted, "I see now... You must be so tired, my dear." Anna compassionately slid over to Katherine's side. "Help me deliver this to the major. I'm sure he can arrange some men to bring your bags to my house."

"Your house?"

"Oh, never fear, you angel of mercy, I'm sure father won't mind such a noble guest. Of course, it is a humble house, and you'll have to share my room, but it is the only room in Savannah..." Anna rattled on, dragging Katherine by the arm into the hotel/headquarters.

Katherine looked back anxiously at him, but he merely smiled and waved. "Don't worry, Katherine. You're in good hands. I'll pay a visit in an hour and take you to Ainsley."

Lockett turned around and glared at his men lounging on the hitching post. "What are you men gawking at?" he snapped. "Back in line! We got a wagon train to unload."

Chapter 5

"James," Katherine said simply as she slid her arm through his and allowed herself to be escorted toward the field hospital. She was more quiet than normal, and he wondered if it was because of her accommodations.

Katherine Moffat had seldom shared in her young life. There had been no need. She had everything that one could want as the daughter of Big John Moffat. He guessed that she did not like sharing a room, especially with a stranger, although given Anna's personality, they would not be strangers for long.

Katherine would get used to sharing a room, he decided. She'd have to, because there was no other way.

As they neared the tent hospital, he changed his mind. Perhaps, the reason for Katherine's muted behavior was not due to sharing, but due to the nervousness at seeing Ainsley and other wounded men. Even Lockett wasn't immune to the sight and smell of the place, but that was nothing compared to experiencing it for the first time.

He wanted to tell Katherine that she didn't have to do this, but he knew that would only provoke a sharp reaction from her. It would all come as a complete shock to the young debutante, but there was no stopping her. She had come too far and broken too many of the barriers as to the conduct of a "proper lady" to stop now.

"What are your intentions with Anna Tucker?" Katherine asked abruptly as the hospital tent came within sight.

"Intentions?" he said in a mystified voice.

"Yes, intentions. Miss Tucker seems quite taken with you. She talked on and on."

"On and on?" he mumbled.

"Is that story about you saving Ainsley true?"

"First of all," he began, "I've no intentions with Miss Tucker. I hardly know her. She's very friendly, but that's her nature. I'm certain there is nothing more to it than that, Katherine. Now, as for Ainsley, yes, it is true that Patrick and I did carry him away from General Ruggles's trap..."

"And the part about carrying him across the field under fire?" she interrupted.

"Yes, we..."

"And the part about leading a charge with only Ainsley's sword and men without any ammunition for their guns?"

"Yes, well..."

"And that's how you became an officer?"

"Yes, that's all true," he finished in a soft, almost embarrassed voice.

"You, an officer?" There was a hint of disbelief and mocking in her voice.

He doubted that she knew how she sounded. Such lording conceit came naturally to her, he mused. She could be a funny girl. There were times when she showed such interest and excitement in seeing him, like today in front of the hotel, but he always felt that interest was driven by a curiosity more than anything else. With a sigh, he remembered what he had told himself many a time, that Katherine Moffat would always think of him as a poor farmer and nothing more.

She was not like her cousin Ainsley in that respect. Ainsley saw him as what he could be, while Katherine could not picture him as anything except what he had been.

"*Lieutenant* Lockett. I never would have believed it," she muttered to herself and made no further comment.

"Yes, an officer," he said humbly.

They walked in silence until they reached the large white tent, halting before the flap. The smell of the place was strong, and he looked at Katherine with that question on his lips again. She seemed to know what he was thinking. With a decisive nod, she faced the opening again and stepped through.

Her eyes scanned the misery. Men laid with bandages on heads, arms, legs, and stumps. One armless soldier thrashed in a seizure as an overworked twelve-year-old orderly struggled to hold him down so that the stump would not rupture and bleed anew. It was a flurry of activity in that corner between the patient, the orderly, and the doctor. Katherine's eyes could not leave the scene even though the rest of the tent tried to ignore it, like it was an everyday occurrence.

There was additional background noise from a moaning captain. His dazed and feverish eyes fixated on Katherine. "Ma?" he questioned.

Lockett stiffened uncomfortably as Katherine took it all in. She shouldn't be here, he thought to himself, but she took a hesitant step forward and then another. Slowly, she made her way deeper into the tent, scanning each cot.

Finally, Lockett strode past her and turned to the left. "Over here, Katherine," he said softly. He looked down at his friend.

Ainsley Stuart's eyes were closed, and his bony chest heaved softly as he rested. His brown hair was damp, and his left hand tremored oddly.

"Ainsley," he whispered gently, "Ainsley, wake up. You have a guest."

His eyes fluttered open and took a moment to focus on Lockett's face. The blue orbs were cloudy and rheumy, as if covered with some sort of mist. From the obtuse look, Lockett wondered if Ainsley comprehended the words, but then the filmy eyes looked to the person on the other side of the cot. They widened, and his lips formed around the name.

"Katherine?" he croaked in a raspy, disbelieving voice.

She nodded, and a relieved smile slowly came across his face.

In that moment, Lockett realized that Katherine's presence was exactly what her cousin needed. He could almost feel Ainsley's spirits lifting.

"I came as soon as I could," Katherine declared, dropping to her knees so that she was eye to eye with him. A tear rolled down her face, and gently, she clasped his clammy hand. "I'm going to make sure that you heal up real fast."

"I know," Ainsley smiled weakly in relief.

* * * * *

Orrin Long looked out the second floor window of the hotel/headquarters, unthinkingly gripping the ledge with all his strength, remembering the shocking sight from hours earlier.

The initial astonishment of seeing Katherine Moffat here in Savannah had not passed yet. Of course, four days prior, he had received a telegram from Big John Moffat warning him that his daughter may be on her way to Tennessee to find her cousin. The powerful West Michigan businessman naturally wanted him to send her back to Kalamazoo forthwith.

When he had first read the telegram, Orrin Long thought his future father-in-law was overreacting. He couldn't imagine that Katherine would travel all this way. Surely, she had come to her senses and turned back, probably before she even reached Indiana.

But she had not turned back. She was here in Savannah!

However, it was not the sight of her graceful walk that made Orrin Long wrench part of the window sill free, rather it was sight of his soon-to-be fiancée arm in arm with another man. And not just any other man, but James Lockett!

He had no idea that she even knew Lockett!

Surely, it must be some sort of nightmare, he thought. It couldn't be happening. Why was she arm in arm with that plebian farmer?

The week before he had taken such pleasure in convincing General Halleck that Lockett and his men were a band of unreliable cowards. Now, the satisfaction was not enough. Orrin Long knew now that he was not done with Lockett.

After today, he vowed to do far worse.

April 24

Colonel Blair looked out at Lockett from behind the neatly stacked papers and ledgers. His hair was carefully coifed behind his receding hairline so that it seemed to wrap itself in one smooth wave from the sides of his head directly into the long moustache that looped from behind his ears. It was a bushy, reddish-brown curtain that obscured most of his lips.

"Lieutenant Lockett," Blair addressed him, "You always seem to be itching to enter the fray so when the general first gave me this order, I immediately thought of you. How about taking care of some bushwhackers, Lieutenant?"

"I always do my duty, sir, whatever the order."

"Yes, yes. What the general needs is the safety of our supply line. It seems the Rebs have been ambushing a wagon train or two east of here. Bushwhackers. Bandits. Murderers. Highwaymen. The general has ordered me to send one company to find and destroy these bushwhackers. Up to that, Lockett?"

"Yes, sir."

"I knew you would be."

"A question if I may, sir?" Lockett added, thinking back to his first days in the war. As one of Birge's Western Sharpshooters, their first assignment had been to rid Missouri of the roving bands of bushwhackers. It had not been an easy task for infantry. The mounted bushwhackers had proved too mobile for men on foot. They would ride away whenever the threat seemed too great and would then reappear to cause chaos when the odds were more in their favor. Only when the bushwhackers had made the mistake of entering into a conventional, stand-up fight at Mount Zion had the Federals been able to make any inroads.

Colonel Blair nodded with some annoyance, "Go on."

"Will we be given mounts, sir?"

"Mounts?" Colonel Blair said in a puzzled voice, "Whatever for? We are infantry, Lieutenant."

"I realize that, sir, but…"

"There are no contradictions, Lieutenant. The orders are clear. One company of Blair's Independents is to march. Find the bushwhackers in their lair and destroy them." Blair looked down at the written orders. "It's very clear, Lieutenant. It says nothing about mounts."

"Yes, sir."

"I'm surprised at you, Lockett. Asking for mounts? I was told that obstacles meant nothing to you. They tell me that you rose up to your new station by your exemplary actions, but now you ask for mounts? Perhaps, General Halleck was right in assigning a different officer to lead this detachment."

"Different officer, sir?" Lockett asked quickly.

"Regulations, Lieutenant. To lead a detached company, one must be a captain. Seeing as how there are no captains in our motley group, I was prepared to ignore this protocol, but the general suggested that one of his staff officers lead the company."

"Yes, sir. I see, sir," Lockett replied, trying to hide the disappointment. The thought of serving beneath a staff officer was not disheartening in and of itself, but he had been looking forward to leading the men on his own, just as he had at Barnes Field.

"Unfortunately, the general could not spare Captain Fulton for this, but he assured me that Lieutenant Long is a highly capable officer."

"Lieutenant Long!" Lockett interjected before he could stop himself.

"Yes," Blair said, giving a disapproving look at the interruption. "He is only a lieutenant, but he is a staff officer. Besides, I'm sure he has date of service on you," Blair chuckled at his little joke.

Lockett completely missed the humor. Like a drumbeat, the name *Orrin Long* reverberated in his brain. He could think of nothing worse than serving under the scum again.

The last time he had served under Orrin, he had been framed for murder. Painfully, the vision of little Amelia's shattered head leapt into his mind. Though his brain kept spinning, nothing could remove that image from his thoughts.

* * * * *

Katherine was returning to the field hospital, having slept fitfully through her first night in Savannah.

She decided that Ainsley needed to be bathed and shaved today. Fixing his haggard appearance was the first step to his recovery, she thought to herself.

She was wondering what the second step could be when she happened to look up and saw a handsomely dressed lieutenant standing in the road, hands on his hips, barring her path. With his brass buttons shining, he looked the very image of a hero, and it took a moment for those thoughts to clear her mind and recognize the actual person.

"Orrin!" she cried out in surprise and rushed forward into his arms.

The strength of her reaction had a cathartic effect on Orrin Long's imposing presence. His face dropped its imperious glare and broke into a pleased smile.

"Orrin, whatever are you doing here?" Katherine exclaimed happily.

"I might ask you the same thing, Katherine," he replied, "However, I am here because I am on General Halleck's staff."

"A staff officer! How wonderful! That is an honor... isn't it?" she added with less certainty.

"Quite."

"You must have made quite a name for yourself in battle. We received your telegram the very day I left. Your courageous stand against such odds left me breathless!"

"I can hardly believe it myself," he said smoothly of his lie.

"Oh, Orrin!" she said, happily hugging him again.

"Now, my dearest, where were you headed?" he asked in a concerned voice.

"The hospital, of course, to see Ainsley."

"Ainsley? Here? Wounded?" He feigned surprise. "I had no idea."

"Yes, he was wounded at Shiloh. A Rebel shell sheared his foot clean off. He looks so weak and pale, Orrin."

"Your cousin has always looked weak and pale."

"Oh, shame on you, joking about such a matter," Katherine castigated him.

"But I can't allow you to go to the hospital, Katherine. It is through camp, and that is no place for a lady."

Anger flashed in Katherine's eyes, but he quickly quelled it. "I must accompany you, my dearest. Let us go see your cousin, Ainsley."

As the smell of decay reached Orrin Long's nose, he felt his stomach twisting and heaving. The carnage of Shiloh started to creep into his head. Unbidden, the images of blood, death, and waves of butternut clad Rebels came into his mind. The coppery smell of the blood and the unmistakable odor of black powder filled his nose. Somehow, he was not in a wretched hospital tent anymore but in an even more wretched field of killing and butchery.

He had tried hard not to run that day, and been successful for the first sequence of the battle, but then the fear had been too much, and he had run for his life. His mind started to replay the shriek of the shells, and he could swear that he felt the earth quiver like it did when those shells had landed and torn clumps from the land.

His face showed the strain of the thoughts, and Katherine mistook the whitening of his face as compassion for the maimed and wounded. She warmly reached out for his hand and gripped it quietly as his stride slowed. With a squeeze, she silently encouraged him forward, and they made slow steps to the cot where Ainsley Stuart slept.

The two of them loomed over Ainsley briefly before his eyes fluttered open. The sight of Orrin Long did not seem to surprise Ainsley, which surprised Katherine. Impassively, Ainsley looked up at them.

Wordlessly, Orrin Long's gaze ran over Ainsley from head to toe. The son of Senator Stuart did not look well. His face showed beads of perspiration, and his shirt was damp with sweat. His bony arms were limp on the cot, while his hands tremored slightly. His pants were crusted with dried blood and surgical plaster. Finally, Orrin Long's eyes settled on the stump where Ainsley's foot should have been.

Stuart was in bad shape and probably wouldn't live, he surmised, which served the fool just as well. The slightly built scholar was a tender-hearted dupe with none of his father's backbone.

"It's gone," Ainsley said eventually, causing Orrin Long to lift his gaze.

"What?"

"The foot. It's gone," Ainsley said simply. "Staring at it won't make it come back."

"I'll get some water," Katherine said, excusing herself.

Long turned to watch her depart. He didn't want to be here, especially alone, and scoured his brain for the proper excuse.

"We're a long ways from Kalamazoo, Orrin."

"Yes." It was obvious that he wasn't all that interested in a conversation, but that didn't seem to stop Ainsley.

"You survived in one piece, I see."

"Yes."

"Happened to me near the sunken road. Where were you?"

Orrin's head snapped up suspiciously. There was something in Ainsley's tone that he did not like. "The Peach Orchard," he answered, his smooth face studying Ainsley's more closely. Despite the sweat and pallor, Stuart's eyes were alert.

"Nasty fighting there," Ainsley remarked. "That was where Henry lost his arm and leg." He pointed to a captain two cots down. "How did the Sharpshooters fare?"

"Well."

"Your uncle? He is well?"

"Unscathed."

Ainsley nodded, and there was an awkward silence before he added, "A staff officer now?"

"Yes," Long answered slowly, wondering how Stuart knew that. Katherine had not known of his promotion. Then he realized that Stuart must have talked to Lockett.

If Stuart had talked to Lockett about that, then Lockett had probably told him about the night at Pittsburg Landing...

A scowl began to spread across his face.

Lockett had told Stuart about their encounter at the Landing the night after the first day of battle! Stuart knew his secret!

Subconsciously, he adjusted the red kerchief around his throat, even though the bruises had faded by now.

Katherine returned with the water for Ainsley. "What's wrong, Orrin?" she asked, noting the angry look on his face.

He smoothed his thin moustache with two fingers to buy himself a moment. "Nothing wrong, my dear," he answered in a pleasant voice, "Much to do, I'm afraid. You know, the price of being a staff officer."

"Of course," she replied.

"My dear Katherine, I will see you later," he said with a kiss on her cheek.

April 25

The day was annoyingly humid again.

There were always a few humid days in Kalamazoo, Lockett reflected, but nothing this oppressive. He felt like he had grown an extra layer of skin, sticky to the touch, which rubbed against the over-insulating feel of the blue wool. Beads of perspiration were already beginning to appear on his forehead despite the early morning hour, and he was not the only one feeling every degree of the temperature.

For over an hour, he and his men had waited. The grumbling had started almost instantly, and Lockett had thought about letting it go. After all, their opinion of Orrin Long was nowhere near as low as his own, but he snapped at the men to keep quiet.

While his men found it unusual that he was so short-tempered today, most attributed it to the early morning hour and nothing more.

Still, the grumbling went on silently. The minutes in the hot sun and thick air dragged on. Finally, Lieutenant Orrin Long came riding up, but he was not alone.

Lockett nodded and said nothing when informed that Congressman Willey from Kentucky would be accompanying them. He could see little good coming from the addition, but he knew that he had developed a prejudice against politicians in general. Unsuccessfully, he tried to push it out of his mind.

Despite the swirl of thoughts, his stony face showed none of it. The men, on the other hand, could be heard snickering behind the two riders. Utterly bald and with a considerable paunch, Congressman Eustus P. Willey shifted uncomfortably in the saddle.

The heavy set Congressman and the young staff officer rode at the head of the column, pointedly conversing only with themselves. Lockett felt no slight at it; he preferred it that way. The less he spoke with Orrin, the better.

But his men, not realizing the past history between the two, took offense at the slight to their lieutenant. They guessed that it had to do with the fact that James Lockett had once been a private like them. They had no idea that there was so much more to it.

Lockett walked with his men near the head of the column.

"It's going to be a hot day for a walk, sir," Adie Graham said to him. The cherubic cheeks of the young private were already apple-red, and the wisps of hair sprouting from beneath his hat were soaked and clinging together.

"Just make sure you take a swig from that canteen once in a while, Adie. I don't want to have to carry you all the way back to Savannah."

"Yes, sir," Graham grinned, pleased that his lieutenant would address him with such familiarity. Ahead of them, Orrin Long and Congressman Willey rode their horses, kicking up a dust cloud that the men had to march through. "How come you don't ride a horse like the rest of the officers?" he added conversationally.

"Cuz he don't have the money to afford that," Levi Thickle commented quietly from behind Graham, but not so quietly that Lockett could not hear.

Adie shot the older private a warning look, but Lockett took no offense. "That's true, but I also just don't like ridin' horses much. Just don't care much for horses, Adie."

"Don't care much for them?" The look of surprise on Graham's face nearly made Lockett laugh.

"I'm good with them when they're hitched to a plow, but not with a saddle. I'd rather walk. It hardens the feet."

"I s'pose that's why you can march all day and never get tired, sir."

"Probably, Adie. Probably."

Despite the dust and humidity, the men were in high spirits so far. A few were whistling *We Are Coming Father Abraham*, a popular marching tune. Many of the men chatted, and Prosper T. Rowe always seemed to be laughing at some joke. His unrestrained and hooting cackle rose above all other sound.

Lockett had half a mind to restrict such exuberance. Bushwhackers were liable to strike at any time. There was no predicting them. He had learned that in Missouri. The problem with bushwhackers was that they always knew the land and had nothing better to do except lay in ambush.

But he decided against imposing stricter standards on the march until later. Garrison duty had not been good for morale, and the men needed this, so he decided to let them enjoy this for a little while longer, just until they got a little further away from town.

Private Elmer Hunt's doughy face folded into a grimace, and he rubbed a grimy forefinger against his large, misshapen nose. With a shake of his head, he watched another fellow soldier duck into the woods and crouch behind a tree, dropping his drawers just in the nick of time.

A few men snickered at the unfortunate soldier, but most did not. Most were personally familiar with the "Tennessee Trots" by now, the painful stabbing sensation at a man's abdomen. No one was ever really sure what caused the ailment, although some men were sure it had to do with fouled water sources.

A long blade of grass dangled lazily in Prosper T. Rowe's open mouth. With a sudden movement, he snatched it away and clucked, "No prob'm findin' our way back, boys. This trail w'are leavin' is better 'n breadcrumbs!"

A few soldiers snorted in amusement.

After the high-spirited start, the pace of the march had slowed as soldier after soldier would duck off into the woods. Their comrades shuffled their feet just a little bit more to make it easier for the afflicted man to catch up. Ever slowing, the column moved along the narrow dirt road.

As Lockett walked behind Orrin Long's horse at the head of the column, he wondered if the men were just generally out of condition. Most had arrived here deep in the heart of Tennessee by steamer. Few, if any, had marched here, and garrison duty involved little real marching, no matter how hard he drilled them.

In the end, he concluded that the "Trots" were the real culprit. He had seen a similar dose of it in Missouri and knew the Trot's agony and how it weakened a man's whole spirit.

But glowering from atop his horse, Orrin Long had no sympathy, even though he had seen it while they were in Missouri.

"Straggling," Long began, "Is a surefire sign of poorly disciplined men, Lockett." He stopped and glared, disappointed that the farmer's face showed no reaction. "If these were my men, Lockett, I promise you, there would not be such straggling."

"They *are* your men today," Lockett replied, immediately regretting that he had opened his mouth.

Long's face flashed sharp disapproval at the retort, but the flood of words that Lockett expected did not come. Rather, he slowly, with odd deliberateness, lifted his cap from his head and smoothed his wavy brown hair.

How the man kept himself so clean was a mystery to Lockett. He knew that he did not share the fresh, clean semblance.

"These *shirkers*," Long said, motioning with his cap to the men behind him, "Are an embarrassment to me and to Congressman Willey. It is unacceptable! Do you hear me, Lockett?"

"Sir…" he began, his anger rising that Orrin would have the gall to call someone else a shirker, particularly his men.

"Say nothing, Lockett!" Long snapped immediately, a despotic look on his self-satisfied face. His voice became slightly shrill. "I will not abide any more straggling."

"Sir, there is little…"

"Shot! Lockett, the next man who leaves the column will be shot!"

"Shot?" he said in a bewildered voice, wondering if Long was serious, "But it's the Trots."

"The Trots?"

"Yes, sir," he replied, forcing himself to say the second word, "It must be bad water at camp. Half of the men are sick with it. There is nothing that can be done about it right now."

"Excuses? I want no excuses, Lockett." He paused and adjusted his red scarf. "You will shoot the next man to step out."

"I will not." Lockett's voice sounded oddly tinny and perplexed in his own ears. He took a breath to gather his thoughts quickly.

"You are disobeying a direct order?" Long questioned, a pleased look on his face, as if he had planned this all along.

"I will not shoot a sick soldier for stepping out for a moment to relieve himself. If the man is to be shot, then you will have to do it yourself."

His voice sounded more controlled now, and the gray eyes did not waver as he glared with quiet contempt and icy conviction. He left unsaid his next thought, *if you do shoot one of my men, I'll shoot you next, you bastard! Court-martial and hanging be damned!*

But before the exchange could go any further, Congressman Willey returned in a slow gallop. Heeling over clumsily in his saddle, he reined in his horse. For a moment, Lockett thought the congressman might fall to the ground.

"You seem to have some sick men, Lieutenant Lockett," Willey said with a pondering tone, as if the observation required great powers of deduction.

"It's bad water, Congressman. It happens when you stay in one camp too long, especially with so many wounded and dead around you," Lockett explained.

"Ahh," Willey nodded thoughtfully, "Are you still fit to fight? What about the bushwhackers?"

"My men will still fight like tigers, Congressman," he promised in a serious voice, ignoring Long's derisive snort.

The rotund Congressman seemed intent on starting a conversation. He pulled a flask from his pocket and took a long pull. He held it out to the lieutenant walking alongside him, but Lockett shook is head and politely declined.

Leaning back slightly in the saddle, the Congressman looked away and said, "Lieutenant Long tells me that most of your men were gathered from those who ran at Shiloh."

Orrin would know, Lockett thought bitterly to himself, but he answered in a composed voice, "A few were, Congressman, but not most. And those who did run that first day were often victims of circumstance, not cowardice."

"Any man who would not stand to defend the Union is a coward unworthy of the uniform!" Willey suddenly expounded, sounding like he was making a speech on the campaign trail. "Why, I should think that an officer would know that! Any man worth his weight should happily stand to defend the Union, against any odds!" Willey waved his free hand wildly and lost some balance in the saddle for a moment.

The congressman had a voice that could be heard across any field, and Lockett was certain that the comments had reached his men's ears. Fighting the urge to look behind him, he looked up at the politician.

Congressman Willey returned the stare with a look of condemnation. "How long have *you* been an officer?" The congressman clearly knew the answer to that question, but Lockett did not take the bait.

Maintaining his poise, he replied, "Congressman, if we find these bushwhackers, you will see my men's courage."

"If?" Willey questioned, "If?"

"Yes, if, sir," Lockett maintained stubbornly. "Bushwhackers are not like the regular army. I know. I chased bushwhackers around Missouri. They will run and hide, attacking only when they know they have the advantage. I'll be surprised if we even find a trace of them, much less see them."

"You fought in Missouri also?" Willey said in surprise, "Did you know Lieutenant Long when you were there?"

"We had some interaction," he answered coyly, looking directly at Long. Subconsciously, he reached up and touched his own red Kalamazoo Sharpshooter's scarf. The sweat-stained knot was so soiled and worn, it was impossible for Congressman Willey to notice that it was the same insignia that Orrin Long jauntily wore.

"We had some interaction," Lockett repeated to himself.

Chapter 6

Adie Graham took another long drink out of his canteen. His early exuberance had long since faded, and the bright color in his face had drained away. Closing his eyes, he leaned back in the thickening grass. The rest break hadn't come soon enough for him.

Neither the sound of Levi Thickle's "hurumphh", nor the sound of the approaching wagons stirred him. All he wanted to do was sleep and pray for deliverance from the horrible pains in his stomach.

He knew it was the Trots again. They had not come on so suddenly last time, but he recognized the gut twisting agony. He had missed all of the action at Shiloh, infirmed by the Trots.

The echoing of distant cannon and the steady stream of wounded back into Savannah, where he waited, had only added to his frustration that fateful day.

How he had wanted to join his comrades in the fight!

But it had been no use. He had been so weak that day that he couldn't even stand. The fact that he recovered so quickly a couple of days later convinced his old comrades that he was a coward and was then pawned off onto Lieutenant Lockett and his motley company.

He would show them! He would prove them wrong, he thought as he lay in the grass. They all thought him a coward, faking an illness to avoid battle. But he wasn't afraid of the Rebs! He had been sick!

His old regiment was on the way to Corinth now, having no need for a "shirker" like Adie Graham, but he'd show them. He would find action today with Lieutenant Lockett and then onto the capture of Corinth. He'd show them all. He was sure of that as he drifted off to a tense sleep and prayed that this time the Trots would not be so severe.

While Adie Graham wandered into slumber, the rest of the company curiously watched the wagons, which were pulled by the most worthless team of mules that they had ever seen. Slowly, the small train of five wagons came to a stop, and the newcomers made their way over to the lounging soldiers.

Levi Thickle watched McManus, who had led the train back from his picket post, speak with Lieutenant Lockett. "That man sure as hellfire has the Lieutenant's ear," Thickle commented to no one in particular.

"No mistaking that," someone else agreed.

While Levi Thickle had no particular qualm about the lieutenant or the unsociable McManus, he didn't like the cozy relationship that the two shared. Clearly, the Lieutenant shared things with McManus that he did not share with the rest of the men.

"May we?" a voice interrupted.

It was one of the newcomers from the wagon, motioning to a bare patch of ground next to him.

With a snort and a nod that the newcomer took as a 'yes', the man sat down next to Thickle. He was well-dressed and middle-aged with an expensive looking watch chain poking out from the inside of his jacket. His fragile facial features and dainty moustache made Levi Thickle's tobacco colored, weather-worn appearance look all the more hardened.

"Now, who'ur you?" Thickle grunted with no disguise of his less than positive impression. He then made a show of eye-balling the man from head to toe.

The newcomer cleared his throat. "Doctor Orvis Wilhelm, U.S. Sanitary Commission."

From the blank look he received, Wilhelm half-thought that the soldier had never heard of the U.S. Sanitary Commission. Yet, most soldiers were very familiar with it and even more thankful for it. Most soldiers' worst nightmares involved being on the surgeon's table, but without the Sanitary Commission and its volunteers, that nightmare would have been doubly so.

"On your way to Savannah?" Prosper T. Rowe asked personably. A new blade of grass dangled in his gap-toothed mouth.

"Yes, as a matter of fact. We have medical supplies from Nashville. I hear conditions in Savannah are dreadful."

"Ain't so bad," Thickle said, concentrating on a hawk flying high overhead, "There are worse places to die."

Wilhelm looked at him with alarm, but Thickle continued to watch the hawk, or was it a buzzard, flying high circles over their lunch spot.

Wilhelm looked from the craggy eyed soldier to the friendlier, gap-toothed one, but all he received was a shrug from Rowe.

"Well, ahh," Dr. Wilhelm cleared his throat again, "Hopefully, we can prevent a few more from dying."

"As long as you leave'm all their limbs," Thickle said abruptly. Without a second look at the startled doctor, he rose to his feet and wandered over to the clump of trees beyond them and relieved himself.

Still perplexed, the doctor watched him go and did not look away until he realized what the soldier was doing. With a reddened, confused look, Wilhelm looked over at the gap-toothed private again.

"Don't mind Levi," Rowe said, flicking a weevil off his hardtack before jamming it into the side of his mouth and breaking off a chunk, "That's jus' his way. He has his reasons."

"Ahh, yes, umm, of course."

"So-ah, ya see any'm bushwhackers on your way?" he asked, washing down the brick-like hardtack with some tepid water.

"Bushwhackers!" Doctor Wilhelm said with a wide-eyed look, "Thank Heavens, no!"

Lockett walked slowly back to the picket post with McManus, knowing that this would be no short lunch break. Despite Orrin Long's earlier harangue, Congressman Willey insisted on being given ample time to digest his food, and Orrin all too eagerly agreed. At least it might help some of the men, Lockett thought humorlessly, as he looked at a few of the sick ones dozing in the grass.

"James," McManus began, using his Christian name because they were out of earshot.

Ironically, they had both remonstrated Ainsley Stuart about such informality just a few months ago, but Patrick had trouble calling his lifelong friend anything but 'James.' Twenty years of friendship and habit were hard to overcome.

"If there are bushwhackers out there, then the Sanitary Commission wagons are the luckiest fellows this side of the Mississippi. We heard them coming from a good ways off."

Lockett nodded, though his mind was on the conditions back at the tent hospital. While the steamers brought some supplies, and conditions were improving, they could use even more medical supplies, not to mention doctors. There were just too many wounded.

"James?" McManus queried.

"I'm listening, Patrick." He turned back to his friend. "So, what are you saying? You think this is a wild goose chase today?"

"You know as well as I do that we're on one. Only blind luck will bring us any bushwhackers."

"Would you rather accompany wagon trains between here and Nashville? Either we get lucky and clear out the bushwhackers this way, or we may end up as nothing more than an armed escort for wagon trains."

The thought of that much marching just for the humiliation of being relegated to such duty was not a pleasant notion. "I ain't interested in guarding baggage," McManus grumbled.

"Even garrison duty would be better than that," Lockett agreed.

"Especially for you," McManus added with his mood lightening, "Especially now that Big John Moffat's daughter is here in Savannah of all places."

"Aw, not this again. I had to hear all about this from you when we were mustered in with the 12th in Niles, and now again?"

McManus shrugged. "If the shoe fits," he started before laughing, "Besides, it is either her or that sweet Miss Tucker."

"Oh, c'mon," Lockett complained, but the teasing from McManus was a welcome respite from his dark thoughts.

It was just a hint of Patrick's old jocular personality, how he used to be before Martha, his wife, died. It was just a hint, but even the possibility that Patrick could someday return to that persona made Lockett feel a little less dreary. That was one of the problems with the war, he thought, there seemed to be no end in sight, and even if there was, everything and everybody seemed to have been irrevocably ruined.

Ahead of them, they could see Private Sandie Holmes leaning against a tree, eyes closed. The smoke from the young Illinois store clerk's pipe drifted back to them, and the momentary ease that Lockett had felt at the good-natured ribbing quickly evaporated. "Private Holmes!" he barked, startling the young private.

Tow-headed with an angelic face, Sandie Holmes turned around immediately, his nervous blue eyes wide with surprise and fear.

"Private, open your eyes and take that pipe out of your mouth this instant! You are on picket duty, and that means I expect you to be constantly alert, not half asleep against this tree."

"Yes, sir."

Lockett glared at him.

Grant's entire army had been caught by surprise at Shiloh. Were it not for Major Powell's unauthorized pre-dawn patrol, all would have certainly been lost. The Army of Tennessee would have been captured in their own tents. Surprise was the ultimate weapon, and he would be damned if he let his little patrol be so lax. The mere thought stirred vicious passions in him. These were his men. Their lives depended on him.

"Private, I'll have you whipped if I find you like this again on picket duty! Sure to God, I will!"

Holmes's eyes widened even further with growing alarm.

Lockett shook his head and looked away, surprised at his own anger. Without another word to Holmes or McManus, he stalked off through the woods, out beyond his sentries.

Beyond their view, he licked his lips and frowned. His own anger startled himself. Certain kinds of men needed that kind of reaction to enforce discipline, but he had to admit that his reaction had not been a conscious decision.

Absently, he looked at his hand. The calluses that he was so used to were beginning to soften somewhat. If he didn't get back behind a plow soon... He sighed and let the thought drift away.

Taking a deep breath, he lifted his eyes and followed the winding ribbon of road down into the valley. The long stretch of road made him pause on how far he was from Kalamazoo. Down that road, through the valley, into the opposite hills, and then keep going until the air was cool and the water clean. Michigan was a long, long ways away, he reflected.

He was about to turn around and seek out Sandie Holmes again when his eye caught movement at the far end of the valley. Not sure what he had seen in that flicker, he tried to focus on the specks in the distance. Then, he saw it! Dust! It was dust being kicked up! Dust caused by riders!

There was no Union cavalry in these parts, and that meant just one thing. Rebels! Bushwhackers! And they were unknowingly headed right for his resting men.

Lockett tested the weight of the rifle in his hand. His revolver was still holstered, and the Stuart family sword was secured in its scabbard. Gently, he tapped the trigger guard of the rifle. It was a scuffed, but clean, Lorenz rifle that he had picked up after the battle of Shiloh. He wished that he had been able to find his old sharpshooter's Dimick that he had discarded to carry Ainsley. But he had not been able to find it. No doubt, some other battlefield scavenger had beat him to it, probably some Reb found it that first night.

But at least, he had the Lorenz. He knew officers were not supposed to carry long-arms, but he felt naked without it.

His company waited in two groups near a bend in the road. The larger group, now under Orrin's immediate command, waited in the woods just beyond the bend. They would be able to give the approaching horsemen a volley full in their face.

The second group, Lockett's twenty men, stood at nearly a ninety degree angle from the main body. From their position in the trees, they would fire into the left flank of the bushwhackers. Lockett was confident that the double hammer blows would be decisive – after all, this was his plan.

When he had originally returned from sighting the approaching enemy, he had quickly begun organizing an ambush. Orrin, naturally, had tried to assume authority, but his plan of splitting the men into parallel lines on opposite sides of the road had been quietly discarded.

With a tact and calm that Lockett felt quite proud of at this moment, he had privately explained to Orrin that such a plan would probably kill as many of their own men as the enemy. It was then that Orrin had seized upon Lockett's strategy. Not surprisingly, Orrin had declared the plan as his own, but it didn't matter to Lockett at this point. His only thought was the approaching bushwhackers.

"Do you hear'em?" Bosworth said to Lockett, "I hear'em."

Graham looked at the sergeant. "How can you possibly hear them, sarge? I don't hear a thing."

"Quiet," Lockett commanded with a hiss, "Just hold your fire until they are directly across from us, that's when Lieutenant Long's section will open fire."

"Yes, sir," Bosworth answered, and the others nodded.

Lockett's eyes were drawn across the road to where Orrin and the main body of men waited, just inside the tree line. His last reminder to Orrin had been to hold his fire. That had drawn an angry stare, but it was better safe than sorry. Still, he worried what Orrin might do. He had seen Orrin run in Missouri.

But this situation was different, he assured himself. In Missouri, Orrin had run when no one else was looking. This time, Orrin did not have that, and Lockett hoped that the responsibility of command would tame those quick feet.

The plan was solid. The ground was perfect for an ambush. The Rebs were unsuspecting. Yet, he struggled to dismiss the clawing sense that something was doomed to go awry.

With a quick shake of his head, he reminded himself that if there was anything that the prior battles had taught him, it was that nothing ever went exactly to plan. Still, they were ready, he chided himself.

His men, concealed behind trees, had their rifles ready, as if they too could hear the sound that only Milton Bosworth heard, or at least claimed that he heard.

At one end, McManus wetted his thumb and ran it over the targeting apex of his Dimick. Lockett had already told him to try to spot the leader of the bushwhackers.

Like most Union soldiers, Lockett thought of the bushwhackers more as a half-led mob, certainly not like fighting the regular Confederate soldiers. Bushwhackers were skittish to begin with, usually held together by the sheer personality of the leader of the band. If Patrick could kill him in the first swipe, he liked their chances of routing them.

Next to McManus were two men Lockett was curious to see in battle, Levi Thickle and Adie Graham. They had not been part of his company at Barnes Field. Like the rest, they were cast offs that no one wanted. He didn't hold that against them, but he wanted to know who he could count on.

Thickle leaned against a tree stump on one knee. He didn't give the slightest hint that battle was imminent. In fact, he looked like he might fall asleep at any minute. The worn, weather beaten face looked oddly peaceful and at ease, not creased with its normal, acerbic frown.

Next to the older man, the young Adie nervously toyed with the hammer of his rifle. He was barely containing his nervous energy. Every once in awhile, he would suck in his lower lip and chew on it.

And on down the line, each man waited. Finally, Lockett's ears perked up.

"Hear it now, sir?" Bosworth grinned.

Lockett nodded and looked off through the opening in the forest, far down to their right.

Through the gap, he could see the sliver of road from which they would come. His eyes strained to see the approaching horsemen, and seconds seemed like an eternity. Then suddenly, the first rider sprung into view.

That momentary image of the rider flashing into and out of view startled Lockett. The horsemen all wore large floppy hats, much like Lockett and many of his men. As expected, they were a patchwork of homespun clothing, and the riders carried themselves with a jaunty confidence, shotguns holstered in their saddles. Their guidon fluttered in the breeze as they rode...

A guidon? Lockett thought wildly. Bushwhackers don't carry flags or banners.

"They're Secesh cavalry," Bosworth muttered quietly, echoing his own thoughts.

"They ain't bushwhackers," another man agreed in a whisper.

The company of forty riders continued on. Closer and closer they came... 500 yards... 400 yards...

Fighting regular cavalry was different than fighting undisciplined bushwhackers, but Lockett put it out of his mind. It didn't matter. They still had the element of surprise, and their first volley would decimate the horsemen, cavalry or bushwhacker.

300 yards...

Had Orrin noticed that they were not bushwhackers? Lockett suddenly wondered.

250 yards…

"Fire! Fire!"

Disbelieving, Lockett and his men heard Orrin Long's shrill voice.

With their eyes wide in shock, Lockett's men watched as Orrin's section opened fire on the unsuspecting cavalry but from a wildly extreme range. They had squandered their opportunity for a surprising, devastating blow!

"Steady!" Lockett hissed down his line, wondering how his mind was able to stay focused and clear when half of it was raging in fury at Orrin's blunder.

His men looked nervously at him.

"Steady," he heard Bosworth repeat in an angry whisper at someone.

"Let them get closer," Lockett added softly, "When I give the word, and only then! Let them get closer."

Adie Graham bit his lower lip until blood ran and looked away from the horsemen and back to the lieutenant. The officer seemed wholly unworried about what had happened to their carefully thought out plan, he decided. He relaxed the panicked grip on his rifle. If Lockett could look so unconcerned, then it must not be as bad as it seemed.

The distant Confederate cavalry swirled on their mounts, caught totally by surprise at the ineffectual volley from the far end of the road. The thick cloud of gun smoke up yonder, just before the bend, clearly identified where it had come from.

They had been unsuspecting, never guessing that the Yankee garrison would stray so far from town, but the range had been too great. There was not a single rider down.

"Ch-ah-rge!" the cavalry captain yelled, taking off down the road in a full gallop, unsheathing his saber and raising it over his head as he leaned forward over his horse's neck, quickly gathering speed. The rest of his men followed close behind.

It might have appeared as a bold and impetuous charge, but the Yankees had wasted their chance, the Rebels knew. Now, while the blue bellies were reloading their weapons, this was the prime moment to attack.

150 yards... 100 yards...

The horsemen were closing the distance swiftly when Lockett heard Orrin's panicked voice scream, "Retreat! Retreat!"

"Aim!" Lockett ordered in an unruffled voice amidst the pounding of hooves.

He stood rock solid, one hand on the hilt of the Stuart family sword. The other gripped the barrel of his rifle, which he would use as soon the others had fired. He concentrated on the rushing horsemen, gauging the moment in which to release his men's fire.

He resisted the temptation of glancing down to where Orrin had been waiting. It was a total disaster. Retreating was no option, Lockett knew. The whole patrol was bound to be captured piecemeal by the mounted Confederates. The only chance they had was to win this skirmish!

"Fire!" Lockett yelled, half-blinded by the immediate sheet of flame that erupted on either side of him.

Acrid smoke from the black powder filled the air, and its splash of lead washed over the horsemen.

The volley was woefully incomplete, but it was still enough to throw off the unsuspecting Rebels, who thought they faced only a panicky enemy to the front, not a poised one on their left flank as well.

Lockett watched the galloping captain get batted from his horse, as if the man had just run into a low hanging limb. Patrick's shot had not been wasted.

Horses and riders tumbled beneath their volley. One horse, unable to avoid the suddenly collapsed animal in front of it, stumbled over the obstacle, cart-wheeling grotesquely and throwing the rider a good twenty feet.

Others crashed into or narrowly averted the fallen, but the charge was stopped cold. The riders swerved and tried to steady their mounts and their own confusion. In avoiding the carnage in the middle of the road, the horsemen split into two groups.

One half of the remaining horsemen were on same side of the road as Lockett and his men. The other half of the cavalry swerved to the far side of the road.

Instantly examining what their first volley had done, Lockett guessed that they had knocked down between five and ten, an excellent first blow. Yet, in the split second of watching the dazed horsemen yank their mounts onto opposite sides of the road, James Lockett knew that he had only seconds to make the decision.

They had three options. They could stay in the woods and continue the skirmish, but without Orrin's section they would be outnumbered two to one.

They could run like Orrin, but that was no option. They would slowly be picked off by the mounted cavalry, one by one.

Or they could do the unthinkable... They could charge the cavalry.

The decision was clear in his madly whirling brain. "Charge!" he cried at the top of his lungs.

They had one chance, and that was to break the Confederate horsemen while they were disoriented, confused, and leaderless. It was the only way.

He tossed his still loaded rifle to Patrick, knowing his old friend would know what to do – find another Rebel officer.

Lockett broke from the woods, his long legs running at full speed. He pulled out the sword.

The horsemen on the near side of the road stared in shock as Yankees suddenly appeared from the woods, a scant 30 yards of grass away.

Lockett did not need to see if the others were following his mad rush. He could hear them. It was not the unsettling yip-yip of the Rebel yell; it was a deeper, bear-like bellow.

The Rebels swirled in tight circles as they struggled to calm their mounts and make sense of it all. Lockett headed for the one Confederate who seemed the least distressed. Sword whirling above long black hair, the man was trying to rally the rest of the horsemen to meet the new threat.

As Lockett sprinted towards him, a solitary rifle joined the pandemonium, and a crimson mist erupted from the Rebel's upper chest and toppled him – McManus's handiwork again without a doubt.

The Rebel's spooked mount made one tight circle and then dashed away.

Lockett angled toward the next closest rider. The man had his saber out and sent it crashing down on the onrushing infantry lieutenant. Lockett blocked the overhead blow with his own sword. A tremendous clang sounded as the blades crashed together. For a moment, Lockett worried that the elegant Stuart family sword would shatter upon such impact. Numbing vibration ran from his wrist down to his shoulder, but the blade did not break. Much like Ainsley himself, the sword was tougher than it looked.

He reached for the Rebel's sword wrist with his off-hand, yanking the man from the saddle. In the next moment, he found himself plunging his blade into the soft flesh of the man's stomach.

He twisted up just in time to see one of his men receive multiple shotgun blasts, but four other blue-coated men dashed around their fallen friend and threw themselves upon the horsemen who had fired the shots.

Another Rebel had Lockett in his sights but never got to fire his weapon as Bosworth clubbed the man from behind.

Lockett hurried to the next cavalryman and slashed from the blind side at another startled Rebel. But there was also a comrade nearby who whirled his mount around. The comrade had seen him coming. His horse reared back, hooves flailing in the infantryman's face.

He ducked and pulled the revolver free, firing as he hit the ground. As inaccurate as he was with the weapon, it was still point-blank range, and the lead ball slammed into the animal's neck.

The brown mare whinnied in terror while Lockett scrambled backwards to get away from the hooves, firing as he went. The third shot hit the suffering beast in the head. He fired again and then again, and the horse fell, trapping the rider beneath.

The dying beast barely missed landing on Lockett. So close, in fact, that Lockett could smell the animal's last steaming breaths from its snorting nostrils.

All around him, desperate fighting raged. Men swung rifle butts, jabbed long bowie knives, and fired revolvers if they had them. A few cavalrymen got off blasts with their preferred weapon of choice, shotguns.

McManus leapt up and dragged one from his saddle, pummeling him with a bare fist while the Rebel tried to hold off the Bowie knife in McManus's other hand.

Levi Thickle and another comrade swung their rifles like clubs at a horseman.

Two more of his men fell as cavalrymen wielded shotguns and revolvers with deadly impact.

Wide-eyed and frozen in place, Adie Graham seemed entranced as one horseman charged toward him. At the last second, the spell was snapped, and he tried to dodge out of the way, but he was too late. While he avoided getting trampled, the horse's front quarter slammed into him, sending him flying and knocking him senseless.

Lockett rose to his feet, knowing his men were fighting bravely, but it was obvious that the tide was turning against the outnumbered foot soldiers. Some of the riders from the far side of the road were now joining the fight. The shock of the first attack had dazed the cavalrymen, but it had not sent the Rebel troopers fleeing as Lockett had hoped. Now that the moment had passed, the Rebels were gaining the upper hand.

THUMPPP!

A bullet crashed into the horse flesh at Lockett's feet, and he looked up to see a cadre of cavalrymen re-forming for a charge into the melee.

His own men were already clustering together, their only defense for charging cavalry. No one wanted to face a charging horse alone. The only defense was to cluster together, make a pack of men and steel sizable enough to deter the horsemen from literally charging straight over them.

But the clusters were too small. They were about to be overwhelmed, Lockett realized. The thought of surrender crossed his mind when a yell sounded from the forest where Orrin's men were supposed to be, and a few scattered rifle shots added to the din. It took him a second to realize that those shots had come from the woods. All of his men had not obeyed Orrin Long's order to retreat.

The others were rejoining the action!

Movement beneath him drew his attention away from the woods, and he saw the trapped rider at his feet struggling to pull his short shotgun free from beneath the weight of his dead steed. Just as the man succeeded in wrenching the weapon free, Lockett pistol whipped the man.

More rifles sounded from the forest, and a few men broke from the wood line. Prosper T. Rowe and Otto Klugge roared as they led the newcomers into the fray. Half-stunned himself, Lockett saw that the group had taken the time to slide their menacing two foot long bayonets onto the end of their rifles.

Sensing that they were now out-numbered by the Yankees, one Rebel cried a sudden, "Retreat!"

With a sense of wonder, Lockett watched the remaining cavalrymen disengage, scooping up two mountless comrades as they did so, disappearing back down the road.

Bosworth whooped in triumph, and then the others joined him. For men who had so often suffered defeat, victory was sweet.

Chapter 7

Milton Bosworth finished scratching the casualty report onto a scrap of paper with the stub of a pencil.

"Who should Halleck have sent to Corinth now, eh? Thought we were only fit for garrison duty! Showed'em better than that! A damn sight better," he remarked to Otto Klugge as they supervised the grave being dug by the two Confederate prisoners.

"Ja," Klugge said simply, stepping away for a moment. His gnome-like face split into a wide grin.

It was the first time that Bosworth could remember the former Chicago dockman doing that.

"Never would have stood and fought like that with my old colonel," Bosworth commented blithely, "He would have run just as fast as Lieutenant Long did."

"Ja," Klugge grunted. He had no idea what the talkative sergeant was saying, but it didn't dim the elation of the moment. There was nothing like the elixir of victory, big or small, although Klugge would not have agreed so readily with Bosworth if he knew what was being said. Otto Klugge still viewed all officers with contempt.

However, if pressed at this moment, he might have given Lieutenant Lockett a temporary reprieve from such scorn. It would have been much easier to join Lieutenant Long in flight, but instead the young lieutenant had chosen to fight. Perhaps the stories about Lockett at Shiloh had been true. Klugge had thought them to be fictitious or at least exaggerated by the impressionable Adie Graham, but perhaps not? If any man ever led a regiment without ammunition on a charge, maybe it could be this lieutenant. And if that part of the story was true, then perhaps the part about Lockett having once been a mere private was also true? Still, that type of justice was hard for the old German to believe.

At Shiloh, Otto Klugge had been under arrest. He had missed the slaughter along the Tennessee River, which was just as well. Over a third of his old regiment never returned; the other two-thirds had bolted and run.

"The lieutenant wants you to take this to him," Bosworth said, handing him the scrap of paper.

"'Vas?"

Bosworth shrugged and pointed at Lockett. "Guess he wants to see you."

Lockett was standing by himself, looking at one of the Sanitary Commission wagons which was now being turned into a mobile hospital. Turning, he saw Klugge waiting for him. "That has to be the luckiest Reb soldier around, Otto."

The German looked at him blankly.

"... to be wounded with a wagon full of medical supplies and two surgeons on hand."

Lockett didn't add that the Rebel was extra lucky that there were two doctors and not just one. One, for the Rebel – another for Congressman Willey, who insisted upon having the insignificant bump on his head treated before any "Secesh scum".

The split lump just above Willey's eye served him right, he thought, running off like a frightened rabbit, or a moose in his case. Despite that, Congressman Willey had not softened his rhetoric. The way he was talking, one would think that he had led the charge against the Rebels.

Klugge held out the scrap of paper, and Lockett read it aloud. "Six dead Rebels, three wounded, two others captured... Should have been more. Those last two were lucky to get away. Still, I shouldn't complain, eh, Private?"

Klugge looked at him blankly again, unsure how to answer, if indeed he was supposed to at all.

Lockett's eyes turned toward the graves that the prisoners were digging. "Ourselves? We lost three good men, but it would have been more without you, Otto, a lot more."

Klugge looked at him in puzzlement.

"I know you're the one who turned and led the men back into the fray, Private Klugge. Thank you."

Klugge nodded. He understood the last two words.

Lockett's eye caught a figure rapidly approaching, and Klugge turned to see Orrin Long stomping towards them. The German didn't bother to hide the look of disgust on his scarred stevedore face.

Lockett chuckled at the reaction. "Best be goin', Private Klugge. Looks like Lieutenant Long has something to tell me. Go," he added, nodding his head in the other direction to get his message across.

Klugge understood the gist and departed.

Long scowled as he approached. "What is the meaning of this, Lockett? You have given orders that we will head back to Savannah in 15 minutes? I am in command here."

* * * * *

"Yes, we'll rally round the flag, boys, we'll rally once again,
Shouting the battle cry of Freedom!
We will rally from the hillside, we'll gather on the plain,
Shouting the battle cry of Freedom!"

Prosper T. Rowe and John Messern led the tune as usual, but for once, the rest of the company was equally ebullient. Bosworth in particular could be heard singing lustily, albeit off tune. Yet, there was one soldier who was in no mood to join in. Private Sandie Holmes felt more like crying than singing.

All that kept flashing through his mind was the sight of the Rebel cavalry charging down the road. His neck had loosened now so that he could breathe again, but he remembered the utter constriction that his panic had caused. His legs still ached from the furious sprint away. Lieutenant Long may have had a head start, but Sandie Holmes knew that he had quickly outdistanced the officer, and he had never even considered turning around to fight like Otto Klugge and Prosper T. Rowe had done.

The terror had been even worse than Shiloh. The swiftness with which the cavalry moved shocked him, and the sound of pounding hooves still reverberated in his ears.

He thought about his young bride back in Kankakee. What would she think about being married to a coward?

What kind of terrible mistake have I made, he thought to himself. I never should have volunteered.

He looked over at the two Rebel prisoners marching ahead of him. They had been chatting personably with Adie and Prosper T. earlier. They looked far from frightening now, but that did not make Sandie Holmes feel any better. Right then, he realized that he couldn't take any more of this. He wasn't cut out to be a soldier. He didn't know how or when, but he knew that he had to desert. Somehow, some way, he had to get out of here.

* * * * *

The high spirits carried them all the way back until they sighted Savannah. Even Lockett found himself whistling softly to the tune, although his reasoning was slightly different than that of his men. While he knew they had won the skirmish, it was tempered by the knowledge that the victory should have been more complete.

Yet, he rejoiced in seeing the weather-beaten town of Savannah. It meant no more Orrin Long. He had survived being under Orrin's thumb. For once, Orrin had not gotten the best of him, and he could look forward to being the lone officer of his company again – not needing to worry any more about Orrin's incompetence or potential for treachery.

In addition, Colonel Blair would be pleased with their victory over Rebel cavalry. They had learned from the prisoners that they had butted heads with a company of Confederate Kentucky cavalry. Private Messern was from Kentucky, and Lockett reflected on what a strange war this was.

The people of Tennessee had voted not to secede, yet the state had joined the Confederacy anyway. Most of Savannah had maintained a Unionist sentiment, yet the majority of the Federal soldiers still eyed the locals with a deep suspicion.

So odd, he thought, so very odd.

April 26

Lockett awoke the next morning with an unburdened spring in his step. Even the discovery of a bullet hole in the upper sleeve of his uniform did not diminish his swell of optimism. Not only was yesterday's triumph fresh in his mind, but a rare break in his duties meant that he could look in on Ainsley at the tent hospital.

The constant care from Katherine Moffat was starting to have an effect. It had only been a matter of days, but the sunken hollows around Ainsley Stuart's eyes and mouth were less evident now. More importantly, the glint of life was back in the pale blue eyes.

As Lockett looked around the tent, it seemed to him that many of the others were looking better too. He couldn't tell if it was his own positive mood tainting his vision, or if Katherine's and Anna's daily visits were having a palpable impact on the wounded.

Anna was chatting with one of the surgeons, Doctor McClutcheon. He watched her for an entertaining second, feeling the surge of her personality even from a distance. Her irrepressible nature could only be described as invigorating, he thought to himself.

A few minutes later, she made her way over to him.

"Lieu-ten-ent Lockett," she said with a bright look, "The conquering hero returns."

It wasn't surprising that Anna knew about their skirmish, the whole town did now. Marching into Savannah with the prisoners had caused quite a stir. The word had spread ahead of them, and by the time his company had reached the center of town, it seemed that every person in Savannah had turned out to watch the procession. It was almost like a parade.

She looked at him with a pleased smile, waiting for his response, while he self-consciously shifted from one foot to the other. Though her comment had been meant as flattery, it made him strangely uncomfortable.

"Still have the sword I see?" Ainsley commented cheerfully, catching Lockett's eye. A bolt of pain crashed through Ainsley's body from his unseen foot, but a second later, he forced the tired smile back onto his bony face.

Katherine was behind Ainsley and gave Lockett a hard stare before turning away wordlessly. He blinked in surprise but did not ponder her behavior for too long as Anna joined him at his shoulder and said, "See how well he is doing, Lieu-ten-ent? Why, the first words out of his mouth are about his sword."

"He does look rather spry," Lockett answered with a teasing look, "Perhaps I should give his sword back to him? He may have use for it."

"Only to protect myself from these coddling women."

"Oh, shush now, Lieu-ten-ent Stuart. You know you love every minute of it."

Ainsley reached up and pulled Lockett closer, whispering, "She doesn't know how true that is. I am rather spoiled. Sometimes I feel bad for the other lads that they give me such attention."

"It looks like they help everyone," Lockett observed. On the other side of the tent, Katherine gave some water to a captain from Indiana. She noticed him looking at her and quickly turned her eyes away.

"She's been a little out of sorts all morning," Ainsley observed.

"Odd. Oh well, nothing is going to ruin my day today."

"I've already heard the gossip, but you give me the real details. Tell me about the skirmish."

"It's good to be on the winning side for once," Lockett whispered conspiratorially. He looked over his shoulder to make sure that Katherine was busy adjusting the bandage on another soldier, "But you know what is best? For once, I survived being under Orrin Long without some calamity."

General Halleck's staff had nearly finished loading the papers into the wagons. Slowly, painstakingly, with agonizing attention to detail, the wagons were given their burden. Captain Fulton stood by with his checklist, making sure that all was loaded and in the proper sequence. The general was finally heading south to join the rest of the army.

Corinth beware, Lockett laughed to the empty room as he watched the proceedings below.

He had been waiting in General Halleck's outer office for quite some time now, but there was enough activity outside the window so that he did not notice the delay.

How would Orrin feel about getting closer to the action again? Nervous to be sure, he supposed. But then, Halleck and his staff would never get too close to the battle, not like General Grant would.

It had been an hour since Halleck's chief of staff, a crow-faced colonel, had told Lockett that the general would see him in five minutes. Time had passed, and he had not seen anyone, even the crow-faced colonel. On top of that, he still had no idea what he was doing here in the first place.

Could Blair's Independent Regiment be heading south with the others?

But he quickly discarded that option. If that was the case, Halleck would have sent for Colonel Blair, not him.

"He must wish to congratulate me on our victory," Lockett mumbled softly. But it seemed hardly significant enough to merit that, he knew.

Finally, the door opened, and Halleck's chief of staff ushered him into the room.

Balding and overweight with a sagging, smooth face and wide bug eyes that made him look as if he had just received some scare, General Henry Halleck did not look like a military leader. In fact, he looked half-senile, but that was in complete contrast to his reputation. For as long as anyone could remember, the former West Pointer had been nicknamed 'Old Brains'. But while his mental acuity had impressed others, Lockett did not see anything special. After all, how could anyone but a fool choose Orrin Long to be part of his staff?

"Sir," he saluted.

"Have a seat, Lieutenant," General Halleck said in a gravelly voice.

"Yes, sir. Thank you, sir," he answered, trying not to sit on his scabbard as he lowered himself into the stiff-backed chair.

It suddenly occurred to him that he was meeting his second general in the past month. He never would have guessed that, never in a million years. Back in Kalamazoo, his brother, Daniel, would be stunned.

"I'll be blunt, Lieutenant," Halleck said, looking Lockett squarely in the eye, "News of your *cowardice* is another black mark on your men."

"What!" Lockett reacted instantly. His hand clenched the arm of the chair, and he felt as if he had just received the heaviest of blows to the stomach. The wind rushed out of him, and his stomach balled into a knot. "Cowardice?" he managed to utter. "Sir?"

The word rang in his ears. The tips of his fingers began to tingle, and his eyes flapped in disbelief. For once, there was no imperturbable reflex to mask his emotions.

"Silence!" Halleck thundered at the interruption, "I will not stand for insubordination as well!"

Orrin!

Lockett knew immediately what had happened. *Orrin Long!* It had to be.

"Lieutenant Long informed me of how you panicked and ran, that only his personal bravery was able to carry the day."

"That is a lie!" Lockett snapped, clenching the arm of the chair, forcing himself to stay seated.

"Silence!" Halleck bellowed again, "I will tell you when to speak, soldier! One more outburst and you are finished! Do you understand?"

"Yes, sir," he returned in a barely audible quiver.

"Lieutenant Long's report was confirmed by Congressman Willey, so there will be no disputing the truth, Lockett! If Colonel Blair wasn't already so short on officers, I wouldn't give you another chance. Be thankful that I am such a generous man."

He did not hear the rest of Halleck's diatribe. He didn't need to. It was obvious what had happened. Orrin Long had done it to him again! Now, he was being branded a coward! He could think of nothing worse!

Ten minutes later, he left the general's office and wandered out to the front of the hotel. Halleck's staff waited patiently on the front steps so they could begin the trip south.

He felt as if his heart had been ripped out. Shaking with anger and dazed to the point of irrationality, he stopped in front of another staff officer. "Where's Long?" he demanded in a menacing voice, his hand locked in a death grip around the hilt of the Stuart family sword.

"He left this morning with the advance party," the staff officer answered, taken aback by the murderous look on Lockett's face.

With a cry, Lockett turned. With all his strength, he fired a punch into the beam holding up the overhang in front of the hotel entrance. He wasn't sure if the audible crack was in the wood or in the bone, but he knew now why Katherine Moffat had looked at him with such disdain.

Orrin Long!!!

II
A Prayer For Redemption

Chapter 8

"I'll kill 'em!" Bosworth vowed upon hearing of the bald-faced lie.

Word of the treachery, and the company's subsequent disgrace, had spread like pure wildfire through the camp.

"That lyin', cheatin' bastard! I'll kill'em!" Bosworth repeated.

"Only if Lieutenant Lockett doesn't slit his throat first," Rowe remarked blackly. Even his easy-going persona had been usurped by a serious, even grim, shock.

"I've never seen him so mad," Graham agreed.

"You think he might kill someone?" another asked worriedly.

Graham shook his head. He couldn't imagine the lieutenant doing something like that. On the other hand, he had never seen such a look on anyone's face before.

The debate carried on around McManus, but he was the only one seemingly oblivious to the jumble of voices. His peculiar behavior did not go unnoticed.

One by one, the others looked strangely at him as he silently whittled a thick stick with his long Bowie knife, a tool wholly inappropriate for the task. They all knew that he was the lieutenant's closest friend, and he did nothing? Said nothing? Just intently whittled with a face that was a mask of concentration?

Most could not fathom it or took it to mean that he did not care. However, after a few more minutes, at least one of them understood the act to mean something very different.

Otto Klugge could not make out the English words sputtering around him, but he recognized the deep, dark thoughts that swam behind Patrick McManus's veil. With each slice of the wood, McManus was working closer and closer to some sort of planned retribution.

McManus still didn't know what had possessed him to take the Bowie off a dead Texan the day after Shiloh. For certain, that part of the field had been picked clean, and the fact that the Bowie knife had been left behind pointed to its limited value.

When they had left Kalamazoo, old Sergeant VanderJagt had impressed upon him and James that items like a large Bowie knife were of limited use and just became one more thing to weigh you down on a long march. He supposed that he would leave the knife behind when it came time to leave Savannah, whenever that was.

Well, he thought to himself, it would not be soon enough for him or James.

He knew that James espoused that the reason he had joined the Army was to keep Daniel at home, but McManus knew better. James wasn't completely selfless. Volunteering had as much to do with escaping the farm and finding what else was out there. James was cautious with his words and not a blow-hard adventurer, but James wanted to see what was outside of Kalamazoo too.

They had expected that there would be danger involved, but little did either of them know that there would be as much to fear from the connivances of a fellow Michigander as from the Rebels. What Orrin had done to his friend burned McManus nearly as much as James, but he knew that James had righted his reputation before, and he would do so again.

The trick was to get away from Orrin so that more lies couldn't be perpetrated. Maybe it would die down if it was allowed to? Or maybe it would just fester?

Truthfully, he felt a little responsible that he hadn't seen it coming and somehow prevented it. Next time, he vowed. Next time, he would not let this happen to his friend. James couldn't look in all directions at once.

Adie Graham jabbed McManus in the shoulder. "Well?" he demanded, "What do you think?"

"About all this?" McManus asked, looking up from his whittling.

"Of course, about all this!"

"It'll pass, but I'm damn sure gonna watch his back from now on," McManus vowed to a murmur of agreement.

* * * * *

Lockett looked into the peacefully flowing waters of the Tennessee River. Ever so gently the dark waters went by, an unbroken plane, save the occasional twig or leaf.

While the river was tranquil today, his thoughts were anything but. Two days had passed since General Halleck's upbraiding, but the anger still bubbled fresh inside of him. His hand throbbed from punching that wood post, but he wanted nothing more than to have that pusillanimous cheat in front of him.

Orrin Long! Orrin Long! Every thought was on Orrin Long.

Thanks to Orrin, there were many in Missouri who considered him a murderer, and now thanks to Orrin, there were many in Tennessee who considered him a coward.

He was certain that the number of misinformed grew with each day. That was how it had been with the Sharpshooters. By the time he had seen his old comrades again, just before the battle of Shiloh, Orrin's Missouri lie had taken root. Many of his old comrades had turned against him. Orrin's version of events had gone unanswered without Lockett there to defend his reputation. Friends like Luke Bailey, Matthew Bauer, and George VanderJagt could only do so much to save his name.

For a moment, he wondered how the Sharpshooters were doing. Luke had been wounded at Shiloh. Had he survived? Had he returned to his unit already? How serious had it been?

He had not heard back from his letter to Matthew on Luke's health. No doubt the Sharpshooters were near Corinth now, near the action, he thought wistfully.

That was where Lockett and his men wanted to be, but Colonel Blair had made it very clear that any action for Blair's Independent Regiment was even further off now, and people were holding Lockett responsible for that.

Red faced, Colonel Blair had stared at him. The Colonel's hand had been a white knuckled fist resting on a neat stack of ledgers. Atop that stack was General Halleck's own handwritten rebuke to the Colonel.

Of course, the men had backed Lockett's version of the story, but General Halleck had scoffed at the notion that Lieutenant Long and Congressman Willey were lying. Naturally, the men would support Lockett over a staff officer. The staff officer was gone, and Lockett was still the company's officer. Common soldiers may be ignorant, but they weren't stupid, Halleck had declared. What soldier would want to incur Lockett's wrath now? Better to side with the officer they were stuck with than with the one who was going away.

All in all, it put Colonel Laurent Blair in a terrible position. He had not been a soldier for long, but Blair knew plenty about political in-fighting from his bank, and this event had driven a wedge through his already fractious officer corps.

Renaud had expressed sympathy to Lockett; Fulkerham was full of condemnation. Eventually, the rest would side with one or the other. Then, above all else, this disaster meant one thing. It was a black mark on Blair's Independent Regiment, and they were now assured of a long stint of dreary garrison duty and baggage guarding. This wasn't what he had committed so much of his personal treasure to do.

April 28

Katherine Moffat watched the two young orderlies, boys really, carry the body of Lieutenant Donley from the tent. It was a sad moment. The gentle faced Hoosier had expired during the night.

Privately, Katherine was surprised that there weren't more like Donley. Though the men put on a brave face and could at times be as quiet as school children, many had suffered such serious injuries that Katherine could not imagine the pain. She had been more than a little skeptical when Dr. McClutcheon, had told her that only about 10% of the arm amputees and 20% of the leg amputees would die after the gruesome surgery. The survival rate seemed impossibly high, but as she looked around the tent, she decided that Dr. McClutcheon had been truthful and not just trying to assuage her worries.

Ainsley was doing well, and she was certain that his recovery would be complete, or at least, as complete as could be without a foot. God had smiled on Ainsley, she reflected. Even Dr. McClutcheon had hailed his recovery as a miracle. Katherine tended to agree with Ainsley, who swore that the quick attention of James Lockett and Patrick McManus had led to a miracle.

Still, Katherine was in no mood to celebrate James Lockett. She couldn't believe that he had tried to lie to her and with such a straight face! She had caught him trying to explain himself to that annoying Anna Tucker, spreading rumors about Orrin.

"... Orrin ran, fast as a rabbit," James had complained to Anna.

Anna had replied with that sickly sweet voice, "I knew what they were saying about you had to be untrue. Why, after your actions at Pittsburg Landing, how could anyone believe such a story!"

"I should have known that Orrin would twist the story around."

"But how could you? Such a dishonorable deed! Such a scoundrel! How could you have guessed that he would do such a thing?"

"If anyone could guess, it would be me, Anna. I've dealt with Orrin before. I know him."

It was with that statement that Katherine could take no more. The slander! It was preposterous! When she stepped around the corner, Katherine took satisfaction in the startled look on James's face.

To think that she had ever smiled upon him! Mother had been right. He was nothing but a worthless, ignorant farmer!

"Katherine..." James had begun.

"Don't Katherine me!" she snapped back, enjoying the thrill of power and control at cutting him off. "I heard everything! Lies, vicious lies! How could you? And after Orrin saved your men!"

"He didn't..."

"Yes, he did," Katherine interrupted again, "He told me. He told me everything! How you panicked and fired too early, how you ran."

"He's lying," James replied in an even voice.

The patience in his voice was unsettling, making her madder still.

"You're the liar!" she shouted, her voice hitting higher pitches as she did so.

"He's a shirker, Katherine. Ask..."

"You're the worthless one! How dare you slander Orrin! He's from one of the best families in West Michigan. His uncle is..."

"Katherine, listen to me," James said, patiently holding up his hand.

"Listen to you! Why? You're just a poor farmer out to..."

James swallowed his tongue at the comment and looked away.

"...out to, out to... Give me that sword, James Lockett. You're not fit to carry the Stuart family sword!"

That comment finally drew a flicker of emotion from James. With a charge in his gray eyes, he glared at her. "That is not your decision to make. This is Ainsley's sword. If it wants it back, I will gladly comply!"

Katherine looked at him. "Then I shall ask him!" She turned on her heel and left in a huff. She'd see what Ainsley had to say about it.

But she had hesitated until now to broach the subject with her cousin. She didn't know the reason for her reluctance, probably because James was like a brother to her sibling-less cousin. The truth would hurt Ainsley, but it had to be done.

"Give the sword back?" Ainsley replied in a voice that sounded even more aghast than surprised.

"Yes, he should give the sword back," Katherine maintained resolutely, "He's not fit to wear it."

"What? Why?" Ainsley asked, "Is this what has been bothering you since..." It suddenly dawned on Ainsley what had transpired. He had been reluctant to open the subject about Katherine's beau, hoping it would take care of itself, but he could see now how foolish that thought had been. She needed to hear the truth about Orrin Long.

"James is a coward and not fit to wear your sword," Katherine declared.

"James is no coward, cousin. Far from it."

"He is! Didn't you hear? He ran out on Orrin and..."

"He didn't run."

"What?"

"He didn't run."

"Yes, he did. Of course, he did. He ran and forced Orrin to fight those Rebels all by himself!"

"You're wrong, Katherine," Ainsley said, ire strengthening his raspy voice, "You don't *know* James like I do. There isn't a braver soldier in the army, Katherine. He would never run. You've been... misinformed." He looked at her, hoping that his gentle, polite approach would have effect, but there was none.

"No, I haven't," she insisted, "Orrin told me everything. Orrin..."

"Orrin told you lies," Ainsley interrupted bluntly. His face flushed, and his upper lip began to tremble in anger.

Katherine gasped. "You don't know…"

"Now damn it, listen to me, Katherine!" Ainsley cut her off. The words and intensity coming out of her mild-mannered cousin's mouth made her hesitate, and Ainsley continued on.

"I should have told you about him before, Katherine." Truth be told, Ainsley Stuart didn't know Orrin Long very well personally, but James had told Ainsley enough – about Orrin's thievery, his brutality towards women in Missouri, how he had run out at battles, about how he had framed James for murder.

Ainsley didn't know Orrin that well, but he knew James Lockett. He trusted James. If James said this about Orrin Long, then it was true. Anything about James Lockett running out on his men was ridiculous, and he would never believe it. Even if Lincoln himself had written the report, Ainsley would not believe such a thing.

"You believe James over Orrin!" Katherine cried in astonishment, filling the awkward pause that Ainsley had left. She looked as if she had been pricked with a pin. "How could you?"

"Because I know James! Katherine, James would die before dishonoring himself, or me, or you for that matter."

"Ainsley, you are so wrong! How can you say such things? How can you discredit Orrin like that? He comes from one of the finest families in West Michigan, and James is… is not to be believed." Lowering her voice to a whisper, "He is a *murderer*, cousin."

"That was not his fault. You are wrong about that."

The utter lack of reaction on Ainsley's face stunned Katherine. She had expected the last statement to be a bombshell to her high-minded cousin, but he was not surprised at all by it! He seemed to know all about it! Impossible! Katherine felt like she was in a dream world, surely this couldn't be happening? "You don't understand, Ainsley. In…"

"Yes," Ainsley interrupted again, "I know all about Missouri."

"But…"

"James is no murderer, Katherine. He has killed, but the circumstances are not as you think."

"What?" Katherine repeated in a mystified voice that trailed off, "You're talking crazy."

"Ask him, Katherine. He'll tell you about it. He'll tell you what truly happened there." The resolute look made her pause.

She turned away, not knowing what to say or think. This had not gone as she had planned.

"No!" Katherine cried out finally.

With startling reflexes, the bed-ridden Ainsley reached up and snatched her arm. "You must believe James!"

She pulled herself free and ran from the tent.

* * * * *

The Federal major with the long black beard looked down at the gaping wound in the back of the dead Rebel lieutenant. With his foot, he rolled him over. Lifeless eyes stared back.

"Sorry, sir," the sergeant said, trying to soothe the Rebel's horse.

"We needed him alive," the officer growled.

"Din't want to let another git away, not like that last one who hopped the hedge. Helluva rider, that one was. This one wasn't the same man. No doubt at that."

"Next time, shoot the horse, not the rider, you damn fool!"

"Yes'r."

The major checked the bloodied saddle bags on the mount, wiping the residue on the horse's flank.

It had been blind luck that they had stumbled upon the rider heading south. The young man had given himself away by galloping away at full speed at the mere sight of the blue uniforms.

Sure enough, the saddle bag contained some coded messages. The major was doubtful that anyone back at camp would be able to decipher it. They needed to catch these riders alive so that they could learn more, although he knew the spy that he hunted was careful.

The coded messages were dropped on some schedule at some unknown location. Even the messengers retrieving the information would likely know nothing about what was on the paper or even who left it, but the retrievers would at least know the location. And with that knowledge, they could lay a trap.

He folded the papers and stuffed them into his saddle bag. With a scowl, he slapped his leather riding gloves across his other palm. This was a missed opportunity, he knew.

April 28

Spent another Sunday evening in the company of Anna Tucker. Her father believes that I'm calling on her. I suppose I am.

Evenings with Anna are entertaining, and it surprises me how interested she is in all that I do. I find myself amazed at how she knows everyone from Colonel Blair to Dr. McClutcheon. She has always been like this, I suppose. It can be humorous from time to time. She knows more about what is going on than I do.

Sunday evenings are a rare bright spot for our dreary weeks. Guarding baggage is degrading, and morale is suffering. Despite my best efforts, I sense discipline rotting away. We need to return to action.

It is odd that I write that, I know. For so long, I was in no hurry to see battle and silently derided those enthusiastic fools who clamored for a fight. Any dreams of glory for those eager ones have been dashed, drowned in a sea of blood. Yet, despite the horrible carnage that battle brings, I know we need it. The war will not end without it. And now, our redemption can only come with it.

--- diary of James Lockett

Katherine Moffat rose quietly from her bed. The scent of spring flowers wafted through the open window. Whatever it was, she did not recognize the sweet smell.   Southern honeysuckle, she wondered?

Across the room, Anna slumbered peacefully, as she always did.   A thin ray of moonlight ran from the window and across Anna's cheek.   Even when she slept, she looked cheerful, Katherine mocked.

The heavy black of night told Katherine that morning was still well off, and with a muted sigh of frustration she gave up any hope of falling asleep.   Pursing her thin lips, she rubbed a clammy hand against a damp face.   She despised this heat and humidity.   It was so astoundingly oppressive – so much worse than any summer stretch in Kalamazoo, and it was not even June yet!

But it wasn't the weather that kept her awake tonight.   It was the deep hurt that she felt, the utter wrenching of the betrayal. There was no justification for it, she thought angrily for the millionth time.   Why would James lie to her and try to push the blame onto her gallant Orrin?   The gall of his behavior would forever sever him from warm feelings.

Pondering on the ungrateful farmer was a complete waste of time, she knew, but no matter how she tried to put James out of her mind, she could not.   Hour after restless hour disappeared.

It wasn't the first night that she had trouble sleeping in Tennessee.   After the first day in the putrid tent hospital, every time she closed her eyes she saw images of pain and disfigurement.   And that horrible smell of infection grew stronger in her nostrils! She had finally gotten used to the smell, but that was no consolation tonight while she turned over again in bed.   Tonight, it was all James Lockett's fault.

How could he have betrayed her like this?

Slinking quietly from the room, Katherine wandered the bare wood floors of the Tucker house.   Anna and her father had been gracious hosts, yet Katherine still felt little at ease around the father, and she plain disliked the daughter.

Admittedly, they had opened their home to her, shared their food with her, and generally treated her like family.

But that type of reasoning danced quickly from Katherine's mind. She wasn't the type to balance her opinions once they were made.

At the far end of the house, Katherine was surprised to see light coming from beneath the study door. The room was usually locked, and it was the only place the Tuckers had asked her not to go. Reverend Tucker was a very orderly man, Anna had explained, and he liked his tiny study just so.

Katherine had never given it a second thought. Her own father was the same protective way about his work. His ledgers... his ledgers... How he had punished her once as a young girl for marking in his ledgers! Other than her announcement that she was going to Tennessee, that had been the only time where she had ever seen Father truly irate.

Reverend Tucker must be inspired tonight and working on a sermon, Katherine surmised. James had once told her that he thought Reverend Tucker spoke extemporaneously, but after living with the Tuckers, Katherine had found that he put in a great deal of time alone in his study, reading the Bible and working on his sermons.

She thought about venturing down to the room to speak with the Reverend, wondering if it would ease her mind about James and permit some rest. But any thought of disrupting the Reverend's inspiration dissipated. Before she could get half way down the hall, the light peeking from beneath the door blew out, and the door swung open. Caught off-guard, Katherine froze and listened to the Reverend's footfalls disappear down the hall and into his bedroom.

Knowing that she still could not sleep and having no idea what she had hoped to accomplish by getting up in the first place, Katherine turned around and went back to bed.

* * * * *

The fly twisted in the spider's web. At first, the large fly looked as if it had barely grazed the soft, willowy strands.

The gentle breeze fluttered the spider's creation, and it looked impossibly fragile against nature's power. Yet even if the breeze was to turn into a gust, the web would weather the storm, Lockett knew.

And as the fly was learning, the web was equally strong against the fly's best efforts. With each struggle, the fly only became more hopelessly entangled. With a silent nod, Lockett watched the fly until it could no longer move. The spider was nowhere to be seen, but there was little doubt that the spider's dinner would still be there when it returned.

"You're not listening, James," Anna Tucker said, interrupting his daze. She set down the Bible from which she had been reading. "Is Joshua boring you today?"

He looked up from his thoughts with a blank look.

"Or is it me?" Anna asked with a soft voice, "Am I boring you today? I do not feel myself."

She was not herself today. He had noticed that right off. She was oddly subdued as if her thoughts were elsewhere, and the vivacious smile seemed to come only with effort. Something troubled her, but he felt oddly hesitant to pry into the introspection.

"It is not you, nor me, nor anyone else," Lockett answered gloomily. He eyed the gray, yet still dry sky.

"Oh, James. You are thinking too much again, aren't you? Patrick warned me that you could be like this." Her eyes started to twinkle, letting him know that she was joking. Whatever weighed on her mind, she seemed able to set it aside, unlike himself.

"Thinking too much," he nodded, "But what is your excuse?"

"I wasn't the one lost in thought, looking at an ol' cob web."

His only response was a light snort, and there was a quiet pause for a moment. Finally, Anna added, "Someday, after the war is over, James, I would like to leave this place."

"Leave?" He looked absently at the coating of dust on his boots.

"Leave."

"To go where?" he asked, not paying her full attention. The sole on his boot was starting to come free. He'd better get that fixed.

"Oh, I don't know," she said lightly.

"Hmm," he answered, looking up at that moment. Her eyes twinkled, but her face was serious, and he was unsure what she was insinuating.

After the war? After living through Shiloh, the mere suggestion of the war ending so soon was ludicrous to him. They would be fighting for years, until all was ash and dust. He wanted to believe that the war could end, and a month of sitting in quiet little Savannah did make the war seem further away. And Halleck *was* finally moving south on Corinth. But it was a slow march and a long war.

Yet James Lockett felt a perverse surge of conflict in his bones. On one hand, he wanted the war over and done with, that was the entire reason he had volunteered in the first place – to end it as soon as possible, to end it before his foolish younger brother could get himself killed. But on the other hand, if it ended now, he and his men would be left totally dishonored. They had fought bravely, but if the war was to end now, they would all be known as contemptible cowards. And he would return to Kalamazoo, slinking back into a county that had heard nothing of him except that he was a murderer and now a coward. On top of that shame, the heavy burden of the plow would wait for him too, and he wasn't ready for that. Not yet anyway.

If his prolonged silence bothered Anna Tucker, she did not show it. Rather, she lightly brushed his arm and said teasingly, "You look such a mess, James Lockett."

He blushed slightly, because he *was* as dusty as an old saddlebag. His light blue trousers were discolored by sweat and dirt. He had taken his little company on a long, fast march today – four miles by his estimate. "I surely don't look like one of Fulkerham's men," he agreed.

Tyler Fulkerham was taking great pains to have his company present themselves "properly", as the West Point expellee was prone to say.

"I am glad you're not one of his men either," Anna remarked, "He punishes his men so. Why, even their buttons must be shined to perfection! And the punishments! I saw one poor boy forced to hold rifles extended from his shoulders for hours today. Any time he let the rifles drop just one inch, another soldier was ordered to jab him with a rifle butt."

Lockett nodded. Fulkerham's men brushed their coats and polished their buttons like they were a ceremonial guard, not a baggage guard. While Lockett drilled his men on the speed of their rifle loading and hardened their feet with quick marches, Tyler Fulkerham paraded his men around the meadow as if they were preparing for a gubernatorial demonstration. Fulkerham openly enjoyed comparing his prim and proper company.

Lockett did not want to take notice of the comments, but now the two companies themselves were starting to antagonize each other. The rivalry developing between the two was far from friendly.

Of course, Lockett had no mind to bring the issue to a head. As long as Colonel Blair allowed him to drill his men as he saw fit, he did not want to do anything that might jeopardize this independence.

Chapter 9

May 6
Dear Brother,
It has been a good while since I last received a letter from you. I trust all is well, Daniel. As before, I am here in Savannah. The weather has been quite hot, like July in Michigan, and very dry without any rain. We have been choking on dust as we search for bushwhackers. There aren't too many around here, but there are still a few. The locals say his name is Bloody Bill Coulter. Last week, he nearly killed a mail carrier. The mail carrier escaped but lost his post. Maybe that is where your last letter ended up! I don't think the folk in Richmond will find news of mother and the farm as interesting as I do.

Do not bother to send me more stamps in your next letter as I had requested. A group from the Christian Commission came through last week and gave out free envelopes to write home, and I bought stamps for five cents. Five cents! The sutlers make a fortune off us, but stamps are hard to come by out here, so we pay double or triple the price. Besides, there is very little else to spend money on here in Savannah.

I trust there has been more rain in Michigan than here. I pray so. Write as soon as you get this.
Your brother, James

* * * * *

Lockett watched the pinkish orange hue hug the hilltops. It was amazing how the sun could sink behind the horizon and

131

give it the power to glow like a candle. He watched this show every night, and every night, he was amazed and then drifted into thought.

Tonight, his wanderings lingered in Kalamazoo, which lay so very far away beyond the Tennessee hills, back where the land was conveniently level.

Farming was a peaceful life. He never had to worry about deceit and lies. The earth never lied. It required attention and a strained back, but it never lied.

Men lie. Men deceive. Men betray others. Men like Orrin Long.

A soldier's life, that was what he was leading now, but Lockett was beginning to wonder if he should. He did not seem cut out for it. It was not the battles that plagued him. That was where he felt the most comfortable. How his brother would find that hard to believe! Despite the shriek of the shell, the zips of the Minié balls, and the impenetrable walls of smoke, he knew he could keep his wits about him. No, it was not battle that bothered him.

To be a soldier, one needed to be just as aware of "friends" as of the enemy. Patrick said one needed to know politics and how to thwart the deceit that men spring on one another. Orrin had done it twice to him, and still he knew he was flummoxed by the game. So too must General Grant be, having lost twice to General Halleck. The scale there was much grander, but the story much the same. How could anyone remove Grant from command? It was absurd! Yet Halleck had found a way to do that to Grant! Twice! Lockett prayed that General Grant would find a way back. The army needed him, not a slow-moving windbag like General Halleck.

Lockett cursed silently. It wasn't what one did; it was who one knew.

Farming wasn't like that. The earth didn't care who you knew. It only cared how hard you worked.

He stewed on those thoughts until Anna Tucker returned to the front porch with a glass of warm lemonade. He knew that he was becoming too used to this. She teased him with a smile sweeter than the drink. It caused him to chuckle, and she responded in kind. How he loved the sound of that laugh. It was like nothing he had ever heard before. She was the songbird cheering an otherwise dreary day. His brief military "career" was in ashes, but if in return that meant more time with Anna Tucker, then all was not so bad.

But the smile faded from his face as he saw Milton and Patrick quickly walking toward the Tucker house. He could tell by the purposefulness of their strides that something was wrong.

"L'tenant," Bosworth blurted out as he saluted, "We gots a prob'm. Sandie Holmes has done run off."

Desertion? The word flashed through Lockett's mind. There was no greater crime in the army. It was punishable by death. Every soldier knew that.

But it was not what lay in store for the angelic-faced Holmes that Lockett selfishly worried about. It was the reaction of Colonel Blair. Blair had given him free rein despite it all. He had given him a second chance after Otto Klugge's "desertion". He had ignored that black mark from Orrin and let him continue with training methods that Fulkerham had deemed ill-suited for a real army.

Truthfully, Colonel Blair had been surprisingly supportive so far.

But that could all change. One desertion could change everything.

"We gonna fetch the fool back?" McManus asked, solemn-faced.

Lockett nodded with a determined look. "Don't have much choice. And don't have much time either." He looked to the orange hue in west. They had about a half hour of light left, at best.

"Anna," he said, turning toward her, "I need to ask your father about borrowing your horses."

She looked from McManus to Bosworth to Lockett. "We have three, including Thunderbolt."

* * * * *

Thunderbolt was as big of a horse as Lockett had ever seen. Purely black with powerful hindquarters, the horse was nearly a full head taller than the other two mounts.

"You sure you can ride him?" McManus asked dubiously. He knew his old friend did not particularly like riding a horse, which was one reason that he was the only officer in Blair's Independent Regiment without one. "That's no plow horse."

"Ride him? Of course," Lockett scoffed, but truthfully, he was not so confident. He was more at ease with a horse hitched to a plow.

The giant black beast stomped the ground angrily with his right hoof, anxious to go. He snorted, his nostrils gaped, and his black eyes seemed to study Lockett.

"He's a handful, son," Reverend Tucker warned, "But you'll never have a better ride." He leaned close to Lockett. "Anna don't like me to ride him none, but I still saddle him when Anna's not looking. He's the fastest horse I ever saw, son, and I've seen some in my day."

"Sir, it's getting darker by the moment," Bosworth pointed out.

"Right, let's get on with it," Lockett said self-assuredly. He put one foot in the stirrup and pulled himself into the saddle. He sat there for a moment, his lanky figure towering above the others.

He pulled on the reins to point Thunderbolt down the road, when the animal reared up on his hind legs, front legs flailing vigorously, tossing him in an instant.

Lockett landed with a thud, and Thunderbolt's front legs returned to the ground, one hoof stamping impatiently again.

McManus and Bosworth laughed so hard that it looked like they too might fall from their saddles.

Reverend Tucker gave Lockett a helpful hand underneath the armpit. "Sorry, L'tenant," he clucked, "Forgot to tell you that

Thunderbolt doesn't like strong direction. You'll not need to kick your heels in with him. A gentle nudge is all he needs to run like the wind. Same with the reins."

"Right," Lockett answered. Thunderbolt seemed to be looking at him with bemusement, and Lockett shook his head. "Crazy horse."

Darkness fell quickly.

With its thick cloak and only a quarter moon illuminating the road, they reined in to a walk. The odds of finding Sandie Holmes were not good and dropping.

A heavy cloud drifted across what little moon there was. "Gonna storm," Bosworth commented knowingly, sniffing the night air, "Sure as hellfire, I can smell it."

Ahead of them was Haney's Corners. They were a good ways from town now, and there was no sign of Sandie Holmes. Even with the two to three hour headstart, Lockett would have been amazed if Holmes had made it this far on foot. Privately, he was amazed that Holmes had the energy to desert at all. After all, he had marched the men hard today. When he had dismissed them, most were footsore and anxious to cook a meal or rest.

Yet, Sandie Holmes had deemed that the time to desert.

There was a certain logic to it that Lockett had to admire. Say what you would about the shirker, but he had endurance. He was a good marcher.

"Check Haney's?" Bosworth asked.

He could smell the smoke from the chimney and see the light in the window in the distance. Haney's Inn was the only structure marking the crossroads, nothing more than a dilapidated two story inn and tavern for travelers.

"No drinking, Sergeant," Lockett grimaced as he looked at the place.

"Sir? Never crossed my mind." Bosworth smiled in the darkness at his officer's friendly rebuke. "Why, a tavern, that's no place to drink at all. Never, sir, never."

Lockett grunted, his mind already back on Holmes. He doubted that a deserter would show his face in a local tavern, particularly one like Sandie Holmes. He didn't seem the type, but then again, he never would have guessed that Holmes would high-tail it in the first place. "Might as well take a look around."

The darkness hid his gloom. They would return empty handed, and Tyler Fulkerham would be proven correct. Lockett could already see Colonel Blair's face and those hawking, accusing eyes.

As they neared the wooden structure, he was surprised to see five horses tied to the hitching post in front.

"Didn't know they did such good business," McManus remarked.

Lockett grunted in acknowledgement while Bosworth added a comment or two. He never heard the sergeant's remarks because he stopped paying attention. His mind was too busy thinking. Five horses? It did seem rather odd.

"Go around back, Patrick, just in case," he ordered, unaware that he had cut off Bosworth in mid-sentence.

McManus nodded and headed off. Bosworth spoke up again and asked, "S'pectin' trouble, sir?"

"There are still some bushwhackers around, Sergeant, and I don't like the look of five horses tied up together. Besides, if Holmes is in there, he might try to skedaddle out the back."

The sweet, pungent smell of good tobacco greeted Lockett and Bosworth at the front of the little tavern. Lockett gripped his rifle before pushing his way through the planking door. He was nervous. Rarely did Blair's little garrison force ever leave Savannah in the night. It was the shadowy bushwhackers who owned these hours.

As he and Bosworth pushed through the door shoulder to shoulder, his eyes rapidly took in the little room.

The long, worn bar top was empty, and Lockett sensed more than he actually saw the nervousness on old man Haney's face as he shifted his feet behind the bar. The little tavern was ominously silent, and Lockett felt the chill of the breeze on the back of his neck.

The appearance of their blue uniforms had abruptly halted the laughter from the four rough-looking men at the back table. Each looked like they had been living out of the saddle for a while with dirty faces and long, snarled beards. Even the baby-faced one looked like he had seen the rough end of a stick a few times in his life.

Lockett felt their icy cold eyes on him as he took in the playing cards, a nearly empty bottle of whiskey, small pile of money, and a much larger pile of ripped open envelopes.

One had a gun belt slung over the back of a nearby chair, and the man snuck a peek at it, judging how far away it was.

The other three glared at the intruders with plain disgust. The looks of hatred were not tempered by the fact that the soldiers had their rifles at the ready in their hands.

Were they bushwhackers or just harmless local citizens? Lockett wondered. That was the problem with uniform-less bushwhackers. They blurred the lines of who was a friend, who was a foe, and who was an innocent bystander.

One of the men, the baby-face, twisted his mouth and spat a wad of tobacco with remarkable accuracy into a spittoon ten feet away. The young man's eyes never left the two soldiers who stood just inside the tavern.

As the tobacco arced through the air, Bosworth's eyes drifted for just a second to examine the flight. In that moment, the baby-faced man leapt up and darted for the gun belt.

The reverberating echo of Lockett's shot shattered the night as the heavy slug flung the baby-faced man backwards.

The last time Lockett had heard a rifle shot in such enclosed quarters, little Amelia had died, but he did not remember that at this moment.

Blood pumping, he dropped the still smoking rifle with a clatter and reached for his holstered revolver as one of the other card players stood to free his weapon from the holster.

But Bosworth's eyes were back to the front and center now, and he fired just as the man succeeded in pulling the gun free. The sergeant's shot blasted the man backwards, and his dying hand sent one shot straight up before he toppled over onto his back.

Lockett dove behind the cover of the bar, while Bosworth flipped over a long table and crouched behind it. He could see Bosworth looking with concern at the spent rifle in his hand. While Lockett still had his sword and Starr revolver, Bosworth was now unarmed until he could reload the rifle.

Old Man Haney, hiding behind the bar, yelped to no one in particular, "Y'all just killed Bloody Bill Coulter's kid brother!"

Overhead, boots pounded on the landing that overlooked the area.

There was at least one more upstairs!

Suddenly, a shotgun blast ripped a gaping hole in the table, just missing Bosworth. The bushwhacker above them had luckily guessed the wrong side of the table, but what about the other two at the poker table?

He heard feet tramping above him again, and Lockett angled his head upward. He had no shot at the landing from his position, only Bosworth did.

"Milton!" Lockett hissed as he flung the revolver across the scarred wood floor. The gun sounded strangely loud as it scraped along the boards, and Bosworth greedily snatched it up. He bolted to his feet, firing a quick succession of poorly aimed shots above them.

Wood splintered and the heavy boots thudded away from the edge.

"You're clear!" McManus bellowed from the back of the room.

Lockett peeked over the top of the bar and saw that Patrick held one bushwhacker prisoner at the end of his rifle, and the fourth lay face down on the ground, unconscious.

Without hesitation he vaulted over the bar.

"Third door down!" McManus shouted instructions as Lockett leapt up the stairs three at a time.

Bosworth looked at the revolver in his hand, but Lockett was already recklessly charging upwards.

Reaching the third door, he pulled the sword free and kicked in the door, darting to the side as he did so, pinning his back against the hallway. But there was no shotgun blast or smoking revolver to greet him.

He charged into the room with a fearsome cry, sword flailing, but the room was empty except for the curtain fluttering from the open window... and a chair in the middle of the room.

It took Lockett a moment to realize what he was looking at, to realize that the battered, bloody mess tied to the chair was not just a person, but Sandie Holmes. Were it not for the uniform, he doubted that he ever would have made the association.

The angelic-faced Illinois clerk sat slumped forward, only the vigorous roping kept him upright. His face had been so badly smashed that it was swollen like a pumpkin and purple like cabbage. The bloody gashes over his eyes and a split lip were starting to coagulate. Thick blood stained the collar of his uniform and dripped down into puddles in his lap.

As Lockett stared aghast at his soldier, he heard a horse whinny and start to gallop away.

The butcher! He scowled furiously. The bushwhacker was getting away.

Lockett slipped the sword back into the scabbard and vaulted out the window, just as his prey had done. Through the stygian night, he felt himself drop like a rock, and he landed heavily, rolling to his side. His ankle hurt a little, but he did not waste a moment as he ran around to the front of the building for Thunderbolt.

The giant black horse seemed to be waiting for him. He stamped the ground impatiently and snorted as his rider grabbed the reins from the hitching post.

The instant Lockett flung himself into the saddle, Thunderbolt dashed forward. He could feel the animal's incredible strength surge beneath him. It seemed that instantly they were at top speed, but then Thunderbolt kept going faster and faster.

He could see nothing in the black of night, and Thunderbolt hammered down the road at a frightening rate. Long, powerful strides carried them, and the night air rushed by like he was being carried by a tornado.

Thunder cracked and lightning illuminated the horizon ahead of them.

There! He could see the other rider now. The man looked impossibly far away. The bushwhacker's headstart surely was too great, Lockett thought.

But no such defeatism entered Thunderbolt's equine mind. The beast ran on even faster. Deeper into the darkness they went – faster, faster, faster. Thunderbolt dashed around a bend that Lockett never saw, and lightning lit the entire horizon again.

There! They were gaining, and quickly! Lockett could hear nothing but the wind rushing past his ears.

Closer, closer.

The night sky again lit up, and he saw the bushwhacker look over his shoulder. It was impossible to see the man's face, but he could imagine the look of shock at seeing the giant black horse closing ground so rapidly.

The bushwhacker veered left into a field just as darkness again overtook the momentary brilliance of the lightning. Through the meadow they crashed. There was no hesitation in Thunderbolt's stride, no fear of the unseen, and he carried Lockett ever closer to the butchering bushwhacker.

His bouncing hand found the hilt of the Stuart family sword, and he pulled it free, all the while trying desperately to stay astride his flying steed. Thunderbolt pulled alongside of their prey, and the storm again turned night into day.

In that second, Lockett took in every detail of the bushwhacker known as Bloody Bill Coulter: the long red beard, the harsh brow overhanging spiteful eyes, the gnarled nose, and the mouth curled in contempt. This was the face of a killer. There was no mistaking that — wildness, cunning, a predator.

But it did not deter Lockett. His grip tightened around the sword, and he slashed violently at the red-bearded man. It was an awkward attempt, going over Thunderbolt's neck and across his own body, but his blood was up. He was no longer James Lockett the farmer; he was the James Lockett of the Hornet's Nest!

But the butcher reacted with stunning grace and ease. Sliding himself to the side while flawlessly staying in control of the galloping horse, the bushwhacker easily avoided the blow.

The awkwardness and viciousness of Lockett's attempt pulled him from his own saddle. His upper body dangled out over open space while his lower body fought desperately to stay astride Thunderbolt. His left hand wrenched on the reins. It was his only point of leverage.

Thunderbolt slowed and swirled, but he did not buck or throw the half-askew rider, despite his foolish actions. With a powerful neck, Thunderbolt held position and gave Lockett a chance to gather his balance. Still clutching the sword, the palm of his right hand found the saddle's pommel, and with a strength developed from years behind a plow in the thick Kalamazoo soil, Lockett hauled himself back into the saddle.

A gap had opened up between Lockett and his prey, and lightning flashed again. The bushwhacker was making for the woods, but doggedly Thunderbolt's powerful flanks starting moving again, carrying them swiftly towards the trees.

The idea of charging through the trees in the darkness did not appeal to Lockett, but it almost seemed too late. They were flying again. The wind whipped through his hair. Anna's father was right, he marveled, he had never seen a horse like this either.

Suddenly, an obstacle emerged through the darkness. It was large and stationary – a bush or a hedge! And they were going too fast to go around now!

He had never jumped anything larger than a fallen log in life. Fence jumping had always been something for the imprudent and adventurous, certainly something that ran against the cautious nature of the young farmer named James Lockett. And this barrier looked even higher than a fence. Lockett wanted to pull on the reins for all he was worth, but he knew it was too late for that.

All at once, Thunderbolt's mighty flanks heaved upwards, and they were soaring. Higher and higher, until he could hear Thunderbolt's hooves scraping against the very top of the brambles.

They had cleared it! Or rather, Thunderbolt had cleared it! He had done little more than hang on for dear life.

As they descended, Lockett felt himself pitch forward slightly. He wasn't ready for the landing and the sharp impact of the ground tossed him over Thunderbolt's front quarter. Unlike a regular cavalryman, he did not have a loop connecting his sword to his wrist, and it went flying out of his hand as he flew headfirst through the black of night. Lockett raised his hands in front of his head instinctively and crashed into the bushes, tumbling heels over head, cartwheeling, before coming to a rest with his head just a few inches from a tree.

He gasped for air, and there seemed to be none. For a moment, he feared he was dying, but then painfully, the air trickled back into his lungs.

It took him a minute or two to recover from having the wind knocked out him. Thunderbolt snorted angrily nearby, as if disgusted by the performance of his rider. Lightning snapped overhead, and Lockett struggled to his feet.

Bloody Bill Coulter had escaped.

* * * * *

Lockett's headlong flight through the brambles left his face looking like he had been attacked by a pack of angry squirrels, and he was still annoyed that it had taken him so long in the dark to locate the Stuart family sword that had flung from his hand.

For a while, he feared that he would never find it but vowed to himself that he wouldn't leave the stretch of woods until he recovered Ainsley's heirloom.

Scraped, dirty, and grumpy, he returned to Haney's Corners where McManus waited with two bushwhacker prisoners and two bushwhacker corpses. All in all, it was a good haul for a night's work, but McManus could see from the determined scowl on Lockett's face that he wasn't happy about the one who got away.

"I ain't no Rebel, 'Ten-ant. You hear me?" Old man Haney's face was flush with either anxiety or alcohol as he came over to Lockett. "I ain't harb'rin' no Rebels, sir. I ain't friendly like with no bushwhackers like Bloody Bill Coulter. No, sir, indeed. They all pay for their drinks. 'Sides, they were five of 'em with guns. Even if I could afford to turn anyone away, it wouldn't be five murderers like 'em."

Lockett could smell the whiskey on the old man and wondered if he had done anything but drink in the time that had passed, but he ignored the tavern keeper and turned his attention back to McManus.

"Holmes?"

"Inside the tavern with Milton," McManus answered.

Lockett brushed past Haney without a word or glance, but the old man simply followed him into the building.

"'Ten-ant, I tell you, I ain't no Rebel."

Lockett ignored the comment again and looked at Bosworth who sat in a chair next to the sprawled Sandie Holmes. "That the post?" he asked Bosworth, pointing to the bag at his feet.

It had been the pile of envelopes on the card table that had tipped Lockett off to the bushwhackers' true identities. They had robbed the postal carrier and were gambling over the contents of the letters for entertainment. The small pile of money on the table had probably come from the envelopes, he guessed.

"No, sir, that bag isn't the post," Bosworth answered uneasily, "Pat already put the mail on the horses."

"Then what's in the bag? Something they stole from the postal carrier this time?"

"Worse 'n that, sir."

"Why don't you have a look-see?" Old Man Haney cackled, annoyed that the Yankee officer had completely ignored him.

"Old man, the Lieutenant can still have you dragged off in irons," Bosworth warned. "I'd be happy to hog-tie you myself."

"Let me see," Lockett said, stooping down to open the bag.

"The carrier di'n't git away this time."

"Good God!" Lockett gasped.

He had seen plenty of death and destruction so far in his short stint in the Army. Still, the contents of the bag turned his stomach, and he fought to control himself from vomiting. Inside the bag was a crudely hacked off head.

"They cut his head off and stuffed it in his own mail bag, sir," Bosworth added unnecessarily.

Lockett retched. There was a reason the man was called 'Bloody Bill'.

Old Man Haney made a tiny snort, and Lockett turned on his heel with a suddenness that caught everyone off-guard. He button-holed the old man and lifted him to the tips of his toes. "Think that is funny, do you?" he snarled. His gray eyes sparked with anger, and his face contorted. Lightning flashed behind him, and Old Man Haney now knew fear as Lockett spoke. "You can always join him in that bag. There's nobody out here but us. Who would know?"

Haney babbled but made no coherent words while the tips of his toes brushed the floor futilely. Bosworth was rooted in place.

"You think I'm going to be fooled?" Lockett growled, throwing the man backward so that he landed on his rump. "We can always bring in one more bushwhacker body."

Haney scrambled backward like a crab and then was on his feet, hurrying out the backdoor.

Bosworth stood up from his chair. "Should I go get him, sir?"

"No, let him go. He's harmless and might even be telling the truth. Besides, we know where to find him."

Bosworth nodded. "Okay. Now what, sir?"

Lockett looked down at Sandie Holmes. He was alive, but nowhere near conscious. The boy's face looked like he had been caught in a stampede, and Lockett couldn't imagine receiving a beating so severe.

Now what indeed? Holmes was a deserter. Deserters were hung. But as he looked at the grotesquely swollen face, he had a hard time envisioning young Sandie Holmes swinging from a rope.

And then there was the problem of trying to explain all this to Colonel Blair.

Chapter 10

The lamp did a poor job of illuminating the little room that was Colonel Blair's office. From the corner of his eye, Lockett saw Tyler Fulkerham sitting smugly in the shadows, next to a neat stack of the colonel's precious ledgers. Despite the insufficient lighting, Lockett could easily make out the pleased look on his fellow lieutenant's face and wished that the colonel would dismiss him. It was bad enough to bear Blair's accusing scrutiny without Fulkerham's bemused smirks.

"And you found these bushwhackers *how*, Lockett?" The hard stare bore right through him, adding to the nauseating swirl in his stomach. The ire would not be easily assuaged.

He paused before answering which caused Blair to answer his own question. "I'll not have my men off fighting private wars, Lockett! You hear me? I give you leeway in the training of your company and no more!"

"Yes, sir."

"Again, tell me how you found these bushwhackers."

"Yes, sir. Bloody Bill Coult-"

"Bill Coulter!" Blair snapped, "I'll not have my men referring to him by any other name! You want to make him a legend, Lockett?"

"No, sir."

"Now, tell me."

This was the moment of truth, the moment that Lockett had pondered the entire way back from Haney's Corners. The easy thing to do would be to admit that Sandie Holmes had deserted.

But hadn't the boy suffered enough already? Lockett himself had once been threatened with the noose, and were it not for Lieutenant Simon looking after him, he may never have returned from Missouri. Didn't he owe Holmes the same second chance?

Of course, Lockett had been innocent – in a way – of murdering little Amelia, whereas Holmes was definitely a deserter.

And protecting Holmes had numerous consequences. His own men knew Holmes was a deserter. Would he set a bad precedent by protecting Holmes? Would the men lose some respect for him? Would they be encouraged to desert themselves? What did he owe Holmes anyway? The man had been a lily from the start. Why stick out my neck for him?

But it wasn't just for Sandie Holmes. It was for himself. He enjoyed commanding his own company. He enjoyed the free rein. A deserter could change all that. Desertion was an indication of a serious, serious morale problem.

Much to his chagrin, Lockett had reflected that it would have been much better if they had never run into the bushwhackers. He could have returned with Holmes, and no one would be any wiser. It was the fact that he was returning with two prisoners that made this impossible to cover up.

He stopped in mid-thought for a moment, half-stunned at what he was deliberating. Lying! Before this war, lying was as foreign to him as flapping his arms and flying like a bird. Lying?

Even though he had worked out a story, he couldn't open his mouth. He had been planning on beginning with, *it all started during the march yesterday. Private Holmes had struck up a conversation with a local and learned that the bushwhackers could be at Haney's Corners that night.* That was the beginning of what he had practiced in his head. But at this moment, it sounded utterly flimsy, not like the lies that Orrin Long could spin.

And so, he found himself completely speechless.

Colonel Blair looked at the perplexed glaze on his face with growing annoyance.

"Holmes deserted, sir," Lockett blurted out finally with a dumb-founded tone.

The word hung in the air like a poised axe-blow.

Deserted.

Colonel Blair seemed startled by the news, and he looked quizzically at Lockett, causing him to repeat. "He deserted, sir."

"Yes, I heard you the first time, Lieutenant. I'm waiting for the remainder."

"We went out to retrieve him and stumbled upon Blo-, er, Bill Coulter's men, Colonel."

"I see," Blair said in a low voice. The voice was pondering, but the face was furrowing and going from red to purple. "Stand at attention, damn you!"

Lockett supposed his shoulders had slumped, for that was how he felt.

"Off fighting your own little war, Lockett! Thought you'd retrieve this shirker Holmes before I was none the wiser? Let me make one thing very clear, Lieutenant Lockett! If you ever, *ever* put my men at risk again without informing me, I'll have you back as a Private faster than you can say the word!"

"Yes, sir."

"This is my regiment, Lockett! Blair's Independent Regiment, not Lockett's! Have you spent the sums necessary to outfit this unit? Well, have you?"

"No, sir." He took a quick peek over at Fulkerham. The man was nearly beside himself in amusement. Blair must have noticed his glance, for he suddenly seemed to remember that Fulkerham was in the room.

"Lieutenant Fulkerham," Blair said with a surprising ability to switch from ire to courteousness, "Please excuse us. Lieutenant Lockett and I will finish this in private."

"Yes, sir," Fulkerham answered, leaving the room. Lockett imagined that Fulkerham would be disappointed to miss the dressing-down.

The door shut, and Blair instantly switched from courteous back to boiling anger. "So, you think you are in charge here! That this is your regiment?" Blair began to pace back and forth across the small room while he continued his tirade. "Fulkerham warned me about you, said you couldn't be trusted. Pointed out that you're the reason we are stuck on this humiliating baggage guarding."

"Sir, I'm sorry, sir, I only meant to retrieve…"

Blair slammed his hand on the table, disturbing his neat stack of papers. "Damn you, Lockett! I'll have you digging latrine ditches for the rest of the war, do you hear me? *Do you hear me?*"

There was a long silence, and then Lockett realized that he was supposed to speak finally. "Yes, sir." He tried not to sound too meek but wasn't sure how it came out.

"Now, what do you have to say about Fulkerham's opinions?"

There was a long pause again while Blair patiently waited. "Opinions, sir?" he said in a confused voice.

"Yes, opinions, Lockett. What do you have to say about them?"

"He's entitled to his own mind, sir."

Blair stopped pacing suddenly, and his accusing blue eyes turned their full attention on him. "Do you know why I have ignored them up till now, Lieutenant?"

"No, sir."

"Because I believe this will be a long war, Lockett. We will get our chance. We won't be on baggage duty forever. That is why I let you train your men your own way. Despite being nothing more than a damn farmer, I was told that you would fight, and that you knew how to fight."

"Thank you, sir."

"Don't thank me, you damn fool! I did it because you're the only one who has really seen battle. I gave you the benefit of the doubt."

"Yes, sir."

"And what do you do? You turn around and flaunt my authority! That was *my* man who deserted, not yours! Do you understand what I am saying, Lockett?"

"Yes, sir. I think so, sir."

"I'm a banker, Lockett, not a soldier. I need your help to make these men fight. I know what the regular Army thinks of men like me, and you too. And they're probably right about most of us volunteers... But not me!" He bellowed out the last word like a snorting bull.

He glared at an unseen enemy, and a full minute passed before his gaze turned back to his lieutenant. "Trust me, Lockett," he said in a calmer voice. "I stood by you. But if you'll not stand by me, I won't have you."

"Yes, sir. I'm sorry, sir." This wasn't what Lockett had expected. Of all things, he did not expect to feel so guilty about his past impressions of Colonel Laurent Blair. "It won't happen again, sir."

"See that it doesn't, Lieutenant. You've put me in a fine muddle," Blair continued. "By rights and reputation, you put your lieutenancy on the line by vouching for Private Klugge, and while he did not desert, another of your men did. What would you do in my shoes, Lockett?"

"I don't know, sir."

Blair snorted. "That's no answer. You're not the indecisive, willy-nilly type. You just don't want to say it aloud."

"Yes, sir," Lockett answered. His precious commission flashed before his eyes.

"So, I break you back down to the ranks, is that it?" Blair paused and tapped his cheek, "But I already have a shortage of officers, not even half of what I should have."

"But if you don't discipline me, Fulkerham and the others...well, there is the overall discipline of the regiment, sir."

"Exactly, so you see, a fine muddle."

"Yes, sir."

"And on the other hand, you did bring in some of these bushwhackers who had been so elusive until now. Let's not forget that." Colonel Blair's tone turned more conciliatory, and then he started to chuckle. "You were supposed to point out that last one, Lockett, not me. Come now, am I to be the prosecution, judge, jury, *and* defense?"

"Sorry, sir. Didn't seem like speaking up could change much."

Blair uttered a small grunt. He saw himself as a better judge of men than most, and he could sense that there was more to Lockett's comment than appearances. The young farmer's face was too unrepentant when he had said that, but the former banker let the question drift away.

"Very well," he declared, "Given that you did capture the shirker and bring in most of this bushwhacker Coulter's gang, I'll give you another chance. So, shall we say that you are officially on your last straw?"

"Yes, sir. Thank you, sir," Lockett said, brightening.

"Dismissed, Lockett. And send in Pope on your way out. We're going to need to build a gallows for these bandits and our own deserter."

* * * * *

The sound of the wooden gallows being slapped together hurried Lockett along. He had never seen a man hung before, but he knew that hangings made an impression on those who saw them. He tried not to think about it, but one thought clung to him like the clammy, humidity-induced second skin. *One of the men to be hung was his own.*

Holmes was currently held in the rear cell of the sheriff's jail, and Lockett could not imagine the thoughts that ran through the young boy's mind. He had heard from his men that Holmes was a coward. They said that Holmes had run faster than Orrin Long in their fateful encounter with the Rebel cavalry. How would a coward accept the news that he was to die by the noose? Poor Holmes.

Renaud walked alongside his distracted friend, sensing the conflicted thoughts. He had already pointed out that it was not Lockett's decision. It was clear in the Army's regulations. Desertion was punishable by death, and this was precisely why the Army had regulations, Renaud explained, so that things like this could not be Lockett's decision. There was nothing to feel guilty about, Renaud added.

But Lockett was not convinced. Try as he might to put it out of his mind, he could not. He could only think that it was his fault. He had let Holmes down in the past, somehow. If he had been a better officer, then Sandie Holmes would not have succumbed to his fears so completely.

The clanking of the hammers and the sawing of the boards continued. He saw Prosper T. Rowe hand a board up to Otto Klugge. Half of the crew working on the gallows were from his company. He wondered how they felt about sweating in the humid heat to build such a thing, the final demise for one of their own. Lockett supposed that this was part of Blair's grand design – to have his men intimately involved, just to be safe that there were no more such thoughts in anyone's head.

The other half of the men were from Pope's company. Lockett didn't know why they had been selected, but it was not a random selection. Colonel Blair always seemed to have a reason for things, rightly or wrongly.

Across the way, he noticed Katherine Moffat watching the activity before continuing onto the tent hospital. Mutually, they avoided making eye contact, not that either really needed to, for Katherine was refusing to speak to him and would conveniently disappear anytime he was in the vicinity. It was just as well, because he could not bear facing her at this moment. Things were always so black and white in her mind. She would not see the grayness of the situation that he saw.

In the distance Reverend Tucker dismounted at the tiny white washed church. Though his damaged leg prevented him from moving quickly on his own, he was still a surprisingly skilled rider. It was only when he dismounted that his movements became pained and laborious.

Yet, it did not slow the man's busy schedule.

As Milton had commented once, it was impressive that Reverend Tucker could maintain a schedule so full of travel. He was always riding off to preach to one town or another. With the war on, there was probably a shortage of preachers and more need for them than ever, Lockett mused as he sauntered over.

Reverend Tucker tied his horse to the post. He was dust covered from head to toe due to his long ride, but he did not seem to notice. As the preacher wiped sweat from a reddened brow, Lockett admired the old man's stamina in this afternoon heat.

The preacher's blue eyes watched the tall Michigander approach.

"Causing another stir, I hear, my L'tenant," Reverend Tucker commented.

"Can't seem to avoid them," Lockett replied with a shrug. "Did you have a good ride?"

"As good as can be with this nag." Reverend Tucker lovingly patted the tiny gray horse. "She is no Thunderbolt."

Lockett could not help but grin as he remembered the wild exhilaration of flying through the dark on the giant black horse. "You were right. I've never seen another horse quite like him."

"He can out-race the devil himself, can't he?" The preacher suddenly sounded excited, like an enthused schoolboy. Reverend Tucker obviously loved to run wild and free, and Lockett felt an ooze of pity emerge for the preacher. "Anna was right about your face," the old man observed, pointing at him, "Your face does look like Thunderbolt took you through a forest of brambles."

"My own fault. I didn't hold on tight enough."

"Goes without saying, my boy," the Reverend laughed, "Thunderbolt never makes mistakes, only his riders do. Just ask the horse himself." He chuckled again and patted his leg.

"Notice that I was the one coming out with a bum leg, not the horse."

"Do I really look that bad?" Lockett grimaced, touching the spider web of fresh scabs on his face. A day's worth of growth sprouted between scratches, and he guessed he would have to grow a patchy beard for a while because shaving seemed out of the question until his face healed.

Behind them in the distance, there was a cry and a spew of profanity as part of the gallows gave way. One of Pope's soldiers, hammer still in hand, had tumbled to the ground, though he seemed none the worse for wear.

Lockett blushed. "Pardon that preacher."

"If only foul tongues were our worst problem, L'tenant."

The preacher paused and looked at the young soldier, pondering the gentle face and the gray eyes which had no expression. He was clearly a mild-mannered, God-fearing young man, which was what made the actions of James Lockett so paradoxical. "You make a strange soldier, my boy."

There was another curse from the gallows as one man bashed his thumb.

"Don't worry about my ears burning. Cursin' is as much a part of the army as bad food and mud." He paused and added reflectively, "You make a peculiar soldier, but then, I reck'n these are peculiar times."

Lockett nodded with resignation, and the hammering on the gallows began anew, drawing both men's attention.

"I spoke with Colonel Blair, begged him in his Christian heart to spare all three of them," the Reverend lamented.

"He gave no hope," Lockett replied. It was a statement, not a question.

"At least he allowed me to speak my peace," Reverend Tucker said, "I reck'n that's more than most."

"Coming back from another congregation?" Lockett asked, anxious to change the subject from the imminent hanging.

"Ah, yes… Yes, indeed."

"The Lord's work is never done."

"Never indeed, L'tenant. Never indeed." A hint of a playful smile crossed the preacher's lips but only for a brief instant.

"Can I help with your saddlebags?" Lockett asked, noticing that they were full.

"No, no," he replied hastily, "Not necessary, my boy. I'm still capable of doing that myself."

"Sorry. I didn't mean to imply…"

Relaxing, Reverend Tucker answered, "No need to apologize. I'm just a little tired from the long ride. You understand." A board fell noisily from the scaffold. "Wish they would at least bury those other ones though. They're starting to smell." The preacher gestured toward the front step of the sheriff's office down the street.

The two dead bushwhackers were propped up in their open coffins so that passers-by had to look at the faces, frozen in agonized rictus. The colonel's idea was to show the townfolk what happened to bushwhackers, but Lockett could see it having the wrong effect on this town. Once pro-Union, Savannah was developing a growing sense of dislike for the Northern intruders. The presence and actions of the Yankees were making some of them wonder if perhaps, their Secession-swearing Tennessee brethren had been right.

"Those men were murderers and scoundrels to be sure, but that is no treatment for any man."

Lockett had to agree and nodded. There was nothing that he could say.

"Course, sooner or later, Bloody Bill and his brother would have been in this situation, a war or not. They were killers before it even started. Coulter's a regular highwayman, but no one could ever prove it. The war just gives him an excuse to continue his thievin'."

"Exactly the same words the colonel used."

"Speaking of your Colonel Blair, it looks like he wants to see you."

Lockett turned to see Colonel Blair with an odd leather tube in his hand. He wasn't sure that he wanted to see the colonel right now. He was tired from the sleepless night of chasing Bloody Bill, and a growing headache knifed through his forehead.

"Ah, Lieutenant," Colonel Blair said in an eager voice, "I have something that you will want to see." Without waiting for a comment, he began to pull out the contents of the tube. "Arrived on this afternoon's steamer."

Slowly and dramatically, the proud colonel unfurled a brilliant green and blue flag that seemed to flash in the Tennessee sun. "What do you think?"

He sounded as if he had made it himself, Lockett thought to himself with amusement. Then he looked more carefully at the banner. It was one large green triangle on top of a blue triangle with an eagle grasping a lightning bolt across the middle. Lockett was awed. It was one of the grandest regimental flags that he had ever seen. Colonel Blair had clearly gone through great expense for it. Across the bottom in golden thread were the words, *For Liberty For Union.*

"It's impressive, sir," Lockett complimented. Then he noticed one other word in the corner - *Shiloh.* He knew that it was common practice to sew in the names of the battles in which a regiment had fought, but Shiloh?

"The flag of Blair's Independent Regiment," Colonel Blair announced to Reverend Tucker, but Lockett did not hear anything except his own thoughts.

Shiloh? Admittedly, Lockett and roughly half of the regiment had fought and bled there, but it seemed to him that Blair's Independent Regiment was taking credit for the blood that others had shed. Again, Lockett could feel someone else taking his credit, and it stirred the poison that still lingered in his veins.

Trying to hide his anger, he turned away and looked down the far end of the street. His jaw was clenched, and he was forcing his temper down when his eyes caught something that was out of place.

He could not quite pinpoint it at first. What was it?

"Lieutenant?" Colonel Blair said, annoyed that his subordinate had turned his back on him and seemed to be ignoring him. "Lieutenant!" he commanded again, this time louder.

"Something is not right," Lockett began, taking a step towards the Sheriff's office.

"Lieutenant Lockett..."

Finally, it registered what was missing.

"Where did they go?" Lockett said to no one in particular. His eyes were still riveted away from Colonel Blair.

"Where did who go?" Colonel Blair replied tightly. He stepped forward to Lockett's side, but anger was etching itself into his face. The furrows plowed more deeply across his wrinkled brow.

But Lockett did not notice. All of his attention was fixated further down the street. It seemed strange, but...

"My God! Bloody Bill Coulter's here!" he gasped.

His hand slid down to the butt of his .44 caliber Starr revolver. The rounded heel of the three pound weapon still felt awkward and unnatural to him, but it provided some reassurance.

"Coulter? What nonsense is this, Lockett? And you know what I think about..."

"There!" Lockett pointed, realizing what had stirred his consciousness. "The coffins are empty."

Blair watched for a moment.

Lockett slowly began to walk forward towards the empty coffins.

"Empty? That doesn't necessarily mean... I mean, it is broad daylight, Lieutenant. The brigand would never dare!"

"It's Coulter," Lockett replied without looking back, his pace quickening.

"Now, look here..."

Blair never finished his sentence as a howling, terrified scream split the air.

"That's Holmes!" Lockett cried of the ghastly noise, running forward.

The soldiers working on the gallows dropped their hammers and looked around in confusion. They could not tell where the screams had come from, or what was going on, but Lockett knew, and he was already rapidly closing on the sheriff's office when someone dashed out. Seeing Lockett heading straight for him, the man raised a drawn weapon and fired.

Lockett veered right and dove for the safety of the alleyway next to the dry goods store. The shot cracked the heavy afternoon air, and dust kicked up behind his heels as he landed just out of harm's way. Another shot splintered the corner of the wall.

Bloody Bill!

He leaned out from his cover but quickly ducked back behind the protection of the alleyway. Freed from the jail, one of the bushwhackers blasted away with a six-shooter in each hand. The shots splintered the edge of the wall.

Boots pounded on the planking in front of the jail now. There were two more shots, both winged the water trough where Colonel Blair kept his head down.

"They're getting away, Lockett!" Blair yelled just as another shot plunked into the water.

Lockett cocked the hammer back on his revolver. At Shiloh, he couldn't have hit the side of a barn with the thing, but while his men drilled over and over again on the speed of their rifle reloading, he had been busy too.

But shooting calmly at trees was nothing like the blurring haste of an actual gunfight.

He drew up the courage to lean out around the corner, but a few more shots at the water trough gave him second thoughts. The boots were moving on the planking again, sounding more faint with each step.

He gritted his teeth and was about to launch himself out into the open when something occurred to him. The bushwhackers weren't going to get far on foot. They had to have horses somewhere, and he had not seen any out on the street. He looked over his shoulder to the back of the alleyway.

The horses must be out back, and he could cut them off.

The only reason that the bushwhackers went out the front was that there was no back door to the jail, forcing the bushwhackers to loop around, Lockett decided.

He darted for the other end of the alleyway and heard a horse whinny from the low clump of scrub pines across the way. The low-hanging evergreens were just tall enough to hide a horse. He took a step out into the open when he heard the crunch of gravel from behind.

How a bushwhacker had gotten behind him, he had no idea, but he whirled, finger on the trigger.

"God sakes!" Lockett exclaimed, snapping the Starr upwards, "I nearly shot you!"

"Glad you didn't," Reverend Tucker replied, unfazed as he limped over to Lockett's side of the alley. "Figured their horses were out back too?"

"Must be behind the pines. What are you doing here?" he added, as he peeked around the corner. "This is no place for a preacher."

The gray haired preacher frowned. "I was fightin' in Mexico before you were even born. Don't lecture me about danger." The frown still on his face, he added, "'sides, my daughter's taken a shine to you. She'd never forgive me if I let ya get ya'self shot."

"Yes, sir," Lockett allowed himself a quick grin as he waited for the bushwhackers to show themselves. "I'd offer you a gun if I had an extra."

"I'm a man of God now, Lieutenant. I'll take no firearms anymore. My wife, God rest her soul, made me promise to swear off ever taking up arms again, and I'm a man of my word."

Lockett stood at the corner of the alleyway and waited for the bushwhackers to come around the far end. He didn't have to wait long.

159

Seconds later, Bloody Bill Coulter emerged in the opening, spinning frantically while he gestured to the two freed bushwhackers to hurry. A corpse from each of the coffins, one of whom was Coulter's younger brother, burdened the two former prisoners. They clung to their loads like a man might hug a tree. The boots of the corpses dragged across the ground, creating swirls of dust behind them. They all moved deeper into the opening, unaware that Lockett followed their paths with his revolver.

"Surrender!" Lockett ordered, stepping out with his revolver leveled at Bloody Bill Coulter.

Coulter raised both six-shooters, but it was impossible to beat Lockett's already poised weapon.

But as Lockett fired, one of Coulter's comrades, accidentally cut in front. He still held a corpse, and the lifeless body would have blocked most shots, but by luck, the bullet zipped over the shield and found the man's neck, sending a great fountain of red blood in the air.

However, Lockett did not see this. Bloody Bill fired both of his guns. One shot smacked into the wood of the building just behind Lockett's ear, but the second shot drew blood as it sliced across the very top of his forearm. Momentarily nerveless, Lockett's gun fell from his hand as he stumbled back into the protection of the alleyway.

It had been the slightest of grazings, and it only took him a moment to catch himself, but his Starr rested forlornly out in the opening, teasingly beyond reach, and he cursed his stupidity. If he had just fired first before alerting them to his presence...

"Lockett!" Coulter yelled. The inflection of hate was unmistakable. "You killed my brother!"

The bushwhacker had learned him by name, Lockett realized with a start.

But Coulter was interrupted by the startled voice of his remaining henchman, "Behind us!"

Lockett could hear the man drop his heavy, lifeless load, and he peeked around the corner just in time to see them duck into the pine scrub. In the background, it was clear what had prompted the bushwhacker's urgency. A dozen blue jackets had dropped their hammers and saws for their rifles.

Lockett clenched his fist to test his strength. The wound in his forearm was just a scratch, and he retrieved his revolver. Blood dripped over the cuff of his sleeve and made his hand slippery, but he wasn't ready to let Coulter escape so easily. Lieutenant Pope and his squad were hurrying, but they were still too far away.

Gun in hand, he dashed to the edge of the pine scrub and peered through the branches of the first low hanging tree. He saw nothing.

There was no sound of galloping horses, and he guessed it was because the trees in the grove were not tall enough to conceal a mounted rider. Coulter and his cohort had to be leading their horses away by the reins until they could get deeper into the grove, and that meant there was still a chance of catching them.

He carefully worked his way deeper into the grove, cautious of an ambush.

Finally, he found an open patch between the densely growing evergreens, complete with a fresh pile of horse dung. He was trying to decide which way to go when the crackle of rifles sounded.

The ragged staccato was immediately followed by the sound of horses galloping away. Lockett threw caution to the wind and ran blindly through the scrub. He burst through the thick evergreens in time to see Coulter and his henchman, their bodies low over the horses' necks, as they urged their mounts on.

They were well out of effective range, and Lockett heard Pope futilely shouting at his men to fire their now empty rifles. It was no use. The rhythmic gallop of the horses grew fainter and fainter.

Bloody Bill Coulter had escaped again.

Leaving Pope and his men to deal with the dead bushwhacker and two discarded corpses, Lockett headed back to the jail.

A small crowd clustered around the doorway and parted before him. Reverend Tucker was kneeling over Sheriff Willows.

The old lawman was on his back, a hand limply atop a stab wound in his abdomen. Blood smeared the entire area of his ample stomach and coated the floor around him.

"Before he passed on, he said that Coulter shaved his beard. Didn't recognize him until it was too late," Reverend Tucker explained. He paused to look down at the sheriff. "Bob was a good man," he lamented sadly.

Above the preacher, Colonel Blair stood with a face of shock. "Broad daylight," Blair murmured in a quiet voice, as if he didn't want the growing crowd of on-lookers to hear him, "The murderers came in broad daylight?"

"What about Holmes?" Lockett asked, looking at the L-shaped bend beyond the first cell.

The open door of the first cell seemed to mock the blue coated soldiers, but it was the jail cell around that bend that Lockett was most interested in. That one held Sandie Holmes.

"We won't be needing those gallows after all," Colonel Blair said numbly, "Private Holmes is dead. His neck is split wide open from ear to ear." It was then that Lockett noticed the trickle of vomit on the colonel's uniform. "A gruesome sight," Blair added unnecessarily, and Lockett imagined that this was probably the first time Blair had ever seen the victim of a violent death.

"I got one of 'em," Lockett said, "But Coulter got away."

Colonel Blair nodded blankly. How would he write this report? The bushwhacker's escape would be another black mark on his regiment's ever deteriorating reputation.

Chapter 11

It was cloudy, yet the sky refused to rain this day.

Days before he had prayed that somehow Holmes would not be hung, but this was not the outcome that Lockett had envisioned.

Holmes was dead.

A few bystanders lingered nearby, watching the unfinished gallows being disassembled. It stood like a mocking monument to their latest defeat.

Lockett idled next to McManus, away from Bosworth and a few others from his company. Though there was no crowd today, it oddly reminded him of the last time he had seen a crowd gather in a town center. That place had been Kalamazoo, and though it seemed a lifetime ago, it had not been too many months since the whole county of Kalamazoo had gathered to listen to Captain Vincent's call to arms. The excitement and rush to volunteer had been unmistakable then.

But there was no excitement today, and the empty scaffold seemed to herald that the dark times were far from over. He noticed Lewis Dell, the storekeeper, looking at him. Embarrassed and ashamed for some reason, Lockett looked away.

"What are you thinking, James?" McManus asked in a voice so quiet that he had to strain to hear him.

"Thinking? Nothing. Why?"

"Good. I thought maybe you would be thinking about Missouri."

"Missouri?"

"Yes, Missouri.   It could have been you up there in Missouri."

He nodded and was slow to reply. "Yes, it could have been me, couldn't it?" Lockett's mind went back to those bitterly cold days. Had it not been for Lieutenant Simon's plan for him to leave town with the sick sharpshooters, who knew what might have happened after the death of little Amelia? Her little pixie face flashed into his head, quickly followed by the sneering, mocking countenance of Orrin Long.

He had been trying to save her. In the end, he had failed there too.

May 11

A wry grin emerged on Reverend Tucker's face.

"Is this a social visit?" he asked amiably as he limped down the steps in front of the little church. He wore a white shirt, damp with sweat even though it was not buttoned to the collar. He dabbed a white handkerchief against his perspiring forehead.

"I'm afraid I need to talk to you about something," Lockett replied hesitantly.

The preacher could not miss the look of concern, and in a fatherly voice he answered, "Well, then, how about a seat in the shade? It's too dadgum hot in the sun today."

Lockett couldn't have agreed more. The baking sun and still air made for another oppressive day. Unthinkingly, he adjusted the bandage on his forearm. Bloody Bill's shot had just grazed him, but the combination of heat and bandage chafed him. At this point, the chafing was worse than the wound itself.

"Colonel Blair asked me to talk to you," Lockett started as he followed the preacher to the shade of the large willow tree. The patch of grass next to its trunk was worn, and he guessed that Reverend Tucker often took refuge from the Tennessee heat beneath its huge canopy.

"Oh?" Reverend Tucker replied, "I thought perhaps ya had come to ask me something about Anna." He gave a teasing smile, but Lockett was in the dark as to what the joke was.

He looked blankly at the preacher.

"Never mind, my boy, what is it that Colonel Blair wants from me? I'm intrigued."

But the preacher still pondered his original assumption. As a father, he had envisioned how someone would come one day to ask for his daughter's hand. He had never imagined that it might be a soldier from a far off place like Michigan.

He liked James Lockett. Indeed, the tall farmer turned soldier had displayed more admirable qualities than most, but the idea that Lockett might be the one asking to take his daughter away left Reverend Tucker with a concern that could only grow.

There would be trouble for all when that day came, but before the preacher could continue down that line of thought, one word from James Lockett snapped his attention back.

"...*Traitorous*..."

"What?" Reverend Tucker said with sudden alarm.

Lockett cleared his throat awkwardly, "The colonel is concerned about your, er... secessionist feelings."

A startled look flashed through the preacher's eyes but disappeared just as quickly.

"It was your sermon last Sunday, you see."

"My sermon?"

"I know. I tried to explain to Colonel Blair that he was mistaken, but someone has told him that your sermon was designed to rouse support for the Rebels."

Colonel Blair had then gone on pointedly to make it clear to all present that he disapproved of his officers fraternizing so closely with the citizens of the town, particularly ones who voiced support for Secession. It was obvious that the comment was directed at Lockett, and in a voice that dared no discussion, Colonel Blair had gone on to reiterate that this was Tennessee, and they were fighting an insurrection – that Tennessee had attempted to secede. With his icy blue eyes burning with scorn, he had turned to Lockett and warned that old loyalties die hard despite what it appeared. No good could come from becoming too involved with any Southerners, he stated.

"Rouse support for the Confederacy?" Reverend Tucker queried, bringing Lockett back to the present.

"Yes. I tried to tell him that he was mistaken."

The preacher laughed softly, "Lieutenant, I believe you should have told your colonel that his information was mistaken, not the colonel himself. He is not the type of man to let a comment like that pass by. You'll never get far in the U.S. Army with that lack of tact."

Lockett shrugged. "I don't intend to get far. Never thought I would be this far. I only volunteered to end the war. I'll be back at farming when this is done."

This time, it was the preacher's turn to nod, but the look on the older man's face seemed to suggest something else.

"You look like you don't believe me, sir."

"I don't. You're not the farming type."

The statement shocked Lockett. He had never thought of himself as anything else. Even now as an officer in his country's army, he still thought of himself as a farmer. This was just a brief interlude, almost like it was someone else's life for the time being. "Farming is all I've done my whole life up to now, Reverend."

"Farming was what you had to do. It doesn't mean that it is what you were cut out to do."

"Sir?"

"I saw you chasin' down Coulter. I saw the calm, and I reck'n you got a knack for finding action. You're still the only officer here to have seen any fightin', right?"

"But that is all a fluke."

"Maybe, but I reck'n it isn't."

"But the war will end one day, sir, and I'll go back to farming."

The preacher gave a shrug of surrender. "You are probably right, son, but funny things can happen to a man. Just look at me. I would have sworn that I'd be a cavalryman for the rest of my days. There was no greater thrill than charging through battle on a snorting steed! The comradery! The carousing! And look at me now!" He laughed heartily. "Funny things can happen to a man."

Lockett had a hard time picturing the gentle-faced preacher as a hard-charging cavalryman. "Sir, about the sermon?" he added, not wanting to get diverted.

"Ah, yes. So, Colonel Blair thinks it was pro-Rebellion?"

"I tried to explain that it wasn't. I know you couldn't utter one secesh word, but Colonel Blair, well, that is another matter."

"I suppose I shouldn't be surprised. I reck'n with emotions in this state, a sermon about the evils of fighting could be interpreted in many ways."

"I guess neither side would be happy with that message."

"And how about you? Would you be happy with such?"

Lockett paused and looked at the ground for a very long time. "I understand what you are saying," he said slowly.

"I didn't ask if you understood it."

"No, sir, you didn't." He looked up, and there was an unflinching glint in his gray eyes. "Fighting is not good, sir. Especially in this war. It is hell on earth. What I saw at Shiloh, I pray I never see again. Whole rows of men wiped out in a single moment. Bodies everywhere. Torn, ripped, like butchered animals. They were gruesome deaths, sir. Only God knows how many gruesome deaths."

He paused for what seemed an eternity, and Reverend Tucker could see that the young man's mind was somewhere else.

The Hornet's Nest... The pounding of the Rebel cannon... The butternut rows cut down in the thicket, time and time again... Brothers in arms killed right at this elbow... Lifeless eyes staring back up at him... The worry and fear in Patrick's eyes and in his own heart... Ainsley scurrying back through the belching earth to tell them that they were about to be surrounded... Carrying Ainsley, praying against all hope that he could hang on... The sickly warm liquid of Ainsley's lifeblood soaking his shirt as they carried him...

"But you still disagree with my message?" Reverend Tucker eventually asked, interrupting Lockett's imprisoning memories.

"Yes," he answered immediately. "Some fights need to be fought. And this is one of them." He paused to let that sink in. When the preacher looked as if he was about to reply, Lockett hastened, "But I will be glad when the fighting is over."

There was a look of remorse, almost bitterness in the Reverend's eyes, but he did not probe further. He knew a granite answer when he heard one. They looked at each other, and in that instant, James Lockett realized that it was something that they would never agree on.

"It will not be over soon, James," the preacher said in a gentle voice.

"I know."

Tucker sighed and took a long, audible breath. "Now, about Colonel Blair, what would the good colonel like me to do about the sermon?"

"Just keep your sermons off that subject, sir. You don't want to be branded a sympathizer. General Halleck's orders in Missouri were very severe to sympathizers. If he gives the same order in Tennessee, I would hate to see you branded as such."

* * * * *

Katherine Moffat eagerly opened the letter. Mail had never been so important to her. When she had first arrived in Savannah, she had dreaded it, fearing it would be another demanding diatribe from her father. Tending to a wounded cousin or not, it was no reason for her defiance. That was what the letter was sure to say.

But a letter from her father had never come.

And in a way, that was even more distressing. Didn't they care anymore? Maybe her father had really meant it when he said that she would be disowning herself.

She had never seen her father so frightfully angry. While she had often heard of his temper and short fuse with business associates, he had always treated his daughters with a gentle touch. To Katherine, he was always Daddy, not Big John Moffat, and certainly not the Big John Moffat that others described.

But that was before she had insisted on going to Tennessee to nurse Ainsley back to health.

Though she had not expected a favorable response from her protective parents, especially her mother who always chided her on being a 'proper lady', the strength of her father's explosion had caught Katherine off-guard. She had never seen anything like it, but she took pride in the fact that she had not backed down. She had stood her ground.

Without arrogance, she knew that few could have weathered that storm. Truly, she was Big John Moffat's daughter. That stubbornness of character had come from him, not her mother. She could still see that face, red as fire, and the thick sinews of his neck, taut and straining. His bellow had literally shaken the walls of their Victorian home.

There had been no hint of a middle ground, no suggestion that in time, his anger would fade, but she was not too worried. She was his eldest daughter, right? He would come to see that she was correct. She was convinced of that eventuality.

The day would come when she would return to Kalamazoo with a healthy Ainsley Stuart, and such a day might not be too far off. Ainsley was improving, and Katherine knew that the improvement was due in no small part to her efforts. It had been imperceptible at first, but when she thought back to those first few days, it was clear now.

It was the most satisfying thing that she had ever done in her life. It was tangible. Even the strain between her and Ainsley over James Lockett was not slowing his recovery.

She still wished her cousin would yield to the truth, that James Lockett was a coward and jealous slanderer of her faithful Orrin. It was impossible to understand how Ainsley could believe James over such a fine figure as Orrin.

Orrin was renowned and respected in all of the finest circles in West Michigan. He was a young man with prospects. Everyone said that about Orrin.

James was just a farmer. Why, if it hadn't been for her and the chance meeting with Ainsley, James would still be nothing but a farmer! He was not at all like Orrin, who was destined for success.

But all Katherine could do was shrug her shoulders and try to point out these facts to her misguided cousin. She supposed that she should not blame Ainsley. After all, James had saved his life, and Ainsley should show some loyalty and respect for that singular act. Even so, James had pushed that too far, and Ainsley would sooner or later come to the realization of his error. It was sad, because part of her still liked James and his thoughtful, if at times, quaint musings.

If there was one culprit for James's bizarre behavior, it had to be Anna Tucker. Katherine was convinced of that. Somehow, that Southern accent and those dark eyes had infatuated James, and under her spell, he had lost his Christian way. That was the only explanation that she could offer. James had once been a decent, well-meaning fellow — for a farmer.

But as Katherine opened Orrin's latest letter, she put all such thoughts aside. Hungrily, she delved into the neatly scripted note. She often thought that Orrin had done himself a disservice by joining the army and wasting such perfect handwriting and poetic prose. Admittedly, he could sometimes wax on and wane into such detail that she would get lost, but there were always those poetic phrases in the beginning and the end.

She skimmed through the body of the letter as he spoke about the impending doom of Corinth and the overall Confederacy. In exacting detail, he told her how General Halleck's army was poised over the town like a hammer ready to fall. With the list of regiments Orrin described and all of the important colonels and generals that he was interacting with, it was impossible for Katherine to conceive how the Rebels could put up any defense.

Katherine had heard others complain about General Halleck, but Orrin's description of his commander made her realize how foolish those soldiers were. She could not understand why those men wanted a barbaric drunkard like General Grant when they had a leader like General Halleck, who planned out everything in such perfect detail. It was no wonder that this war was still going on, she thought, given the ignorance of the average soldier. Fortunately, they had men like Orrin to lead them, or they might actually lose this war!

She skipped down to the bottom of the letter where Orrin usually spoke of how her beauty inspired him, giving him strength and courage. Occasionally, he would gently reproach her on her independence and about leaving Kalamazoo for Tennessee, but other times, he would applaud her compassion for tending to her stricken cousin.

Katherine read and re-read the letter. Finally, she meticulously folded up the paper, knowing that she would re-read it at least once more tonight. Carefully, she slid the letter back into the envelope as she always did. Her past hesitancy about the man was long gone now, and she castigated herself on her momentary interest in James Lockett. She could understand her mother's confusion now. Whatever had gotten into her?

Katherine walked over to the rough-hewn corner stand of drawers that she shared with Anna Tucker. She flipped the envelope over to the front and gave it a parting kiss as she pulled open the top drawer where she kept all of Orrin's letters.

She was about to set the letter on the pile of old envelopes, when she blinked in confusion. In puzzlement, she stared at the backside of an envelope. Looking at it for a few seconds, Katherine felt an anger rise in her – someone had read the letter and put it back wrong!

She always gave the envelope a parting kiss and put it face up! Always!

The Moffat ire surged through her as she realized what had happened – Anna Tucker had been reading her letters from Orrin!

The nerve of her, Katherine stormed, stomping her foot on the ground. How dare she read my private letters!

First, she had poisoned James. Now, she was going after Orrin! Well, there was going to be no taking this lightly, Katherine resolved.

* * * * *

Lockett walked Anna Tucker back to her house. He had bumped into her in the telegraph office where she was giving Lieutenant Pope some freshly baked bread in the hopes that it would help settle his stomach. Pope had been fighting the Trots for quite a few days now.

The fact that Anna had been merrily chatting with the sallow faced officer did not bother Lockett, nor did the fact that she was friendly with many of the soldiers. It was part of her personality to make strangers feel welcome. He had seen it with some of the wagon trains that had come through town. She loved to talk and listen, to see what was going on outside of little Savannah, Tennessee. She was a bit of a romantic adventurer at heart, trapped in a small town and always yearning to know what was on the outside. A five minute chat and a friendly wave to someone she would never see again were as much a part of her as the curly hair that cascaded past her shoulders.

She might talk to other men, but none of that bothered Lockett because he knew he held a special place. Her eyes always grew brighter when she saw him, and she would detach herself politely from any conversation to join him. Secretly, he loved when that happened and took pride in the envied looks.

Today, she wore a bright yellow dress with a light blue belt that accentuated her hips. Giving him that sunny smile again, he wondered if garrison duty was such a bad thing after all. The bitterness that he felt from Orrin's latest mark of dishonor seemed to fade every day in her presence.

"Just wait on the porch, James," she said, "And enjoy that nice breeze." For once, the terrible heat had lessened, and it was almost comfortable with the soft wind that blew. "I'll fetch the Bible," Anna added.

Lockett sat in the narrow rocking chair and rocked. In moments like these, he found it easy to forget why he was in Tennessee. The blue uniform and its responsibilities ceased to exist, and he would listen to that soft, sweet Tennessee voice read passages out of the Bible. On occasion, she would explain passages that he did not understand, but mostly he just enjoyed the sound of her voice.

Except today he did not have the luxury of time.

"I'm afraid that I can't stay more than a couple of minutes today, Anna," he said. "I have preparations to make..."

"Ah," Anna smiled mischievously at him, "For this picnic or fair that your colonel wants to host in a couple of days?"

He blinked and grinned in amusement. "How did you know that?"

"It's a small town, James. It does not take much for word to spread of most everything, but particularly a piece of news like that. It would be nice to think about something other than the war, if only for a little bit."

He nodded in agreement. Indeed, it would be good to think about something other than the war.

Chapter 12

The high-pitched squeak of the oiled piglet erupted prematurely, as if the little skittering animal knew what was coming. The men of Blair's Independent Regiment crowded around the hastily built pen, ready to see which company would capture greased lightning.

The sun was warm and soothing. The sky was the bluest of blue. Only a light haze of clouds far up covered any part of a sky that looked as if it had been washed in divine waters. It smelled like spring, even though it was closer to summer now. The men's spirits were high, forcing Lockett to admit that perhaps there was something to Colonel Blair's unexpected order for a day of relaxation and entertainment for the men.

For once, there would be no work, no marching, no drilling, no chasing after ephemeral bushwhackers. This day was to be devoted to games and enjoyment. This was a day for greased pig catching, eating, a horse race, and a few other organized diversions.

Whether it was some stirring of conscience, Lockett did not know, but clearly Colonel Blair felt this was a time when the men needed a morale boost. The bushwhacker's audacious rescue and Sandie Holmes's murder were still fresh in everyone's minds. Today's objective was to put something else in that place.

A large roasting hog was already in the pit, paid for with the colonel's own money, but few paid attention to the food just yet. Everyone was gathered around the tiny greased piglet that scampered about the enclosure with five soldiers stripped down to their waists chasing after him. Lockett and the rest of the company laughed with gusto as the piglet skittered into and out of harm's way.

Each company had selected one man to put in the pit. Lockett could see by his own company's selection that they had a sense of humor about it and were more interested in laughing than in the honor of having their company catch the piglet.

As excitable and clumsy as ever, Milton Bosworth chased after his prey with the agility of an ox on a sheet of ice. Loud guffaws burst forth as he collided with the equally clumsy man from Pope's Company. They landed in a heap, and Fulkerham's man tripped over them.

Oblivious to the crash behind it, the piglet dashed away only to find another private waiting for him. But adroitly, the piglet reversed course and ran back from where he had just come. Without breaking stride, the ham bounded up onto the low pile of men just as they were sorting themselves out. In one clean hop, the piglet landed on Milton Bosworth's back and then jumped to the other side.

Even greater laughter burst forth and continued as Bosworth rolled over, knocking Fulkerham's man down just he was getting to his knees.

The piglet, of course, still had one man to avoid, but thanks to his greasing, he slipped right through the man's arms like a figment of imagination.

Standing next to Lockett, Reverend Tucker laughed uproariously, clearly enjoying himself to an extent that Lockett had never thought a preacher capable of. "Good ol' fun, Lieutenant!" he guffawed. "I'd forgotten how entertaining this could be! Haven't seen it since we were at my sister's in Murfreesboro! What a good many years ago that was!"

Lockett nodded and grinned. It was reminding him of home too.

The pig dashed between the legs of Williams's corporal, leaving the man gaping and looking backwards through his open legs.

"Hah!" Reverend Tucker laughed again, "Anna will be sorry she missed this event!"

Renaud's man was a little bundle of unbridled energy. Like a hunched whirlwind, he kept chasing the pig around the pen, darting between the others just like the pig. But like a pig's shadow, he never seemed capable of catching up to the runt.

"Where is Anna?" Lockett asked, not taking his eyes off of the spectacle, "I thought she was going to come."

"She is. She is... look at that!" Reverend Tucker laughed again, as Williams's corporal succeeded in grabbing the pig and hoisting him off the ground like a man carrying an armload of firewood. "He's got him!" But the pig squirmed free, slithering from the man's arms and sprinting back around the increasingly dusty surface.

"Tarnation, that's a quick little pig!" Reverend Tucker exclaimed before turning his attention back to Lockett. "Don't you fret none, Lieutenant. Anna will be here. Miss Katherine had the excellent idea that this might be a good opportunity for some of the wounded to get fresh air. Anna's helping her fetch'em over here."

The piglet squirted free from another man's sprawling grasp. But this time, the swine bounded right into the waiting arms of Milton Bosworth who grabbed one hind leg with a thick hand and tucked the bounding animal under his other arm with crushing pressure. Trapped, the piglet squealed, squirmed, and jabbed a snout into Bosworth's armpit, but there was no escape.

"I'll be damned," Prosper T. murmured in gap-toothed wonderment. "Er... sorry, Reverend." He snatched his floppy hat off his head, and his thin, angular face turned deep red. "Didn't think we'd be the one to win."

"Damned indeed," Reverend Tucker whispered conspiratorially, giving the surprised private a gentle elbow in the side.

The piglet squealed loudly, but not loud enough to drown out Bosworth's cry of triumph.

Lockett was still grinning five minutes later at the memory when he felt a light tap on his shoulder.

"My Lieu-ten-ent," Anna Tucker smiled warmly, sliding an arm through his.

"There you are," he replied, "You missed Sergeant Bosworth catch the greased pig."

"Oh, no," she smiled, "We all saw it."

"You did?" he answered, knowing that at her height, the only way to see the event was to be in the first row around the pen.

"We all saw it," Anna continued, "From up on the hill." She pointed to the small rise beyond the pasture. "It's good for those poor boys who'd been cooped up and all to get some fresh air, but I'm 'fraid many of them became winded by our little walk. So, we decided to take a break on the hill, and that was when the fun started with the greased pig. Why, I hadn't seen such fun since…"

"Murfreesboro," he interjected with a knowing smile.

"Why, yes! How did you know?"

"Your father told me."

"Ah," she nodded. "That was somethin', wasn't it? It was good to see those poor boys smile, if only for a little while."

Lockett nodded, wishing that Ainsley had been one of those up to the jaunt here, but despite his progress, Ainsley was still a long way from that type of mobility.

Anna noted the look on Lockett's face but continued, "It warmed my heart to see their expressions. Warmed Katherine's too."

Lockett chuckled, knowing that if Katherine's heart had indeed been warmed, she never would have said so to Anna.

But despite Katherine's obvious disdain for her, Anna Tucker still only saw the good in Katherine Moffat. It was a real Christian trait, he thought, and she put him to shame for he knew that he could not constantly see the good in everyone.

The zealous efforts of Prosper T. and his fiddle caught Lockett's attention, and he watched and listened for a moment. It would have been excellent dancing music, but there were few women in the crowd. In spite to the Colonel's open invitation to all of Savannah, only a few of the townspeople had turned out for the festivities.

It would surely be disappointing to Colonel Blair who was becoming increasingly aware of the glares and abbreviated looks that he and his soldiers were receiving.

There had been no direct troubles to date. His soldiers had conducted themselves well enough to this point, but the weight of a few hundred soldiers amongst them was grinding away at many of the folks.

The fact that today's concept was a complete contradiction to the warning he recently gave Lockett about Reverend Tucker's sermon and getting too close to the locals was impossible to miss.

Lockett was not sure if such vacillation was a character flaw in the wealthy banker, or if his own points about the Reverend's sermon had been so well received that it changed the colonel's mind. Truthfully, he doubted that it was latter.

He guessed that the colonel was hoping for two birds with one stone when it came to today's festivities. It was supposed to be a chance for his soldiers to unwind, but also for the townsfolk to see that the Yankee soldiers were not to be feared.

Yet based on the limited attendance, it would not have the desired effect.

Still, that did not dampen the men's enthusiasm as they laughed and reveled in the entertainment of the day. Two of Renaud's men joined Prosper, one another fiddler and the other with a wooden flute. Some of Pope's men danced a jig.

Tyler Fulkerham approached Lockett and Anna. His uniform was freshly brushed, and the buttons shimmered in the sunlight. Ramrod straight, he appeared taller than Lockett. His face was freshly shaven, save his combed goatee.

Fulkerham removed his hat and formally said with perfect confidence, "Miss Tucker, would you do me the honor of a dance?"

Lockett felt a bite of anger and jealousy. Fulkerham rarely missed the opportunity to jab at him about the impropriety of socializing with a Southerner, yet here he was asking her to dance. The hypocrisy jarred him, but the reaction was short-lived.

"Alas, Lieu-ten-ent Fulkerham, I've already promised the first dance to Lieu-ten-ent Lockett. Perhaps, later?"

Tyler Fulkerham's mouth opened slightly and then clamped shut. "Uh, yes, perhaps later," he said stiffly.

Anna's arm tightened around Lockett's, and she led him closer to the music. When they were out of earshot of Fulkerham, Anna said to him with a devilish smile, "I'm afraid, our dear Lieu-ten-ent Fulkerham is not used to rejection."

Lockett grinned. Her comment was true, but he had trouble fully enjoying the moment, because now he had another worry. "Anna," he whispered in a pained voice, "I don't know how..."

But before he could finish his sentence, McManus interrupted him by hurrying over.

"Jame-, er, sir," he said pointing, "Up on the hill."

Instinctively, Lockett's hand slid towards his sidearm, but it wasn't bushwhackers. It was three soldiers in blue on their horses. They had reined in to study the goings-on before starting to trot toward the gathering.

Lockett looked around for Colonel Blair but did not see him.

"I better see what they want. Excuse me, Anna," he added, disengaging from her arm.

Without need for any spoken command, McManus followed after him.

As they neared the trio on their horses, Lockett could see that it was a major, a sergeant, and baleful looking private. He saluted the major.

The senior officer returned the salute but remained in the saddle and said nothing for the moment, looking right past Lockett towards the gathering beyond them.

The major had coal black hair and a thick tangled beard, which gave some fullness to an otherwise narrow face. Between the layers of dust on his uniform and the peeling skin on his sun burnt nose, he was clearly no staff officer, but he gave no indication of who he was or why he was here. He was a hard-looking man whose flat glare finally turned back to Lockett.

"Colonel Blair's men, I presume?" His upper lip curled slightly in contempt, matching his tone.

"Yes, sir. I'm Lieutenant Lockett. Do you want me to take you to the colonel?"

The major did not answer the question. Instead, he commented, "A picnic? You are having a picnic?"

He turned towards his sergeant and added, "No wonder we have the problems that we have. It's a God-damned picnic!"

Lockett gave no response to the man's disgust and stood rigidly still. It wasn't his place to explain the colonel's logic, nor did he think it would help much.

Still ignoring Lockett, the major continued. "There are even a few Rebels down there, by God. Look at that, will you?"

Lockett wondered if the major was referring to the townspeople.

"Little wonder, sir. Little wonder," the sergeant added obediently. He had a hoarse, raspy voice and a curious way of rapidly bobbing his head while spoke.

"While the three of us ride a hundred miles, sleeping rough every night, break our backs to protect this army, this entire regiment throws a party for the Rebels!" He spat at Lockett's feet.

"Revolting, sir. Revolting."

"It's worse than that, sergeant. Damnably close to treason… Certainly, dereliction!"

"Dereliction indeed, sir. Der-re-liction!"

Finally, looking at Lockett, the major lowered his voice an octave. "And you, take me to Colonel Blair this instant."

"Of course, sir," Lockett replied, only too happy to leave this man with someone else, although he did feel a twinge of sympathy for Colonel Blair.

By the time that he had returned from Colonel Blair, happy to have been dismissed by the former banker, the dancing was over. He felt some relief at having missed the dancing, although he would not have felt that way if he had known that Fulkerham had taken the opportunity to dance with Anna more than once.

The music had stopped, and the eating had begun.

Lockett took a seat at one of the tables while Anna took the opportunity to chat with Doctor McClutcheon and a few of the wounded. Most were a sorry lot. Bandages and slings, two were missing fingers or a hand, one an arm, and one an eye. All of them seemed to be wearing uniforms that were two sizes too large for their shrunken bodies, but as they saw Anna Tucker return to them, each and every one brightened. She was their "Tennessee Angel".

Lockett knew most by name now. They were good men and good soldiers, although for many, their soldiering careers were done. They would return to their farms and shops not quite the same as they had left, but at least they were returning.

The bench shook slightly as someone sat next to him. "Y'all's enjoyin' yourselves," Lewis Dell said, taking a large bite of pork. The Savannah shopkeeper chewed loudly, adding between swallows, "Wish more of us had come out to see this... might give'm another impression of y'all." The small, clean-shaven man with furry eyebrows looked beyond Lockett for a moment. "What's goin' on over there?" he asked, taking another large bite as he did so.

Lockett followed the gaze to the small cluster of men. In between the heads, he saw Lieutenant Renaud. "Probably the wrasslin' matches," he replied, knowing that Renaud had volunteered to officiate the one-fall matches just to make sure that things did not get out of hand.

Dell grunted in reply and lifted his plate in Lockett's direction. "You should get some, 'tenant Lockett. You could use some meat on your bones. At your size, you're liable to waste away once the fighting starts again for y'all."

"You don't think we'll be here on garrison duty for the rest of the war?"

Dell shook his head, not quite catching the fact that the Michigander wasn't serious. "Sure seems like it to some of 'em, I'm sure. But eventually, y'all will move on. That's the nature of things. Was in the army once myself, ya know. Fought down with the Texicans. Ol' Mex-e-co. Yup, me and Preacher Tucker back in our days. Seems a long time ago now."

"How was the Reverend in the army?" Lockett queried. Since the preacher had mentioned that fact when they had been in the alleyway, he had been very curious to know more.

"That was before ol' Tuck became a man of God. By golly, he was one of the best cavalrymen we had down there. No one could ride a horse like him."

Lockett nodded appreciatively. The lame preacher did ride with skill.

"Hell bent for fire, he was! More 'n once I saw him charge through a storm of musket balls and never a scratch on him. Half those around him would be torn to shreds but never a scratch for ol' Tuck. Touched by God, he clearly was. Made it through those scrapes. One ball of fire, he was, yup."

"So what happened to him? I mean, most people would never guess... he's a preacher now."

"That came later. His wife tamed him if's you asked me. Sarah was a quiet, quiet woman, not at all like Anna. She takes after her father. Yup, Sarah was a real quiet, pious woman, like most womenfolk 'round here, I reckon. I reckon it don't make no sense how ol' Tuck fell for her, but he did. 'Fore ya knew it, ol' Tuck was no more a hell-raisin' horse soldier. He was a Bible-thumpin' soldier of God." Lewis Dell cackled. "Yup, I reckon ya never know the ways of the Almighty."

Lewis Dell looked over at the wrestling match and spotted Reverend Tucker who was watching with great interest. "Ol' Tuck was one dadgum good wrassler in his day too, 'tenant. Not big but quick, ya know. Quick as lightning, yup." He stopped and watched the preacher lean heavily on his hickory cane. "Kinda of funny that for all his daring in ol' Mex-ee-co that he ends up lame jus' ridin' his horse through a pasture here. Funny how things work."

"Yes, ironic," Lockett agreed.

"Course, from time to time, I still see some of that adventurous spirit in young Anna. She's got some of that ol' Tuck fire, yup."

Lockett grunted in acknowledgement.

"Really now, 'tenant. I reckon you better git some of this pork, before your men eat every last bit."

Patrick McManus rubbed the back of head with a sour look as the cheers and cries of amiable derision sounded again from the soldiers forming a massed ring around two new wrestlers. With the back of his hand, he wiped a trickle of blood from his nose and spat angrily into the ground.

Everyone had already turned back to the next match, and McManus was glad for that at least. He didn't need any words of encouragement when he felt this mad. Angrily, he jammed his hands into his pockets and silently berated himself.

He hated losing, especially at wrestling. He should have won, he thought furiously. Some would have been happy to win two matches, but he wanted to win them all. He underestimated the speed of his larger opponent. That was obvious now in retrospect.

Across the way, he saw James chatting with Anna Tucker. It was odd to see James so at ease with a girl. Heck, it was odd just to see James next to a girl, he mused as he tried to lure his thoughts away from the lost wrestling match.

James had never had time nor interest in women back in Kalamazoo. The rich, black dirt of the farm had always dominated James's attention.   At any time on any day, McManus knew that could wander over to the Lockett farm and find his friend up to his neck in effort, hefting that plow in the heavy soil, dunging the fields, clearing the crops, always something.

But now, here was James talking so carefree with Anna!

McManus couldn't help but reminisce that it was like when he had started courting Martha at the Kalamazoo County fair. It hadn't been that long ago, but it seemed like ages.

He had made a mistake by volunteering for the army. He knew that now. He should have listened to James and stayed behind when all of his friends were volunteering for the Kalamazoo Sharpshooters.   It never occurred to him that something could happen to Martha in his absence. If he had been there, he could have nursed her back to health. He was sure of that.

But what was done, was done. She was gone, and he would never see his smiling wife again.

Strange how he struggled to imagine life without her, he thought. Their time together had been so brief.

He had not known what to do or where to go from there. So, when James suggested that they re-enlist, this time with the 12th Michigan, there was really no decision to be made. He blindly followed his friend back to the army, persuading himself that by protecting his friend, he could bring back some reason to keep living.

* * * * *

The nervous twinge in the pit of Lockett's stomach slithered upward to his throat, constricting it.

The coarse looking major was standing next to Colonel Blair, waiting for the rest of the officers to gather. He had hoped against hope that the black-haired officer with the fierce scowl would be gone by now.

As each man entered, they all received the same glare of superiority. Even Fulkerham's polished buttons did nothing to ease the judgmental stare that bore down.

Colonel Blair stood red-faced and silent. Whatever the major had said had shaken the normally self-confident former banker, and an awkward silence hung in the air as they waited for the last to arrive. The momentary good spirits coming out of their so-called fair were already a distant memory, even though it was only hours old.

Finally, Enoch Pope entered the room, stopping in mid-stride as if physically struck by the mood. The major's animus drilled in on Pope pitilessly.

Lowering his gaze to the floor, Pope quickly shuffled to a seat next to Lockett, shoulders hunched, as if it made him less visible.

"What's going on?" he whispered ever so faintly.

Lockett gave the most imperceptible of head shakes, while Colonel Blair strutted to the door, closing it with an anxious purposefulness.

"My time is too valuable for formal introductions," the major began.

Lockett thought that he heard the man then add, '*and I care nothing to know any of you regardless*', but then Lockett decided it was merely his imagination filling in a logical blank.

"I am Major Axford. I'm here on the direct orders from General Halleck himself."

With unexpected theatrics, he threw a small package of papers on the table in front of them. None of the lieutenants made any move.

"Go on," Major Axford urged, "Look at them. That is why I am here."

Slowly, Lockett and Fulkerham reached first for the papers while Axford continued talking.

"While you and your colonel throw a party for the people of Savannah," he declared with an intentional pause, "They are stabbing you and your brethren in the back!"

Lockett felt his jaw tighten, but he did not look up. Instead, he stared uncomprehendingly at one of the pages that he pulled from the pile, and Enoch Pope looked over his shoulder.

"What is it?" Pope asked dumbly.

"Spies," Axford said darkly, "An entire nest of them."

"But what are these?" Fulkerham said puzzlement, looking at another page from the sheaf. "These words make no sense."

"It is in code," Axford snapped, sounding like a headmaster addressing a dunce. "This was taken recently from a Rebel sympathizer trying to sneak through our picket lines around Corinth — damning information, information originating from Savannah. Some of this information is on river and wagon traffic that passes through *your* little station."

He paused for dramatic effect. Slowly, he looked from officer to officer.

With a concluding scowl, he added, "There is also a detailed report on the regimental positioning around Corinth. That could not have come from here, but the fact that someone is keeping the Rebels advised of the traffic passing through Savannah is troubling, very troubling."

"But if it is in code, how can you tell that?" Fulkerham asked.

"The Rebels aren't the only ones with spies. We now have the key to read this."

With more dramatics, Major Axford reached inside his jacket pocket and slowly pulled out a folded piece of paper. After unfolding it with exactly deliberateness, he placed it face up on the table in front of Lockett and Fulkerham.

"This particular sheet is from their spy in General Halleck's camp, but you will get the idea of how damning this is once you see it."

Both men leaned forward and silently read the translated version. It was indeed detailed information on the whereabouts of different brigades and generals. However, there was one sentence that truly caught Lockett's eye. It described the location of the Kalamazoo Sharpshooters in their advance position.

Blinking in surprise, Lockett felt some envy for his old comrades. They were up front and center on the push into Corinth.

The honor was a far cry from Lockett's current position guarding baggage and garrison duty. He felt a moment of self-pity before his thoughts were interrupted.

"Then why don't you just arrest the traitor supplying it?" Pope added softly. It was not meant to be heard by the major, but he heard it nonetheless.

"The spy, or should I say spies, because it is too much and too varied of information to have come from one man, won't sign his name to the document." Major Axford snorted at the question. "They are too smart for that. The information is somehow consolidated and then left for a courier to retrieve. If I had that information on who the spies were, then I would not need to visit this, this place..." He waved his hand at those around the table and said the last word with an air of disgust.

"So, what do you want us to do?" Lockett finally spoke up cautiously.

He found it odd that Colonel Blair was as silent as could be. Perhaps he had already had this same conversation with the major? Perhaps he wanted to see how his men reacted? Perhaps he had been so shamed by the major for their attempt to ingratiate themselves with the locals that he was speechless? The timing of Major Axford's arrival could not have been worse, Lockett mused.

"As we identify these traitors, you and your men will be necessary to perform searches and arrest them. We should probably require all citizens to swear to an oath of allegiance, arresting all who won't, but the general has not authorized that... yet."

"Don't see what good that would do. A spy would just swear to anything, right?" Pope thought aloud.

The stare that he received from Major Axford caused Pope to shrink back in his seat and promise himself that he would not open his mouth again.

"Do you have an idea who this spy is?" Lockett asked slowly.

"Spies," Major Axford corrected. "Spies. There is too much information, from too many different areas, not just Savannah, to have come from one person. And I will develop some ideas over the coming days while I am here. The general seems to think that it might be coming from this bushwhacker that escaped you."

He paused to look accusingly at each of them.

"I, on the other hand, have always found bushwhackers to be unreliable sorts, more interested in themselves than any cause, and certainly not as organized as this one. Why, most bushwhackers can't do more than an 'x' for their name, much less write these complex missives in code."

Lockett nodded slightly. He had to agree with Major Axford on that point.

"I will be here for a few days, observing and asking a few questions. I have no doubt that I will develop a few suspicions on who these vermin might be. We may make some arrests, or maybe we will observe them a little longer. Regardless, I will then be relieved by a captain that General Halleck is sending to keep an eye on this town while I move further north up the river to see what else I can learn. But know this, this little berg is a hive of Secessionist activity and traitorous actions! There will be hangings here, mark my words!"

Tyler Fulkerham picked up more of the sheets of paper. He studied them even though he could make no sense of the code. "This confirms my suspicion from all along," Fulkerham declared, "These people are not to be trusted, despite how they say they voted."

* * * * *

It was quiet in the hospital tent when Lockett entered.

One soldier read the Bible, slowly mouthing the words.

Doc McClutcheon was peeling back another soldier's bandage, wrinkling his nose at the disappointing smell and giving a grimace that the soldier couldn't miss. The soldier knew all too well what the odor and disappointing look meant, gangrene. The arm would need to come off. What little pallor was left in the poor man's face quickly drained to grayish white.

But Lockett paid little notice. His mind was elsewhere, and he knew that he only had about five minutes to spare for Ainsley today.

"You are coming from Anna's today, I see," Ainsley remarked with an amused grin as Lockett took a seat in the rickety stool next to his friend.

"What do you mean? How did you know?" he said with some surprise.

"I can tell by that odd look on your face," Ainsley laughed.

"Oh," Lockett mumbled, turning more serious, "I didn't realize…"

"It stands out on you, my friend, because you are usually so solemn."

"Sorry."

"Don't apologize," Ainsley chided good-naturedly. "I, for one, certainly wouldn't begrudge you that. She's an enchantment, as any man in here would tell you. I would spend every moment with her that I could if I were you, duties permitting."

"And leave my friend alone constantly in this tent?" Lockett answered with a shake of his head.

"I'm hardly alone, and besides, Katherine takes good care of me and many of the others as well. I never would have guessed that my aristocratic cousin would be so dedicated to something as dreadful as this. I'm fortunate in many ways…"

Lockett pursed his lips and nodded slowly. It was one of the many reasons that he admired Ainsley so much. Few men in Ainsley's position would ever use the word 'fortunate' to describe themselves.

"Where is Katherine anyway? I hardly see her nowadays."

"Probably for the best," Ainsley answered. "She's still rather sore at you, both of us really, for our opinions on her beau." He paused, deliberating on whether or not to add something. "She also has this crazy idea about Anna that would likely provoke you. So, it is probably best that you steer clear... at least for a while."

"What?"

"Yes, I guess perhaps my cousin is a bit jealous?" Ainsley added with a touch of wonderment. "Perhaps, Katherine had more feelings for you than I realized, or perhaps she just thinks that all men should orbit around her."

"She's mad that I am spending so much time with Anna?"

"Bit more than that, I'm afraid. She has this daft notion that Anna is interested in 'taking Orrin away from her too'."

Lockett snorted in amusement. "Well, that is plum crazy. Has Anna ever even spoken to Orrin? What in the world would give Katherine that idea?"

"Apparently, Katherine is convinced that Anna has been reading the letters that Orrin sends. I guess she think that Anna wants to horn in."

"Reading letters?"

"I know, it's ridiculous, and I'm sure that she is mistaken. But she claims that she always puts the letters back in the dresser that she shares with Anna. Last time, she noticed that the letter was not the way she had left it."

"This place must be getting to her," Lockett lamented. "That's ridiculous. Why would anyone want to read those love letters?"

"I know," Ainsley agreed. "I told her that she was seeing things, and even if the letter had been touched, perhaps it was because Anna was looking for something else. After all, they share the drawer."

* * * * *

May 17

Another week has passed without hearing from Daniel. I cannot understand why I have not heard from him or any of my other brothers. Mother cannot read or write, but still the lack of communication causes me fear. That bushwhacker Coulter is out there, but the mail has not been interrupted lately, so he is not the cause.

Events in Savannah trouble me as well. We have doubled the patrols and are searching any travelers. We have others who watch the landing all day, but it is not obvious who this spy is. I sense more unease in the citizens of Savannah. I fear it is not due to guilty consciences as it is to the suspicion we all view them with now. These are uncomfortable times. I remember what happened in Missouri, and I pray that the spy is found before Halleck orders harsh remedies against the local citizenry.

--- the diary of James Lockett

* * * * *

Lockett escorted Anna home after visiting her father at the white-washed church. She was more quiet than usual, and her thoughts were elsewhere as they walked along.

But it wasn't just Anna, Lockett knew. The entire town was reserved. And it was not dislike in their eyes when they looked at him; it was fear. They knew the soldiers were looking for a spy, and even the whiff of accusation could mean death to them. The threat of a hanging was not an empty threat. They would no longer be innocent until proven guilty in Savannah. They were guilty until proven innocent.

God in Heaven, Lockett thought, this was feeling more and more like Missouri. Would they ever be able to trust their neighbors? How could they ever be one country again after things like this? Most of the soldiers were already under the impression that they were judge, jury, and executioner. Alarmingly, only a few saw this as a terrible burden to shoulder.

"You're quiet today, Anna," he said in a voice that did not disguise his discomfort.

"I know," she answered, still not looking at him, "This Major Axford has the whole town on edge. He is constantly prowling around, asking all sorts of leading questions. Even when he is still, I can see him watching and writing himself notes in that journal that he keeps."

Lockett nodded. "He keeps track of who is talking to who."

"And now your colonel has you searching anyone traveling? How can you search anyone traveling from one spot to the next?" She blushed, "I'm sorry, I don't mean you, just you, it's just that…"

"It's okay."

"We are all guilty it seems." There was an awkward silence and neither of them knew what to say. "Do you know what it is like, James, to have someone watching you all the time, certain that you are guilty?"

He bit his tongue. What could he say? He cursed the way events were moving, moving to put him and Anna on opposite sides. If only it would pass soon… If only things would go back to how they were a few days ago…

Maybe once Major Axford moved on and was replaced by this captain that General Halleck was sending, then things would improve? He could only hope.

"The information your army captured from this spy must have been very damaging for such a response," she added.

"It was very good," he nodded, "He's a very thorough and efficient spy. The information was recent too."

"And this captured courier did not reveal the identity of the spy?"

"No, apparently, he doesn't know anything. Or maybe he was killed. Not really sure that the major said one way or the other. He just said that the system was set up by a cautious and clever man, or men. Major Axford is certain that there's more than one behind all this."

"I see," Anna murmured. "I find that all too difficult to believe."

"Yes, but Axford is certain of it."

"Savannah is too small for something like that to occur without the rest of the town knowing."

Lockett could only shrug. "Perhaps, you're right. Renaud and I think there are just two spies. Some of the information in the dispatch could not have come from Savannah. It was too detailed about Halleck's dispositions around Corinth. There must be another spy in Halleck's camp near Corinth. Perhaps when they catch this other spy, his capture will lead to the one here?"

"Yes," Anna nodded, brightening slightly. "Maybe when they catch that one things will improve."

"You still look sad," he commented.

"Of course," she replied with a slightly imploring tone, "You talk so easily about catching a spy here, here in Savannah. I have lived in Savannah all my life and have known everyone here all my life. I hate the thought that something could happen to one of them. I can't believe one of them would be a spy. I don't want to see any of them hung."

Lockett nodded. He empathized with her, but a spy was a spy. The information pointed to Savannah, and this spying could lead to defeat, to more deaths in Halleck's army, to more deaths in his old Sharpshooting company.

"You'll hang this spy when you find him?"

It was a simple, unequivocal answer. "Yes."

* * * * *

May 23

Another week has passed, another week of fruitless marching and searching in the brutal sun. Any enthusiasm for the hunt has faded quickly. It is a tiresome, futile ordeal. There is not the slightest idea who this culprit is, nor the slightest idea of where to or how to look.

We watch the town and search travelers, what few there are. Not one shred of evidence. I still do not understand how one could regularly pass this information along. Other than the river traffic, there is little consistent travel here. How could the spy get the information so far south consistently? Clandestine night rides?

Renaud thinks that the spy might be a crewman on one of the steamers. Even if not the actual spy, that would make for a convenient way to transport the information. But we have found nothing on any of the passing steamers either.

We will never know who this spy is!

--- the diary of James Lockett

* * * * *

Night fell across the Tennessee River, and James Lockett forced the persistent questions of spying from his mind. This was not the time for it.

He stood with fifty others around a fire. Overhead, a blanket of stars watched the soldiers at their prayer meeting. It was a struggle, but he locked away the worries of the army, and he tried to focus on things holy.

Prosper T. had just finished in leading them in a hymn, and Bosworth handed Lockett a well-worn prayer book for him to recite from in the flickering firelight.

But before he could continue, Renaud came up from behind and tapped him on the shoulder. After whispering in his ear, Lockett handed the book back, "You'll have to lead tonight, Sergeant." Then, he followed Renaud back to Colonel Blair's quarters.

"And what's the bee in his bonnet this time?" he asked sourly. He did not like being taken away from a prayer meeting.

"Co-men-su-ate wiz ze times," Renaud shrugged, "Maybe zey found ze spy, eh?"

"We're not that lucky, Pete."

"Mebee, mebee not. Becos if we did, we could stop humpin' around all ze darn hills, eh? Would be fine by me."

They went to the small farmhouse that Colonel Blair had confiscated from its absent owner. The room glowed with light, and Lockett could already see a number of silhouettes around the table. Great, he thought, they were the last ones again. Colonel Blair was a stickler on tardiness.

Stepping inside, he was vaguely aware that his fellow lieutenants were sitting at the long, narrow table, but it was the presence of the man speaking to Colonel Blair that drew Lockett's eyes. His back was to him, but Lockett knew that form anywhere. He felt Renaud's cautionary hand on his shoulder, pulling him back gently, as he had instinctively taken a confrontational step forward.

The blue-coated officer turned around slowly, aware that he was being watched. With an arrogant smile, Orrin Long returned Lockett's hateful gaze.

"Lieutenant Lockett," he sneered. There was a telling look on the bastard's face. Like a blow to the stomach, Lockett then noticed the difference in Orrin's uniform – a captain!

The air was heavy and foul all of a sudden. He could feel the others looking at him, waiting for something. No one moved, and an eerie stillness settled over the room.

In a flash, the frustration surged up through Lockett, and he thought about grabbing Orrin by the throat. He remembered the feel of the man's neck in his hands. He should have killed him at Shiloh when he had chance! Could he finish the job here and now before the others broke it up and locked him away? The penalty would be worth the crime, if only he could succeed in totality.

Orrin was clearly pleased with himself, and the look of pleasure on the scoundrel's face only made Lockett more angry. He remembered the fear in Orrin's bulging eyes when he had throttled the coward at Pittsburg Landing. How he wanted to see that again!

"Sit down, gentlemen," Colonel Blair ordered abruptly. His voice was louder than expected for such a small room and full of command, as if he sensed the debate in his lieutenant's head. The command had its intended effect and snapped Lockett from his delusion.

They sat, and from the corner of his eye Lockett noticed the smug look on Tyler Fulkerham's face. Another surge of defiance fueled Lockett's veins, but he forced himself to look at Colonel Blair who had already begun to address them.

"...would like to think that Captain Long is here with news that one of the spies has been captured and has news of who the others are. Unfortunately, that is not the case. These spies are alive and well. General Halleck is so concerned with this that he has sent Captain Long to us." Colonel Blair paused.

The colonel's words were said evenly, but Lockett understood the underlying tone of resentment. And with good reason, he thought. This was a direct slap in the face. General Halleck thought them all so incompetent, including the colonel, that General Halleck needed to send one of his valued staff officers.

Orrin Long was back.

Chapter 13

Orrin Long kicked off his boots and sat on the lumpy mattress. He frowned. In Kalamazoo, this hotel would have been considered a rat's hole. Savannah was typical Southern squalor, he thought contemptuously.

When General Halleck had first informed him that he was sending him personally back to Savannah to root out these vipers, his first reaction had been fear.

Lockett was in Savannah, and the man must certainly be desperate enough to try anything by now. He wished that he could have brought Lockett up on charges for assaulting him at Pittsburg Landing. Of course, that would have exposed the fact that he had fled the field and been hiding down at the Landing. No matter, he would have his revenge in time.

That momentary fear had receded from his worries as he had comforted himself with the fact that he had General Halleck, and therefore, the army and its discipline on his side.

Buoyed by that realization, he turned his mind to more constructive matters. This was a golden opportunity. General Halleck wanted a spy to hang; Long himself wanted to inflict pain on James Lockett.

What if he could tie the two together?

* * * * *

"But, sir, a door to door search!" Lockett exclaimed. He stood alone before Colonel Blair. This was beginning to look like Missouri all over again. "Imprisonment of any *suspected* sympathizers? Suspected by who? With no proof?"

"That," Colonel Blair replied pointedly, "Is the order that *Captain* Long was sent here to deliver." Blair dragged out the word captain, making his displeasure clear. "Don't complain to me about this order, Lockett. It came straight from General Halleck, and we wouldn't be in this mess if it weren't for you." Blair paused and glared angrily at him, "Were it not for you, I doubt that General Halleck would have so low an opinion of me as to send a snot-nosed brevet captain to order *my* men around!"

"Sir..."

"Damn your hide, man!" Blair thundered. "I don't want your lip, nor your objections. This is an order!"

"Yes, sir."

"Thank you, Lieutenant." Blair said after a pregnant pause. "Now, you may continue with your point."

"Lieutenant Pope, sir, has informed me that to search a home, we need a search warrant and to imprison..."

"Damn your hide! Damn your hide!" Blair bellowed again, "Maybe you *are* an ignorant farmer like Fulkerham says! A search warrant? My God, man! Do you know what habeas corpus is?"

"Ah, no, sir." Lockett shook his head.

"Well, your precious President Lincoln has suspended it. And don't tell me you didn't vote for the man, because I know you must have."

"I voted for him, sir."

"If we had just voted for a compromise candidate, it never would have come this."

"Yes, sir," Lockett answered his frustrated colonel, unsure where this was going. "But we can't put people in prison for no reason other than Orrin Long doesn't like them."

"Damn it all, Lockett, aren't you listening to me? Lincoln suspended that privilege. Orrin Long and General Halleck can do whatever they damn well please here. Whatever they damn well please..." He repeated darkly.

Lockett was quiet. This was what he had feared, but he had to try, even though he knew that Laurent Blair was not the man to whom this argument needed to be addressed. He was as powerless as Lockett to stop these forces. It was an act of selfishness, but he made the argument anyhow.

"But, sir, this kind of action will turn the whole town against us."

"Hah! And you know what General Halleck would say to you, if he bothered to answer at all? He would say, who damn well cares if we turn a bunch of old men and women against us! You think the Rebs would be that much greater of a threat with someone like lame Preacher Tucker or old Lewis Dell toting around a Palmetto musket? Do you, Lockett?"

"Sir, enemies can do more than just carry a musket. They can spy for instance. This will create a whole town of spies."

Blair paused, still fuming. "We don't have a choice, Lieutenant."

Lockett looked at the floor. It was only a matter of time until this went terribly wrong.

* * * * *

Lockett had Bosworth pick ten men from the company. "The ten who are the least likely to be tempted," he had instructed the sergeant.

Thoroughly, and with their lieutenant quietly expressing apologies, they searched the Wheeler house. It was a tidy little home next to the livery.

He supposed that the Wheelers were picked first because one of the old man's two boys had signed up with the Confederate cavalry at the outset of the war. Of course, the other son was wearing Union blue somewhere, but that did not seem to count for anything.

Searching a few houses a day, while maintaining all of the patrol routes, seemed a futile gesture to Lockett. After the first house, there would be no surprise. The spy could easily hide things now before being searched. The only thing he could figure was that Orrin Long thought that the threat of door to door searches might cause the spy to give himself away. If that was the plan, he doubted it would work. This spy was a steady fellow by his guess – if the spy was here in Savannah at all.

* * * * *

The steamer belched more acrid, black smoke into the clear blue sky. Its furnace and boiler would not come to a rest until after the crew finished securing it to the reinforced dock. Gently, the brown water of the Tennessee River drifted past the side wheeler.

Well-used would be a polite description for this steamboat, Lockett mused to himself. She was one of the many workhorses that plied the waters. Her twin black stacks towered above the pilothouse, looking stark against the dusky white of the rest of the boat. After countless hours of exhaling clouds of black smoke, her once white paint grew increasingly obscured as one looked from the water line up to the black stacks.

With a clatter, the gangplank was roughly hauled out and slammed against the dock, drawing a flurry of curses from one of the mates. With angry gesticulations, he berated the other crewman, who eventually slunk off to wait near the crates on the foredeck.

The mate turned on his heel and waved the waiting soldiers to cross the gangplank and begin the offloading. Once the soldiers were aboard, the mate crossed to the dock and headed towards Lockett.

His gait was unsteady, as if drunk, although maybe it had more to do with the unsettling sway of dry land on his sea legs. Lockett wondered.

"I oughtta leave that half-brained fool with you when we shove off," the mate grumbled to him as they stood shoulder to shoulder and watched. The smell of whiskey wafted by as he continued. "He ain't got no sense, always banging around in that old scow like she is invincible."

Lockett grunted in response, and the mate continued. "This old tub is nearing the end, worm eaten in the keel by this point, no doubt. God forbid we ever grind against even a sandy bank. It will rip the bottom out like peeling a potato."

There was confusion on the foredeck about which crates stayed and which were to be off loaded.

"No, those ones, Hobbs!" the mate shouted and shook his head.

"Gotta do everything myself," he grumbled and headed back aboard, leaving Lockett gratefully alone.

Telling Bosworth that he was in charge, Lockett left his company sweating over the unloading of supplies. The once inactive and boring life of garrison duty was quickly becoming a memory as Blair's Independent Regiment marched circles around Savannah and "inspected" houses daily, all the while keeping an eye on the supply line for Halleck's army.

With a pensive look on his face, Lockett quickly walked through town. He glanced at Anna's empty porch. Most likely, the reverend was at the tiny church, and she was with Katherine in the tent hospital.

But the wanderings were quickly wiped away by the shriek from up the street. Looking up, he saw blue coats outside of the Widow Magruder's house. Was it Orrin Long again?

Halleck's lackey had already threatened to put three "suspected sympathizers" in jail.

Each of Lockett's strides fired a new memory, and each memory stoked his anger. By the time he reached the tiny, two room house, his eyes were blazing, and he was ready to end it all with Orrin Long, consequences be damned!

He saw Lieutenant Williams's sergeant picking through the freshly dug dirt in the garden outside her house.

"What's going on here, sergeant?" he barked. He knew what the sergeant was doing. He was not looking for evidence of a traitor; he was looking for family valuables, like a set of silver.

Narrow-faced with tobacco-stained, canine-like teeth, Sergeant Philyaw looked up. His stubble growth face was full of belligerence at the interruption. "What does it look like... sir?" He only added the last word after a deliberate pause and with a contemptuous tone.

Lockett snatched the man by collar, his face twisting in pent up wrath. "You are dangerously close to insubordination, sergeant."

The movement had been swift, and the wiry officer was stronger than Philyaw had guessed. Sensing that the officer was not to be crossed at this moment, Philyaw blanched. "She's the spy, sir," he said meekly. "We're here to arrest her."

"The old widow?" Lockett replied incredulously.

With one hand wrenching the man's collar, Lockett propelled him through the front door. The widow's tiny front room looked as if it had been hit by a twister. Drawers were pulled out, their contents scattered across the bare wood floor. One of the two chairs around her tiny table was tipped over, and an empty water pitcher lolled about forlornly on the floor.

There was a cry of protest from the back room as another blue coated soldier mindlessly tossed the bedding to the floor and searched the bed.

"A spy?" Lockett said harshly to the sergeant. "This old woman is a spy?"

"Is true, sir," a private next to the fireplace said. There was a look of disdain in the husky private's eyes. Like many in Williams's and Fulkerham's companies, they viewed James Lockett as a disgraced, Bible-thumping officer.

Lockett walked over to him, and the man continued to give him an unconcerned stare. It caught him totally off guard when Lockett spun him around without another word and slammed him hard against the wall. He never even got a hand up to stop himself, and the private's fleshy face was the first thing to hit the wall.

With the officer's hand still pressing his face firmly into the wall, the private felt Lockett's other hand reach into his pocket.

"I suppose this is yours?" Lockett scowled, holding up the dainty, colorful scarf that he had taken from the man's pocket. "For your girlfriend?"

The old woman clearly did not have much, and the fact that one of them would take what little she had only made Lockett more wrathful.

"The old woman's a spy," the man angrily retorted, spittle dripping down his bearded face.

Lockett could feel the man's muscles tense, and he prepared himself to fend off an attack. But the private held back, knowing that there were few things worse than striking an officer.

"She's a Reb spy," he repeated, straining to control his anger and putting a hand up to his bleeding nose.

"And your proof?" Lockett asked, his eyes catching sight of it just as the man said it.

"That Reb flag right there!" The private pointed to a scrap of cloth that had been sewn into a crude Rebel flag. "Hung that out her door when the Rebs came through," he explained, "Said so herself."

Lockett bit down the curse and released the man, "And how do you explain that?" He pointed to the small Stars and Stripes next to the Rebel flag. The private looked blankly at him, so Lockett walked him over to the scrap. "Soldier, you got a brain the size of a pea! She's got a Rebel flag for when the Secesh come through town. She's got one of ours for when we come through. She does that to protect herself, not because she's a spy."

The widow Magruder had stepped out of the second room, followed by the two soldiers who had been tearing the bedding apart. Curiously, they watched the exchange.

"Well, Private?" Lockett demanded, looking at the bent old woman who could scarcely walk. "Tell me, private, is this your great villain?"

There was no reply.

"What are you going to tell me now, that she has Confederate money? I know a fair number of our soldiers who hold some as souvenirs too. Does that make them spies too?"

The commotion had attracted a small crowd of citizens outside. Unbidden, his eyes latched onto Anna and her father in the front. He turned toward Sergeant Philyaw, "Where's Lieutenant Williams at?"

"With the rest of the company on patrol, sir," Philyaw muttered, "Left me in charge."

"You are done here, sergeant."

"Yes, sir," the sergeant said after some hesitation and with obvious bitterness.

"I suggest you leave and allow the old woman to put the place back together."

"Yes, sir," he replied in a barely audible tone.

The crowd parted for the soldiers, and Lockett watched the blue jacketed men leave. It was terrible, he knew, but the worst part was that it was just the beginning. If this spy wasn't caught soon, Orrin Long would have this town torn to pieces. Worse, there wasn't anything he could do about it.

Lockett took the tiny Rebel flag and stuffed it into the old woman's hand. "I suggest you burn this, ma'am. You have no need for it anymore. The Rebels won't be back here, ever."

The woman cackled and her words echoed in Lockett's ears for the rest of the day and night, *"Brave words, Lieutenant. Brave words."*

* * * * *

It took a week for Lockett's fears to turn into reality.

By the time that he arrived at the little Sheriff's office, the same one where Sheriff Willows and Sandie Holmes had been murdered by bushwhackers, a small crowd was already starting to gather.

Inside the structure he could see blue uniforms moving around. He hoped one of them was Colonel Blair, and that he could talk some sense to him.

Lockett had been summoned by the desperate urgings of Martha Dell, the shopkeeper's wife. He had run the whole way, leaving the old woman far behind, but he listened to her long enough to know the story.

Of course, at this moment, Anna held tightly to his arm as he towed her through the gathering sea of Savannah's humanity, only half-listening as she repeated what Martha Dell had already told him.

"They've arrested old Lewis! He's no spy! He just an old man! He's no spy!"

"Stay here," Lockett said bluntly as he entered the Sheriff's office.

Subconsciously, he looked to the center of the floor. Sheriff Willows's blood stain was still plain to see. The copious blemish on the scarred wood detained his gaze and would not let it go.

Standing just beyond the mark, Lockett sensed more than saw Orrin Long's self-satisfied smile. And beyond him, Lieutenant Williams's men stood guard over the first jail cell.

Peering from behind the bars, Lewis Dell stood up when he recognized Lockett's tall frame enter.

"They got the wrong man!" the old shopkeeper bleated. He wiped beads of perspiration from his red face. "Lieutenant, you hear me? Y'all got the wrong man! I ain't no spy."

To Lockett's dismay, there was only one other officer there, Orrin Long. Colonel Blair must not have heard of the commotion yet, but he would, judging by the continued murmurings of the crowd outside. It was calm to this point, but there was no guarantee that it would remain so.

Long leered wolfishly. "Got our man, Lockett." He patted a notebook in his hand, which Lockett recognized as Major Axford's.

He must have left it with Orrin before leaving for points north, Lockett thought with some surprise.

"The clues were right in front of you all along."

"Old Lewis?" Lockett snapped, unable to restrain himself any further. "The shopkeeper? Based on what?"

The insubordination was plain in his tone, but Long was too caught up in his own success to notice it.

"I was reading Major Axford's observations, and it just came to me, clear as could be."

He paused and waited, finally forcing Lockett to ask, "What? What, Orrin? What is as clear as could be?"

"This spy is gathering information from all over. The entire area is a nest of vipers, like Major Axford already knew." He paused. "There are spies, probably too numerous to truly figure out, but they must gather in one place to share information."

He paused again, and Lockett realized that it was a conscious affectation. Orrin wanted the drama of his statements.

"They consolidate their information and then deliver to points south. Too much for one man." Pause. "Too much for one area, but not so much for multiple people to do... And then share it with one central point. They gather at the store to share their information with the shopkeeper. Every time I looked in there, there were people lingering, talking, plotting, no doubt!"

"You arrested a man because townsfolk like to gather in his store to chat and gossip? Don't you ever stop in Burdick's Dry Goods back in Kalamazoo? There are always people gossiping in there! That's what people do in a general store!"

"It's more than gossip," Long sneered, "Mark my words, he's fully capable of producing these coded missives that the major showed you."

"Fully capable," Lieutenant Williams echoed, reminding Lockett of Major Axford's sycophantic sergeant.

"And now that he's arrested, he'll tell us all his secrets," Long continued ominously. "And if it he doesn't, we'll tear that store apart. We'll find those codes and other evidence. Mark my words, we got the right man."

"Old Lewis?" Lockett replied, struggling to keep his voice even. He knew that he could not afford to lash out now, at least for Lewis's sake. "He's an old, old man. How is he getting this information passed south of here? He can't ride that far anymore at his age. Plus, he's in the store six days a week and in church on Sundays. If he was gone even for a day, it would be noticeable. How's he getting it to this courier?"

The last point gave Orrin Long only the briefest of pauses. "We'll find out, we'll find out."

"Besides," Lieutenant Williams added with a leap of creativity that surprised Lockett, "He doesn't have to ride anywhere. He can pass along the information using the steamers that go south of here, someone who works on the boat could do it for him. And that person could then pass onto the courier who slips through the lines!"

"Someone on a steamer?" Lockett answered skeptically. "It's not always the same steamer running through here. He's got an accomplice on every steamer?"

"Maybe," Williams answered, stepping forward belligerently and thrusting his chest forward. He didn't like being challenged.

"Indeed," Long said, his finger tapping his cheek thoughtfully. There was a strange gleam in his eye. He looked even more satisfied than before. "There could be an accomplice on a steamer. That is a brilliant thought! Good to see that there is some semblance of intelligence among the colonel's officers. I'll have to mention that to General Halleck."

Williams positively glowed at the last statement.

Lockett couldn't stop himself from frowning. Orrin was enjoying himself too much. He wondered if Orrin really did think that the old shopkeeper was truly guilty. Or was he just enjoying a chance to aggravate me, arrest someone that I like?

Arrest an innocent, knowing what that will do to me based on past history?

None of the questions, or possible answers, made him feel any better. Lewis was still in jail and would probably stay there until he could figure out who the real spy was.

Damn that Orrin Long and this damnable war!

His fingers brushed the wood of his holstered revolver. Wildly, he dreamt of wiping that smile off the Orrin's face once and for all.

But Orrin Long was oblivious to the murderous thoughts across from him. In excitement and delight, he repeated his phrase from earlier.

"Yep, he's the man, and the clues were right in front of you all along, Lockett…"

III
Decision

Chapter 14

Bloody Bill Coulter licked the dribble of drink from his upper lip.

"Give me enough men, and we could conquer the world." Despite all of the alcohol, his voice was still the same coarse rattle as always.

"We'll show 'em Yanks," the boy across from Coulter answered.

Though he had consumed only an eighth of what Coulter had, he teetered perilously to one side, only catching himself by leaning into the other new recruit. The others in the room guffawed in drunken laughter at little Tommie Wexler.

"You'll hold your drink bett'r after killin' some Yankees," Coulter laughed.

He knew what men wanted. Men wanted drink, money, women, and blood. He had promised all that in spades to these boys, his new recruits.

Most were from families that never would have considered allowing their kin to ride with a bandit like Bloody Bill Coulter before the war. But like Tommie Wexler, these new recruits had seen their views harden. They could not sit by while the Yankee invaders assaulted the homes, the very mantel of Savannah and its outlying farms.

All of the new Yankee actions played perfectly into Bloody Bill Coulter's hands. The ranks of his bushwhackers were starting to swell like never before. He had once been whittled down to two, but now there were ten, and each day promised more.

And now that he had men again, he could act. The question was what to strike and when. Most of the men wanted to strike directly at the Yankees conducting the searches.

Coulter nodded appreciatively to their thoughts, but he had no intention of trying to stop the Yankees from their foolishness. Attacking those patrols and searches promised little in the way of money, guns, liquor, or anything useful to him. Besides, the more that the Yankees kept ripping up farmhouses, the more recruits he would have. He was more interested in the Yankee payroll. Up river, his conspirators would let him know when the shipment would come by steamer. That was an intriguing thought.

But in the meantime, there was another one to gnaw on – how to kill James Lockett?

* * * * *

Orrin Long smiled wolfishly after his junior associate left the little room. His plan was not yet complete in his mind, but at least he knew that he had an ally now. He had someone to help set the destruction of James Lockett in motion.

Since he had returned to Savannah, it had not taken long to discover that Blair's motley camp was divided into two fiefdoms, one that protected Lockett and another that realized Lockett was the cause of their present demise.

This had been easy to determine. After all, sitting in just one meeting of Blair's officers, it was plain to see that there was a chill between Lockett and some of the other officers, a tension that transcended past the officers right into the companies themselves.

His problem had not been discovering Lockett's foes. His problem was quietly finding out who would be willing to do something about it. Which ones would be willing to fracture a code or two to rid the regiment of their cancer? Which ones would realize that the end was more important than the means?

He had now found at least one who was willing, a man who knew he could be helped by having friends in the right places.

The irony of it, Long smiled, was that Lockett himself had planted the seed for what was growing now into a full-fledged plot. It would start with the steamboats.

May 25

The regiment has lost its first soldier since Sandie Holmes, a private in Lieutenant Pope's company named Bryant. It was an accident. The man's best friend tripped and fell. His rifle discharged. Pope said there wasn't much left of Bryant's face, and Bryant's friend is distraught beyond words naturally.

Consequently, Colonel Blair has ordered all patrols to march with unloaded weapons now to prevent further accidents. He reasons that bushwhackers are no longer a problem. They have not been heard from in quite some time. My immediate reaction was negative, but I kept it to myself. In the end, the unloaded weapons may be for the best. More than anything else, it may save the accidental death of some poor Savannahan whose house is being searched. With each house we search, I am plagued by visions of little Amelia. I did not believe in ghosts before, but now I am not so sure. At every house, I see her peering out the windows at the approaching soldiers. One moment, she is the innocent girl. The next moment, she is...

--- the diary of James Lockett

* * * * *

Tommie Wexler crouched in the thick woods, his freckled face hidden deep in the shadows. Impatiently, he watched today's detachment of blue-coated soldiers march by.

Bloody Bill had his men keep tabs on all such movements. All roads from Savannah were watched. To date, the bushwhacker chief took no action, which frustrated Tommie greatly. He had defied his mother and father to join Coulter, but all he had seen so far was drinking and talking. Talk. Talk. Drink. Drink. Talk and more talk. He wanted action! And he wanted it now!

Perhaps, today was the day. Maybe today Bloody Bill would decide to inflict some pain on the Yankee soldiers. Tommie knew that Bloody Bill was up to any fight, especially against some Yankee. In fact, Tommie himself was downright scared of the bushwhacker.

The man's bloodshot, ice blue eyes seemed to see everything, not to mention see right through him. There was a visceral wildness to them, like some beast in the woods.

And yet, the predatory fear that Coulter could instill was somehow channeled with a cunning calm, like a prowling animal that patiently stalked its prey, and Tommie knew the one thing that Bloody Bill wanted.

He thanked God that he wasn't that Yankee, Lockett. Bloody Bill would have no mercy for him! The Yankee had better hope that he wasn't taken alive. For a moment, Tommie felt sorry for him, but then he remembered the soldiers throwing his ailing mother to the ground, holding their rifles on his father, and leering at his young sisters. The compassion disappeared in an eye blink.

It was about time that Bloody Bill put that fear into the Yankees too. Maybe today would be the day. After all, this small detachment that marched out of town was led by the tall Lieutenant Lockett.

This might be the day for action…

* * * * *

"Think w'all find this thar spy today, sir?" Prosper T. Rowe said good-naturedly.

They marched in column, two abreast down the empty farm lane.

Lockett smiled in response. He wanted to laugh and agree with the unspoken criticism. These patrols were worthless. They would never capture a spy this way.

But he was the leader, and he knew that he could not share the luxury of a common soldier's cynicism anymore. "Today could be the day, Private Rowe," he forced himself to answer.

Rowe gave a long, cackling laugh. "Yessir," he said between hoots, "Today is the day. Who do ya think it is, sir? Some farmer whose boy is a Johnny Reb?"

"Now, if I knew that, Private, the search would be a bit easier, now wouldn't it?"

Rowe cackled again. "Yessir."

Lockett hid the grin that he felt. There was something about Prosper T. that made people want to smile. It was a good group of men that he had. He was lucky to have them, he thought to himself, dregs of the army and all that they supposedly were.

Lockett and his detachment of twenty men marched on. Today's destination was the Giddings farm. Giddings, his wife, and four daughters were regular attendees at Reverend Tucker's church. Lockett knew them all now. He doubted that the Giddings could be spies, but orders were orders.

At least, his men were the ones conducting the search. He could assure the Giddings of good treatment during the search, something that he couldn't promise about the other companies, except for Renaud's men. Even Pope, harmless as he was, did not have a strong enough sway over his men, and these intrusions were always rife with temptation.

A refreshing breeze swam through their column as they made their way across a broad meadow surrounded by trees. The early growth of spring, launched by the massive rains in April, was now slowing due to a lack of May rain.

The farmers would be starting to worry about that, Lockett thought to himself. How had May been in Kalamazoo? Had it rained? Was Daniel able to keep the farm up? It had been so long since he had heard from his brother.

"Sir!"

It was Prosper T. who saw them first. With a bony finger, he pointed to the edge of the wood line across the meadow. Ten horsemen meandered out of the elms, revolvers in hand. They wore floppy, brimmed farm hats and mismatched home spun. There was no banner.

"Bushwhackers!" Adie exclaimed.

Even from this distance, Lockett recognized the man in the rear of the group, gesturing for the horsemen to spread out some.

Where did Bloody Bill get all those men? Lockett wondered. Then he forced the thought from his mind. There was no time for such wanderings. The horsemen were already urging their mounts forward, and Lockett's column of twenty blue coats had nothing to greet them with except empty rifles, as per Colonel Blair's orders.

"Company, right face!" Lockett ordered. His voice was loud but calm, much calmer sounding than he actually felt. His men turned on their right heel to face the attackers. Instead of a wrong-footed column, they were now two neat rows of ten. "Rear rank, load weapons!" He could sense his men's uneasiness. There would not be enough time to load a rifle before the horsemen were upon them. "Front rank, fix bayonets!" Eagerly, the front rank obeyed, and there was the clank of metal sliding over metal as the long blades were slotted in place.

The horsemen were now charging forward in full gallops. Their loud whoops filled the air until overcome by the percussive sound of their pounding hooves. One bushwhacker fired an exuberant shot into the air as he rode.

"Die, Yankees!" another shouted, barely audible over the on-rushing horseflesh.

But Lockett's men were steady. The locking of the bayonets had solidified their resolve. If the horsemen tried to stampede through their little line and break them into smaller pieces, the bushwhackers would feel the pain of the long, gleaming silver spikes.

With his right hand Lockett pulled out his Starr revolver and removed the Stuart family sword with his left. He could hear two ramrods rattle in the barrels behind him and found himself wondering which two men were so quick.

Sod flew as the bushwhackers charged across the meadow.

"Bayonets!" Lockett ordered unnecessarily. His men already had the metal spikes thrust forward.

Some of the bushwhackers began firing their pistols, but it seemed that they were more intent on crashing their mounts straight through the blue line. Then at twenty yards out, they began to swerve off, like water passing around a rock in a stream. They rode across the front of Lockett's line and then around the flanks, firing and whooping as they went.

Lockett fired his Starr at the lead rider and missed.

Most of the bushwhackers were careful not to get too close to the prickly line of shiny bayonets, veering away in plenty of time. Their paths took them on an arc nearly twenty yards away from the Yankees, and they continued to discharge their revolvers. Most fired from their bouncing mounts with amateurish accuracy, high and wild, more frightful to look at than anything else.

Bloody Bill Coulter stayed back and let his men make the first pass, stalking them from a distance, but his eyes were solely on one man, Lockett.

While most of his horsemen safely avoided the bayonets with room to spare, one horseman was slower than the others in banking away. His path took him within five yards of the line.

Adie Graham leapt out from the row and braved the dashing horse.

The horseman switched his aim to the soldier lunging toward him, but he had been caught by surprise. He was too late, but Adie Graham had misjudged the thrust of his bayonet at the speeding rider. The blade slid narrowly in front of the rider while Graham's momentum carried him into the horse.

The extended barrel caught the startled rider across the chest and knocked him sidewise in the saddle, ripping the weapon from the Graham's grasp.

Then the horse's rear flank collided with the off-balance young soldier, sending him flying backwards.

Spinning, Graham hit the ground in a heap. Awkwardly, he flipped over his shoulder and laid face first on the ground.

But his effort had been enough to make the rider lose his balance too. One foot slipped from the stirrup, and the reins fell from the bushwhacker's hands. With one foot remaining trapped in the stirrup, the bushwhacker dangled upside down.

The horse, freed of the reins, veered away from all of the commotion, dragging the perilously hanging rider back through the meadow. The rider looked as if he had been beheaded as the grass obscured his crown.

The rest of the bushwhackers curved around and regrouped. They saw a couple of Yankees on the ground and were sure that more had to be wounded. Encouraged, they charged forward again.

"On Lockett! On Lockett!" one of the bushwhackers shouted. The nine horsemen bore down on the lone officer standing on the right end of the frail Yankee line.

Lockett fired the last bullet in his revolver, and then threw it to the ground. There was no time to reload it, and he switched the sword into his right hand. He had heard their battle cry and knew they were heading straight for him. The bushwhackers were thirty yards away and gathering speed when a bullet snatched his hat from his head, and he felt the air around him alive with their shots.

At that moment, rifle cracks, much deeper sounding than that of a revolver, erupted from behind him.

The rear rank had finished loading!

First, there were just two shots and then eight more echoed. The ten heavy Minié balls ripped into the charging horsemen. Two well-aimed shots exploded the chest of the lead rider. A second rider was also unhorsed. The tally was only two bushwhackers, but the shock of it was enough. For most of the bushwhackers, this was their first armed encounter with the enemy, and in shock, they reined in their mounts, paused momentarily, and turned around. Not bothering to give Bloody Bill Coulter a second look, the bushwhackers raced back into the woods.

Bloody Bill Coulter scowled at Lockett from across the field. "We'll meet a'gin, Lockett!" he yelled hoarsely before following after his retreating men.

Lockett turned to his men. "Reload," he said in a businesslike voice.

They did, and they waited for the bushwhackers to give battle again, but Coulter and his bushwhackers were gone. They had not lost one man, although two were wounded.

One of the wounded was Levi Thickle, and Lockett watched Prosper T. Rowe tie a bandage around the man's arm.

"Is the bone broken?" Lockett asked as Thickle winced.

"Don't think so, sir," Rowe answered for Thickle. "Pistol bullets don't pack the same wallop. Looks like it went through the muscle and nothing more."

Lockett nodded approvingly. That meant that Thickle stood a good chance of keeping his arm. Many amputations were done because the bullet had snapped the bone, making a gap. Because there was no way to reconnect the separated bone, many arms came off.

Luckily, it looked like Thickle and the other wounded man, Private Thomas, could recover. "How about Adie?" he asked Rowe.

"Just dazed, sir. Amazingly enough. I war' darn sure he broke his fool neck the way he went a-tumblin'. But it don't look like he broke a thing, sir. He'll be right as rain."

Again, Lockett nodded approvingly. A small grin slid across his face. "Isn't that the second time that a horse sent him flying?"

Rowe chuckled and nodded.

"You'll have to think of an appropriate nickname for him, Prosper T."

"I was thinking the same thing, Lieutenant." With a wink, he added, "How 'bout 'Little Mule Kick'?"

Chapter 15

"News travels fast around here," Lockett remarked to Ainsley Stuart.

Ainsley reclined in his cot with one arm behind his head, casually interrogating him about his latest brush with the bushwhacker.

"There's not a whole lot to do around here except talk, James. Most of us are bed-ridden for a good portion of the day. Besides," Ainsley joked, "I need to keep track of the whereabouts of my sword."

"My cousin thinks that he might need it back," Katherine butted in. She hovered over them, a soiled bandage from another man's wound in her hand. For a moment, Lockett thought this was about soiling the Stuart name again, but Katherine's harsh tone and hawkish look was directed at Ainsley, not him, for once. "Go on," she prodded Ainsley, "Tell him your grand idea."

"She'd make a good big sister." Ainsley allowed himself a small grin and pointed at her reproachful gaze. "A born natural at it, except that I'm her older cousin, not her younger brother." The mild rebuke had no effect.

"What's she talking about?" Lockett finally asked. "Grand idea?"

"I was only commenting to my dear cousin what my plans in the army might be in a couple of months, once I sufficiently recover from this wound."

That he could speak so simply about such a gruesome injury and so matter-of-factly about recovery was a testament to

Ainsley's spirit. The bloody stump was still fresh in Lockett's own memory.

"You know that they will be moving me and some of the others in a few days, or a couple of weeks perhaps. A nice little boat ride north, maybe Louisville I hear."

Lockett nodded. Anna had already relayed the possibility to him. She was much more in touch with the latest camp rumors than he was.

"Once I recover, James, I will again need to be useful to my Army, to this Grand Cause."

"And you would want your sword back then? Of course, I would give it back, Ainsley, but what would you do? You have... you have no... well..."

"No foot, James. It was a foot," Ainsley said testily, but then his voice switched back to pleasant optimism. "A man can serve this Army without a foot, James. I can still ride a horse. In fact, I bet I'm still a better rider than you!" Ainsley was the only one who laughed at his little jest.

"The cavalry won't accept a one-footed man, Ainsley. As bad as they could use a good man like you, they still wouldn't do it."

"Not the cavalry, James, a staff officer."

"A staff officer?"

"Sure enough. The ones who keep the generals organized and communicate with their commanders. A man needs a good mind and the ability to ride a horse and carry a message."

"God knows you'd be a better staff officer than..." Lockett caught himself at the last second, remembering that Katherine was still next to them, "Better than most, but why? How?"

"How?" Ainsley fairly laughed at the question. "I *am* the son of Senator Stuart, remember?"

Lockett nodded. He sometimes did forget that his generous and easy-going friend was a son of privilege.

"Being the son of a Senator does have its benefits. I have no doubt that some general would take me, if only for the presumed access to my father."

Lockett looked blankly at him for a moment. Ainsley probably would be a good staff officer, and he had seen action. Ainsley knew what battle was like, something that Lockett doubted most staff officers understood.

And Ainsley did have the connections to land a staff officer post, but it was the resolute look on Ainsley Stuart's narrow, still health-pinched face that convinced him. Ainsley wasn't ready to let go of the fray, and Lockett could understand that. He too had once been forced from the fight and had wanted nothing more than to jump back into the maelstrom. "Well then, I guess you'll be needing your sword back sometime."

"James!" Katherine huffed. She glowered at him, red in the face, trying to find the words. But apparently, the right ones would not come, and she stomped the dirt floor once. This seemed to make her even more agitated. Flummoxed for words, she smacked her lips before stomping once more. Then, she turned on the ball of her foot and stormed out of the tent.

"Oh, well," Lockett laughed, "She was already mad at me to begin with."

Ainsley chuckled with him for a minute before turning serious again. "One thing though, James, about the sword."

Lockett nodded for him to continue.

"I want you to return it to me... after the war, *personally.*" Ainsley lifted Lockett's hat which had been lying absently on the cot. Pointedly, he placed his finger in the ragged hole made by one of the bushwhacker's shots. "Do you understand what I'm saying?"

Lockett's gaze narrowed. "You know I can't guarantee that, Ainsley. None of us can."

"I know."

"I don't like to make promises that I'm not sure I can keep."

"Do it this once, and I'll tell you why. Because when James Lockett promises something, he keeps that oath. You're too good of a friend, James, and I've seen how you react when the lead starts to fly. I want my friend to return that to me when this is all done. I know that no man with an ounce of courage can guarantee that in this war, just tell me that you won't do anything really stupid."

Lockett took Ainsley's extended hand. "Agreed."

It seemed a simple thing to agree to at the time.

* * * * *

Lieutenants Fulkerham and Williams stood beneath the shade of a tree and watched Lockett's men revel in what they were calling a victory over the bushwhackers. Despite their best efforts, Fulkerham and Williams knew their own companies were becoming a little envious of Lockett's ragamuffin band. The relaxed dress and luck for finding action was slowly eroding the discipline that they had worked so hard to instill in their companies.

"It would be one thing if we were in different regiments," Fulkerham frowned, "That would be one thing indeed, but for two companies in one regiment to be working so differently is untenable."

Williams nodded. "It's eating away at us all."

"And now he has even more of the colonel's ear. Now we will be marching with loaded weapons again. I cannot fathom how the man has let Lockett get away with it."

"Having *him* here now isn't helping either," Fulkerham added, looking in the direction of Orrin Long who was walking towards them. "As much as the man is supposed to be looking for a Confederate spy, it seems to me that he is doing his own spying on us and reporting back to General Halleck."

"It should make the colonel pay greater attention to the passage of regulations with the general's own aide here," Williams answered carefully.

"It should, but it doesn't seem to be working that way. Colonel Blair doesn't care what Captain Long has to say. I believe Colonel Blair has come to the conclusion that Captain Long is the liar, not Lockett."

"Rubbish!" Williams spouted, but Fulkerham said nothing.

Long strode up to them, and the two lieutenants saluted. "Watching Lockett's menagerie?"

"Two more dead bushwhackers," Fulkerham pointed out without enthusiasm.

"Two more wounded of your own," Long answered, "And they never did make it to that farm to check for spies."

The lieutenants nodded obediently.

"General Halleck will not tolerate continued failure. One only need look at General Grant's demotion to know that."

Fulkerham wondered if that was supposed to be a threat. If it was, it was too heavy-handed, and he supposed that the captain must be referring to Colonel Blair or someone more senior than himself.

"We need to start hanging people. Then, they'll come forward with who these vermin are," Williams declared. "Maybe start with that shopkeeper who is still sitting in that jail cell."

"It may come to that," Long replied boastfully, "But before that, I have another idea. I'll be offering a reward for information leading to the capture of the spy."

"A reward?" Fulkerham questioned.

"Twenty-five dollars. Twenty-five dollars of my own money."

Williams gaped at the sum. That was nearly double what any of his men made in a month.

"That should loosen some tongues!"

May 27
I sent another letter to Daniel today. I implored him to write. I cannot understand why I get no response. It could be my own impatience. Kalamazoo is a long way away. But I am nervous at the lack of news. Daniel is probably struggling with the farm, but that is the only way for him to learn. I suppose that he could be so bone-tired each day that he has no gumption to write.

But I would still want one short letter. Patrick received one today from his sister. No news on the Locketts, but I suppose that is probably good news. I asked Patrick for them to check on Daniel.

Back here, Colonel Blair was happy with my report today. We carry loaded weapons again tomorrow. Luckily, that lesson did not come one day too late.

--- the diary of James Lockett

* * * * *

"They tell me that you are someone who knows the value of a nickel and can be trusted to keep your mouth shut," Orrin Long finished in conclusion.

The slack-jawed man at first gave no reaction. The flesh of his heavy brow hung sleepily over a lazy eye, although the other one followed the uniformed officer with interest. Finally, he tugged on his thick beard and nodded wordlessly. Finding some ash and grit in his beard, he pulled it free and flicked it away with his thumb and forefinger.

Overhead, the tramping of soldiers and clamor of cargo being off-loaded continued. It would take another hour for the small group of soldiers to finish unloading the *Tonana*. Then the steamer would continue south tomorrow on its biweekly supply run.

The smoke-tainted confines of the room made Orrin Long claustrophobic, but he had to consummate this deal and needed a place away from all eyes. "It's very simple. I give you half now and half when you finish."

The slack jawed, bearded stoker gave another open-mouth nod, and Orrin Long wondered if the ignoramus had what it took to pull this off. He needed someone with at least a little bit between the ears.

"Half now, half later," the man repeated.

"Right," Long said, still dubious.

"And the reward too."

Long's pencil thin moustache wrinkled in momentary distaste. Perhaps the stoker was not so dull-witted after all?

"I get the twenty-five dollars too, at the end, of course."

It was said as a statement, not a question. His good eye stared straight at Long, but it was the lazy eye, which seemed to look right past Long's ear, that unsettled him more than anything else.

The stoker waited patiently and combed through his thick beard with his fingers while he waited, searching for more grit.

Long was of half a mind to dicker with the man. This was getting expensive, but he decided against it. He needed the man's silence, and it would be well spent if it caused the death-knell of Lockett. "You'll get the reward too, as long as you keep your mouth shut." He scowled.

"I can guarantee that," the stoker said confidently.

There was the sound of a crash outside the room, and a look of panic crossed Long's face.

God in Heaven! He figured it would be plenty private to talk in the squalid little room.

He yanked the door open and looked into the hall. Breathing a sigh of relief, he saw a crate that was tilted against the stairs at the far end of the hallway. The narrow hallway must have made it sound as if it had been right outside the door. Some careless fool up top must have dropped the crate down the opening while crossing.

Returning his attention to the stoker, Long chided himself on his anxiety. He had nothing to be nervous about. He was in total control, and this time, he would take care of Lockett completely. There would be no recovery from this. And if he squared this just right, Lockett would be swinging from a noose to boot.

"Then we have an understanding. You know what to do."

"Yep," the stoker replied.

The stoker closed the door, and Orrin Long departed through the far staircase, not bothering to pick up the crate that still lay at the bottom of the stairs. He took a long stride over it and continued up to the main deck.

"You buffoon!" McManus whispered when the coast was clear. He poked Bosworth in the shoulder, "You clumsy mule, what was that?"

"I fell," Bosworth said meekly.

"I know that. If it wasn't for me putting that crate on the stair…"

"Well, praise your quick mind."

"Praise, indeed."

"How was I to know there was a tool box on the floor behind me? All I did was take a step back."

McManus waved an exasperated hand.

"'Sides Captain Long is a fool. Ain't no way a crate like that is going to fall all the way down those stairs without splintering."

"He's no fool," McManus said ominously, "He's up to something. I told you he was up to something, didn't I? No reason for someone like'm to go below deck on a filthy steamer like this."

Bosworth nodded.

"As soon as I heard that he was putting his own money up for the reward, I knew there was something rotten to follow. There's nothing that man does for the good of us all, certainly not with his own money! The man is a greedy skin flint."

"Could you hear what they were saying?" Bosworth asked. "I couldn't hear nothin' through that door."

McManus shrugged. "Nothing I could make out. My ears aren't what they used to be."

"Too many loud bangs'll do that to ya."

"All I heard was the end."

"What in the tarnation is he planning with a stoker from a steamer?"

"Nothing good. That stuffed shirt doesn't deal with men who got dirt under their fingernails unless it's for no good."

"Probably."

"Oh, I know for sure," McManus declared, "In Missouri, he used a fella called Hiram Walker. The man didn't do one good day's work in his life, joined the volunteers for the booty to be sure. Anyhow, Lieutenant Long used Walker for all the dirty work he was cooking up."

"He's a captain now, Pat. It's Captain Long."

McManus grimaced and said nothing.

"We need to tell the lieutenant about this," Bosworth recommended, "I'm sure he'll know what to do."

"We'll tell him, but I don't know what good it will do. Whatever it is, we'll need to catch Long red-handed. It can't be hearsay, 'cause we already know that we'll lose that battle."

* * * * *

Had someone else brought him the story, Lockett would have waved it off, but this was Patrick, and Patrick knew all about what Orrin was capable of.

Lockett chewed his lower lip and paced while he pondered, "Does sound like he's up to something."

"Can we talk to the colonel?" Bosworth asked hopefully.

"Not a chance, and tell him what? We don't know anything."

"We know what our own gut is telling us," McManus answered, "But we hear you."

"So how did you end up on the *Tonana* anyhow?"

"We've been keeping an eye on things when we can. Since Orrin arrived, Milton and I have been trying to watch him, especially since he announced this reward."

"You've been following him?"

"More or less. Adie's pretty good at it too. People don't pay him much attention, and Orrin doesn't know him either."

"Adie?"

"Don't worry. He's a kid, but he's up to it."

"Just don't get caught," Lockett cautioned. He didn't need any of his friends running afoul of Orrin Long also.

"We ain't gonna get caught," Bosworth laughed, "That there Captain Long is so absorbed with hisself that he has no idea we're watchin' him."

"All the same, be careful about it."

"Yeah," McManus added to Bosworth with a smirk, "Don't go taking any more steps back without looking first."

Lockett looked quizzically at him.

"Inside joke, sir."

"What should we do, Lieutenant?" Bosworth asked, ignoring McManus's gentle jibe.

"What should we do?" Lockett shrugged. "I don't know. Not much except keep watching. When there's something solid, I'll talk to Colonel Blair."

"The problem with that," McManus began, "Is that by the time we get something solid, it might be too late."

"You're probably right, Patrick, but there is nothing else I can do about it."

After the officer had departed, McManus turned to Bosworth. There was a strange glint in his Irish blue eyes. "There's nothing he can do about it, Milton, but there is something *we* can do about it."

"There is?" Bosworth said with a puzzled look.

May 28

The morning sun was plenty high in the sky, and Long pulled out his watch chain and checked the time again. Where was the man!

He tried not to show his frustration, but damn it all, where was he? He had been told that the stoker was the man for the job.

The stoker was late. Had he taken that money and run out on him? It seemed unlikely. The stoker was too greedy to do something like that. He would want his second half, and then the reward too.

But where was he? The *Tonana* would have her steam up soon, and his little trap for Lockett would be foiled. Where was that damn stoker?

* * * * *

There was a yelp from the dark grove of trees that was halfway between the *Tonana* and headquarters. It was a short, canine howl, but there was no one around to hear it other than the occupants of that small patch of forest.

"He bit my hand," Bosworth complained, shaking his hand and wiping a drop of blood on his jacket. "Like an animal, Prosper T."

"I tol't ya, it ain't no difference, Sergeant. There ain't no one 'round here to hear him. Ya didn't have to clamp your hand over his mouth when we dragged him in here."

"Yeah, but look at this mangy dog of a man," Bosworth grumbled. "I've heard of men dying from their own horses biting them, and most horses ain't less clean than 'im." He pointed angrily at the stoker.

The slack-jawed man from the steamer looked up at the six soldiers who had dragged him into the woods. "And I'll do a whole lot worse to you too!" the stoker added, full of belligerence. "Let go of my arms, and I'll show you!"

"You got a good grip on him, John?" McManus said to John Messern, who had the stoker's arms pinned behind his back.

Messern bobbed his head.

"Good. Now, you," McManus turned to the stoker. "You sure are full of big words for someone who is in a heap more trouble than you realize."

Dramatically taking his time, McManus pulled his long Bowie knife free from its leather sheath. The menacing blade had recently been sharpened to give it a frightening edge and a devilishly sharp point.

The belligerence raced out of the stoker like water from a sieve. "W-what do you want?"

"We want to know why you were talking to Captain Long," McManus continued with the interrogation.

"I ain't got any idea what you're talking about. Captain who?"

"Oh, you got an idea," McManus said. He gave an almost imperceptible nod, and Otto Klugge moved next to John Messern.

The big stevedore took one arm while Messern took the other. With the added weight, the stoker found that he was completely anchored, unable to move even an inch. His eyes locked onto the blade of the large knife.

It was the size of man's forearm, and in its well-maintained sheen, he could see the eyes of the Irishman holding it. They were the most remorselessly cold eyes that he had ever seen.

"W-what do you want with me? I don't even know you!"

"We saw you talking to Captain Long on the *Tonana* yesterday." The voice was slow and deliberate, in total control.

"Y-yesterday?" the stoker said shakily, his eyes never leaving the Bowie knife.

McManus nodded and took a step forward. "Yesterday." The voice lowered an octave, threatening.

"Y-yes, y-yesterday, I do remember... do remember talking to a captain now that you mention it."

"And what did you talk about?"

"Talk about? N-nothing important. No, sir."

With another nearly imperceptible nod from McManus, the stoker felt his arms get twisted. He howled.

"My arms! You'll break my arms!" he managed between gasps.

"A stoker with busted arms ain't no good," the Irishman said.

The stoker howled again as they applied another iota of pressure.

"I want to know *exactly* what you were talking about."

"Nothing important!" His voice was a pitch higher than before.

McManus's blue eyes and the whites of his teeth flashed as he snarled, "I'll whittle you down like stick if I have to!"

The Irishman's fist locked around the stoker's throat. "Let's start with the ears, since you already heard the question, you won't be needing them anymore."

A high, whistling sound of terror escaped from the stoker's throat, and his eyes bulged, moving side to side since he couldn't shake his head in response.

"Is that a 'no'?" McManus asked, releasing his grip on the throat and stepping back.

"But, but…"

"I think you have a lot more to fear from us than from a yellow-bellied officer who can't do his own dirty work."

The stoker nodded violently in agreement. "Okay! Okay!" he gasped, "He didn't pay me that much."

"What did he want? Where were you going?"

"I was on my way to see your colonel."

"Why?"

"To claim the reward, tell him that I had been given a message to deliver from the spy."

"What?"

"Yes, yes," the stoker chirped, worried that the soldiers didn't believe him, "It's in my shirt pocket. There's a letter. It's what I was supposed to hand over and say that the spy had given it to me."

"You're crazy," McManus remarked as Bosworth pulled a folded piece of paper from the man's shirt and handed it to Adie Graham. "They'd lock you up as an accomplice."

"No, no, Captain Long said he would use his influence, say I had showed my true colors by turning the spy in. I was then to get out of town on the *Tonana*."

McManus wanted to say that the stoker was a fool for trusting Orrin, but in this case, Orrin probably would have kept his word. It certainly would be in his best interest to get the witness out of town once the false testimony was delivered. Either that or maybe kill the man shortly thereafter, maybe as some sort of accident or escape attempt.

"Who was Captain Long trying to frame?"

The stoker blinked uncomprehendingly back at McManus.

"Who were you going to say was the spy?"

"Someone called Reverend Tucker."

Bosworth looked at McManus. They were both thinking the same thing.

It was no accident that Orrin Long had singled out the preacher. It was clearly a shot directed at James. The only thing worse would have been to single out Anna, but they both supposed that would be too much of a stretch to believe, leaving Orrin to settle for the father.

"Oh, no!" Adie Graham exclaimed, looking up from the letter. "Look at this. You were going to give this letter to the colonel?"

"Why?" McManus asked.

"'Cause it says here that the lieutenant has switched sides and is going to give'em information."

McManus scowled. Orrin was going to leave nothing to chance.

The stoker tried to shrink backwards from the murderous look, but the other soldiers still had him pinioned in place.

"What now?" Adie asked.

McManus turned the full power of that look back on the stoker. He holstered the Bowie knife, but that didn't help the quaking knees of the stoker. "You're going to take this piece of shit back to the *Tonana* with Otto and John and make sure that he gets on it." He took a step toward the stoker, "And if I ever see you back in this town again, I'll kill you. You understand?"

The stoker nodded. "No prob'm there, no prob'm there," he said hastily, head bobbing.

"Milton and I are going to go show this letter to the lieutenant."

The soldiers shoved the stoker out of the forest, and with Adie in tow, they took the man back to the steamer.

Once they were alone, Bosworth exclaimed, "Good God, Pat, you can be one scary son of a bitch when you want to be! You almost had *me* soiling my pants!"

Chapter 16

The orange glow of early morning gave its hue to everything, including the lone figure struggling to carry two heavy buckets. Lockett watched her straining with the load. She was a reed-thin shadow moving in the ethereal haze that rose off the drought stunted grass. He watched her, wondering exactly what brought him here. He patted the object in his pocket as if to reassure himself and sighed at his indecision.

The letter that Milton and Patrick had delivered to him yesterday was causing an indecision that he was not accustomed to. The letter and the stoker should have been the evidence to combat Orrin Long, shouldn't it?

He wanted to believe that it was, but he could not convince himself. The seed of doubt had been planted so deep that he could not shake the hesitation. He had lost battles of hearsay with Orrin before, and then there was the letter itself.

The letter had been written with a heavy hand, in such excessive force and in child like block letters, that it would be difficult for him to prove that it was Orrin's handwriting.

He paused, wondering how Orrin had intended to prove the writing was Reverend Tucker's.

Then, Lockett realized Orrin's devious logic. Orrin didn't intend to prove that it was the Reverend's writing, only that the preacher/spy had taken a conscious effort to disguise the truth. It would be odd that it was not in code, like the rest of the spy's communications had been, but Orrin probably had a story for that too.

Damn it all! Patrick had secured the letter, but they couldn't prove that it was Orrin's plot. He wanted to deliver that letter to Colonel Blair, to have his day of judgment once and for all. But Lockett knew deep down that it was a foolish impulse. He would lose. It would still come down to his word against Orrin's, and there was no need repeating those defeats.

The impotence had eaten away at him for the entire sleepless night, and that was what brought him here. He knew there was nothing to say to Katherine Moffat, no way that she could help, but he felt oddly compelled to seek her out.

Finally, she saw him watching her as some water sloshed out of her buckets. The long tendons of her slender neck protruded in exertion. "That lazy Bill," she began, speaking of the twelve year old orderly, "wasn't around, so I had to fetch my own water."

Even though she had been in Savannah for some time now, it did not take much for Katherine to summon that Belle of Kalamazoo voice.

"Can I help?" Lockett replied, not bothering to mention that he had passed the "lazy Bill" on his way here. The boy was ankle deep in the grave that he was digging.

Katherine took a few more dogged steps and then relented.

"What do you want?" she said testily. "If you're waiting for me to show you the proof that Anna is incorrigible, I have given up. Given up, you hear?" She drew out the words with long intonations for emphasis. "Even if I caught her red-handed, I doubt you would believe me. You'd have to see it with your own eyes. So frankly, I've given up, James Lockett. I can't see any other way of proving this to you, so there."

"I'm not here to talk about Anna," Lockett answered calmly. "If you would rather talk about something else, that's fine." They walked along for another minute in silence, neither knowing what to talk about. Finally, Lockett said, "What is the latest news from Kalamazoo? It's been ages since my brother wrote."

Katherine snorted, "How would I know? I've been disowned, remember? My father warned me when I left, and he's a man who doesn't go back on his word."

"You haven't heard from him since you left?"

She shook her head. "Not once."

"Moffats are stubborn," he joked, but Katherine either did not grasp his jest or chose to ignore it. After a short pause, he added, "He'll come to his senses eventually, Katherine. Why, Ainsley is getting better everyday. Soon, they'll move him north, and eventually you'll take him back to Kalamazoo. When your father sees a healthy nephew, he'll change his mind."

"You obviously don't know my father."

True, his rosy statement of compassion did not sound like what he had heard about Big John Moffat, but he felt compelled to try to lift Katherine's spirits. "He'll change his mind, Katherine. He'll see that you are serving your country just the same as Ainsley and I have been."

Katherine turned abruptly and stared in astonishment.

"What?" Lockett asked, puzzled by her reaction.

"I never thought of that. Do you really think that is true? I am serving my country?"

"Of course," he said, genuinely dumb-founded. "How could it not be?"

"Serving my country?"

"Of course. Just the same as Ainsley and I have been. You don't have to carry a gun to serve. God knows that you've seen plenty of unpleasantness in this hospital. This has been as nasty and discomforting work as there is. The suffering you've seen…" he paused, his throat thickening at visions of misery. "Well, there are plenty of boys here who will be forever grateful to you, Katherine, whether your father understands that or not. I know Ainsley will be forever grateful, and so am I."

She looked at him, and surprisingly, her blue eyes began to soften. "Thank you, James."

They looked at each other with a gentleness that neither had managed in a long time. It reminded him of when he had first laid eyes on her, back when he had fallen into her mother's cellar while delivering some apples. In these moments where her guard was down, she was like a completely different person, he realized. Beneath that haughtiness there was still this touch of innocence. He knew that he was staring, and he told himself to look away.

Surely, the stare would cause her guard to go back up.

Yet, she met his eyes and maintained the same oddly gentle look.

For a continuing moment, there was silence between them. The orange glow of the dawn radiated behind her.

Then, the moment was gone.

She snapped her head down, having seen something behind him. "You're needed," she said firmly as she quickly wiped her eyes.

Lockett turned to see Bosworth heading quickly towards them. What now, he wondered.

* * * * *

Lockett and his men were just out of sight, and the dust was only now settling back on the tired road.

"They're gone," Sergeant Philyaw said, his tongue licking yellow stained teeth in anticipation.

"Yes, they are," Orrin Long answered, though his eyes did not waver from the empty road.

"Shall I go see the colonel now?"

Long shook his head. "Wait a half hour. We have all the time in the world now." He felt more confident than he did earlier. It had been surprisingly easy to get Lockett out of the way. It was merely a matter of finding a family who Lockett was friendly with, which wasn't hard, and then announcing that evidence had surfaced which demanded a search.

He wasn't sure how Lockett had done it, but he was convinced that the failure of the stoker to materialize was somehow related to his former private. So this time, he made certain that Lockett was out of the way.

It was the same plan as before, but this time with a more dependable accomplice. On top of it, Sergeant Philyaw came cheaper than the stoker, merely settling for the reward and nothing additional. Whether or not the man would want more in the long run was another question, but Long felt confident that he could control him.

The truth was that Sergeant Mick Philyaw would have done it for nothing. He was a man with a long memory when it came to those who had crossed him, and he wanted nothing more than to get rid of the pious officer. Men like Lockett were why this war wasn't over yet. A few good beatings and burned homes would go a long way in teaching these Southern traitors a lesson, but as long as men like James Lockett protected and coddled them, they would never be one country again. Philyaw would have helped Orrin Long rid the regiment of its affliction for free, but if Halleck's man was willing to pay him to do so, all the better.

"At half past then," Philyaw said, departing.

Orrin Long leered at the empty road. "This time, Lockett, you're trapped."

* * * * *

A pall of silence hung over Colonel Blair's room.

To Fulkerham and Williams, it was a hush of revelation.

For Renaud, it was an ominous quiet. The French Detroiter could not believe what he had just heard. The timing was far too convenient. The accusation could not be true. In fact, it stunk like a bald-faced lie.

Yet, the man presenting it was one of their own, a sergeant even. Renaud knew that Colonel Blair could not dismiss it out of hand, ridiculous as it was.

Sergeant Philyaw stood at attention before Blair's officers, fully aware that he had created the swirling, muted energy which dominated the room. Words, mere words, but he might as well have physically jostled the officers, such was their reaction.

Renaud's glare burrowed into Philyaw, but Philyaw was unfazed by the intense gaze, and that only fed the righteous anger building in Renaud's Gaulic veins. It was no coincidence that this was brought to Colonel Blair now, he thought. The sergeant had waited until Lockett had departed!

The room stayed deathly quiet, but the words still hung there, *"Reverend Tucker is the spy."*

Standing at perfect, albeit diminutive, attention, Sergeant Philyaw waited for Colonel Blair or one of the other officers to respond. He ran his tongue over his tobacco stained teeth, but he wasn't nervous.

To Renaud, Philyaw's face bore the look of a scavenger who had just stumbled across a meal.

"The Sergeant's testimony confirms what you suspected earlier, Colonel. If the preacher's sermons encourage Secession..." Orrin Long left the sentence unfinished, satisfied that gentle prodding was all that was needed.

"Shall I form a party to arrest the traitor?" Lieutenant Williams asked, clearly chomping at the bit to do so.

Colonel Blair said nothing. Calmly, he smoothed his sweeping mustache, trying to look contemplative. Like Renaud, Colonel Blair felt odd about the timing of the accusation.

But the accusation was coming from one of the regiment's men of responsibility. And everything that Williams had always reported of the sergeant was that he was utterly dependable, although the former banker thought Philyaw was the type of man who made tellers edge back from the barred window.

Philyaw claimed that he had overheard Reverend Tucker talking to an unknown man about the latest troops to pass by on the river. It seemed unlikely, Colonel Blair thought to himself. Over the past few weeks, he had come to view the country preacher in much the same light as Lockett. The man was harmless at worse, an amiable friend here in Savannah at best. He cursed himself for ever mentioning his one-time suspicion of the sermons to Captain Long. Comments in passing could prove damning, he now realized.

"Colonel?" Long prodded.

But it was Renaud who jumped into the lull, re-questioning the witness. "And 'ow did you say you 'eard Reverend Tucker telling zis 'man' about Illinois artillery passing by on ze river?"

"I was behind the church, sir!" Philyaw gave a stentorian answer that was unfit for such a small room. He stood stiffly, seemingly a model non-commissioned officer with his sharp salutes and strict attention to discipline.

Blair winced at the man's loud response. The voice was perfect for the openness of a parade ground, but in here, it made the walls vibrate. For a moment, he wondered what could possibly be Philyaw's angle. What was to be gained? Then, Colonel Blair remembered the reward. That damned reward was nothing but trouble, he thought with an invisible sigh.

He found himself doubting the story, but he had no concrete reason to dispute Philyaw's honesty.

"And what were you doing behind ze church, sar-jeant?" Renaud continued.

"In the trees relieving myself, sir!"

Blair pursed his lips and looked at Captain Long. There was something too smug on the washed face of Halleck's man. There was no surprise at the accusation. Indeed, he almost looked as if he had been expecting it.

But Laurent Blair also knew that he had little choice. The accusation could not be ignored. A search would need to be made of the church and the Tucker residence. Besides, Blair soothed himself, he couldn't imagine that they would find anything incriminating against the preacher. "Search the house and the church, Lieutenant."

* * * * *

Tommie Wexler watched Lockett and his Yankees tramp into sight. Deep in the forest, the thirteen year-old swatted at a fly that buzzed around his head. It was the only swatting that he figured he'd be doing today.

Twenty Yankees would be too many for Bloody Bill Coulter, especially since everyone in town knew that the Yankees were marching with loaded weapons again. When they had fought last time, the Yankees had started with unloaded weapons, and still they managed a draw. That fact vexed Tommie Wexler.

Why hadn't they wiped out the Yankees? Everybody knew that a good Southern boy was worth any three Yankees. Maybe it was really worth two, not three, Wexler daydreamed. He had missed the last ambush, and with dreams of grandeur, he lost himself for a moment.

After the brief diversion, he brought himself back to the present. If only they could lash out at Lockett and this little party. There wasn't much down this road, just the Brown's farm. Tommie didn't care much for the Browns. They had some hag ugly girls and dullards for boys, but he still wished for a fight against the Yankees. He would show them this time.

But he had overheard Coulter telling some of the older men that they would not fight unless the odds were in their favor, so Tommie Wexler contented himself with following Lockett. Maybe Lockett would break his men into two detachments. If he did that, then the odds might be good enough for an attack.

* * * * *

Renaud and Pope watched Lieutenant Williams's detachment of blue soldiers move towards the Tucker's small house.

"I don't like it, Enoch," Renaud said, turning to the thin officer. Pope gave an open-mouthed nod but said nothing, allowing the French Detroiter to continue. "It's too convenient zat James is away right now. Philyaw intentionally waited. I know it."

"Captain Long wouldn't be so smug if James was here either," Pope agreed. "I wish there was something we could do." His sallow face and thick lips pressed into a grimace.

"Is your 'orse fresh?" Renaud asked.   He knew that it was. "Put your sar-jeant in charge for ze time being and go find James. I'd feel better if 'e knew what was going on."

"Yes, sir," Pope answered. Technically, he was senior to the French Detroiter, but Enoch Pope was the type who preferred to receive orders.

"Best 'urry, in case Colonel Blair looks for you later."

"Uh, okay," Pope said, hesitating.

"Just go, Enoch."

"Okay," Pope said. He hurried off.

"Doesn't feel right," Renaud said to himself as he headed towards the Tucker house.

There was little in the way of explanation as the soldiers crowded into the small home.

"Where's the preacher?" Orrin Long asked Anna roughly. The reply that he was off serving a congregation east of here drew little more than a snort from the captain. He didn't really hear anything besides the fact that the preacher wasn't there.

"What is the meaning of this?" Anna asked, her pleasantness starting to give way in the face of the intrusion, but she received no answer from Captain Long or Lieutenant Williams.

Williams shouldered his way past her, leaving her startled as the soldiers broke into two groups to search the house. Williams took one section to one end, while Orrin Long took the other.

"What's going on?" she said to Renaud who was arriving in time to bring up the rear.

Renaud looked at the genuinely mystified gaze on her normally cheerful face. She was still calm, but he could sense her unease. The disturbed look on his own face probably didn't help. "Is all righ', Anna. Jus' a fool and 'is wild idea."

She looked blankly at him, and Renaud felt compelled to continue but only as he gently pulled her by the elbow. He needed to keep an eye on Orrin Long and his men. He now wished that he hadn't sent Enoch off. He could use another set of eyes to watch what Williams and the others were doing at the other end of house. "Is okay, Anna, becos zey're looking for something zat couldn't possibly be 'ere."

Long and his men stood in the crowded hallway. "This door is locked," he declared, turning on Anna with accusing eyes.

"It's my father's library," she replied innocently.

He gave a harsh laugh, sounding like an expectant coyote. "So? Open it."

She glanced reluctantly at Renaud, but he nodded reassuringly. Soon, five soldiers began to search the room under the supervision of Orrin Long.

"This is all preposterous," Anna remarked to Renaud as the soldiers fanned out across the library, "But I suppose that is what everyone says."

She watched with plain dismay as her father's private sanctuary lost its orderly precision. The neat pile of paper on the corner of the desk was scrambled and then discarded. The small bookshelf had its contents removed, shaken for loose items, and then put on the floor. Her father's precious copy of Milton's Paradise Lost was thrown recklessly over a shoulder after a short look. One soldier courteously replaced the item with an embarrassed look, but Sergeant Philyaw and two others took obvious pleasure in creating a mess. It bothered Renaud that the key witness of all this was an active member of the search party, but it seemed too late now to voice that objection.

"This drawer is locked," one of the privates reported.

"Open it," Long ordered Anna with another cold glare. His dark eyes flashed malevolently, and for a brief second, Anna began to feel the suffocating grip of fear around her throat. It was as if she was cornered in her own house by a predator. Maybe it helped that Renaud was standing next to her, but she shook off the feeling.

"There is nothing of yours in there," she replied tersely.

Long scowled. His upper lip curled contemptuously. Now, if only Renaud would leave them alone, he thought silently. Lockett's ally was a complication that he had not counted on. "Open the desk, or we break it open."

Reluctantly, Anna retrieved the key from beneath a Bible that had yet to be examined. She unlocked the drawer, and the soldier pulled the drawer open. Curiously, it was completely empty, not even a scrap of paper. Anna said nothing and stepped back beside Renaud.

The private looked up from the empty drawer with a quizzical look. Who would lock an empty drawer?

He slid it shut and then opened it again. This time he ran his fingers against the bottom of it and then gave a tap. It was hollow. "There's a false bottom," he remarked with surprise, removing the loose paneling.

Renaud could feel himself leaning forward slightly to see what was in the drawer.

"Ah, ha!" Long cried with expectant triumph. Perhaps, his insurance policy would not be needed after all!

The private removed two silver candlesticks from the drawer and held them out for the two officers to see. "Nuttin' else in there, sir."

"With two armies traipsing back 'n forth, you'll find a whole mess of folks hidin' their valuables," Anna said, giving Orrin Long an acid look.

"Put the candlesticks back, Private," Renaud said with some relief. For a moment, he had feared that Long had been right. "We're not here to look for family heirlooms."

Long said nothing, but his eyes did wander over to Sergeant Philyaw across the room. It was too bad that Philyaw had not been the one to find the false bottom, he thought to himself. That could have worked perfectly.

Philyaw blinked in acknowledgement. He was thinking the same thing.

But the look of recognition did not go unobserved.

Renaud saw it too, and it stirred his innate suspicion. There was something too familiar in the response. How did Philyaw know Long so well? Why would they look at each other?

Renaud's eyes followed while the sergeant went back to emptying out a small chest of drawers. Philyaw was a small, foul-mouthed man, but he always kept closely in line. Like many of the others, Philyaw paid more attention to his uniform than anything else. The buttons were always polished and tight all the way up to his neck. There was never a half-opened jacket, whatever the heat, but today, the top two buttons were undone.

While it was not unusual for Renaud's or Lockett's men to carry on with a button or two undone, it was never the case for one of Williams's or Fulkerham's, and Renaud stared curiously at the aberration.

And then he saw it. A fleck of white?

When Philyaw bent down to examine the lowest drawer, there was a fleck of white inside his jacket. It looked like... a piece of paper?

Why in God's name did Philyaw have a piece of paper tucked inside his shirt? Renaud wondered.

He took a few steps closer to the man, and then it hit him. Philyaw, the key witness, was going to plant evidence!

"Sar-jeant," Renaud said softly, now looming over the man.

"Sir?" There was annoyance on the man's weasel face.

"Come with me, Sar-jeant."

"Sir?" The annoyance faded into concern.

"Is there a problem?" Long intervened.

"No problem, Captain," Renaud said smoothly, "I just want to speak with ze sar-jeant for a moment."

"We are in the middle of a search right now, Lieutenant?"

"Please, sir, if I may 'ave a moment's indulgence." Renaud did his best to show proper deference and hide the scorn that he felt.

A scowl flashed on Long's face, but he didn't want a scene for no apparent reason. The little French Detroiter had no way of knowing what his accomplice was up to, he decided. "Very well, but be quick about it." He ignored the look of concern on Philyaw's face.

Alone on the front step of the house with Philyaw, the pleasant face that Renaud had sported for Orrin Long turned into one of menace. The French-Detroiters's dark features and heavy brow furrowed together.

"Let me see what is inside your jak-et, sar-jeant." It was said with a hard-edged, threatening voice that Philyaw had not seen from him before.

In the background, Renaud could see Colonel Blair and Lieutenant Fulkerham coming down the street, quickly walking towards them.

"Sir? I don't understand, sir." Philyaw stumbled on the words, stalling, praying that Captain Long would stick his head out the door.

"I said, let me see what you 'ave in zere." The glare from Renaud froze Philyaw. "If you make me remove it myself..."

"Nothing, sir."

"I know zis came from Captain Long. I can see ze paper!" Renaud declared, his voice rising and stepping closer. He pulled on Philyaw's unbuttoned collar, plainly revealing the piece of paper.

"No, sir," Philyaw maintained, but he didn't sound so sure of himself now. "It's only some paper I snaffled for the latrine. The Reverend'll never miss it. He's got enough paper in there to outfit a regiment."

"I swear to God, sar-jeant, if you make me take it out, I'll 'ave your 'ide whipped raw."

Slowly, Philyaw pulled the rumpled and sweat glazed parchment from his jacket. It was small, like a piece of personal stationery. Renaud's out-stretched hand had nearly taken possession of it when Colonel Blair's call froze both men.

Philyaw drew his hand back as Renaud looked away.

"Lieutenant!" Colonel Blair repeated.

"Hold on, sar-jeant," Renaud growled. Colonel Blair was now waving him over. "You stand right zere 'til I come back."

Philyaw held the paper tightly in his hand while Renaud jogged over to Colonel Blair, looking back once to make sure that Philyaw didn't move.

"Captain Long's search will have to wait for later," Colonel Blair began, not noticing that in the background, Sergeant Philyaw made a quarter turn so that his back was to the two officers.

Quickly, Philyaw crumbled up the small piece of paper and jammed it into his mouth where his stained teeth worked it over.

"They captured another courier south of here," Colonel Blair informed Renaud. "And he says he was to retrieve something from our spy *this very night* at someplace called Yoder's Corners. Lieutenant Fulkerham has already organized twenty men and taken the horses from the baggage train. We leave immediately to lay a trap for this devil!"

"Yes, sir."

"Inform Captain Long. No doubt he will want to accompany us. I leave you in command of the camp, Renaud."

"Yes, sir," he answered.

Events had swung very quickly. Perhaps, today would be the day they would capture this spy after all.

* * * * *

Lockett's men collapsed wearily in the grass beneath the trees. The shade made little difference. The day's smothering heat meant that his men were drenched in sweat again. He knew he was marching them hard today, and he tried to tell himself that it was for their own good. But despite his best efforts, he had to admit that the pace had more to do with his own impatience and frustration.

He could hear their grumbling. He could always hear their grumbling. Usually, it was only half-serious as his men took pride in their efforts.

But today, there was some earnest dissatisfaction with the patrol. It was hot, and he didn't blame them for bellyaching. He reassured himself by reflecting that he was sweaty and dusty too. Unlike the other officers, he marched on foot with them, not riding along on horseback. He would bear the same burden as they. Still, it was not much of a salve for his conscience.

"Wild goose chase again," McManus commented casually as he idled up to him. "Another Orrin special."

They had departed in a hurry, because Long had convinced Colonel Blair of the necessity of this patrol, saying there was evidence against the Brown family. Supposedly, the bushwhackers were using the farmhouse for shelter from time to time. Hearsay evidence to be sure, but such was the case that every wild rumor must be investigated.

Naturally, they had found nothing at the Brown's farm, no evidence, only indignation. The men had behaved, but it was impossible for them not to draw the civilians' hatred. By definition, they were intruders in someone's home.

His men disliked these missions and so did he. He looked at his old friend with a sad nod. "Another wild goose chase is right, Patrick. These damn fool rumors..." he added with frustration.

"Always a waste of time," Bosworth agreed, as he joined them.

They had talked often about it, gone over it a hundred times since Orrin's arrival. Spy or bushwhacker, it made no difference to the outcome.

"We'll never catch bushwhackers or a spy like this. It's jus' like Missouri all over again. We need horses if we're going to do this right." McManus wiped a hand across his reddened face.

"We can still catch the spy like this," Bosworth offered, "But we'll have to be lucky."

"Maybe," McManus answered, "But luck always seems to be against the man who depends on it. Even if we catch'm, it's the spy in Corinth they need to catch. What's the use of catching a spy reporting on troop movements up in Savannah when there's one down in Corinth reporting on Halleck's actual plans? If what you said about those documents is true, James, then what's the point of this anyhow?"

Lockett frowned. He wanted silence and time to think. He didn't feel like going through this again.

"What do you think, sir?" Bosworth asked, trying to draw him in.

Lockett relented with a shrug. "You're right. We all know it. Colonel Blair knows it. Everyone but Halleck knows it."

"I'm still not even sure what we are looking for when we do these," Bosworth added.

"A sworn statement declaring them the spy?" McManus chuckled. "Maybe an original copy of what Major Axford showed the officers?"

"That would be something, Patrick. You should have seen this translated dispatch, the one that Major Axford showed us... Amazing detail." He shook his head at the thought. "All of Halleck's brigade dispositions, laid out in detail, Patrick, right there on the paper. Only Heaven knows how this spy got so much information. It even listed off some of the units. I still can't believe that one of them was our old Kalamazoo Sharpshooters. From the sounds of it, they were in some light skirmishing with Rebs west of Corinth. I guess that Captain Vincent must be rounding them into shape."

"More'n likely it's old VanderJagt who's roundin' the lads into shape, not the Captain."

Lockett gave a small nod and grin. He missed the old sergeant. The veteran of the war with Mexico had taught them a lot.

"Sounds like that dispatch is all the Rebs would ever need to know," Bosworth chipped in.

"All that was missing was exactly which day Halleck would decide to attack."

"Mebbe, but with the speed that old Halleck is moving, who needs a spy? The Rebs can figure it out for themselves."

Lockett snorted at the comment and looked at the farmer's field across the pasture. If they didn't get some rain soon, there would be no crop, he thought to himself. It was early, but these fields needed some water. He could empathize with that.

For a moment, his mind left Tennessee, 1862, and he was back in Kalamazoo, 1857. His father had been dead and buried just over a year, and a rare dry summer was threatening the crop. It was more than a boy should have needed to bear, the responsibility for the survival of a family. They *were* dirt poor farmers as Katherine Moffat had angrily pointed out once.

He reflected on his last meeting with Katherine, remembering the dawn's glow behind her and the look in her eyes before Milton had interrupted them. She was a difficult girl to make sense of to be sure, but he was glad that they seemed to have moved past this nonsense about Anna and the letters.

Maybe he had been too hard on Katherine. The strain of all this was surely enough to crack most. Maybe he should have had less of a reaction to her initial statement. People needed to blow off steam in different ways. If anything, maybe he should have directed more ire towards Orrin since he was, in a way, responsible for their disagreement. They were his letters after all…

"Rider coming, sir," McManus straightened suddenly, pointing into the distance.

Instinctively, Lockett's hand reached for his rifle. Bushwhacker?

But as he looked up, he saw a blue coat and watched with surprise as Enoch Pope reined in his horse.

* * * * *

"Take my horse, James. I can bring the men back," Pope added. His normal blank appearance was given an unusual look of urgency by the dust that caked his face. There was even the glimmer of excitement in his normally dull eyes.

Enoch Pope also sensed foul play.

And while he hadn't liked James Lockett at first, the young farmer had been distant towards him initially and eager to assume responsibility, Pope had since come to appreciate that it was just the Michigander's way. There was no ego about James Lockett, at least not a harmful one.

Pope knew that he himself was not a very good officer. He didn't like the responsibility and sometimes his men took advantage of that. He also was not the type to assume control of a situation, which he knew a good officer should do. He guessed that the rest of the officers saw these short-comings too, and probably sometimes delighted in them, but Lockett wasn't one of those. Lockett treated him with respect whether he deserved it or not. So it pleased Enoch Pope that he could do a little something for Lockett in return.

But Lockett shook his head at the offer. "Not necessary, Enoch. We'll get back when we get back."

"You're sure?"

Lockett nodded in response, hiding his true concern. As he had listened to Pope relate the recent events in Savannah, he had felt a chill settle into his bones and did his best to let that gray-eyed mask fall into place.

Naturally, he knew better than anyone else what treachery Orrin was capable of. The fear for Anna and her father was real, but rushing back would only look worse for all of them in the colonel's eyes. His men were on patrol. It would be like abandoning his post for personal reasons. That would be how the colonel would see it.

"Well, okay," Pope answered uncertainly.

"I can't do anything more. My sudden presence would only make more trouble. Besides, how would it look to Colonel Blair if I abandoned my men and went racing back to Savannah?"

Pope nodded his sallow, long-nosed face. "Yes, I suppose that could be true." He paused. "As long as you are sure."

"I'm sure," Lockett replied, looking earnestly at Pope, "But I thank all you the same. I know you didn't have to ride out here."

Pope smiled in pleasure, "That's what friends are for, James."

Lockett pivoted, ready to order Bosworth to round up the men for the march back. He would not take Pope's horse and rush back, but he could speed this march up. Except that when he turned, he found to his surprise that Bosworth had read his mind.

The men were already formed on the narrow little road.

* * * * *

Whether the march back actually lacked the normal soldierly chatter, or if it was just that his mind was elsewhere, Lockett would never know. What he did know was that he heard nothing at all as his brain spun round and round.

Anna and her father were now Orrin's target, and the guilt weighed heavily on him. The Tuckers had done nothing to bring this on themselves! Had they never known him, this never would have happened to them!

Lockett ground his teeth. Anyone he came in contact with seemed to suffer, and not just because of Orrin. Even before this, Anna Tucker had faced the contempt of Katherine Moffat. Patrick's wife had died. His own father had died. Little Amelia had been killed. He was a curse!

He wanted to believe that Orrin's latest attempt would fail. It was too ridiculous to consider, but he knew that Orrin would try again, and the Tuckers were certain to be the target. Orrin had found a soft spot.

Orrin and General Halleck were trying to turn Tennessee into Missouri, and for what? To find a spy reporting on ship traffic? How about the greater problem of finding the spy reporting on Halleck's own plans?

"You all right, James?" McManus whispered from next to him as they marched along.

The scowl remained etched in Lockett's face. He knew such vitriol was useless, but he was impotent to stop it. Why couldn't Orrin just let old grudges go like Katherine had?

McManus's words were a mere buzzing in Lockett's ears as he continued to churn uselessly.

The biting sense of lack of control burned him. He wanted to run all the way back to Savannah. He would throttle Orrin this time, and this time, he wouldn't let go!

This was going to be an interminable march back, like when the Kalamazoo Sharpshooters had trudged back from their disastrous first skirmish in Hallsville, Missouri.

"Kalamazoo?" Lockett whispered as he stopped in his tracks. "Kalamazoo?"

The thought struck him as if he had just run around a corner and smacked into a closed door.

The column marched by.

"Kalamazoo Sharpshooters?" he murmured to himself.

His heart was pounding. The cloud that had hovered in his mind suddenly parted. Like a stage curtain being drawn, James Lockett suddenly saw something new, something that seemed unreal but was impossible to ignore.

"My God!" he mumbled silently, as the life drained out of him.

He flashed back to Axford's captured dispatch. The translated words now stood out on the page, as if in flaming red. The dispatch said *Kalamazoo* Sharpshooters!

The dispatch called them by their old name! His old company had ceased to be known as that to the rest of the army months ago. While the current and former men of the unit still preferred to call themselves by that old name, the rest of the army knew them now as one small part of Birge's Western Sharpshooters!

How could that dispatch use their old name when no one used that name anymore? How was it that a dispatch could single out the Kalamazoo Sharpshooters? It should have said Birge's Western Sharpshooters!

There was only one reason that he could think of.

"It can't be," he said to himself. But he knew that it was.

254

The Kalamazoo Sharpshooters! Surely, that was how one Kalamazooan would describe it to another. That was how Orrin would have described them to Katherine!

There was not a second spy in Halleck's headquarters making detailed observations. The spy was here in Savannah!

God in Heaven, there *was* a reason for someone to read Katherine's letters!

His throat tightened. Seconds ago, he had felt nothing but guilt about Orrin's accusation against the Tuckers, but now...

Now, he felt the intense pain of betrayal!

For a childlike moment, he wished that he could pull the thought back, but he knew that he was not wrong. There were not two spies, one in Corinth and one in Savannah. *It was one spy, and it was Anna Tucker!*

Chapter 17

Renaud watched Lockett's patrol return. They were moving quickly, and he wondered what he would say to Lockett. Despite his caution of never letting Philyaw out of his sight for more than a second, the piece of paper had disappeared, and with it, any evidence of Orrin Long's treachery. He suspected that Philyaw had eaten it while Colonel Blair had addressed him, and in that flash, Renaud had lost the proof that he needed, that Lockett needed, that the Tuckers needed.

He had searched the area thoroughly and even had the obstinate Philyaw strip down, but the piece of paper was nowhere to be found. And Philyaw was proving an intractable and fearless liar about the whole episode.

* * * * *

The men had marched quickly back to Savannah, but to Lockett, lost in his private agony, it had been an eternity. The anger closed off cogent thought, and the despair drained him of all energy. Still, he wanted to see her face.

How could those endearing dimples and bright eyes have done this to him? He had been played for a fool! Oh God, how stupid he had been!

He knew nothing of women, and he should have realized that in this war, little was ever as it seemed. One never knew which way was up, which way was down, who was a friend, who was a foe.

What a fool! He should have known better!

With his men dismissed, he tried to listen to Renaud, but the French Detroiter was speaking so quickly that he had trouble understanding him, not to mention that all he could see was the Tucker house looming in the distance.

"… setting a trap now at Yoder's Corners." Renaud paused to catch his breath.

"James, 'ave you 'eard what I said? Do you understand me? Long was going to 'ave Philyaw plant evidence inside ze Reverend's 'ouse!"

Lockett nodded, but Renaud still wasn't sure if he understood. "James?" he added with some exasperation.

"Where's the paper now?" Lockett asked, his eyes still on the little parsonage.

"Zat bastard must've ate it while I was saluting Colonel Blair, becos when I got back, it was gone. 'ad 'im strip down and still couldn't find it! If ever zere was a born liar, it's Sar-jeant Philyaw!"

"Lots of born liars," Lockett answered in an ominous voice.

"'ow do we prove Philyaw to Colonel Blair? I can report it to ze colonel first thing upon zer return?"

"You won't get anywhere without proof. Your word might carry the day against someone like Philyaw, but you'll get nowhere against Orrin Long without hard proof. All you would do is elevate yourself on Orrin's list of enemies, and that'll do you no good."

"But what are you saying? Drop it?"

"That's exactly what I'm saying. Remember it, but leave it to me. I appreciate what you tried to do but don't expose yourself more. You leave this to me. This is between Orrin and me. Now, I have something that I need to take care of. Excuse me."

Lockett's jaw clamped shut, and he blew out a long breath through his nose as he walked toward the house.

The long-legged stride became ever more brisk with each step, but his mind was moving even faster. At a stone's throw from the house, Anna Tucker appeared on the front stoop. Immediately, his feet grew heavy over those final steps.

"James? Are you all right?" she said with concern, seeing the lost look on his face.

He forced himself to move the final two steps. "I suppose, I should be the one to ask you that."

"I told Lieu-ten-ant Renaud that it wasn't necessary to find you," she said, ushering him into the house. The parlor looked in order now, but he could see the study door open and the mess of books and papers still to be cleaned up. "He's such a fine gentleman, not like that Captain Long."

"You're unhurt?" Absently, he looked away from her and at the study again.

"Yes," she answered, somewhat perturbed by his odd demeanor.

"They checked your father's study, I see."

"They checked nearly the whole house."

"And the bedroom?" he asked, walking down the hall.

"The bedroom? No?" she replied, lurching in surprise to follow him. "They left when the colonel appeared, although I don't know why they left so suddenly. I assume Colonel Blair finally talked some sense into them."

When Lockett ignored her, she added with confusion, "James? Where are you going?"

He stopped at the edge of the bedroom. In the corner, he could see a tiny chest of drawers. One of the colorful combs that Katherine sometimes used in her hair was on top of it. It caught his eye, and he stopped to stare at it.

"James?" Anna queried again, stepping around him to place herself between him and the beckoning room.

But he did not answer.

He looked over her head at the chest of drawers. "Did they go through Katherine's belongings?" he asked.

"Katherine's?" she replied with confusion. "I already told you that they did not come into the bedroom."

The bewilderment sounded genuine. Could he be wrong about her?

He brushed past her and pulled out the top drawer. Just as Katherine had described, there was the pile of letters.

Anna grew quiet instantly.

Picking up the top letter, he quickly skimmed it.

He wanted to be wrong, but he could think of only one reason that the sharpshooters had been described so specifically as the Kalamazoo Sharpshooters. Few knew that name anymore. Was it in the letter to Katherine?

He didn't see the word in this particular letter, but there were many letters in the pile.

Gently, he laid the envelope back down, careful to place it face up.

"So they never found the letters, Anna?" He craned his head around with a slow deliberateness.

She gave no answer to his question, and his gaze hardened. Still, there was no reaction, just an innocent look.

But he knew now not to be surprised. He knew now that Anna Tucker was a very, very good actress.

"They never found the letters," he explained aloud. "Never discovered that all the information a spy would ever want was conveniently spelled out in the letters from a staff officer to his girl? No, they would never figure that out, but you did."

He paused, wanting to see some reaction, even a look of satisfaction on her face. Her cleverness had finally been recognized.

Yet, Anna still gave no reaction. Her features were steady as she returned his hard gaze. No denial. No agreement.

"And I wondered how many congregations your father was serving with all those trips of his! How perfect could it be for you, Anna? All the information laid out for you and an inconspicuous means of travel."

He grimaced.

"And one damn *fool*," he fairly shouted the last word, "Of a soldier who could give you just enough protection from prying suspicions!"

Fool. The caustic word resounded within the walls of the tiny bedroom.

Finally, her face softened, "We never meant to hurt you, James."

He could feel himself blushing, both from embarrassment and anger. He had been such a God-damned fool!

"Please, James, can't we..."

He had prayed that his suspicions were wrong, but the Tuckers were the spies, and now Reverend Tucker was riding towards a trap that Colonel Blair was setting.

"Where's your father?" he asked harshly.

"What?"

He closed his eyes and started to walk past her, but she did not move and blocked his path.

"Never mind. I know where your father is." He skirted past her, his steps sounding strangely loud down the hallway.

Her father was walking straight into a trap. How could this be happening! Everything he had worked for, fought for, and, most of all, hoped for was slipping through his fingers.

"Where are you going, James?"

"Yoder's Corners," he said with determination, "To save your father."

"Yoder's Corners? How do you know about Yoder's Corners?"

"That's why they broke off the search, Anna. They're setting a trap for him."

Chapter 18

Thunderbolt trotted down the road, sensing his rider's indecision. Lockett knew he had been deceived, and he wanted to wallow in the self-pity, just like he had when his father had died.

But he forced his mind forward. This was no time to think about what could have been. This was a time to think about the present.

On impulse, he looked behind him. For a second, there was another rider, but in a blink, the vision was gone. It felt like someone was watching him, but he shook his head to clear the paranoia. There were enough real problems to worry about without inventing phantoms.

He knew what would happen to him when Colonel Blair and the others captured Reverend Tucker. With Orrin so close at hand, there was no doubt that he would find a way to force the guilt of the Tuckers onto him. Lockett knew he would not be able to defend himself from the landslide of circumstantial evidence. After all of the time that he had spent with the Tuckers and his own checkered past, there would be no defense. He would be branded a traitor, lose his precious commission, and then most likely, they would hang him next to the preacher.

No, there was only one thing to do — stop Orrin from proving the Tuckers' guilt.

And the only way to do that was to prevent Reverend Tucker from being captured or killed at Yoder's Corners.

Lockett wasn't sure how he would do it, was hardly even sure where Yoder's Corners was, but he had to try. He looked behind him again, and this time there was no mistaking the presence of another rider. With her dress flapping behind her in the wind, Anna Tucker quickly closed the gap.

"What are you doing here?" he snapped when she reached him, slowing her horse into a trot alongside his.

"I'm comin' with you. If you're going to get to my father in time, you'll need to know the shortcuts to Yoder's."

With that, she turned off the road. After a moment's hesitation, Lockett nudged Thunderbolt to follow her. Through wide pastures and narrow deer trails, they raced as fast as the terrain would allow.

He never would have found his way without her. And despite the fact that he rode Thunderbolt, he found himself struggling to keep up. She was surely her father's daughter, riding with ease and confidence, like an old cavalryman.

After an hour and a half, she reined in and looked him square in the eye. The wind had blown her curly brown hair back behind her face, which glowed crimson with excitement and exertion. She had never looked more beautiful to him than she did at that moment, but her beauty just made his anger all the more palpable.

"You're sure that you want to do this?" she asked skeptically, looking at his scowl.

He wasn't sure if the question related to concern for him, or just confusion about why a loyal Yankee soldier was on his way to save a Rebel spy. He looked back at her unflinchingly.

"You mean rescue your father?"

"I mean help a Rebel," she said bluntly.

"Help a traitor?" His face was a mix of determination and resignation, "I'm here, aren't I?" It wasn't much of an answer, but it didn't seem like he had much choice if he wanted to save his own skin.

"Are you doing this for me?"

So beautiful, he sighed. He had trusted her. He had felt a closeness to her that he had never felt before. He wanted to laugh aloud at her question. She had betrayed him, used him!

The bitterness boiled. Should he laugh aloud at this?

But he couldn't laugh, couldn't show the contempt that would have been natural. He had fallen in love with her, he realized.

Instead, he asked himself the same question. Was he doing this for her, or for him? For his neck? He wasn't sure.

His only response was a confused shrug.

Perhaps it did not matter. It seemed like he had long since lost the ability to dictate his own fate.

"We never meant to hurt you, James."

She said it with complete sincerity, a look of hurt in her eyes. He wanted to believe her, but what was to be believed anymore?

"I never intended it to work out this way."

"You would just play me along until the war was over? Then what?"

She bit her lip and shrugged. "I don't know. I don't know what I was doing."

"We don't have time for this now, Anna," he frowned. "Is that the hollow where your father intends to leave his message?"

She nodded. "Through there."

"Stay here," he ordered, "If they so much as *see* any of our faces, we are all finished."

And that was the problem, Lockett knew. Not only did he need to stop them from killing Reverend Tucker, he had to get to the preacher before his face was seen, and all without Lockett's own identity being revealed.

He dismounted and led Thunderbolt by the reins. He wished he could do without the large horse, but he feared the need for a speedy escape. At least Thunderbolt was quiet. The animal seemed to sense what was needed.

They disappeared from Anna's sight, following a deer trail down into the hollow through a clump of trees and into a dense thicket. It was thick growth and reminded him of the heavy foliage surrounding the Sunken Road at Shiloh.

At Shiloh, the growth had broken the cohesion of the Confederate lines before the Rebels had even been fired upon.

The growth was his friend again, but this time it was because it shielded him from sight.

He decided he had gone as far as he could with Thunderbolt and looped the animal's reins around a tree limb. He removed his scabbard and hung it from the saddle horn. He didn't need any encumberment or clumsy clanging now. With his rifle in one hand, he crept deeper into the growth.

Where would the trap be? Yoder's Corners was a larger area than he had envisioned.

He suspected that Colonel Blair and the others also had not expected such a wide area to cover. Where would they wait? Or would they search the woods actively? Split up and find the spy?

It was difficult to say how Colonel Blair would approach it. Would the presence of Orrin Long affect Colonel Blair's thinking? Maybe the presence of a staff officer would make him more aggressive, maybe they would sweep the area rather than lying in wait? In some ways, Lockett hoped so, because he felt confident that he would hear them before they could hear him.

Caution slowed him. He couldn't afford to make any noise as he crept deeper into the woods. He could be walking into an ambush at any moment, but by the same standard, time was of the essence. He had to find Reverend Tucker quickly.

The woods were quiet, save the soft rustling of the leaves in the tree tops. The shelter of the forest prevented any wind from reaching him, and he could feel the beads of sweat slowly dripping from his temples. He carefully stepped around a section of dead leaves and listened. There was still nothing.

It seemed that he was the only person here, but his heart was beating heavily because he knew that there were others out there, somewhere. He skirted an open patch and went between some tangled bushes.

There!

He stopped dead in his tracks. In front of him, he saw both his last hope and his greatest fear, one on the left and one on the right.

To his left, Reverend Tucker rode his horse slowly through the narrow opening between the trees, screened by a tight cluster of young pines. He could not see what Lockett saw — a blue coated soldier crouching behind a tree, patiently waiting for the soft beat of the hooves to come into the clearing.

Lockett took a quick breath. He recognized the soldier as one of the men who had chased the greased pig with Milton Bosworth. That day seemed so long ago now. Private Nelson was his name, he vaguely remembered.

He was running out of time!

In a second, it would be too late. Reverend Tucker would reach the end of the pines that separated him from Nelson, and even if Nelson was to miss the shot, he would be sure to see the preacher's face.

Lockett gritted his teeth and raised his own rifle. Private Nelson had never done him any harm and was doing exactly what he had been ordered to do.

But for Lockett, there was only one thing left to do.

Automatically, he leveled the rifle against his shoulder and looked down the long barrel. Gently thumbing back the hammer, his eyes traced over the nub at the end of the weapon. He focused in on Nelson's chest.

Concentration came with difficulty as his finger slowly closed around the trigger. The sweat poured off his forehead, running into his eyes. He blinked. Time was running out... running out fast!

He focused again on Nelson's chest. If the man had been wearing butternut or gray instead of blue, he would be dead already, but all James Lockett could see was the blue, the same blue as his uniform, the blue that was pouring out its blood.

Nelson tensed, sensing that his prey was nearly in sight.

Lockett's face contorted in concentration, and he tried to focus his shooting eye along the barrel once more...

But he couldn't do it!

He closed his eyes and tilted his head back in resignation. He couldn't do it.

He couldn't shoot his own, even if it meant his own life. It was over.

Lockett lowered the rifle an inch and watched Nelson thumb back the hammer on his own weapon. Then another blue coat materialized next to Nelson. He had been blocked from Lockett's vision by Private Nelson and the tree.

There were two of them!

And Lockett found himself doubly relieved now that he had not killed innocent Private Nelson. It all would have been in vain anyway.

But then his eye glimpsed something else. His heart skipped a beat as his brain seized upon an idea.

In the crook of the tree, ten feet above Nelson and his comrade, there was a bee hive, a very large nest. Without a second thought, Lockett steadied his rifle and fired with no time to spare.

Surprise registered on Nelson's face at the sound. His comrade shuddered sharply, causing Nelson to think that his friend had been shot. But then something dropped on Nelson's shoulder, and he looked curiously at what had fallen.

"What's..." his friend began in a befuddled voice. The voice was drowned out by a growing roar.

Lockett's shot had been clean through the middle of the hive. The large caliber shot exploded it and sent large chunks downward. Even from where he stood, the irate buzzing sounded impossibly loud, but Lockett didn't bother to watch the swarm erupt from their home and dive down on Private Nelson and his comrade.

He never heard their yelling as the two soldiers ran pell mell through the woods, because Lockett was already on his way to grab Reverend Tucker.

The preacher had stopped in his tracks at the very edge of the pine screen. The rifle shot did not seem to be aimed at him, and he peered futilely into the pine boughs. Behind him, Lockett blew a quick whistle, and the preacher turned around in the saddle. With a wide arm, Lockett motioned the astonished preacher to follow him.

Reverend Tucker pulled on the reins, and satisfied that the preacher was following him, Lockett took off in a sprint back to gather Thunderbolt.

This was no time for caution, and he ran like a madman through the woods. He could hear shouts behind him. He had stirred up a hornet's nest, literally and figuratively. The tree branches slapped across his face, and he stumbled over roots, but he did not slow.

He leapt over a trickling creek and a fallen oak in a single bound. His heart was pounding, but he did not feel tired in the least. He was fueled by the overwhelming hope that he still might be able to pull this off.

Finally, the majestic form of Thunderbolt appeared ahead. Lockett unlooped the reins, grabbed the scabbard that was still hanging from his saddle horn, and swung himself into the saddle.

"What's going on?" Reverend Tucker asked, reining in just as Lockett pulled himself up.

"A trap!" he answered, turning Thunderbolt around, "Come on! Before they see us! Anna is back here!"

They picked their way through the growth as fast as their mounts would allow. At every moment, he was terrified that he would see a blue-coated man pop up from the growth and spot them, but it never happened, and he found Anna just where he had left her.

With his face damp with perspiration, gray eyes glinting with determination, and a hard-set face, he looked all business as he reined in next to her.

"I heard a shot," she said anxiously. She started to lean toward him, as if she intended to hug him. He ignored her.

"Come on!" he said sharply, "We're not done yet and neither are they. We still have to get out of here!"

"That is the easy part, my boy!" Reverend Tucker grinned as if he was enjoying himself. "Follow me!"

They traversed the woods through a series of deer paths and creeks, once crossing frantically over a road, but there was no one with them except for their shadows. Lockett was amazed at the man's knowledge of the trails and woods. He was not unlike a bushwhacker, Lockett mused. Reverend Tucker knew this land like he knew his own hand.

Lockett couldn't believe it, but it looked as if they had escaped.

Chapter 19

The cross-country jaunt ended an hour later, and they paralleled the Tennessee River. It was the long way back to Savannah, but they were safe and decided it was time to water the horses.

Reverend Tucker had been riding with an ease and grace that Lockett could only imagine, but the aging preacher stiffly pulled himself from the saddle. "Too old for this," he moaned as he balanced himself with his cane and stretched skyward.

Lockett gave no reply and let Anna take the three horses back through the trees to the water, leaving him alone with her father.

The older man smiled. "Now, ya know, ya wouldn't be such a bad rider, son, if ya jus' relaxed a little in the saddle. Don't make it too much work."

"Yes, sir," Lockett answered. The instinctive response amused the reverend, and it irritated Lockett. Sir? He thought to himself. This was no *'sir'*. This was a Rebel and a spy at that!

"Now, y'all mind tellin' me what in tarnation is going on?"

That question had multiple meanings, but Lockett choose the simplest interpretation. "They captured your courier. Colonel Blair, Fulkerham, Long, and about twenty men were waiting for you."

"Twenty men? They marched to Yoder's Corners?"

"They borrowed the wagon train horses."

"Those flea-bitten bags? Hah!" he said, "We could've walked out of there, even with my ol' leg." Then, he turned serious. "So, they were waiting for me?"

269

"For the spy," Lockett corrected, "They still don't know it's you… and Anna." He left unsaid that Orrin Long was out to frame the old man.

"But you do? You knew?"

"I finally figured it out." The words left a bitter aftertaste in his mouth and after a long pause, he added, "Unfortunately."

The reverend nodded thoughtfully, his face full of fatherly concern. "Never meant for it to work out this way, L'tenant."

It was said in such an amicable and unassuming way that it only further irritated Lockett. Didn't the man realize the gravity of what he had done?

"You're a spy, Reverend!" he blurted out. "A Rebel and a dishonest one at that!" He could feel the anger working up in him. "You're supposed to be a man of God! Why? How can you lie like you did?"

"We'll never see eye to eye on this, L'tenant. Should I even bother to explain my motivations?"

"Damn it all!"

The reality and finality of everything was sinking in. For the first time in his life, Lockett had found himself getting comfortable, and all of that was smashed now. He had never courted anyone before. There had never been time, nor interest really, but Anna Tucker had been different. She was full of the sun's brightness and energy. He had come to hunger that everyday and had even allowed himself the sin of thinking about what life would be like after the war.

He had never contemplated losing her, certainly not like this. And not only had he lost her, *he had betrayed everything he believed in!* He had helped Rebels escape and nearly shot one of his own in doing so!

There was an unmistakable irony to all this, he knew. In Missouri, he had been accused of a cold-blooded murder that he did not really commit. Then in Tennessee, he had been accused of cowardice when all he had shown was courage. But now… Now, he *was* guilty! He had helped traitors escape, and no one knew it… yet.

"What now, L'tenant?" Tucker asked.

"What now!" he snapped back. Lockett glared at the man for a moment, and then he shook his head with resignation. "I don't want you to be found out, sir, either of you, but I can't let you stay in Savannah and keep spying on us."

"Wouldn't matter much now, son. Our best information came from Orrin Long's letters, and now that he is here in Savannah, there's no more letters. I s'pose, we're victims of our own success." He began to chuckle then stopped since there was no humor on the soldier's face. "Leave town?"

"Leave town."

"I s'pose we can go to Murfreesboro. We have people there, my sister."

"It's more than you deserve," Lockett said bitterly.

"I s'pose if I was in your shoes, L'tenant, I would find that a fair statement."

"Ambrose was never pressed into service, was he?"

"My son? No, it was all part of the disguise. He wanted to volunteer outright. He made it look such as he did to make it safer for Anna and me."

There was silence while Lockett looked off into the empty woods.

"And what about Anna?" Reverend Tucker asked eventually.

Lockett did not shift his gaze. "What about her?"

"She never meant to harm you, son. Neither of us ever did. She's quite taken with you, Yankee and all."

"Obviously not enough to stop her from lying to me."

"By the time she realized it, it was too late, L'tenant. I can see the hurt on my daughter's face so clearly. Your forgiveness would mean everything to her."

"Forgiveness! You both turned me into a traitor!"

Reverend Tucker ignored the outburst. "She never meant to fall in love with you, L'tenant, but she did."

Lockett wanted to react angrily, with some sort of cry of derision. Loved him? She had betrayed him!

She had turned him into something that he would not have thought possible! Katherine Moffat had been right! Anna was not to be trusted. He wanted to react accordingly... but... but... but he couldn't.

All he could do was lower his eyes and wonder how it was that he could be so confused.

He was a traitor himself now.

Chapter 20

"Came this way, sir," the private reported to Lieutenant Fulkerham and Captain Long.

There were ten of them picking their way through the Tennessee thickets, hot on the trail of the spy. While Colonel Blair and the others had returned to Savannah and were probably already there by now, this party was doggedly on the trail of the spies.

They splashed across a small creek, and the ex-West Pointer noticed the large number of hoof prints in the mud on the creek bank. "Looks like some others have joined up, sir," the private reported, echoing Fulkerham's own thoughts.

"How many?" Orrin Long said warily.

"Five to ten more, sir," the private estimated.

Tyler Fulkerham looked curiously at Captain Long. What if Lockett had not been lying? What if Long really was a coward who ran at the first shot of battle? If ten bushwhackers had joined up with the spy, then his little detachment might be out-numbered now. Tyler Fulkerham did not like the idea of chasing a party like that with a commanding officer who was a coward.

* * * * *

"Y'all need to talk," the preacher said with a paternal tone, taking the horses' reins from Anna. Leaning heavily on his cane, the gray-haired preacher trudged off, leaving the two of them in an uncomfortable silence.

273

Neither could utter a word, and Anna eventually sat on a fallen tree and looked at the ground. She knew there was nothing she could say to make it better. She had always prevented herself from thinking about this day, even though she knew it would come.

Lockett absently watched a crow fly in and land in the treetops. The sun was on its downhill slide. There would only be a couple more hours of daylight. They sat there, wordless for what seemed an eternity.

"We better get on the move again," he said finally, turning to look at her. "If…" He never finished his sentence and flinched at the sight of tears on her face.

"If only I could go back in time…" But she was not capable of finishing the sentence.

A wave of pity, regret, and some other emotion that he didn't recognize swept over him.

Anna Tucker had always been so strong. He had never seen her like this. She was the one who labored with Doc McClutcheon in field hospital. No task was too overwhelming for her. The smells, the sounds, the sights, she had maintained that energy through all of them. She did her tasks with a smile and optimistic energy that carried those men from one day to the next. No hurdle was too great.

But this was not the same Anna Tucker. This Anna Tucker looked frail and vulnerable. Before he could stop himself, he went to her side and put his arms around her. "It's all right, Anna," he soothed, though he did not know what the words really meant.

She was soft and warm and eased into his embrace, burying her face in his shoulder. The long brown curls obscured her face and dangled down his side.

There was more that he wanted to say, but he couldn't bring himself to it. The past was past, and the future… Well, there was no denying that there was no future anymore. Despite his pounding heart, he couldn't utter any words to change that unalterable fact.

"If I had known you would come into my life, I never would have started," she lamented. "Why couldn't I have been born in Kalamazoo?"

"If you had, you wouldn't know the person that I am now," he said, stroking her hair. "You would have looked past me like most people. Just another poor farm boy, scratching in the dirt."

"No," she maintained, "I would have seen the real you. I could never look past you."

He held her tighter and took a deep breath before forcing out the words. "It was not to be, Anna." She squeezed him tighter, but the verbal response came from the trees beyond.

"Very touching, Lockett."

Anna's head jumped off his shoulder, and they looked into the coarse features of Bloody Bill Coulter.

* * * * *

"I'm curious, Lockett," Coulter said, his Colt revolver aimed at Lockett's chest. "What are y'all doing out here? Why are y'all ridin' so hard? Y'all's been harder to track than a rabbit in a br'er patch."

"Does it matter?"

"Don't!" Coulter ordered, as Lockett failed to inconspicuously slide his hand to his holstered revolver. "We'll kill you soon enough, Yankee scum, but all in due time."

"We?"

"Boys!" Coulter gave a whistle and four more bushwhackers emerged from the trees.

A fifth one led Anna's horse and Thunderbolt by the reins. "Got their mounts."

"Tommie Wexler?" Anna exclaimed on seeing the boy. "What are you doing ridin' with this murderer?"

"I would be careful, who you call murderer," Coulter growled, "Who's the one with the murderin' Yankee?"

"James is no murderer," she said, uncowed by the gun that the bushwhacker brandished.

275

"They're all murderers," Coulter laughed, drawing nods from his men. "Yankees, murderers, every single one of them!"

Lockett eyed Coulter's weapon, praying for an opportunity that was not there.

Coulter followed his gaze and licked his upper lip in pleasure. "Nowhere to go now, Yankee."

He paused, wanting his prey to cower or say something, but his only reward was a flat, gray eyed mask.

"Now, what's the story, Lockett? We've been following y'all since you left town. Desertin' and stealin' the preacher's daughter?"

With a sideways glance Lockett saw their two horses being led by the young bushwhacker called Tommie. His rifle protruded awkwardly from Thunderbolt's saddle. With a silent sigh, he remembered that even if he had the weapon, it was still unloaded since he had not had the time to correct that after firing at the bee hive.

But there were only two horses, and no sign of Reverend Tucker.

The glimmer of hope within him died quickly though. Not only would that be one man against six, but the reverend's vow against firearms made any potential rescue impossible.

The malice-lined, stubble face of Bloody Bill Coulter was marked with an evil smile. "Cat got your tongue, Lockett?" Before he could answer, Coulter added, "Changed my mind. Don't really care what ya have to say."

He cocked back the hammer on his Colt. "Know how long it takes to die from a gut shot?"

He laughed so hard that his head tilted back. One of the bushwhackers joined him in his glee, and Lockett recognized him as one of the former prisoners from Haney's. He was the man whom Coulter had broken out of jail the day they murdered Sandie Holmes.

"You'll beg for mercy! I'm going to make sure that it takes a long time for you to die. You're gonna suffer, Yankee."

But at that moment, there was a commotion from the right. Lockett turned his head, as did everyone else, at the sound of pounding hooves. But while the bushwhackers were frozen in momentary surprise, Lockett was already using the distraction to push Anna into the woods. From the corner of his eye, he saw the preacher's horse charging madly at Bloody Bill, seemingly on its own.

Turning to watch as he escaped, Lockett gaped admiringly as the old cavalryman clung to the side of the horse, his left foot in the right stirrup. The only part of his body that was not shielded was the hand clenched around the saddle horn.

Coulter and his bushwhackers were clearly stunned. Tommie Wexler stood as if rooted, not able to jump to the side until it was too late, and the horse trampled right over him.

The next bushwhacker in line stepped to the side and tried to raise his weapon, but the old preacher righted himself along the side of the horse and swung his cane viciously. The old hickory stick smacked solidly against the man's forehead, and the bushwhacker fell, discharging his weapon straight up in the air.

Recovering from their momentary paralysis, the other bushwhackers fired their weapons at the one-man cavalry. The shots zipped harmlessly over the vacant saddle.

From the cover of the woods, Lockett drew his revolver and fired at the distracted bushwhackers. One shot hit the target square in the middle of the back, and another snapped a tree branch inches from a bushwhacker's head.

The fire from their rear forced the bushwhackers to the safety of the ground.

Lockett looked quickly across the opening for Coulter but did not see him.

With balance and skill that most men couldn't even imagine, Reverend Tucker brought his horse around for another charge. The old man urged his steed forward, toward another bushwhacker. But the immediate chaos of his appearance had now dissipated, and Bloody Bill Coulter rose from behind the shelter of a tree crook, letting loose two shots as the preacher raced across his front. The first shot sailed over the empty saddle, but the second caught the horse in the neck.

Whinnying violently, the animal slewed around until it was pointed in the other direction. Its rear legs folded under itself, and the animal collapsed. With a cry of pain and alarm, Reverend Tucker went under with the horse.

Together, rider and mount hit the ground heavily. The crash echoed throughout the forest, and in dismay, Lockett saw that the preacher was pinned beneath the horse. He made no noise and did not move. For a moment, he wondered if the old man was still alive. Then there was the slight twitch of his hand. In a kitten-weak effort, the preacher tried to pull himself clear, but he was too dazed and irrevocably pinned beneath the large animal.

Lockett's eyes flitted over to Anna. Her mouth was open in terror, uttering a wheezing gasp.

"Oh, Lockett, forgit somethin'?" Coulter heckled. He was shielded from Lockett's vision by a tree, but Lockett could tell by the location of the yell that the bushwhacker was looming near the fallen preacher. "Hey, Lockett! Show ya'self or the preacher dies!"

Lockett shifted his feet, but Anna immediately grabbed his arm. "You can't," she whispered, "He's a killer. He'll kill you both."

"I have to do something, Anna."

He still had no view of Bloody Bill, but movement to his left caught his attention. With his dull red shirt, this bushwhacker was difficult to miss in the green and brown of the forest.

Revolver ready, the red shirt moved cautiously from tree to tree, but it was clear that in the confusion of Reverend Tucker's charge, this bushwhacker had lost track of them and was not sure of the direction in which the Yankee and the preacher's daughter had fled.

Before he could think much about that threat, there was the coarse rattle from Coulter. "Lockett! Show ya'self now or the preacher dies!"

Lockett's brain whirled furiously on what to do next, but then only a breath later, Coulter called out again in a ringing, almost laughing hoot.

"Hell, ya should have minded your own bizness, preacher."

Coulter's solitary, point-blank shot echoed through the forest.

"No!" Anna gasped, choking down a full-throated cry.

"Now, it's gonna be your turn, Lockett!" Coulter gave an insane laugh.

Instinctively, both Lockett and Anna grabbed the other's hand, sensing that they needed to restrain the other.

Lockett clenched his teeth. Despite the betrayal, he felt a tremendous rage. It was like a member of his family had just been murdered. His hand gripped the wood of his Starr revolver with vengeful strength, and he waited for Coulter to show himself. From the corner of his eye, he watched the red shirted bushwhacker work his way deeper and deeper into the forest. That man would soon be so far off-course that he would not be much of a threat.

With a slap and a whinny, Lockett could hear their horses running off. "No horses now, Lockett!" Coulter yelled. His voice was edged with sadistic amusement. "Y'all got nowhere to go, so come on out. I'll kill y'all quick, if ya do." His laugh echoed in the thick forest so that for a moment it sounded like he was right behind them.

Anna stared straight ahead with a look of horror and disbelief.

He felt a compelling urge to say something, anything, but no words came to his lips. Instead, he forced his eyes beyond her, trying to occupy himself with spotting Coulter in the trees.

He had to be somewhere to their front right, he knew, and the red-shirted bushwhacker was to their back left.

There was a third bushwhacker, the one from the jail, and he had lost track of that man.

Even though Reverend Tucker had greatly improved their odds, Lockett still didn't like three guns against one.

"Can you get to the river?" he whispered.

Slowly, her gaze left the ground, but she stared uncomprehendingly at him.

"The river, can you get there?" he repeated.

"Yes," she replied, but her face was so puzzled that he wondered if she understood the words at all.

"Can you swim it?"

She nodded, more perplexed than ever.

"Okay. I'll hold them off and lead them away. Get to the river and cross it."

That statement triggered a sudden reaction from her. "I'm not leaving you!" she whispered back, aghast.

He frowned. It was the look that he had learned as a drill sergeant and perfected. The gray eyes glared, and the furrowed brow spoke of nothing but determination. It was a look that had cowed many a soldier, but it had no effect on Anna Tucker.

"I'm not leaving," she maintained stubbornly.

"That's not a request, and we don't have time to argue," he replied in a harsh whisper.

"No."

"Anna," he said softly in quiet exasperation.

"No."

"Hey, Lockett!" came Coulter's call from beyond, "What's the preacher carryin' here? This saddlebag's mighty heavy. A little offerin' money maybe?" The cackle resounded around them. "The good Lord helps those who help themselves!"

"Anna, you have to trust me," Lockett whispered, ignoring Coulter's hoots, "I'll be right behind you. I'll just make sure that I give you, us, enough time to swim across without having to duck their fire the whole time."

"I don't know…" she started, but he didn't wait.

"Good, it's decided then. Head back this way," he pointed, "And try to enter the water quietly in case they're nearby." He still didn't know where the third bushwhacker was and had now lost track of the red-shirt as well, but he would feel better knowing that Anna was off to safety.

He didn't really expect to be 'right behind her'. Rather, he expected to hold his ground until the end to make certain that she had enough time to swim the wide Tennessee River.

"Only if you're right behind me," she declared, reaching up to grab his chin. Tenderly, she twisted his face toward her. A solitary tear slid down her face. "My father sacrificed himself to save us. He knew what he was doing when he made that charge. Don't let it be for naught." She pulled him closer and kissed him with surprising fierceness. Then she started to back away.

"Wait," he said, removing his belted scabbard. Gently, he handed her the scabbard, and she looked at the elaborate hilt of the Stuart family sword. "Just in case," he added. "It's not much against a gun, but it is better than nothing."

And then she was off, half-running in a bent position. He watched her for a moment and started to wonder if he should follow through with his plan or if he should eventually make his way after her.

CRACK!

He dove to the ground as a pistol ball splintered the branch next to him.

"Over here!" a bushwhacker cried.

Lockett felt the slivers of wood in his scalp. He had found the third bushwhacker, or rather, the bushwhacker had found him. The man was sprinting from tree to tree in an effort to get closer.

Lockett returned fire. Too late, he cursed silently as the bushwhacker went back to ground. They traded a series of quick shots and ducked back behind their respective covers.

Where was Coulter?

It was a stand off, and that would give Anna some time, but he knew that he could not keep this up for long. Was Coulter or the red-shirted bushwhacker sneaking in behind him?

Lockett crouched and waited for another opportunity when a separate shot ripped the dirt next to his feet. Intuition took over, and he dove to the side instantly as another lead ball buried itself in the tree.

Coulter was flanking him, he realized without actually seeing the man. A third ball zipped overhead from a different angle. He was caught in a cross fire between the two bushwhackers!

I can't stay here, he realized immediately.

The lightning bolt of survival instinct surged through him as he rolled to his feet and dashed between two trees, narrowly avoiding the shots that chased him. He bounded around and over nature's obstacles like a rabbit chased by hounds. He frantically searched the path for a suitable place to duck down and continue the battle, but there wasn't one. More shots sounded behind him.

He was running for his life.

And he was running in the direction of the red-shirted bushwhacker.

Chapter 21

Lockett's long legs flew over the ground. Ahead was a three foot drop, cut into the soil by what was normally a flowing creek. But in this sun-scorched spring, it was only a shallow stream in the bottom of a ditch. Blindly, he leapt into it.

And he nearly landed on the red-shirted bushwhacker.

The bushwhacker was a fresh-faced boy whose face was far cleaner than his muddied red-shirt. In fright, the boy dropped his gun. The barrel just touched the water, but the all important six-chambered cylinder was still dry on the muddy bank. The bushwhacker staggered back a step but regained his balance in the ankle deep water.

Lockett landed awkwardly, more out of surprise than anything. He sat on his rear, and the water coursed around his hips, but he had not dropped his weapon. "Stop!" he ordered the boy.

The red-shirted boy was half-bent at the waist, hovering above the weapon. He looked at Lockett and then back to the gun, judging if he could reach down and pick it up fast enough. Once more, he glanced between the two.

"Don't," Lockett warned in a voice without malice.

The boy hesitated. Truth be told, he had joined Bloody Bill Coulter for the adventure and a chance strike back at the Yankees. He had never held a revolver a day in his life until today, and the glamour of riding with the outlaw had suddenly lost its luster, which was why he had been hiding in the creek bank.

"I said, 'Stop'," Lockett repeated clearly, ominously clicking the hammer back on his Starr.

The boy did not move his hand, but slowly, he craned his head around one last time to look at the grim face and steely gray eyes of the Yankee. It was not the face of a vicious cutthroat like the boy had envisioned all Yankees to be. There was a hint of lost innocence in the Yankee's own young countenance, and the bushwhacker imagined that the Northerner was only a few years older than himself.

"You're awful young to die," Lockett warned again, getting to his feet. "Now, step away from the gun, slowly."

And the boy did step back.

They stared at each other, and Lockett found himself wondering what in the world he was going to do with a prisoner.

Suddenly, there was a howl of belligerence and a splash in the creek just beyond the boy. The boy spun around to look, and Lockett instinctively jumped forward, grabbed the boy by the back of the collar, and raised his revolver over the boy's shoulder. Together, they looked into the fanatical eyes and red-stubble face of Bloody Bill Coulter. He had a gun in each hand and grinned demonically at them.

Coulter showed no fear, but Lockett had a clear shot, and he pulled the trigger.

Click.

The metallic clap of the hammer falling on an empty chamber resounded in his ears. He was out!

Coulter gave a great belly laugh, while Lockett grabbed the boy around the neck, pulling him in front as a human shield.

Surely, Coulter would not shoot with his own man in the way, but even so, Lockett knew he had only a matter of seconds.

There!

On the bank, only a few feet away, was the red-shirted bushwhacker's weapon. If he could just manhandle his 'shield' over to it...

"I'm going to…" Coulter started with an even wider smile. He fired one gun into the young bushwhacker's left shoulder, and then the other into his right. "… enjoy this."

The boy screamed in anguish, and Lockett nearly lost his grip as the boy sagged. His red-shirt grew darker, almost black.

Lockett struggled in the slippery mud with his heavy, howling weight, stunned that Coulter would shoot his own man with so little regard.

Coulter fired again from each gun. Each time, he took a step closer, methodically pumping shots into the boy.

Lockett's mind flared in desperation. If Coulter got much closer, he was liable to put one right through the bushwhacker. The young bushwhacker's blood flecked Lockett's face.

Bloody Bill's maniacal laughter rang out, and the boy's body went limp. He felt like two tons now in Lockett's grasp, and Lockett struggled to hold him up high enough to protect himself.

His eyes were still on Coulter, but his mind was on the gun that lay close to the water.

Coulter paused in his merciless murder of his own man. His face grew serious, and his arm stiffened as he finally took aim on the Yankee. He wanted Lockett to know that he was aiming at him, that his last moment was at hand.

But before Bloody Bill Coulter could fire, there was a flash of color. It swooped from the bank down into the creek like an avenging angel, a flowing calico blue and flash of silver. Coulter saw the movement, but it was too late for him to get clear of Anna Tucker and the Stuart family sword. His arms swung upward, but the base of the sword caught one arm full and the tip clanged off the gun in his other hand.

Stunned, Lockett watched Coulter sag to his knees. Both guns dropped into the water.

The dead boy slid from Lockett's grasp, and Lockett lunged for the gun on the bank.

But the elation of the rescue was fleeting. Coulter's knees had scarcely hit the muddy water before he swung a leg out, sweeping Anna's feet out from under her. With a cry, the sword slipped from her grasp, and she landed face first in the water.

Coulter was upon her in an instant. He grabbed a fistful of her hair from the back of her head and slammed her, face first, into the muddy creek bottom. Anna's arms flailed out futilely, and her legs kicked the water in impotence.

Lockett reached for the dead boy's gun on the muddy bank, but as he did so, he found himself knocked forward and thrown from his feet.

The gun slipped from his hand into the water. Before he could open his eyes, a pair of rough hands reached for his throat.

But he rolled and slithered away. He got to a knee and tried to open a mud-covered eye, only to be rewarded with a solid punch to the jaw that knocked him backward.

Landing on his back, the rough hands were upon his throat again before he knew it, along with a weight that pressed his body into the muddy water so that it coursed just over the tip of his nose.

Lockett forced his face upward momentarily, and he opened his eyes to see the third bushwhacker on top of him. The veins in the man's neck bulged with exertion, and the pressure on Lockett's windpipe was unbearable. And then Lockett was back under the muddy water. He knew his eyes were exploding from their sockets, and he could feel himself weakening from a lack of air.

With frenzied strength, Lockett jabbed sharply at the bushwhacker's throat with his knuckles, and the surprise blow rewarded him with a loosening of the grip. He knocked the grasp completely free and heaved himself upwards.

His attacker slipped and fell backward.

Lockett gasped for air and searched in the murky water for the gun. It had to be just inches from his grasp.

But he could see nothing in the roiled, opaque mix. He was vaguely aware of the bushwhacker rolling to his feet and reaching for something. Without thinking, Lockett launched himself forward, pinning the man's arm between their bodies.

He felt the tip of a metal blade prick his pant leg, and on reflex, he reached down and seized the man's wrist.

The bushwhacker fired a short left hook from their close quarters, but Lockett did not lessen the grip on the hand that held a wickedly sharp knife.

Still, his footing was poor, and he found himself struggling backward beneath the superior size of the bushwhacker. His boots were never far from slipping out from under him in the creek mud. The distance between the two combatants widened somewhat but was constrained by Lockett's grip on the man's knife hand.

The bushwhacker struggled to force the blade into Lockett's chest, snorting in wild breaths. There was pure hatred in the man's eyes, and the sinews of his face and neck protruded as they grappled. Each man knew that only one would walk away from this alive.

Finally, Lockett's attacker put every last ounce of weight and strength into it.

It was pure instinct, but Lockett spun as he felt the man commit himself, spinning the man to the bottom of their pile, and he twisted the man's wrist as they fell. They landed in the flat mud just below the steep creek bank. There was a soft, absorbing, muddy gurgle as they landed, and it took Lockett a second to realize that the man had gone still. He lifted himself off the bushwhacker to find the blade buried to the hilt, just below the man's sternum.

He only looked at the bushwhacker for a half second before turning his attention to Anna Tucker and Bloody Bill Coulter, but he was too late.

Chapter 22

Anna thrashed wildly, but she could not hope to break the brigand's leverage. She could feel the thick mud in her nose and mouth, and it seemed she had been underwater for minutes. There was the overwhelming surge of terror. Drowning! Her lungs were starting to cry out in agony, and her arms flapped uselessly in the shallow water.

Her panicked hand landed on a fist sized stone in the creek. Seized by primal instincts, she gripped the slippery rock tightly. Instead of trying to push herself up, she pushed her face deeper into the mud and twisted with all her strength. Coulter still held a gob of her long hair, but his hand slid to the side just slightly as she tried to roll, allowing her just enough range of motion to fling her arm in a back-handed manner. Her face was still under water, but she felt the satisfying crack of the stone meeting skull.

Suddenly, the pressure on her head and hair was gone, and she lifted her face from the water. Her long, curly hair hung over her face like a death shawl, and she greedily took in air. Wearily, she gasped and wiped the hair and mud from her eyes.

As she fell to her side, Bloody Bill Coulter staggered backward. His hands were clamped over his eye near the temple, and blood seeped between his fingers.

Exhausted, she did nothing as the water flowed around her hips. Seconds passed before she remembered that Coulter's guns were somewhere around her in the muddy water.

Between gasping breaths, she thought about looking for them but decided that the powder would be useless now. Instead, she sat there and watched.

Coulter staggered further down the creek, eventually collecting himself. After a number of wobbly steps, the bushwhacker paused and stared at her.

His eyes rolled in a strangely unfocused way and then looked past her. Wrath streaked the killer's face, but with a final curse, he turned and climbed over the creek bank and disappeared.

"Anna?" she heard her name called.

Turning, she could see James running through the creek towards her.

"Are you all right?" he panted. Muddied himself, he knelt down and tried to wipe some of the clumps of mud from her face.

"I'm okay," she nodded. She then noticed the bloody knife in his other hand.

"I'm going to kill that bastard," he vowed, rising to his feet.

"No," she cried quickly. "No. Let him go."

"What?"

"Tommie Wexler and the other one might have recovered, maybe there are even more of them! Let's run while we can."

"Run?" he said, mystified. He shook his head stubbornly. "Coulter's finally going to die... today."

"No, James, no!" she said, clinging desperately to his hand.

Lockett looked at her, barely stopping himself from saying, *'He killed your father, Anna!'*

But Anna did not miss the vengeful look on his face, and she seemed to know exactly what he was thinking. "I know, James Lockett." Her voice lowered an octave. "I know. But I can't lose you this day too. His day will come."

When he had no reply, she added in a voice more commanding than pleading. "Don't leave me now."

She was soaked and muddied. Blood dripped out of her nose. Her hair was matted to her face in flat ringlets, and her thoroughly ruined dress clung to her.

Lockett wanted blood, but he wavered at the sight of her brown eyes imploring him for caution.

"Even if Tommie Wexler and the other one are dead, their weapons are still back there. He'll get them, and we'll have nothing but a knife."

"And this sword," Lockett added. He picked up the Stuart family heirloom from the side of the creek.

As he wiped some of the mud from the blade on his soiled trousers, he realized that she was thinking more clearly than he was. Coulter would beat him back to the spot where the others had fallen. The killer would be armed, and he would have nothing except a blade.

He nodded slowly. "You're right."

"I know the farm across the river and down a mile, James." She seized her advantage. "We'll be safe there."

He looked into her eyes and reluctantly came to the conclusion that he would not kill Bloody Bill Coulter this day.

"Okay, but we don't need to cross the river, Anna." She looked blankly at him, and he pointed behind her. Waiting patiently beyond the creek bank was the massive black form of Thunderbolt. Despite the bushwhacker's spanking, the majestic horse had not bolted for home.

* * * * *

Bloody Bill Coulter picked his dead henchmen clean of their money and weapons. At first, he thought that Lockett would pursue him, but the Yankee must have been afraid to do so, for Lockett did not come.

Coulter looked down at the dead preacher at his feet. The flies buzzed busily around the gaping, grotesque wound in the old man's head. The bushwhacker spat, disturbing the flies for only a second. He had not killed Lockett, but at least he had inflicted some indirect pain on his enemy.

Coulter's head ached, and the gash in his arm throbbed, but it was the double vision that made his actions slow and laborious.

He had never wanted revenge against a woman before, but Anna Tucker would die just as soon as he killed Lockett.

Finally, he reached down and picked up the full saddlebag that had once been the preacher's. It was heavy. There was definitely more in there than just a Bible, and he would go through it in detail once he was safely away.

Coulter cackled as he put the saddlebag on his horse.

He had only ridden a few yards before a startled rabbit dashed from the brush. He laughed as the little animal bolted off in terror, but when Bloody Bill Coulter looked up, he saw something that struck fear in him — a detachment of Yankees!

He yanked on the reins and turned his mount around. There was the crack of gunfire, and the lead slammed into his shoulder, knocking him forward violently. The second shot hit him in the spine, and Bloody Bill Coulter was dead before he hit the ground.

* * * * *

"Bloody Bill Coulter!" one of the soldiers yelled excitedly, looking down at the body.

"Colonel Blair wanted the spy alive," Lieutenant Fulkerham noted as he dismounted.

"Dead now. Dead later. There's no difference," Orrin Long said in a voice that masked the elation he felt. His hand still vibrated from the shots. He couldn't believe it. He had killed Bloody Bill Coulter, bushwhacker and maybe spy! He would be a hero!

"What do you think happened, sir?" one of the privates asked Lieutenant Fulkerham as they surveyed the opening.

"It's the preacher!" another soldier shouted, gesturing to the corpse pinned beneath a horse.

They found two more bodies. Judging by the discoloration on the face and broken neck, one had been trampled to death. The second appeared to have died from a blow to the head.

"Looks like they ambushed the preacher on the way back from one of his churches," Fulkerham speculated.

"But how do you explain this, sir?" One of the men gestured to the two dead bushwhackers.

"They had second thoughts about robbing a man of God and fought amongst themselves?"

"Makes sense to me," Long agreed. "Eureka!" he then shouted. "Look at what's in Bloody Bill's saddlebags! He wasn't just a bushwhacker. Proof that he was the spy too!"

Triumphantly, we waved coded papers above his head.

"Guess General Halleck was right about the spy being a bushwhacker after all," Fulkerham commented.

"Makes sense. Makes sense," Long repeated.

He looked at more of the contents of the saddlebag. "I suspected it all along."

"Too bad for Reverend Tucker," Fulkerham added, "He was in the wrong place at the wrong time."

"Yes, too bad," Long replied absently, without conviction.

Fulkerham looked at the dead bushwhacker. Coulter was giving off a terrible stink. He must have lost control of his bowels because of the shot to the spine, he thought to himself. Well, Captain Long would certainly be a hero now for killing the feared Bloody Bill Coulter. It was then that Fulkerham noticed the nasty gash in one of Coulter's arms. It was deep and wide. It looked too deep to be from a knife. It looked like a saber cut.

Fulkerham looked from side to side but did not see any bladed weapons in plain sight.

Odd, he thought to himself, but it was getting late, and he wanted to get back to camp before nightfall, so Tyler Fulkerham decided to think about it later.

* * * * *

Dawn, and with it, came the now familiar, nauseating swirl of emotions. Just a few days ago he never could have imagined such a revolting, conflicting mixture was possible. All of this still seemed unreal, like a bad dream.

But it was real, and today was the morning that Lockett had dreaded.

The sunlight was bright, and there was actually a cool morning breeze making the temperatures unusually pleasant. The light brown haze of the morning cook fires still lingered beyond the weather-beaten silhouette of little Savannah, but all of that was lost on him.

Three days had passed since Reverend Tucker's death, and so much seemed to have happened.

Orrin Long had returned from that ride a hero. He had killed the bushwhacker and spy, Bloody Bill Coulter. Sadly, Long and Fulkerham's men had been too late to save the local preacher who had just been ambushed by the highwayman. The bushwhacker had killed the preacher, only to meet his own fate moments later at the hands of a righteous Yankee officer, or so the story was going.

And then, there was Corinth itself. The Rebel stronghold that General Halleck had been creeping towards with such temerity was suddenly no more. Just one day after the conclusion of the spy mystery, the Rebels had withdrawn from the vital railroad junction, allowing the ponderous Union army to enter it unopposed.

It struck some as more than coincidental that once the Rebels' spy had been eliminated, Corinth had been hastily discarded. Without their steady advance warning of General Halleck's intentions, there was little chance for the out-numbered defenders to keep it.

Corinth was in Union hands, and Federal spirits were higher than Lockett had seen in quite some time.

But not for him...

He felt nothing but a heavy heart. Not that it even mattered now, but Anna Tucker was leaving.

Savannah was no place for a young woman on her own, and Anna was leaving today to join her aunt in middle Tennessee.

Lockett stood next to the stagecoach, trying to distance himself from her as she bid good-bye to a few neighbors. One part of him wanted to loiter at her shoulder, catching every last ray of her, but the other part wanted her gone yesterday. This part wanted her to be nothing but a memory. Yet, he knew that he would not forget.

The torture of what might have been would linger with him forever.

Damn this war!

Anna turned and smiled tiredly at him.

She had worn a brave face for the past few days, but the red-rimmed eyes told the true story. These had not been easy days for her either. She had lost her past when her father was killed, and now she was losing her future too, or so Lockett wanted to think.

Lewis Dell, freed from jail now with Colonel Blair's profuse apologies, and the shopkeeper's wife drew Anna's attention back as they embraced her and said farewell.

Lockett looked at the ground. Try as he might, he knew that he would not forget.

That smile, those dimples, the playful eyes so alive – he would remember it all for the rest of his days.

Of course, with a war on, that was no ambitious statement, he shrugged. He could always die tomorrow. The bushwhacker's aim could always be true tomorrow, or the Rebel shell could pick him randomly from the line, assuming Blair's Independent Regiment was ever to see battle again.

A soldier tossed the mail bag onto the top of the stagecoach so that he could climb up there to tie it down. Lockett glanced over at the interruption. It was Private Nelson, the same innocent man whom he had almost killed three days ago.

The man's face was still swollen and lumpy, like the underside of a tin that had been battered by hail. He wondered how many times Nelson had been stung.

"How are you feeling, soldier?" Lockett asked, anxious to do something besides think of Anna.

Nelson blinked in surprise. He was unaccustomed to being addressed by an officer unless there was an order attached to it.

"Uh, fine, sir. Jus' fine." Then realizing that his sting-swollen face was being studied, he added, "Had to do somethin', sir. Couldn't just lay 'round no matter how bad my noggin' hurts."

He climbed to the top of the stagecoach and began to strap down the mail.

"That's the spirit," Lockett commented. It felt like the thing to say, even if he didn't feel like being so cheerful.

"Those hornets sure was angry though," Nelson added. "Can you hand me that other strap, sir?" Lockett tossed the worn leather up to him. "Like as not, I'd be mad too if someone just blew up my house."

Nelson chuckled, and Lockett found himself liking the man all the more, making him even happier that he had not killed him. "Yes, sir, like as not, I should just praise God that that damn Reb was such a bad shot. Could've killed me!"

"You think it was a bad shot?" the voice asked from behind Lockett.

He turned, more startled by the words than the voice.

The tone of the question was light not harsh, but Katherine Moffat looked coolly at Lockett. He felt her examining him with those blue eyes.

Private Nelson looked down from his perch. He gently scratched an itch above his swollen eye and made certain that he replied politely. He knew that this woman was Katherine Moffat, who had come to nurse her cousin, and now many others, back to health. Everyone in the regiment knew who she was, and they were grateful for her, but few openly expressed this. Her airy demeanor put most off, and more importantly, everyone knew that her beau was Orrin Long, the same staff officer who had condemned them to a life of baggage duty – rightly or wrongly. Nelson was sure as hellfire that he didn't want to offend someone like that.

"Bad shot, ma'am? Had to be a bad shot. I mean, he could've killed me, instead of missing by a full six feet, ma'am."

Katherine Moffat said nothing and did not take her eyes off Lockett, so Nelson added, "Ain't that unusual though, ma'am, missing high I mean. That's the natural tendency, you see. The rifle's kick can send the shot high if ya ain't careful like. Why, I've even seen the lieutenant here drill his men by telling them to aim for their..." he paused, "er, groin, ma'am just to compensate for that." Nelson paused, and his swollen face turned red. He hadn't meant to paint himself into such a corner in front of the lady.

Katherine still did not shift her gaze, "Is that so, Lieutenant?" She paused deliberately and added, "About a rifle kicking high?"

"It can be a problem, Katherine, especially in the heat of battle when your blood is racing," Lockett answered warily.

"I see. I thought perhaps the person meant to hit the beehive."

Nelson hopped down to the ground. "Meant to hit it?" he asked in puzzlement.

"To spare you," Katherine explained.

"Spare me?" Nelson said incredulously, "Pardon me for saying so, ma'am, but that ain't likely."

"No?"

Katherine was still looking at Lockett even though she was answering Nelson, and it was starting to bother Private Nelson now. He knew he was a patient man, but by God, women could be infernal.

"Ain't likely that they spared me. Why, that Bloody Bill cut a man's head clean off and put it in his own postal bag! No, ain't no bushwhacker who is gonna spare no Yank soldier, especially Bloody Bill Coulter."

"He's got a point," Lockett added.

The implacable shield was across Lockett's face, but he still felt nervous. Ever since he had returned that day, he had felt paranoia that his secret excursion would be discovered. But no one had a clue. No one, it seemed, except for Katherine.

He shook the thought from his brain. It was his own over-active worrying streak, he scolded himself. She knew nothing.

"Of course, you're right," Katherine finally agreed.

"Right about what?" Anna Tucker asked. She had removed herself from her neighbors, leaving only Katherine and James for their final good-byes.

"Nothing," Katherine answered, "Nothing at all."

Lockett had been trying to do whatever he could to distract himself from the reality of this final good-bye, but Katherine's words were more than an artificial distraction. For a moment, he found himself looking at Anna but thinking about what Katherine knew.

"James," Anna said softly.

The sound of her voice brought him back, causing the emotions within him to spin like a storm. What could have been, what was now lost, and the betrayal that he still felt... It made for a dichotomous sentiment.

Oddly, Katherine did not seem to have such a mix of emotions. She embraced Anna Tucker as she would her closest friend. Apparently, the past was the past with Katherine, and she bid Anna a heartfelt farewell. Her warmth startled both Anna and himself.

"James," Anna said when it was finally his turn. She looked at him with those entrancing eyes.

There was much left unsaid between them, and he found himself tongue-tied. He could not mumble a single word. Feebly, he tried to offer a hand for a departing handshake. Anna took the hand and pulled herself close to him. Her grip was like iron, but she gently pulled him down to her height. Standing on her tip-toes, she gave him a not-so-quick kiss on his scruffy cheek.

Then she turned around abruptly, feeling her own pain. She accepted Nelson's hand up into the stagecoach, and then she was gone without another word.

Nelson departed, and James Lockett bit his lower lip as the coach jostled down the rutted road, through the slight dip, and then ultimately disappearing around the bend.

Lost in his own thoughts, he did not realize that Katherine was still standing next to him. The sound of her voice as the coach disappeared froze him.

"So, she got away with it then."

Paralyzed, he felt a strange tingling sensation. Consciously, he took a slow breath and fought to show no reaction. "What was that, Katherine?"

"I said, she got away with it then."

"Away with what?" he asked, trying to sound puzzled. Nelson had already wandered off, and it was just the two of them standing there.

"Your spy got away."

He felt his blood go cold. "My spy? I don't follow you, Katherine."

She laughed as he looked cautiously at her. Her light blue eyes, that at times could look so haughty and arrogant, now looked amused. "I've told you before, James Lockett, you are a terrible liar. You'd do better to stand there and say nothing. It's your voice that gives you away."

"Katherine, you're making no sense."

He wanted to walk away, to leave the discussion in the dust, but he knew that he could not. He needed to find out how much she knew.

He thought of the giant black horse that Anna had given him as a parting present. Could Thunderbolt out-run these problems? Defending himself against accusations had proven time and time again to be futile. The best course of action would be to run before they could hang him. Besides, this time, the accusations would be true.

"Oh, I make perfect sense, James. That is why you are so nervous. It all makes perfect sense, but I must admit that I did not see it until yesterday when I overheard Sergeant Bosworth tell Patrick that you had returned to camp very late the night

Bloody Bill Coulter was killed. You see, until then, it wasn't that clear to me. Then, poof, everything fell into place."

"Go on," he said, giving up on playing dumb. He should not have been surprised. Katherine was the only one who had deduced that his return to Kalamazoo was related to his disgrace with the Sharpshooters, related to the death of little Amelia. Katherine had a quick mind and a talent for such things, despite some obvious blind spots in other areas.

"Oh, don't worry," she soothed, "I'm not going to tell anyone. I just wanted *you* to know that *I* know that Anna Tucker was the real spy of Savannah, not some drunken bushwhacker. My only question is, how long have you known?"

He paused, searching her face for some sign. Then he decided he might as well tell the truth. "I figured it out the day that everything blew up." He spoke with a low voice, even though there was no one around.

"She was using my letters, wasn't she, James? I knew it! I never understood why she would care about those letters until yesterday when I realized what Orrin was putting into them. That would be useful to the enemy."

Lockett bit his tongue.

"Every other day or so, the Rebels were getting an update on General Halleck's plans, straight from the general's own staff!" She chuckled. "I shouldn't laugh, I know, but it is ironic, James, is it not?"

"So, what now, Katherine?"

She chuckled again. "Don't be such a hen. I'm not going to say anything. How could I? It would implicate Orrin in the whole mess, and besides, he's a hero now for killing Bloody Bill Coulter. As far as everyone knows, he killed the spy of Savannah. He's a hero. It's good for his career."

"His career," Lockett scoffed, "His God-awful career! You are some piece of work, Katherine. You and Orrin do make the couple, what a fine fit you two are!"

"Oh, James, don't be that way. I've decided to forgive you for everything that you've done to Orrin. I want bygones to be bygones."

"Forgive *me*!" he cried incredulously, pointing to his chest. He looked at her once porcelain face that had now been freckled by exposure to the Tennessee sun. "I pray that you never see the truth about that man. It will be too much of a shock. God protect you from that." He shook his head. "God protect you."

"What happens now?"

"Now? Now, the war goes on, Katherine. We'll soon leave Savannah one way or another, I am sure. Maybe we'll get a chance to fight again."

And with any luck, maybe I'll get myself killed in the next battle, he thought to himself.

"Onto the next battle?"

"Onto the next battle, Katherine. Savannah was just a brief stop for me. Never fear, there will be more battles for James Lockett."

Historical Background

Readers of the other books in the series will no doubt have recognized that *Lockett's Betrayal* is a bit different.

Whereas *The Boys From Kalamazoo* and *Lockett's Crucible* included battle narratives with a heavy emphasis on historical accuracy, *Lockett's Betrayal* is more of a mystery and adventure novel. The need for unswerving factual content was not such a priority, and the element of fiction plays a greater role in *Lockett's Betrayal*.

However, I was able to include a number of historical tidbits, plus there are a number of areas that I would like to discuss so that the reader can be assured that the context of *Lockett's Betrayal* is factual.

The aftermath of the battle of Shiloh staggered both the North and South. With over 10,000 Confederate casualties and 13,000 Union casualties, the burying of the dead and the tending of the wounded were overwhelming tasks.

Men like James Lockett and his comrades worked busily to bury the dead, aware of the weather and deteriorating condition of the corpses, leading to the usage of shared burial trenches for the Union and Confederate fatalities.

While their immediate work was done in a matter of days, the impact on the small communities surrounding the battlefield was a longer nightmare. They were inundated with enormous numbers of wounded, and labors of mercy lasted weeks and months.

As Lockett related to Ainsley Stuart, the duty of loading the wounded onto steamers, so that they could be ferried to places with doctors and medical supplies, was a state by state affair that left many a Michigander untended on the banks of the Tennessee River. In today's America, where the importance of statehood can be more of a formality than anything else, we can hardly fathom such a process.

It is an important reminder to us that the thought process and context of 1862 is far different from today's. And this lesson can be applied to many aspects of yesteryear's environment, including our amazement at the seemingly mindless courage that soldiers on both sides could display. It was truly a different time.

It was also not uncommon for civilians to travel to the battlefield after a significant battle in those days. There were numerous examples during the Civil War.

As mentioned in Volume I, while the Moffats were one of the founding families of Kalamazoo, and Senator Charles Stuart was one of the most popular and well-known individuals in the state, there was no Ainsley Stuart or Katherine Moffat, nor are they based on anyone. They are simply fictional characters. Yet the actions of someone like Katherine Moffat, traveling to a far-off battlefield in search of a wounded relative, do have their basis in fact.

Similarly, there was no Reverend Tucker or Anna Tucker in Savannah, Tennessee; however, the comments relating to Tennessee's position on the subject of secession are factual. Tennessee did, in fact, reject Secession in a general vote, yet the elected government of the state opted to leave the Union regardless.

While Unionist sentiments were strongest in eastern Tennessee, isolated locales in western Tennessee also displayed surprising consensus in their desire to remain in the Union. However, as the war continued and armies trampled on property and, at times, civil liberties, sentiment in some towns naturally began to tilt towards the Rebellion.

It is just another example of how blurred and confusing things could be, particularly in the border states.

In a conflict such as the American Civil War, where it was brother against brother and neighbor against neighbor, there were spies on both sides. While spying was generally poorly organized and often spur of the moment, there were notable exceptions. Additionally, some of the most successful spies were women, such as Virginia's Belle Boyd and Rose Greenhow.

There are many possible explanations for General Halleck's excessive caution in approaching Corinth. Likewise, there are many possible reasons for General Beauregard's patience for waiting in Corinth against the overwhelming force that approached him. Was one explanation that both sides were affected by particularly successful spies, someone like the Tuckers? Perhaps…

Regardless, the Confederates did eventually abandon Corinth, and Halleck's Federals took command of the vital railroad junction. With the fall of Corinth in May of 1862, some saw light at the end of tunnel. It was wishful thinking in retrospect to be sure. As we all know now, the war had hardly begun. Years of bloodshed remained.

Sadly, this was only the beginning. As Lockett has correctly surmised, there is still much ground for him and his comrades to cover, with many more battles left to fight.

ABOUT THE AUTHOR

A Michigan native, T.J. Johnston is the author of the James Lockett Civil War historical fiction series, including *The Boys From Kalamazoo* and *Lockett's Crucible*. A history lover and long time author, he has degrees from Hope College and Michigan State University. He currently resides in Texas where he is working on subsequent novels.

Made in the USA
Las Vegas, NV
28 February 2022

44734091R00177